Casted

BOOK ONE

THE STOLEN SCROLLS

ASHLEY KUCINSKY

Published March 2023

www.ashleykucinsky.com

ISBN 979-8-9878404-1-2

Cover design by Morgan Lakofka

www.lakofkaportfolio.com

Editing by HR Camarillo

www.hailiecamarillo.com

Proofreading by Kimberly Harmon

www.anhourofyourlife.podbean.com

Content Warning

This is an adult romance with fantasy elements, and is intended for mature readers. Content warnings include, but are not limited to: violence, murder, graphic imagery, violence against women, explicit language, sexual content, infidelity, one allusion to sexual assault, and themes of racial and social injustice. Please read at your own discretion.

Pronunciation Guide

Selah Sharpe Say-lah Sharp
Andren Whitt An-dren Wit
Finix Emrys Fin-nix EM-riss
Myran Mee-ran
Ophida Oh-FEE-duh
Martock MAR-tock
Tomas TO-moss
Cecil SEE-sill
Rior Ree-or
Bodney Bahd-nee
Rashel Rah-SHEL
Della DEL-uh
Pickham PICK-em
Maher May-er
Oberin OH-bur-in
Andalls AN-dahls
Palladria Puh-LAH-dree-uh
Esson ESS-un
Asa Ha'i AH-suh Hi
Lasso Lah-soh
Swyft Swift
Dua Merno Doo-uh Maer-noh

The Prophecy of the Scrolls

Ordained by the Ancient
Borne from flame
Bonded in union
Branded in name
Cleansed of sin
Salvation of all
One Caste to rule
One Caste to fall

Chapter One

If I jump, would they win?

My toes hung over the side of the dam, looming treacherously above the dark water. The strait was swollen and angry after a mid-summer storm had rolled through, and the crisp breeze slapped me in the face. I licked the salt from my lips, a mix of sea air and dried tears I refused to let them see. But they couldn't see me from their shiny white houses, and they wouldn't dare follow me to this place. I could jump, and they'd never be able to reach me again, but I didn't want to give them the satisfaction of winning.

The wind shoved at my back, sending a loose piece of granite plummeting. It plinked against the sides of the dam until I could no longer hear it over the roar of the water below. I lurched, clambering to regain my footing before stepping off the side of the wall onto the security of the stone. Bent over, heaving air in and out of my lungs, I dropped to my knees. They were bruised, and my stockings were torn, but the cool, wet stone soothed my wounds. Yet again, I had let them reach me.

My mother thought the taunting and tormenting had stopped years ago when in actuality, I'd just become better at hiding it. I was practically an adult now, and supposed to be the top tier of society. No reasonable person would expect such ugliness from my peers, but it had only grown worse as we approached our Debut season. I was no competition to the other Ladies, with their perfect Casted features. The men ignored me anyway. But they were relentless in their assaults.

How do you live with yourself, knowing you're a walking disappointment to your parents? You can't possibly think you're attending Debut. What self-respecting Lord would take a wife who looks like a peasant? And that horrid hair. You'd be better off shaving it. Ooh, that's a great idea. We should shave it off for her. Someone hold her down—let's do her a favor. Who can hold that thing down? She's an overgrown swine and I don't want to get dirty. Wouldn't want the rest of Oberin to think we hang out with nasty Selah Sharpe.

They were right; I was too tall and too strong for them to hold me down. But it only took two of them to shove me to the ground when they snuck up from behind. I'd gone through half a dozen pairs of stockings just this week, forcing my Lady-in-Wait to make several trips to purchase new ones. She never seemed upset about the additional task, but I knew she pitied me, which was far worse. I looked like a servant, but nobody paid servants any attention because they weren't Casted. I was, and yet being ignored was preferable to this.

The dam was the perfect escape because it was all the way in Lower Oberin, skimming the edge of our island. The other Ladies wouldn't be caught dead down here among the lesser class. I could walk freely around the market without fear of injury, so long as my parents didn't find out. I stood upright and brushed debris from my tattered stockings, scanning the city center sprawling against the curve of the dam in a crescent shape. The lowly clay huts were one solid mound from this distance, but the bright white mansions jutting from the center of the crescent were easily discernible, down to the gables and arches of each estate. The sun was poking through the clouds after the storm, casting a shadow over the rest of the island. The contrast was nothing out of the ordinary to my fellow nobility, but it left me with a queasiness I couldn't pinpoint, like seeing rotted flowers in a bouquet. Maybe if other Casted could see it from this angle, it would change their perspective. But probably not.

Ignoring my mother's pleas to stay out of the sun, I kept my hood behind my back and made my way into town. The harsh rays would be the least of her worries if she knew I was strolling through Lower

Oberin. It's not that I tried to displease her; it was simply a way for me to funnel my restlessness into something more acceptable. And by acceptable, I meant something she didn't know about. My unfortunate appearance may have been the source of many whispers and side-eyes among the Casted, but it was a welcome advantage when I needed to blend in with the lesser class.

Lower Oberin was particularly vibrant today with villagers hustling about in smears of reds, blues, and greens, easing my worry of being spotted. Midday at the market meant there were hoards of children darting in and out of their mothers' skirts, wiping bright red noses on their sleeves. I realized I had *also* been a child at some point–even Casted weren't exempt from that stage of life–but they were not a common sight. And definitely not in public. Infertility was one of the side effects of our Bloodline, but it made us more *rare*. Or so the Caste claimed. The lesser class just let their children run about on display, spreading germs and who-knew-what kind of disease in all shades of color. *So bright and assaulting.*

It wasn't that I disliked children, or that I was afraid of catching an illness from one of them. When the Original Bloodline was cleansed, all sickness was completely eradicated so I wasn't at risk among them. But I was wildly uncomfortable, seeing them in droves with their gaunt faces and tattered clothes. They wore their poverty like an ugly scar–a brand of their destiny. The grime and destitution ate at me like acid, but the worst part wasn't their condition. It was the pure innocence radiating off of them–the genuine mirth as they ran their grubby fingers over the displays, completely unaware there was another world just up the hill. A world where children went to fancy boarding schools and never played in the streets, and only wore pastels to match their muted features. We learned to read and write and play piano, not how to survive the harsh island winters.

Scanning the rows of produce and goods along the way, I meandered around the market patrons in a zig-zag. A pair of boys splashed through the runoff in the street, but I sidestepped them too late to avoid their splatter. I shook the excess waste water from my gowns, trying not to grimace and draw attention, but the water bled through my skirts and sloshed into my boot. The boys continued to flank my position on the street, carrying on with their ruckus while I looked around for a hasty retreat.

I eyed the shop across from me and decided it was the nearest, and driest, option. It looked deserted, but the sign on the door indicated it was open. *Guaranteed Sponsorship*, the bold lettering boasted. I'd heard of Sponsorship brokers but had never experienced any because I was born from the Original Bloodline and had no need to go through the daunting process of being made Casted. Graciously, the Caste allowed an avenue for those *less fortunate* to join our ranks in the ruling class, though I'd always heard the required Trials were extremely difficult to even attend, let alone pass.

Those of us who were graced by birth didn't speak of the Trials very often. *It isn't proper.* But the impropriety only made me tingle with even more curiosity. My own Scrolling was coming up after Debut, where I'd officially declare myself as a full member of the Caste–*if* I found a respectable suitor–but something nagged in the back of my head. Something I wanted to scratch. I needed to know what signing the Scrolls actually meant for those who weren't raised within this delicate bubble of aristocracy, where it was little more than ceremony.

I kicked at the cobble street and dashed across. *You need to go home, Selah. What if someone recognizes you?* But I was already palming the tarnished brass doorknob before my reasoning could kick in, and then I stepped inside the shop.

Everything was black as my eyes adjusted from the afternoon sunlight, but the smell of damp lumber and copper hit me as soon as I closed the door. Squinting, I just barely made out the shape of a small desk in the center of the shop. The tiny square room was otherwise empty. I didn't know what I expected to find, but it wasn't a vacant space. I shouldn't be surprised to learn the hopes and promises of becoming Casted were just a front. *Oh well, probably for the better.* I turned back to the door to scurry away before anyone caught me lingering in this place, but a clipped voice stopped me in my tracks.

"Can I help you, miss?" It was just over a whisper, but the sound consumed the cramped area. Swinging around, I realized the source was a rail-thin man sitting behind the desk. *How did I overlook him before?*

He cleared his throat while I fumbled to untangle my hair from my hood.

"I, uh, I'm–" My words caught in my mouth, clinging to my tongue despite my best attempt to release them.

"You're here to find a Sponsor?" he said, scooting his chair under the desk and propping his smudgy face against his fist. I shook my head. This was a terrible idea. "Ah, to be a Sponsor." He made the declaration before I had a chance to correct him. "Come, sit." The man extended his free hand to a rickety stool parked in front of his desk. Too embarrassed to confess my ruse, I lowered myself onto the hard wood seat.

"I'm glad to hear you're considering sponsoring a candidate. I've had a higher demand than usual this year and haven't been able to match paying customers up with a Sponsor, and I'm not keen on turning away another prospect." The man adjusted a faded black tie before laying a stack of paper in front of me. "The contract is quite simple. You just need to identify who you'd like your payment sent to, and if you are sponsoring a specific candidate. Do you have an arrangement already?" He raised a thick brown eyebrow at me. I should have explained this was all a misunderstanding, but I foolishly kept going.

"No." At least it wasn't a complete lie.

"Excellent," he said, flipping the papers around to bring a new one to the top. "Can you read or do you need me to go over the Duress Clause?"

"The Duress Clause?"

"No problem," the man said, picking the paper back up. "*The Sponsor acknowledges that any enrollment into the Trials is expressly voluntary, and that the Sponsor cannot fulfill his or her obligation to the candidate while under duress. The Sponsor acknowledges that total and complete termination of life is required to complete a successful Sponsorship of the designated candidate into the Trials. Failure to comply with each aforementioned stipulation will result in a defected candidate and non-payment to the Sponsor's designated beneficiary.*" My head swam with the fountain of words coming from his mouth.

"Termination of *life?*"

He rested the papers on the stack and folded his hands. When he looked up, I realized his eyes were a similar gray hue to mine.

"Yes. But you knew that coming in, right?" I nodded but he looked unconvinced. "Do you have a beneficiary to receive your payment, assuming you successfully complete the Sponsorship?"

"But what happens if the candidate doesn't complete the Trials?" I ignored his question, clambering to piece together what I knew of the Trials with what the man's contract stated. The lower class could become Casted if they weren't born from the Original Bloodline, but they had to prove themselves worthy to have their blood cleansed. And apparently someone had to *die* for them to get that chance. It was no wonder the Casted preferred to ignore the Trials' existence.

"Ah, smart girl." He pulled back his lips to reveal gaps between his yellowed teeth. "Straight to business. I can respect that. You want this page." He retrieved another paper from the bottom of the stack. "The payment information." I craned my neck to read the printed contract, but the script was too small to fully make out.

"What does it say?" The hair on the back of my arms stood at attention, and my skin crawled with unease. I should have bolted from the decrepit office, yet even the heaviest trepidation wasn't enough to dissuade my need to hear the rest of his pitch.

"It's the details of reimbursement for Sponsorship. This here shows the first installment upon completion of your obligation, and the second installment if the candidate completes the Trials and signs the Scrolls. With the failure rates being what they are, we always pay the first half regardless of the candidate's outcome, so you can rest easy knowing your people will get their money." I was anything but resting or easy right now. "We'll make the payment within five days of the Sponsorship to anyone you designate, so long as we can locate them. I suggest you arrange that in advance." He winked. "And here's the amount."

At the bottom of the page, I saw numerals scrawled with several zeros trailing them. Growing up in a home where we had everything at our disposal, I had extremely limited knowledge of money. But that looked like a lot.

"Your sacrifice is no small contribution, miss. Your family will be set for life, even with half the payment. And if the candidate makes it, they not only get the full payment, the candidate gets a whole new life. It's a win for everyone." The man leered at me before nudging a quill and inkwell my way. "Only gotta make an X if you don't know how to sign your name. Right there." The line at the bottom of the page blurred, and my ears rang like a thousand crickets were closing in on us. Whatever air there was left in the room grew stifling hot.

"I have to go." The stool collided into the dirt floor as I shoved it away from my body. The man called to me but I was already fleeing out the door. I had to get out of there before I suffocated.

I waited for the fresh air to hit me as I tumbled into the street, but instead I was met with something so large and so hard, it knocked the wind from my chest and my legs right out from under me. The ground smacked my backside and elbow with a jolt, and the zip of pain flashed in my eyes. I was only vaguely aware of strong hands on my arms, and the faint scent of cedar and salt muddling what was left of my senses. When the hands released me, I was upright.

"Pardon me, miss," a deep baritone voice said as I planted my feet into the ground and willed my knees to hold steady. I strained my neck to look him in the face. He was large, *very large*, with hair and eyes so black they looked like bottomless pits, and skin several shades darker than mine. Even for a lesser classman, his size and saturated coloring was a shock to absorb. The feeling in my limbs still hadn't returned, but it would be a marvel if I walked away from that collision unscathed. *Don't gawk, Selah.*

I clamped my mouth shut when I spied a Casted gentleman in the wake of Tall, Dark, and Huge. This man stood several inches shorter than his hulking partner, but still cleared the top of my head, unlike most Casted males. He looked like he could run great distances, with long limbs that moved with a casual, confident grace. His golden hair was parted to one side, falling across his forehead and around his ears. Translucent blue rested directly on me.

I froze.

"Please forgive my Hand, miss. He is quite the brute." *Miss.* Relief trickled down my spine and I settled back on my heels. My reputation was already shaky, and any sort of scandal would crush all the visions my mother had for me landing a respectable Lord husband. I sighed audibly, but the two men were conversing amongst themselves and didn't notice. His Hand peered at me with a look that could melt steel before rendering a half-hearted shrug and turning back to his intended destination. The Casted man lingered.

"Are you alright?" he said, almost too casually for a Lord speaking to someone he thought to be lesser-born. As I raised my head to answer him, a swatch of red caught my eye. Red with gold embroidery. Where most Casted Lords wore their blue lapels, this man had a very distinctive patch that was now burning into my retinas. *What is someone of such importance doing in Lower Oberin?*

Not Lord, the *Governor* stared at me expectantly.

"Yes, Sire," I said, squirming under his persistent stare. The corner of his mouth dipped ever so slightly, which drew my eyes right back to his face. His lips were full and his teeth were just as bright as his hair. All Casted had a sophisticated polish but this one was exceptionally handsome. My scuffed boots suddenly became very interesting.

The Governor's gloved fingers tipped my chin and leaned my head back towards his direction. His touch felt like fire on my skin, which spread through my cheeks like they were dried brush.

"Are you sure?" I looked behind the Governor to his Hand, who had his wide back toward us as he perused the booths. "Finix is on a mission to find a very specific map, that is only drafted by one mapmaker in the Dominion, who will only be in Oberin for the day. I sincerely apologize you happened to be in his path."

Stepping back to a more comfortable distance that allowed my lungs to reinflate, I smoothed my dress before I brought one hand up to also tame my fiery auburn hair. My disheveled appearance had been my armor walking into town, but I suddenly wished for my ballgowns. *That's a first.*

"Nothing hurt but my pride." The jest escaped before I had a chance to retract it. No working class would speak to a Governor in such a manner, but a toothy smile spread across his face. It ignited a single dimple on his right cheek, and a simultaneous swarm of bees in my abdomen. Even my best ballgown wouldn't be enough in his presence.

"Fair enough," he said. "Can I call a healer to tend to your pride?" My experience with Casted men extended to my own father and my tutors, none of whom had much to speak of in terms of humor. But a godly Governor was flashing a mischievous grin right at me like we were old friends.

"No thank you, Sire. I can manage."

He raised his eyebrows in feigned surprise. "Quite the independent spirit, I see. I like that." He winked. The Governor *winked* at me. "Well, then I will attend to my Hand before he plows over any more lovely Ladies." Before I had time to ponder if all Governors were this charming, I caught his final word.

Cold sweat prickled at my hairline in spite of the excessive heat outside. He continued to speak but his words were coming from miles away. I swallowed hard and maneuvered my pupils to focus on his face. *Get it together, Selah.* It was probably just a colloquial use of the word.

"Farewell, my Lady!" He called after me. I heard that.

No, no, no.

He knew. I glanced back over my shoulder to catch him still watching me, before he pivoted toward his Hand. He definitely knew. I had to get back before word got to my parents. Maybe if I intercepted the message, I could do some damage control. The violent thrum in my chest reiterated there *was* no controlling the backlash that would surely come from my stupid mistake. *Stupid. So stupid. What was I thinking risking this?* I tore off through the marketplace, forgoing my usual path across the dam. It was likely too late, but I had to try anyway.

Chapter Two

Breathless, I rushed through the heavy oak doors of our house and up the winding marble staircase to my chambers. My Lady-in-Wait was in the same spot I had left her hours earlier, poised to ready me for dinner. I wondered if she had stayed like that the entire time before I started shedding my cloak and boots.

"I have to get out of this, Corinna." She didn't flinch at my demand, but her displeasure rippled off her. I stood in the center of the room with my arms above my head, assuming the usual position that allowed Corinna to pull on my afternoon dress. In any other circumstance, I would have chuckled at the irony of my helplessness right then, just after being called *independent*. She sighed loudly when she saw my undergarments were soaked through with sweat, then peeled them over my arms.

Corinna dressed me in crisp, fresh petticoats then layered a soft blue gown over them. I loathed pastels but they were the quintessential fashion among Casted Ladies. Anything to be soft and muted, but my hair and olive skin prevented me from achieving the complete monochrome standard. She pulled the sash uncomfortably tight around my waist, trying in vain to create feminine curves on my muscular figure. I grunted in protest but Corinna only tugged harder. She handed me silk slippers before she made her way to my hair, then froze when she saw its state.

"This is going to take me forever to untangle."

"I don't have time for that, Corinna. I need to get downstairs." Mother was a stickler for etiquette, and she would know something was off if I was late to the table. As if she didn't hear me, Corinna retrieved the brush and circled my head like a hunter moving in for the kill. Intercepting her attack, I flipped my head over and gathered my mane in a pile, winding it into a high knot on top of my head. "Hand me a ribbon."

Corinna rolled her eyes but dutifully retrieved a blue ribbon. She watched me fumble with the silk then yanked it from my hands. I didn't resist, and before I could follow the motion of her deft fingers, she had fashioned it into a neat bow.

I gave myself a once-over in the silver mirror on my dresser. Briefly, I considered smearing on a lip stain to appease my mother, but the last thing I needed was more pigment. My face was still tinged pink from my exchange in the market, highlighting the smattering of freckles across my nose. I couldn't fault the other Casted Ladies for their endless comments. My features *were* garish. Whatever had tipped the Governor off, it certainly hadn't been my looks.

"Thanks, Corinna," I said, then scurried off to dinner.

The dining hall was dimly lit, the perfect veil to my disheveled state. My joints moved stiffly as I sat down in front of my golden charger, each muscle bracing for impact. I poured a glass of wine to the brim, just in case, but my head was already swimming. I'd all but forgotten the run-in with the Casted girls before the Sponsorship Broker, and *him*.

A few moments later, my mother glided in and took her usual seat. If those girls knew how purely Casted my mother was, directly descended from the Original Bloodline with all the delicate features to show for it, they'd never let me live it down. She greeted me with a terse smile and filled her glass to a much more conservative level. I wistfully stared at the second vacant plate across from me, wishing my little sister was here. She was always the best buffer between my parents and me.

But sadly, she was not here to bail me out of this mess. Lilah was attending her final years of school across the island, though she was due home at the end of summer. *After Debut*. As if I didn't already know my younger sister was practically tearing down the wallpaper at her boarding school while she missed such a crucial event of mine, her dozens of letters solidified that assumption.

"Have you had your fittings yet?" Mother interrupted my daydream with so much efficiency, I clinked my wine glass against the table in start. "No respectable tailor will have enough time to prepare all those gowns if you are stalling."

"I will go tomorrow," I said. "I've just been very busy with my studies." The excuse fell flat in front of my mother. I'd been dodging discussions about Debut for weeks, but the stern angle of her jaw told me she was serious this time. Ballgowns for a frivolous parade of courtship were such a trivial concern when I had bigger problems afoot. Much bigger.

"Selah, you cannot hide behind your studies. The impression you make during Debut will impact the future of our family, and *the Prophecy,* and that should be your priority now. We know you are a very capable student." She furrowed her brow into one neat crease. Mother reminded me of fine china, but not in a fragile way. She was the kind that was expensive and untouchable, and would stab you in the gut with her shards if you let her fall. I could always count on her to compliment me, even as she chastised me.

"I know, Mother. I will see the tailor first thing in the morning."

"Thank you, darling." Her momentary approval would all be washed away when she found out about my escapade today. Mother would never tolerate a blemish of that nature, especially in front of a Governor.

She rested her glass of wine on the polished tabletop as my father entered the room. He sat down in one of the intricately chiseled chairs that weighed more than I did. This was the signal for the servants to come alive, silently ushering in our meals on platters. They laid our napkins across our laps, sat out polished silverware, and uncovered each serving in descending order from my father to me. It was all so formal and stuffy, but it was our routine.

I waited for him to take the first bite, nodding his approval, before I cut into my own spread of pheasant and roasted carrots. I chewed as slowly as I could manage, staving off the gurgling hunger that had erupted out of nowhere. All the sensations my body had been hiding behind its panic were breaking through, including a deep throb in my elbow.

"Good evening, my blessings." Father greeted us with his customary endearment. "I hope your day was as fruitful as mine." Mother and I both shook our heads up and down, already aware this was rhetorical and only the precursor to the account of his day. He leaned over to kiss Mother's cheek before gathering his fork and knife. Father was still lean and fair as the other Casted Lords, but he was warmer than Mother in every sense. Perhaps it was the Original Bloodline that hardened its bearers, making them cold, or mean in the instances of my classmates. But I'd never speak such a supposition out loud.

A dense, weighted silence filled the room in a suffocating blanket. Mother watched me like I was primed to erupt into chaos and disappointment at any moment, which in this case, was entirely possible. If Father had been briefed on my run-in, he didn't show his hand, however. He shoveled spoonfuls of potatoes and carrots into his mouth without a single care in the world. How the two of them ever ended up paired together, I hadn't a clue, but Father loved her fiercely. And she gave whatever affection she had to him, which was no small feat given her family's reputation. Mother was descended from the Original Bloodline, and Father was the son of a commoner, made Casted in a twist of fate. They were as ill-fitted as I was to them, yet we were all sharing a meal just as we did every other night.

Tonight was different though. Tonight, there were no mundane conversations and routine interactions. I was quite literally poised in my seat, branding my palm with my silverware in anticipation. I couldn't bear the buzzing in my head and needed to hear my fate. Time to take action.

What I knew of Father's work was only from snippets he shared at dinner every night. He was a Lord like other genteel Casted, but he was also the Dominion's Trade Officer, and it was apparent he took his duty to heart. While Mother had little patience for his political ramblings, I quite enjoyed the glimpse into the inner workings of our world. I waited for a pause in his speech before I took another swig of my wine, dampening my tongue so I could move it.

"Father?" I asked. "Do you know the Governors?" He also took a drink from his glass, though the dark liquid's viscosity was much heavier. Father preferred brandy to wine.

"Of course, why do you ask?"

"My lessons were about the Chancellor's advisors and I realized I did not know who they were. I suppose that is something of importance if my father regularly consults with them." I already knew each Governor of the original three Governors by heart–they were in every heroic story of the War–but the fourth and fifth were revolving doors of young appointed Lords. It was almost as if the Caste knew those roles were disposable, so they found the most forgettable men to fill them. *He's far from forgettable though.*

He set his fork down with a metal *clank*. "That's my little Lady, ever the conscious scholar." He took another drink of his brandy and followed it with two glazed carrots. Dabbing at his face with his napkin, he rested his forearms against the table.

"Three of the Governors were appointed when the Chancellor took his position after the War–Eslo, Gregor, and Donorio. They are commanders of our Armies, Fleets, and Tactics." I was confident the Governor I'd met today hadn't been born until centuries after the War of the Scrolls when the Chancellor rose to power.

"The other two are much younger, and they're actually brothers. The elder brother, Amon, has served for nearly a decade now over the Handlers. His younger brother, Andren, was brought on just last year to oversee the Barrier. It is quite unprecedented to have a set of siblings filling Governorships, but they both seem adept in office. I have not personally interacted with either of them, though." *Andren.* I missed what Father said next because my head swirled with images of golden dimples and white teeth. A young, unprecedented official–that had to be him. I shoved a bite of pheasant in my mouth, allowing myself to taste it this time. *Father didn't know him personally. He didn't know Father.*

"Thank you, Father. I do enjoy hearing about politics." His face illuminated with much more than the spirits he polished off. Though Father had the ashen appearance the Casted shared, he always looked warm and rosy. For years now, I had tried to picture his family before they joined the Original Bloodline, reconciling my rogue red hair had come from his side before the Cleansing had washed it away to match everyone else. We had an oil painting of my grandparents in the hall, but it must have been rendered after my grandfather's Cleansing. Part of becoming Casted meant voiding oneself of individual tones and hues, so I could only guess what color his hair was before. My parents didn't bring it up and I didn't ask, but I passed the portrait every night, fighting the urge to paint it red. Just to see it.

"Selah is going to see the tailor in the morning for her Debut gowns." Mother redirected the conversation to a topic she found more palatable. Politics were too fussy for her.

"Ah yes, that time is quickly nearing." I couldn't be sure, but there seemed to be a glisten in his eye against the murky candlelight. "Have you considered any colors, Selah?"

"Not really." I didn't need to hold pretenses with my father. Mother cut her carrots into tiny slivers as a way of dissent, but Father paid no attention.

"Well, not that my opinion matters in the realm of Ladies' fashion, but I have always preferred you in green. A fine emerald green would be splendid." His eyes danced over his brandy. Mother frowned but didn't dissuade him.

"Thank you, Father," I said. "I will certainly ask about green."

Father drew his lips at the corner, his mouth twitching as if he was about to speak again, but returned to his meal with a soft smile brushing his face. Maybe I was overreacting about everything. The Governor had never met my Father in person. Even if he had detected my status, he had no idea who I was. And with my Father cheering me on, maybe Debut wouldn't be as bad as I thought.

Chapter Three

Debut was as bad as I thought. It was sweaty and awkward and uncomfortable. The kickoff event was an annual mixer held in Lord Olm's ballroom. The Olms were one of the oldest families descending directly from the Original Bloodline, the very banner of prestige among Casted. Lord Olm was a trusted advisor to the Chancellor and his Lady wife was considered the expert in betrothals, though it seemed more like meddling now that I was standing in their estate. The whole scene was reminiscent of an insect under a magnifying glass, complete with the Olms hovering over the balcony to observe our every move. What better way to gather fresh fuel for her gossip?

From the second I entered the extravagant ballroom, I could feel the stares beating down on me like a heavy rain. The insults were barely held inside the other Ladies' pursed, primly painted lips. Despite this being an evening event, most of them wore creamy neutrals with high necks and long, lacy sleeves. Fresh from the tailor, my dress was a rich burgundy with a square neckline and a softer silhouette hugging my hips. The contrast instantly spiked my temperature, moistening my unmentionables and driving me to shift about clumsily as I walked.

The remaining guests bustled to their own seats as I took mine. My discomfort refused to fade as I hid behind the table, only settling around me in a noxious cloud. I battled through the beginning of dinner service under an assault of hot oil lamplight and cramped body heat. The Olms also had an ornate fireplace in the back of the room that was lit "for ambience." All of the men were staged on one side of the sprawling table while the women were positioned opposite their potential suitors. They had the perfect view to watch me roast on a platter of chiffon and silk.

A boyish-looking Lord sat in front of me and I breathed in relief at some kind of distraction. While I knew he was at least nineteen, his appearance suggested he was closer to fourteen. His hair was colorless and fine, slicked down until no individual strands were discernible. I scanned his features, taking in eyes like frightened prey and a soft jawline that would likely never grow a beard. He attempted a smile, emphasizing the lopsidedness of his mouth. I could practically smell his nervousness hanging between us, compelling me to try and comfort him, but only in the most maternal sense.

"Good evening," I said in offering. "I'm Selah Sharpe." The boy fidgeted with his place setting.

"I'm Lord Frier," he replied. I tried to catch his eye but he was looking to the side of my temple.

"I see you have taken your position. Congratulations." Assessing his eagerness to display his title, I assumed it must be new, unlike most of the men here tonight. I only recognized a few faces from primary school and assumed the rest were all older than I was. Casted men were permitted to attend Debut at any point, or even multiple times, in order to find the perfect match. This was my only shot as a woman, and it rattled my very being to set myself on display for a sea of strangers. None of them looked appealing, with their greased hair and pompous tail coats swarming around us like buzzards. Lord Frier, however, was closer to carrion himself, and I decided that alternative was worse.

"Good evening, Lady Selah." The young man seated next to Lord Frier interjected. This one had darker blonde hair that hung in finger curls to his earlobes. Each curl bounced like a tiny spring as he moved his head around. He looked to be a more appropriate age, with squarer features and a long, pointed nose. When he spoke, I noticed one of his front teeth overlapped the other by a millimeter or two.

"Good evening, my Lord," I said as a generic greeting.

"Please, call me Martock. All these titles are quite pretentious." His words passed over the young Lord Frier, who chased a piece of cheese around his plate, notably with the wrong fork.

Next to me, across from Martock, was a girl so tiny I thought she was slouching low in her chair. To my surprise, she was sitting erect. Her straight hair matched her posture, hanging around her shoulders with the front pieces pinned to the sides of her head. It was a bit plain for the event, but I could've been passing unfair judgment on the poor girl. It was possible her family did not have a Lady-in-Wait to help her prepare, or that she was even a Lady-in-Wait herself, especially since she hadn't been one of my classmates. I honed in on her bony hands wringing the tablecloth furiously in her lap, then noted the wrinkles I'd been creating in the linen myself. Neither of us were immune to tonight's torture.

The girl released the cloth, folding her hands neatly in her lap. When she opened her mouth, I watched all her features harden.

"*Ahem.*" She cut Martock off mid-sentence.

"Good evening," he said, bouncing his eyes back and forth between us.

"Good evening, my Lord." She pouted her red lips at him, bold and harsh against her pale skin. "I am Ophida."

"A pleasure, Lady Ophida," he said, turning back to me. But she had no intention of letting him go. Perhaps the men weren't the only birds of prey at tonight's event.

"My Lord, I am not a Lady…yet. Please forgive any misconceptions I may have given you." So she *was* a Lady-in-Wait. "And you can call me Phi." She purred the words, then sliced her eyes my way. Obviously the invitation to use her pet name did not extend to me.

I mentally scanned the contract I had seen in the market, deducing someone had *volunteered* to sponsor this girl. While I couldn't comprehend the incentive, I also realized she would have to find a Casted suitor willing to postpone their marriage until after she signed the Scrolls, *if* she made it to the Scrolling. No doubt it was a daunting task, so her ferocity in her pursuit of Martock's attention made sense. Ophida wasn't going to back down, and neither Martock nor Lord Frier were worth the fight.

To my right, a couple was already deep in conversation. Neither acknowledged anyone else in the room, so I sat through five more courses and saccharine sweet cordial without any further attempts at niceties. Lord Frier seemed content with silence and Martock occasionally stole glances at me whenever Ophida looked away. My legs were getting restless from sitting for so long and my neck ached from craning to see down the row without drawing too much attention to myself. But all the other guests were preoccupied, their cheeks now ruddy from the heat and the spirits.

I was tracing the pattern on the skirt of my dress when the Olms' servants took the final dishes away, signifying the close of the evening. The Ladies paired off with their potential suitors to be walked home, the first intimate moment in budding courtships. I would have rather walked on nails all the way home than be escorted by Lord Frier, or feel the wrath of Ophida to have the company of Martock. But the gravity of my loneliness cut through the layers of my gown until I felt naked on Lord Olm's front lawn.

The sun had dipped into the horizon and the evening air was chilly, making me pull my shawl around my shoulders as I pushed past the gaggle of guests. I was invisible to all of them, which forced a scratchy laugh from my throat. I'd been their favorite target to taunt only a few weeks ago, and now none of the other Lords and Ladies acknowledged my existence. Sure, I was grateful their relentless bullying had stalled, but the silence was just as maddening. How could I reasonably find a suitor in this mix when I never had been one of the Ladies to begin with, and never would be?

Opting for the shorter wooded path away from the main thoroughfare, I sullenly trotted off in the direction of our family estate. While my parents would already be in their chambers, my eyes burned from the inevitable disappointment I was carrying home. I hadn't tried hard enough. I didn't want it enough. I didn't even know what *it* was. I was simply going through the motions of what a good Casted Lady *should* do, but being a spinster sounded more desirable than this. At least I could live out my life without ever setting foot in the Olms' estate again.

Between the fog of my mood and the low lighting, I missed the large rock laying on the footpath and stumbled over it in my flimsy silk shoe. I braced myself to hit the ground, more worried about my dress than my body, but jolted when something grabbed hold of my arms and pulled me back upright. Barely regaining my footing, I pivoted to see who, or what, had followed me down the hill. Golden hair, light blue eyes, and a single dimple flashed back at me.

"My Lady," Andren said with a small bow. Still shaken, I gaped at the impossibly handsome Governor looming over me. He beamed, drawing his eyes from my face down to my dress. I followed his gaze and realized I must have stepped on the hem when I stumbled. The seam had been split at my waist, leaving a sliver of my midriff exposed. Chagrined, I crossed my arms over the tear.

"Sire." I kept my eyes toward the ground until his motion yanked my gaze back to him. He ran his long, agile fingers through his hair, pushing the loose pieces on his forehead into place.

"We really have to stop meeting like this," he said, still smiling. I shifted from one foot to the other as his eyes lingered over my waistline.

"You have quite a knack for finding Ladies in compromising positions."

His plucky grin stretched to his earlobes, and my heart misfired against my ribcage. "I assure you, my Lady, this talent only extends to you." My title sounded so intimate coming from his mouth. I blessed the dusk for concealing my crimson blaze.

"Are you walking home alone?" His question had an edge that made my face burn even hotter. If it got any worse, I feared I might actually combust.

"I was, Sire." He cocked his head as if he was trying to solve a puzzle.

"I find it hard to believe that no strapping Lord offered to escort you."

"I left before anyone had the chance." I balled my fists to brace for his reaction.

"Interesting," Andren said. "So Lord Frier was not to your liking?" It took me several seconds to register that he knew who had been seated near me. *Had he been in the ballroom with us?*

"He wasn't much of a conversationalist." I then added, "Sire" for good measure.

"I don't imagine he would be." His tone was much more relaxed than mine, but there was no scenario where I'd be able to unwind my nerves in his presence. "Might I formally introduce myself now that we have had two quite literal run-ins? I believe I can outdo Mr. Frier's conversational skills by a fraction at least." He grinned at me like a teenage boy, far from the statuesque Governor he was.

"Of course, Sire."

He straightened his back and lifted his chin as he pretended to adjusted his cravat. He was not kidding when he said *formal* introduction.

"My Lady." He dragged out each syllable. "I am Andren Whit, Fifth Governor of the Chancellor's Council." His diction was so exaggerated, I couldn't stop my own grin from betraying me. I bowed with excessive vigor to match his theatrics.

"Sire, it is my honor to be in your presence," I said with a stippled annunciation that would make my tutors proud. "I am Lady Selah Sharpe."

"Selah," he said, showmanship falling to the side. "The honor is all mine. And please, call me Andren. I've had enough formalities for one night."

"Yes, Si–, er, Andren." I corrected, noting the way his name felt in my mouth.

"Given your propensity to accidents, I feel I am duty-bound to see you home safely."

"Sire," I said, clamming back up at the idea of being alone with him. "There are undoubtedly countless Ladies awaiting your escort up the hill. Surely one of them piqued your interest."

"That is awfully presumptive of you to assume I am a participant in Debut," he said. Embarrassment swept over me. *So stupid, Selah.*

"Please forgive my poor assumption."

"Oh, my Lady." Andren laughed out loud. "Your assumption was correct but it was still presumptive of you." I allowed myself to release a single tight laugh with him, loosening the grip on my spine once again.

"I humbly beg your forgiveness, *Andren*." His eyes refused to release mine as the creases in his face softened from his laughing fit.

"I guess it takes a Lady falling on me to grab my attention."

"Well then, I suppose I can accept your offer. It would be the least I could do for falling on you." Andren caught my wrist in his forearm as he hooked his elbow, leading me down the path.

"Selah Sharpe," he said as we walked. "Your father is Lord Sharpe, I take it?"

"He is." The same icy panic seized my chest once again. He *did* know who my father was.

"He has quite the reputation in our court," Andren said.

"Mmhmm." This was it. He was following me home to report my infractions to my father. Each cautious step down the path was carrying me closer to my fate, driving another nail into my chest. I tried to suck in more air, to catch my breath, but it was still hissing out my sides as I deflated.

"He has a very impressive position and his accomplishments are well known," Andren said. *Right foot. Left foot. Inhale. Exhale.* "Which does pique my curiosity when his Lady daughter runs around town unescorted." Even knowing it was coming, my footing still stuttered, but this time I had no obstacle, or Hand, to blame. Andren grabbed my arm and steadied me yet again, but I kept my stare straight ahead and continued to will myself forward. *Right foot. Left foot.*

"Yes, about that." I couldn't think of any reasoning that made sense, so I opted for the truth. "I just like to get away sometimes." I counted the raps of my pulse while Andren walked in silence. I jumped out of my skin when his voice broke through the darkness again.

"I know what you mean." My chest inflated just a bit. *Inhale. Exhale.* " I enjoy getting out and about myself. Why should Nix get all the fun?" I recalled the muscular, dark-haired man that accompanied Andren through Lower Oberin. His Hand, Finix, was presumably Nix for short, though nothing was short about the mountainous servant.

"How did you know I was a Lady when you saw me there?" I stopped on the path, and looked at Andren. A sliver of fleeting light caught the indentation of his dimple.

"Selah, even if you were cloaked in a potato sack and covered in dirt, no one would ever mistake you for anything less than a Lady." I instinctively jerked my hand to a piece of hair that had worked itself loose from my braid. It was far from ladylike, but I was too fixated on the way his eyes drifted over me to ask what he meant. Andren resumed his stroll while I scurried to keep up. *Right foot. Left foot.*

"You don't find it unbecoming that I was down there?" I gulped at my own forwardness. He may have called himself Andren, but he was still undeniably a Governor. *Inhale.*

"Unbecoming? No. Maybe a bit foolish since there are some seedy characters that frequent the market, but not unbecoming."

"I understand." *Exhale.* The breath escaped louder than I intended, and I desperately hoped he hadn't noticed. "I wouldn't want my misgivings to impact my father's good reputation."

"Selah, why would a trip to the market have any effect on your father?" He grabbed my elbow and halted us again. I let my arms fall to my side, but quickly drew them back in when the cool night air touched my bare skin underneath. Andren tipped my chin; I gaped at him wordlessly. *Pathetic.* "I have no intentions of telling anyone where we met. Including your father." *Inhale. Exhale. Exhale. Exhale!*

My eyes darted back and forth between his, searching for the lie. It had to be there somewhere. There was no way a high-ranking official wouldn't turn me in to my family so they could *correct* my behavior. "You're not telling my father?"

He shook his head, letting blonde tendrils fall around his eyebrows. "No, Selah. Everyone deserves to escape sometimes. I just wouldn't turn it into a habit. I won't always be there to save you from imminent harm." The youthful grin overtook the seriousness on his face.

"Save me? You *caused* my imminent harm." I shoved him playfully, holding my breath until he nudged me back. *Flirting.* Governor Andren Whit was *flirting* with me. *Right foot, left foot.* I commanded my feet to move but nothing was registering, and I simply floated down the path as I leaned into Andren's arm.

Before I could get back into a rhythm, we reached the lane of gated estates where my family residence stood.

"This is home," I said, pointing to a nondescript white house with four gables instead of two. Andren led me the rest of the way down the cobble street and parked in front of the wrought iron gate.

"My duty is fulfilled." He bent into a low bow, hand extended toward me.

"I am indebted to your service, Sire." I peered at him from under my lashes while he unfolded himself before me. He took my hands between his thumbs and forefingers, and I envisioned each loop and whorl of his fingerprints branding my flesh.

"I am the one indebted to your company, Selah. If it pleases you, I'd like to find you at the next event."

I resisted the urge to bounce up and down like an excited child. "It would please me, Sire," I said with marked control. "And I can confirm your conversation skills are marginally better than Lord Frier's." We both laughed as Andren released my hands and the shock of night air swallowed the warmth from his touch.

"Until then, my Lady." He took one more long look at me before disappearing into the darkness. I rested against the door for several minutes, digesting everything before I went inside. My body was having a difficult time convincing my brain this was real life with all the emotional crescendos skewing my perception. *Hopeful* was not something that frequented my vernacular, not because I was a miserable person, but because I was never able to visualize anything beyond this island. My life was so small, so simple, that I already knew what to expect. But *this* had blindsided me.

Chapter Four

Three nights later, the second Debut event was held on the lawn in front of Oberin's courthouse, a sprawling green sea adorned with exotic flowers and shapely shrubbery. The courthouse was seated amidst the mansions of Upper Oberin instead of downtown, designating it an asset of the Caste rather than the people of the Dominion. Servants had laid out wool rugs with coordinating patterns, tables covered to their edges in miniature pastries, and strands of ribbon and garland in every inch of space available. Every detail was fabricated with romance in mind, which caused my palms to itch as I walked up to the scene. Andren's parting words had left my insides abuzz for the past three days, and now they vibrated out of control as I scanned the open area for him.

Finding nothing, I resigned myself to an empty table on the perimeter, ready to fade into the scenery yet again. Perhaps Andren would show up later. *Or perhaps he was just being polite.* That annoying tickle in the back of my brain flared, but I swatted it away and leaned against the vacant table to sulk in silence.

Right on cue, Martock pulled the chair out next to me and plopped into it with enough gusto to lift the feet of the table off the ground. He balanced two plates full of petit fours and tarts, one of which he sat in front of me. I shook my head, but he nudged the plate in my direction.

Even if I was hungry, I didn't dare try to eat in my dress or makeup, but Martock failed to take the hint and advanced the plate until it bumped my arm.

"The food is the best part," he said, chewing a mouthful of lemon tart. I was starting to develop the theory he was a lesser classman who had become Casted recently, judging by his manners. Or his absence of manners. But he was the only guest I seemed to be entertaining, so I selected an almond shortbread from the plate and conceded.

"There you go." Martock grinned. He was not traditionally handsome, but his unadulterated youthfulness made me examine him through a different lens. Life with Martock would be easy, possibly even fun. But the notion didn't really excite me like I thought it should, so I dismissed it as quickly as I'd developed it. There was nothing that said I couldn't enjoy his company in the interim, however.

"So, Lord Martock is it?" I asked. "I did not have the chance to hear about you at the mixer."

"Are you always all business, Lady Selah?" Martock cocked his head at me. "Or were you just disappointed we didn't share more time before?"

"I suppose neither," I said, joining his game of dodging questions.

"Yet here you are again, wanting to know more about me." His eyes twinkled under his springing curls. Martock's entire body stayed in constant motion.

"Are you going to answer my question, *Mister* Martock?"

His grin widened. "She *is* interested in me." I doubted he was even capable of holding a title with his utter inability to be serious.

"Unfortunately, my interest is waning," I said.

His mouth stopped working on his dessert, and he swallowed the remainder in one attempt. I watched his Adam's apple bounce. "Quite the business woman, Lady Selah. You really missed your calling in government." Martock dabbed the corner of his mouth with a napkin. It was the first sign of etiquette I had seen from him. I raised a single eyebrow in reply, visualizing working alongside Andren. *Where is he?*

"Oh, alright then. I suppose I've made you work hard enough." He sat back in his chair. I shook the image of Andren from my head and rejoined the conversation. Martock crossed his arms and propped his ankle on his knee, adding at least ten years to his apparent age. "I thought women would appreciate the mystery."

"I appreciate facts," I said, stifling my laughter.

"Yes, yes. I see that. I am Lord Martin Hamerstock, son of Mathis Hamerstock." Lord Martin pursed his lips. I, however, gripped the sides of my chairs until my knuckles went white to keep from springing into the air.

Mathis Hamerstock was a renown novelist, handpicked by the Chancellor's wife to come to Oberin and create new publications after she helped him become Casted. Or so the rumors went. I recalled the worn novel in our study, with its familiar patina and aged scent. I had read and reread the story of the valiant soldier who'd rescued a fair maiden from enemy captives during the War. He tragically died at the end, but I was a glutton for punishment and ran the dagger into my own heart over and over. The writing had been enthralling, and each time I had a new hope the characters would find their happily ever after, as if the ending had somehow changed. Of course it didn't, but Mathis Hamerstock was brilliant. And now his son was sitting in front of me, stuffing his face with baked goods.

"Lady Selah, your mouth hanging open is rather unbecoming," he said. I realized that my mouth *was* agape and quickly snapped it shut.

"I take it you know of my father," Martock said, trying to regain the conversation. He'd gone uncharacteristically still. So Martock could be serious.

"Yes, oh yes," I said, then pulled back when Martock seemed to dim.

"I supposed you would. Most people do." His mouth formed a straight line that matched the crease in his forehead.

"Is...is that a bad thing?" He looked down at the grass beneath us, digging his toe into the earth.

"No..." Martock said. "It's wonderful. He's wonderful. Truly." His voice was monotone, as if he was reading from a textbook instead of describing his father. His very acclaimed, accomplished father at that.

"I can imagine there might be challenges that come with having a famous parent." I recognized I'd gone too far, but it had happened so quickly, I didn't have time to recover. All my efforts were just bouncing off of Martock.

"Yes," he said with a large exhale. "I really am proud of my father—he's brilliant. It's just that, I don't want to be an extension of him. Especially here...." He looked around the crowd. I moved my head up and down in understanding but also seized the opportunity to scan the gathering again. *Still no Andren.*

"Perhaps it's the visionary's gene." Martock pinched a ladyfinger in half. I cringed when the crumbles fell across the spotless linen. "But I hope to find someone who wants to marry *me*. Just me. Not Mathis Hamerstock's son." He paused to absorb my reaction to his last declaration. I shifted my weight to the other side of the chair, trying to escape his imposing stare.

"But if wooing the Ladies with my father is what it takes to snag a decent one, it's a tactic I might just employ." The boyish grin was back and dessert was once again his focus. Martock shoveled a second ladyfinger into his mouth then folded his hands behind his head.

As if she was summoned by a beacon, or by ladyfingers, Ophida approached our table and hovered at Martock's side, turning her back toward me.

"Lord Martock," she said with a curtsy. Without moving her head, she spoke over her shoulder, "Lady Selah." I returned a cordial greeting and folded my hands in my lap. Famous father or otherwise, our conversation was over.

"Good afternoon, Miss Ophida," Martock said, curls once again bouncing across his forehead. He showed no indication that he was miffed with the interruption to our conversation. Perhaps he had several more tactics he wasn't sharing.

"Phi," she corrected. Her voice was as porcelain and doll-like as the rest of her. Tonight she had a rose pink dress with tufted sleeves, and she'd opted to plate her hair in rows. It was slightly more upscale than her last style, but still very childlike.

Before Martock could say anything else, Ophida asked if he would escort her around the lawn. "It's so lovely, isn't it? And those swings look magical!" Martock shrugged and stood up, offering her his elbow with a glance in my direction. I waved my hand at him lazily, waiting for the irritation to kick in. Ophida was insufferable, but I couldn't bring myself to enter a turf war on the courthouse lawn. Martock wasn't the reason I'd let Corinna painstakingly pin my entire head of hair into tight curls for hours. Instead, I shrugged off the exchange and went back to the abandoned desserts. Cake never let me down.

I shifted from side to side in my chair, hunting through the sea of beige and cream for any trace of gold. Either he was attending these events incognito or he was not here. Governors had plenty of other pressing matters, no doubt, and I was foolish to expect anything else. Giving the lawn another once-over to be sure, I swallowed back the bitter twist of disappointment lingering on my tongue.

The restless feeling in the balls of my feet crept in the longer I sat at the table. Andren clearly wasn't making an appearance and I had promised my mother I would make an effort to meet people. *Just put yourself out there. It'll be fine.* My pep talk gave me the gumption to hoist myself from the chair, but I froze when I looked back at the wall of guests. *Were there this many people a few minutes ago?* I swore the number of people had doubled, but I took two tentative steps forward before diverting to the refreshments. Debut was not having a positive impact on my choice in beverages, but liquid courage was a good supplement for the real thing. I took two champagne flutes and emptied the first before I stepped into the churning crowd.

In a matter of minutes, the bubbly fermentation began to make a warm path through my body, until it crested at my forehead. Trying not to shatter the stem of the flute in my clammy hands, I headed straight for the chaos. It was all or nothing at this point. A group of Casted men and women were congregated in a semicircle, sounds of jovial voices and laughter ringing all around them. They were perfectly at ease interacting with strangers, so at the very least, I had something to glean.

I slipped into the epicenter and tipped back the second drink. The immediate effect gave me something to do with my hands so I could fight off the urge to ball myself up and disappear. The secondary effect came next, clouding my inhibition as I barged in on the conversation. Two men talked animatedly with a young woman, eyes bright and cheeks red with merriment. Behind the fog of imbibement, my heart thudded away, demanding I flee before it was too late. But the chatter died down as the three strangers eyed me curiously.

"Good afternoon," the girl said. She must have been a class ahead of me, because I would have recognized her untamed beauty if I had known her, and her chirpy tone was far too nice. She had a mountain of sandy hair piled on top of her head, and her dress was a sleek teal that hugged her in all the right places, revealing a voluptuous curvature that no corset could give me. The girl's nose was straight, set between rounded blue eyes that looked at me expectantly.

"Good afternoon," I said. *Good afternoon? Do people actually say that in social settings?* I had such limited experience in situations like these. The group closed in, and I waited for the snide remarks to hit me. But the girl gave me a wide smile that crinkled her eyes until they were no longer visible.

"I'm Myran and these two nitwits are my older brothers, Willem and Wiles." She leaned her head toward the men. Their faces were not only mirror images of each other's; they possessed the same wide mouth and straight nose as Myran. The trio could have been mistaken for triplets, if such a thing was possible. The replica she introduced as Wiles shoved Myran's arm playfully then turned to greet me. Willem echoed the motions, pushing her other arm so she swayed back and forth between the brothers.

"Nice to meet you. I'm Selah," I said, not sure where to direct my greeting. I paused awkwardly, having made it further in my mission than I'd anticipated. *What now?* I cursed myself for the excessive drink as I reached into my vault for a viable conversation topic, but couldn't rustle anything up. Myran, Willem, and Wiles didn't need the prompt.

"So Selah," Willem said. "Have you staked your claim yet?" He gave me a fiendish grin and wiggled his eyebrows.

"Oi!" Wiles said, leaving me slack-jawed. "Have you found one you fancy?"

"More like one you can tolerate, some right heels prancing around." The two punted lines back and forth without waiting for me to contribute.

"Obviously, she has not found someone worthwhile, otherwise she wouldn't be standing here with you buffoons," Myran said. "And please, Selah, these aren't the ones either. Trust me." Between their jokes and the champagne, I couldn't hold back my laughter. It worked itself from my belly out of my mouth, flooding me with relief in its wake.

"Well, might as well join our ragtag band of Debut's finest," Wiles said. "We're nothing if not fun." *Fun.* I was having fun. For most people, it should have been a common occurrence, or at least a vivid memory. But I couldn't recall anything I'd done that would be classified as *fun*. Sure, I read books and enjoyed going for walks, but those never gave me this effervescent, overflowing sensation. Other people had given me the opposite effect, actually. This was what I'd been missing.

"Which is in short supply out there," Willem said. Myran shook her head, letting her wafts of hair tumble around her temples. She looked out at the lawn filled with Debut hopefuls, and this time I didn't follow suit.

"But seriously," she said. "No one has caught your eye?"

Nobody here, I thought. "Not yet. What about you?" I asked. She was a knockout with all the ideal Casted features–everything I didn't have. There was no detectable reason for her to miss her window for marriage.

"Ah, what about me," Myran said wistfully. "Our father is a professor of geology, made Casted before he married, and incredibly gifted. Don't be fooled by these two," she added. "I spent most of my finishing years shadowing him, trying to convince him to take me on as an actual apprentice, but that's not a consideration our *Lady Mother* was willing to make." Myran's straight nose crinkled in obvious displeasure.

"So here she is, trying to play the odds of some poor chap proposing to her." Wiles and Willem cackled amongst themselves, but Myran was less than enthused. I couldn't blame her. She and her brothers looked exactly alike, but there was a distinct bifurcation in their futures. Her frustration burrowed into me, though I had nowhere for it to land. I wasn't excited about finding a Lord to direct the rest of my life, but I didn't want anything else like Myran did. I had grown such a dense, protective shell over the years, that I didn't know what else was out there to want.

"If only Father's sons weren't completely inept, he wouldn't need me to apprentice." Myran swung back. Both brothers raised their shoulders and nodded in agreement. Myran rolled her eyes, but the shadow still loomed over her face.

"What about you two?" I turned to them, taking the heat off her.

"Us?" Willem gestured to his chest with his thumb, eyebrows dancing under his shaggy mop of hair. "We're here for moral support."

"Can't let our baby sister wind up with the wrong chap," Wiles said.

"They could apprentice *and* take their time finding a match if they weren't so dense," Myran said. "Men have all the luxury."

The three of them continued their volley but I was too distracted to listen. Something else had caught my eye. Something big. Across the lawn I spied the giant silhouette of a man, midnight colored hair standing out like an oasis in the desert.

My pulse tripled as anticipation smacked me in the face. Eyes darting from face to face, I frantically searched the area around Nix. *He* had to be nearby. The drumming came to a screeching halt when the crowd parted and the Governor emerged in all his golden glory. *He's here.* Andren was here, draped in an expensive coat and tails like a gift-wrapped present. Nix walked ahead of Andren and the roar of the party faded into a dull murmur as everyone gawked at the Governor and his oversized pet.

Following my line of sight, Myran turned to see what had me entranced. "Ah, the Governor has graced us with his presence." The four of us watched the show unfurl, while I struggled to stand still. I couldn't rush him the second he walked in. *But I should have.* I should have swarmed him alongside the dozens of other women who were now on his heels as Nix parted the wave of adoration. When Andren came to a halt, they pounced.

I observed the whole scene from a distance while he stood in the middle of his fans and carried on what appeared to be polite conversation. His charm was ceaseless as he looked every girl in the eye, exchanged words, and granted adequate attention to each before he moved onto the next. The women started to dissipate after they got their turn with him, growing tired of competing with the throng of eager Ladies. How... *sad.* As much as I wanted to elbow my way through the mass and steal away some of his attention just like the others, I couldn't bring myself to do it. I'd rather slither away into the grass with my tail tucked between my legs.

The sinking feeling in my intestines was swiftly replaced by broiling, seething horror when I realized Andren had pulled away to focus on just one girl. It shouldn't have affected me in such a way—I barely knew him—but I was choking on a primal wave of possessiveness. In a split second, Andren had confirmed all my insecurities and publicly stepped on them. I wasn't the only girl he'd made arrangements with tonight.

Shadowing myself behind Myran, I stalked Andren and the mystery woman's every move with a razor focus. They made their way to one of the swings, but not before he stopped to grab a glass of champagne and hand it to her. The way he smiled as he did it, dimple visible from my distance, shoved away every rational thought I had left in my head. I was feral with rage and regret for allowing myself to be so gullible. I'd wasted the whole event pining for a ghost, passing up tangible opportunities for connections. Actual, *available* connections.

"Here," Myran said. "You need this." I felt her push a thin, hard object into my hand while simultaneously coaxing my old flute away. I looked down to see the glass I had been holding was empty and that Myran had managed to summon a new one out of thin air.

"Do you know him?" she asked. "His presence seems to uh, bother you." I let loose the empty glass and tossed back half of the new one.

"We've met, but I don't really know him."

Myran raised a fresh glass she had secured for herself and clinked it against the tip of mine.

"Well, I wouldn't worry about... that." She gestured with her glass in Andren's direction. "He's a Governor, and a handsome one at that. I'm sure Debut is like catching fish in a barrel for him." Something about being compared to a fish jerked me back to my senses.

"I'm sure," I said, forcing myself to tear my eyes from the scene. Willem and Wiles had taken a step back for their safety, tracking my movements with caution.

"It's no consolation prize, but there's always Willem or Wiles." Myran snorted. Wiles bowed at me to formalize the offer.

"All the looks, none of the bore of being with a politician," Willem said, pushing his brother to the side. "And you get both of us as a package deal, no matter who you choose. That's the real prize." He tipped his glass toward me and I released a small chuckle. He did have a point, and in a better headspace, I might have actually considered it.

"You make a very compelling argument, my Lords." My voice cracked but I smiled at the duo anyway.

"You hear that?" Willem puffed his chest at Myran. "Finally getting the respect we deserve." I loosened my grip on the champagne flute, melting into the laughter that poured from my core. Though I wanted nothing more than to hide in a corner and lick my wounds, the blissful relief of letting go was far more therapeutic. The siblings and I laughed until my sides hurt.

The three of us idly chatted into the late afternoon, until the sun started to dip behind the courthouse and the guests began fading away. Temptation got the better of me and I stole a glance toward the swing in the corner, but Andren and the mystery girl were nowhere to be found. I sighed, unsure if it was from relief or disappointment. I wasn't going to let Andren overshadow what I'd accomplished today–I was leaving with three new friends, two of whom were technically eligible bachelors.

"Would you like an escort home?" Willem asked, Myran and Wiles waiting just behind him. I smiled graciously at his offer.

"Oh no, I don't live far. But thank you."

He shrugged and gave me a lopsided grin. It was neither devastating nor dimpled, but it still tinged my insides with warmth.

"Whatever pleases m'Lady," he said with a bow. The siblings departed together after we all exchanged goodbyes and promises to see each other at the next event, leaving me walking the opposite way toward my house. I crossed the grass, holding my dress down as I took long strides through the open area.

I yelped and tumbled backwards when something caught my wrist, all of my momentum coming with me. My balance evaded me from the shock, and from my bottomless champagne. I stumbled over my feet and landed into something hard and warm.

"While this one is solely my fault, I'm beginning to think you might be a walking hazard." The landscape tilted and I squinted to hold the figure in front of me still. My mind was a cruel prankster seeking its revenge for my champagne indulgence.

"You broke your promise, Lady Selah." Andren and his blasted dimple gazed down at me while I battled with gravity. He kept hold of my wrist, magnetizing whatever coherence I had remaining to the point where he made contact.

"Have you forgotten already?" he asked when I failed to respond. "You wound me so." Andren pretended to clutch his chest in pain.

"I can't remember a thing beyond the shock you just gave me," I said. "I may be a walking hazard but you are certainly a hazard to my nerves." Each one was frayed and raw, along with my patience. I narrowed my eyes to bring him into focus, only registering a shimmering gold orb in the moonlight.

"Ah, yes," he said. "Your aim hits true. My apologies, my Lady." My bravado waned as he danced around his activities tonight. He cinched his fingers on my wrist and my chest squeezed in tandem. I had to keep it together.

"Apology accepted." I unearthed the strength to reel my wrist back in. Andren held his eyes on me, one eyebrow stitched to his hairline.

"Did you have a pleasant evening?" he asked. More dancing. More pretending. He was a politician after all.

"I did. You?" I returned the inquiry, refusing to meet his stare. Off to the side, I noticed his faithful servant waiting in the wing, watching me like a guard dog. The intensity of his stare made my stomach flutter, aided by the champagne.

"It would have been much better if I had been able to see you." I felt his smile melt into me, but I wasn't ready to thaw. I would not fall victim to his charm, not when I was so obviously his backup plan for the evening.

"Sire, you seemed plenty entertained. I highly doubt my absence was noticed." I was done dancing, but Andren's smile just grew bigger. It boiled my blood.

"So you saw me then?" I didn't dignify him with a response. He apparently saw no shame in his escapades. "And you didn't grace me with your company like you promised me the other night?"

"I don't believe I had time between visitors." My temples throbbed and my eyes were starting to burn. I needed my bed, and I needed to get off the courthouse lawn before I fell asleep there in the grass.

"We can't have that." Andren placed his hands on his hips. "I suppose I'll have to do away with any distractions." His words swirled around my ears, but only every other one was entering. If I could trust my waning senses, it sounded like Andren was flirting with me again. I pictured the hoard of yellow and lilac at his feet, on his elbow, by his side on the swing, and I looked down at my navy gown and gathered the pinched fabric at my waist. *I* was the distraction. He was stalling–entertaining himself, maybe even indulging himself–but growing up the perpetual punchline had made me cynical. It had matured me quicker than I should have, but it had given me a long tenure in identifying a trap.

"Will you join me for dinner this weekend? At my estate?" he asked. "With my parents. Like any good courtship." Every synapse misfired and I teetered on my feet. I looked to Nix but Andren grabbed me by my shoulders and steadied me.

"I–," I was not prepared for that. "I–" This man was giving me whiplash between his gilded words and his murky actions. He'd spent the whole night with another Lady, had the nerve to *laugh* about it when confronted, and was now asking me to meet his family to make amends. Dinner during Debut wasn't an ordinary invitation. It was a vital step in a courtship, but the world was leaning too far for me to take any steps right now.

"Wonderful," he said. "Please extend the invitation to your parents. Saturday, 7:00. I hope you understand my need to be so forward. I won't miss another *opportunity*." Andren turned to me, as if challenging me to say no, but my voice evaporated into the breeze.

"Saturday at 7:00." I heard my own body repeat the information back to him, then cursed my manners for kicking in.

"Until Saturday," he said, stating it rather than asking. He squeezed my fingers before he released me to rejoin Nix. My brain told me I should have been insulted he didn't offer to walk me home, but my nerves thanked me. Nix's eyes lingered a beat too long. I squirmed against the boning of my gown and let my feet drag with each step forward. I was sticky with midsummer humidity wafting in from the ocean, and there was a pebble in my slipper, but I trudged the whole way with a mind full of colors and snippets of voices.

Chapter Five

"Corinna, it looks fine," I said to my Lady-in-Wait, who was making her fourth pass on my hair. She had managed to fashion a crown of sorts out of multiple braids, which wrapped from ear to ear. The remainder of my hair hung in loose curls down my back. I let her have a say in my dress, selecting a cascading sapphire frock. It was a heavier, structured material that drew in my waist with a bodice that laced up the back.

The entire look boasted sophistication, which was something I hoped Andren's parents would appreciate, but it was unbearably heavy. I tried to focus on anything but the suffocating bulk hanging from my body, but could only summon the last time I'd seen Andren. I ran the conversation through my head over a million times, until the phrases sounded like they were in a foreign language. Andren had specifically called the dinner a *courtship*. Never in my life had a single word caused such a visceral reaction.

"How do I look?" I asked Corinna, spinning around for the full effect.

She'd put the whole ensemble together but she indulged me anyway. "Fit for a Governor," she said, her excitement oozing from her pores. I still had a giant stone wall constructed around my emotions, but seeing Corinna like this drove a crack in it.

My parents' reaction had been quite the same. I thought Father would fall from his chair when I told him about my invitation, and theirs, as well. I'd only seen the look on my mother's face one other time in my life—the day Lilah was born. I'd been only three years old when she swaddled the blonde cherub in a rose pink blanket and let me kiss her on the cheek, but my mother's expression was sharply etched in my mind.

"I didn't know the new Governor was participating in Debut this year," Father had said when the shock first wore off. "But I suppose that makes sense. He is serving in a very important position and is still unwed. I imagine the pressure for him to fully emerge into society is quite high." While well-intentioned, Father's statement reinforced my little fortress, building it higher and stronger. The truth had been floating around just under my skin the whole time. I knew in spite of my unfortunate genetics, I still held a prestigious title. Mother's family was one of the oldest in the Bloodline, and though Father's was made Casted in more recent years, he was a senior leader in our society. My credentials were excellent on paper.

Regardless of why Andren extended the invitation, the actions were already a tidal wave in motion. Mother emerged from her dressing chambers an absolute vision in her own gown, leaving no detail untouched. Father's face sparked as she glided down the marble stair-case, completely entranced by the sight of her. I stood near the door, watching silently to not disrupt the scene, though I may as well have been across the sea. Nobody else existed but them. My heart squeezed at the display, and I realized *that* was what I wanted. Whether or not Andren could give me that, I had yet to determine.

We went by carriage to Andren's estate since it was on the other side of Upper Oberin, complete with two footmen to greet us. I gasped at the red brick drive, exquisitely lined with carved shrubbery and blossoming flowers the entire length. The trees formed a green tunnel, transporting me far outside my understanding of normal. The house itself was bright white like all the other estates in Oberin, but it stood twice the size, with a piercing roofline adorned with dormers, eaves, and towering chimneys on either side. I shifted the bodice of my dress, which now seemed dowdy and out of place next to Andren's home.

"My Lady." A tall, withering man in a dark tailcoat greeted me, head bowed. He leaned into a massive wooden door to heave it open, no small task given its size compared to his. Inside the round foyer, a formidable receiving line waited. I strained to lift my foot from the floor, my slippers apparently bonded with the brick porch. When I didn't advance, my mother nudged the small of my back like a defiant child, but Father didn't take the hint and shoveled both of us through the threshold. The only woman standing in the line tilted her head to look at us over the bridge of her nose. I wasn't supposed to be here and she knew it.

Andren intercepted from the side of the door, patting Father on the shoulder and ushering him to the lanky man with shimmering white hair. He gave Father a warm smile and extended his hand. Father shook it up and down in large arcs, like they were old cronies reuniting. When Father finally released him, the man turned to me, scanning me with a hint of something filtering his expression. I knew that look all too well. It was the same debate I'd seen others have when they met me, sometimes out loud. Was I a great beauty or an abomination? Was my existence a mystery or a problem? Either way, the outcome was the same; they always wanted to solve me.

"Lady Selah, this is my father, Lord Allendar Whit." Andren took my hand and passed it to his father, who clasped his other hand over the top of mine.

"An absolute pleasure, Lady Selah," he said to me. A glimpse of Andren in the future flashed in my mind, which set loose a thousand butterflies inside me. He'd be outlandishly handsome his whole life, but the part that really twisted the dagger in my side was the imagery itself. What did that say about me if I could picture him as an old man, but not me? Wouldn't a normal person daydream about passing the years with their suitor? Lilah would already have her monogrammed wax seals made by this point.

"And this is my mother, Lady Helena." He turned me to the woman standing at Allendar's shoulder. I took the initiative to reach my own hand more than halfway between us, leaning heavily on my years of finishing. Helena accepted it with a two-fingered grip, as if I was a filthy rag to be tossed aside. I knew that look well, too. She looked *through* me instead of at me, but I sucked in a breath and rendered a formal greeting. Why did my hands have to be so big, and so sweaty?

As Helena unceremoniously released me, wiping her palm on the side of her gown, two men entered the room. Just from the sudden absence of space in the foyer, I knew Nix was present before I looked over at them. The other man was barely visible behind Nix's elbow, though in actuality he was only a few inches shorter than Andren. His pallor resembled fresh cream, like his mother's, though it lacked the same gossamer texture, but his hair was such a mousy shade of blond it looked prematurely gray.

"Ah," Andren said. "Just in time for the formalities." He sauntered over to the pair and slapped the blonde man on the back hard, knocking him into Nix's arm. "Selah, please meet my older brother Amon, Fourth Governor by title, but not by importance." His brother had been undisturbed by Andren's physical greeting, but he flinched at his words.

"Lady Selah," he said.

I stumbled over my feet at the excuse to move out of Helena's ray of disdain, welcoming Amon's bored handshake. He, too, didn't meet my eye, but instead, kept his gaze fixed somewhere over my shoulder. Either Andren's social affairs didn't interest him, or I wasn't enough of a novelty to earn his attention. Andren had probably courted many others, and I was just another passerby. He'd never explicitly said this was his first Debut; that was just my assumption. *Look at him.* Of course he'd had other suitors. My cynicism was usually an effective weapon at keeping myself guarded from ambushes like these, but Andren had dulled it.

"You have already met Nix," Andren said, moving back to my side. "So we can spare you that torture again." Nix peeled back his lip in a half-smile then pushed through the doorway without waiting for the rest. I stared at his broad back as he walked, watching his sides flex through his clothing. He was much more comfortable roaming Andren's estate than any servant I'd seen. In spite of his size, Nix always wore an expression that suggested he was comfortable *anywhere* he went. It seemed foreign to me that anyone could be at ease in their own skin when it was so out of reach for me, especially someone as conspicuous as Nix. He was the antithesis of Casted.

Andren took his place at the head of the table while the man seated me to his left-hand side, just as Mother sat next to Father in our house. The chair groaned when I sat down, the same sound I imagined Helena making every time she locked eyes with me. Father was placed on my other side and then Mother, creating a sanctuary for me to duck and hide. If I leaned onto one hip and turned my head at just the right angle, I was able to block out all the other guests besides my family.

Nix threw back the chair on Andren's other side and plopped down directly in front of me. This time I got a full smile from him, and it was positively predatory. I worked my facial muscles to appear polite while the rest of Andren's family was seated around the table, but Nix bogarted my attention. How odd for him to get the seat traditionally reserved for family, while Andren's actual family filled in the gaps. In fact, it was odd he even got to sit at the table at all.

"You're in for a treat," he said.

"Excuse me?" I raised my brows at the giant holding a comically small dinner fork.

"Andren's chef is a magician. We found him in Torred and hired him to come back with us. You'd flip if you knew what Andren paid him." Nix's onyx eyes twinkled under the crystal chandelier.

"How... *extravagant*." Extravagant? It was ludicrous. Whatever Andren's mother thought about me, she was correct. I had no business being here, with a handsome Governor, and his handsome Casted parents, and his terrifyingly handsome servant. The chef was probably wildly talented and handsome, too.

Once dinner service began, a hoard of servants flitted in and out with gold platters. *Gold*, not silver. If Nix hadn't given me a heads up, I might've fallen from my chair after my first bite. The flavors were bold and wild, unlike anything I'd tasted on Oberin. Andren gushed about each featured spice and what lengths he'd gone through to procure it. By dessert, I was reduced to an uncultured sow in a dress, taking second chair to the balsamic and thyme reduction.

"Lord Sharpe," Andren's father said. "Andren has told me that you are quite skilled in your role." Father dabbed at his mouth with a napkin. "I'd love to hear more."

"I hope he has not built me up too much, my Lord," Father said. I smiled into my own napkin. At least he was in his element. "I am still newly assigned a larger territory of trade, so there are many things yet to accomplish."

"Have you traveled much into the Andalls?" Nix asked, propped up on his elbows as if Father was about to read him a bedtime story.

My father shook his head. "Not as often as I'd like, but there are some excellent miners I hope to engage. Right now those trade routes are largely underdeveloped because of... ah, the risk," Father said.

Nix nodded knowingly. "They've been giving us hell." My jaw clenched at his choice dinner conversation, but nobody else batted an eye. "I have been collecting different maps of the region. I may have some in my stock that could help." Father lit up like a candle.

"Nix is quite the purveyor of maps, and quite the budding cartographer." Andren spoke of Nix as if he was bragging on his own child. "He has been my Hand since I took Governorship last year and will be sponsored in the Trials this year. I want him as the official Cartographer to the Dominion."

Nix grinned sheepishly and polished off his cordial. "If I can pass the Trials."

Even with the high failure rate the broker had quoted, if anyone could pass the Trials, it was Nix. I couldn't even guess what they entailed, but just from being near him, I knew he could do it. The man didn't have a discernible weakness, and he had already made himself at home among the Caste.

"Your father was made Casted?" I was jostled from my daydream by a clear, orotund voice coming from Helena. I didn't expect that sound from such a tiny body, and I certainly didn't expect the pointed question aimed at my father's head.

"Yes, my Lady." Father tipped his chin, then leaned into my mother's direction. He often used my grandparents' story to segue into his own with my mother. *Had she turned him down during their courtship, he would have volunteered for the Trials just to dedicate them to her.* I had been born into a long line of generational romance–a precedent that set an impossible standard, but also an undeniable drive to find it. That made this whole ordeal very inconvenient considering Casted marriages were arranged out of alliance and pedigree, not love.

"That's quite the...fairytale." Helena stiffened her lips in disdain.

"I would only hope to find a love like that one day," Andren said. He angled his head toward me and winked, twisting my innards into a bow with a single look. Helena gave a *hmph* in protest. Now I knew why Andren sat her so far away.

"Time for a cigar," Nix said, pushing himself from the table.

"Excellent idea," Andren replied. "To the parlor, gentlemen." He led the processional of men out of the dining hall. Nix hovered in front of me, an unreadable expression on his face. If he'd been trying to rescue me, it worked. Helena muttered something about retiring for the night, and ducked out of the back entrance. My very own knight in shining black armor.

Andren was a sight to behold poised in the middle of the parlor. He talked with his hands for emphasis, gliding his long fingers through the air before artfully looping them around his cigar. The way his mouth formed each word, the corners pulling to one side, mesmerized me. He scraped his teeth across his full lower lip every now and then, and my salivary glands malfunctioned. The man could undo me without even looking at me.

When the cigars had burned out, and the decanter of brandy ran dry, Andren presented himself to the corner of the room where my mother and I politely sat in his velvet chairs. As soon as he got close, my pulse skipped into an erratic rhythm.

"My Lady," he said to Mother. "Would you permit me to take Selah for a walk around the gardens? I'd like to show her the rest of the property." Mother nodded, likely resisting the urge to tag along.

"I will bring her back shortly," he assured, and pulled me to my feet.

My stockings clung to the back of my knees, and I all but left my heart on his fancy chair. *Ruining his upholstery isn't the impression I wanted.* Somehow I moved one foot in front of the other and followed him out the door, audience and all.

The backdoor of the manor opened to a beautiful terrace the size of our whole house, illuminated with flickering lamps. Every direction I turned, I was surrounded with peaceful green and delicate blooms. It was straight out of a dream. Outside in the night air, the fog in my head dissipated and I allowed myself to finally be present. Between Andren's parents and his grandiose home, I'd let the events dictate my movements, my speech, and even my reactions so I could fit the mold of all *this.*

"You like it?" Andren spun me around to ensure I took every angle in.

"Oh yes," I said breathlessly. "Andren, this is splendid." Nothing in my life had ever warranted the use of that word outside of an academic setting. But *this* was the definition of it.

"There's more."

The gardens were actually a full conservatory, complete with towering walls of ivy and two greenhouses secured behind a bucolic white iron fence. If I sat and read my favorite books back to back without eating or sleeping, I wouldn't come close to experiencing the level of fantasy Andren had in his backyard. He had the luxury of strolling through this every day, living in this enchantment. His wife would be incredibly lucky to inherit all this.

He spun me to face him, encasing me with his arms on my shoulders. My chest pounded the word on repeat. *Wife.* Even I couldn't deny the way he touched me only reinforced my delusion. It was dangerous for me to have hope like that, but the look in his eye seemed far more deadly at the moment. I was surrounded by greens and pinks and yellows, but the bright blue was all I could focus on. They radiated brighter than everything else, putting me under a spell.

"You were perfect tonight," he said. I'd known I was being evaluated, but the statement still kicked me straight back into reality. Thunder rumbled somewhere in the distance, reverberating in my sternum. The island was notorious for late summer storms, but it felt like the background noise was selected just for me.

"Perfect?" I wrinkled my nose at him, unable to keep up the farce. I wore my emotional turbulence like a jacket. A very large, scratchy jacket.

"My family can be a bit...overwhelming" he said, confirming my transparency. "But they took to you." If that was taking to me, I never wanted to discover what her disapproval felt like. I cocked my head at Andren.

"Yes, my mother is always like that." Apparently I was *very* transparent.

"She's certainly *intense*," I said, unfolding my words carefully.

"Yes, she is." He inhaled with a deep, sweeping pull. "You're also quite hard to read. Do you know that?" *You just read me like a book.* His arms pressed into my shoulders and I shifted my weight, debating if I should slam the book closed or let him continue to flip through the pages.

"I'm sorry," I whispered. I hadn't been friendly or warm enough. I knew I wouldn't live up to their standards, but I'd tried *so* hard to socialize appropriately–like a good Lady.

"Selah, please don't apologize," he said. "I have pursued you without considering how you feel, especially now that you have your first taste of what courting me would be like." He flashed a devilish grin that shook my knees under his weight. Sensing me falter, he pulled me a step closer and moved his hands down to the small of my back. He couldn't say things like that to me and expect me to hear them when he was sharing oxygen with me. I couldn't breathe without smelling the hint of vanilla from his cigar. "So, what do you think?" *I'm supposed to think right now?*

"I—I. I, uh." *I can't speak with your mouth so close to mine.*

"It's too much, isn't it?" His lower lip protruded in the most tantalizing pout. *Good god, it is way too much.* I nudged him back a few inches.

"It is a bit much," I said.

"Of course it is, but here you are still." He laughed, shaking his head and letting blonde strands loose. They landed across his brow, and instinctively I swiped them aside with my fingertips. Another bout of thunder crackled, electrifying the connection with his skin. He let his smile melt from his face, narrowing his eyes and flexing his jaw. *Too much.* Touching him was too forward; a proper Lady would let the gentleman lead the interaction.

Andren pulled me in, closer this time. His breath tapped against my nose and cheeks, and the tops of my thighs pulled magnetically against his. He had me at a scandalous distance. If anyone was spying on us from the windows, we'd earn a strong chastisement on propriety, but I didn't care. I violated all these societal rules just by design, and I wasn't about to make an exception for Andren. Not when his hand pressed against the small of my back, edging me farther into scandal.

"Your hair is one of the greatest marvels I have seen in all the Dominion." He used his free hand to finger a rogue curl against my neck. I had to remember to thank Corinna for her masterpiece, if I had any brain cells leftover after this.

"It's not exactly a marvel to other Casted Ladies." I jerked the strand from his fingers. *Don't ruin this.* He didn't need me to call out all my flaws and insecurities, not when he was near perfect in comparison.

Andren touched the tip of his nose to mine. "They're jealous, Selah. Bored little girls with nothing remarkable to distinguish them from the next." My breath hitched in my chest and my heart hurtled to a stop as he stole back the piece of hair from my fingers. I waited for it to start beating again, but there was nothing but another low drum of thunder. His eyes darkened with the advancing storm. "We could give them something to *really* make them jealous." He couldn't talk to me that way. If he knew what he was doing, he'd be much more careful. Andren slid against me, his body meeting mine.

He knows exactly what he's doing. The crack of thunder crashed into all the places on my body I'd been trying to ignore. Electricity surged through my pelvis at the mere thought of Andren's suggestion. The atmosphere around us condensed with frenetic energy, and the threat of a raging storm. It made me feel dangerous, reckless.

"I fear no one has told you that before." Andren released my curl and took my chin in his hands, pulling my face up to his. We were painfully close to connecting on every plane. God, just a little further. *Please.*

"No," I said, a challenging feat without air in my lungs.

"That's a bloody shame." He spoke against my mouth, lips hovering over mine. We hung there for an eternity, the sweet, heavy build of the storm pushing down on us. Infinitesimally, he moved his mouth to mine and landed with the softest touch. When the sky boomed again, Andren took me completely. His lips to my lips, his tongue exploring me, his hands grazing my curves, his whole body telling me what he wanted. The sky exploded, white lights flashing in my vision, all thought channels intercepted. I'd never recover from this kind of devastation.

Far too soon, Andren released me, leaving me suspended with a moist, cool absence where his mouth had been on mine. My muscles screamed to bring him back. *I* could've screamed if my brain had been functioning properly.

"A bloody shame," Andren said again, looking down at me through heavy eyelids. I was exposed, standing under the churning clouds with Andren's essence lingering on me, but god, it was perfection. Just like him.

"I should get you back before we get blown away," he said, pulling away from me. *Too late for that.* I was surprised my knees didn't collapse when they lost the support of his against them. I caged the urge to argue, far from ready to give up the magic of his gardens, and whatever magic he'd conjured between us. But a loud crack sent me leaping back from Andren, severing the hold he had on me. The storm roiled overhead, and I knew Andren was right.

Our families were still in the parlor where we had left them, too busy reviewing a yellowed map Nix had unrolled across a drawing desk to see us slink in. Glued to his side, Father leaned over the map to absorb everything Nix pointed out. Mother sat back in the armchair, a peaceful smile resting on her face. Allendar and Amon observed from Nix's other side, chiming in about a landmark or passage of interest as Nix continued on.

"The storm seems to be picking up," I said, hoping to avoid any incriminating lines of question as we reentered the room. "We'd better get the horses home before they spook." Nix narrowed his eyes at Andren, then turned his stare to me. *He knows. For the love, it's painted all over my stupid face.* He bore a hole right through my head, emptying all my transgressions on the floor. I could've died if my body wasn't such a defiant twat.

Before anyone else could make a move, a rupturing *crack* slammed against the front of the house, violently shaking the walls of the enormous structure. The sound of glass shattering and wood splintering clattered all around us. I clamped onto Andren's elbow. Nix's approval wouldn't mean squat if the house came down. Somewhere down the hall, a scream rang out, turning my boiling blood to ice.

Andren took off running towards the sound and I scurried after him. Nix pushed past to catch up to Andren but I stayed on my course. That scream had been the shrill pitch reserved only for pain. I would know. We piled in the foyer to find one of the giant trees protruding through the windows above the doorway. The stately walls had buckled under the damage, and the frame was fractured and dangling. A servant sat on the ground, leaning against the wall in a wilted pile. She cupped her palms over her face, blood pouring between her fingers. I ran to kneel at her side.

"Are you alright, miss?" She was young—fourteen at most. Though she'd likely been fair to begin with, her pallor was nearly translucent against the crimson staining her face. There was so much blood I couldn't tell exactly where it was all coming from. I swallowed hard, then flipped up my gown to snag the hem of my undergarment. I used the soft linen to blot the streams of red so I could get a better look. Withholding a gasp, I found shards of glass peppering her skin from her forehead to her mouth. Her eyelid was torn, with a jagged sliver embedded precariously close to the delicate tissue beneath it. I could pull it out with my fingers, but I'd risk permanently damaging her vision on that side. I needed help, but the staff trampled around the foyer in the hysteria of everything; no one looked our way.

"She's hurt?" *The thunderstorm is talking to me.* Over my shoulder I spotted large leather boots and shaggy black hair. Nix crouched at my side, his attention honed on me and not the injured girl

"Yes," I said. "She could lose that eye if she doesn't get help soon." Nix cut his eyes from the girl back to me, and then to my stained dress.

"What do we need to do?" His dark complexion had blanched to a sickly gray, but he pressed his full lips together. In any other situation, watching a squeamish Nix would be humorous, but right then, I wanted to hug him for his noble effort.

"Bring me a bowl of water and towels from the kitchen." Relief returned some of his color. He was eager to distance himself from the gore. "Then I need a needle and thread, and tweezers or pliers—anything you can find." Nix gave a mock salute before disappearing into the calamity.

"You're going to be okay," I whispered to the girl. She'd begun to sob in guttural heaves, and I needed her still to prevent further injury. I ran my fingers over her smooth, brown hair. "We're here. We have you."

Nix was big, but he was fast. He reappeared holding a tray full of my requests, down to the pair of tweezers *and* pliers. Wide-eyed, he stared at me while I took inventory.

"Perfect," I said, and he rocked back on his heels, as if he'd been waiting for my affirmation. I quirked my eyebrow at him curiously, but I couldn't spare any more of my attention. Not when the girl was losing blood at an alarming rate.

Dipping the edge of the towel into the water, I cleared around her wounds before retrieving the pliers. I was going for the worst of it first. Nix sucked in a breath next to me when he figured out my plan. *He better not pass out.*

"Here," I said, tossing him the towel. "Hold this right here. When I give the word, press hard." Hopefully a task could distract him, because this could get ugly quickly. Gritting my teeth, I angled the pliers just so and took a careful grip on the shard to avoid shattering it. Breathing in through my nose, I yanked up with one, swift jerk, then braced for the backlash.

The girl barely twitched, and as promised, Nix held pressure on the open wound. I counted down thirty seconds in my head before sliding Nix's hand from her face. Her eyeball was in tact, and the laceration was nice and clean. I exhaled. *Thank the Ancient Ones.* Moving rapidly, I threaded the needle and bit the end of the thread. I wasn't much of a seamstress, but I had tried to learn many times. Skin couldn't be that much different. But from the first loop, I quickly realized skin had much more resistance and a completely different movement than fabric. *Don't mess this up. Easy.* It was only her sight at stake after all.

Fighting the pressure to keep my hands steady, I fed the needle through to form as tight of stitches as possible. When I tied off the thread, I paused to assess my work, but Nix shook my shoulders and jostled me like a clothesline.

"Holy shit! You did it," he exclaimed. The girl chanced a look at Nix's outburst, and then at me. She reached her hand to her face but I pulled it back gently.

"Let me finish cleaning you up," I said. She held her hand in the air, as if she either didn't understand me or didn't trust me. I replaced the pliers for the tweezers, and got to work plucking the smaller shards from her face, then wiped the blood away with the towel.

"Keep your face clean, and mind the stitches for a week or two. Then you can cut them out," I instructed her. She gave a curt nod in acknowledgement. *So she does understand.* "Do you think you can walk?" She held my stare without moving. *She didn't say no.* I grabbed her under her arm and lifted her torso to try to get her to support herself. Nix offered to help but she was so weightless, I already had her up. I clutched her against my body, picturing the frail little thing hauling around large stew pots and sacks of flour. She had a life of physical labor ahead of her, but she was so *breakable.*

"You're amazing," Nix said after we'd walked her to a settee. "Where did you learn to do that?" Frazzled curls clung to my damp forehead. I swiped at my hair with the back of my hand, careful not to streak more blood across my face. *I have to look like hell right now.* But Nix gaped at me as if I'd just been crowned queen of the whole Dominion. *We don't even have a queen.*

"I had a lot of injuries as a child," I said. The expression on Nix's face was utterly unreadable. My face flushed, and I turned away from his uneasy stare. I'd said too much, and to Andren's Hand of all people. To make matters worse, the Governor himself dashed into the room, looking as collected as he had when we'd first arrived. I took a wide step away from his servants and tried to conceal the blood stains under the folds of my gown. *What a complete disaster.* Andren stumbled when he caught sight of me.

"Selah, I–." He tripped over his own words, assessing my state. I might as well have rolled around the barn with his horses and pigs.

Andren scanned over the servant girl on the settee in the corner. "I'll send for the healer." My golden Governor turned on his heel and walked out of the room without another word. *I ruined everything.* I should have called for the healer myself, like a respectable Lady, but I had to sabotage the only good thing I had going in my life. I scoffed. *It was only a matter of time.*

Chapter Six

Every time I let my mind wander back to the scene at Andren's estate, I seized in sheer mortification. The worst part was having no one to blame but myself. Andren had been a perfect gentleman, but I'd left his house in a disastrous scene. I had the looks of a commoner, and now my behavior had matched. Getting down on the ground, handling his servants, soiling my gown.

I cringed when I heard the butler answer our door, knowing I could only avoid the conversation with Andren for so long. Eventually I'd have to face my embarrassment head on, and hope it hadn't tainted Andren's opinion of me enough to end our courtship.

Clamping my fingers around the velvet wingback chair in our parlor, I prepared myself for Andren to enter. But the doorway was filled top to bottom with a much larger, much darker form. Nix waltzed into the room and helped himself to the adjacent chair before I could offer it to him.

"Afternoon, Lady Selah," he said. I nodded in his direction, still adjusting to the contrast of Nix when I'd been expecting Andren.

I reached for the decanter on the side table and poured a glass of whiskey. Better to prepare for what was coming—sending Nix in his stead had to be a bad omen. It was far easier to have a servant deliver unsavory messages. I lifted the decanter and offered Nix a glass.

"No thank you. I won't be here long."

Well, the fun had lasted longer than I expected. And for someone like me, it was miraculous I'd been invited to a Governor's estate at all. *Time to get this over with.* I tipped the glass back in its entirety, then poured another. Nix raised a single, dark eyebrow but said nothing.

"How can I help you, Nix?"

"You're awfully formal for someone who performed emergency surgery with me just a few nights ago," he said. I gazed at him, unable to conjure a response. *Just put me out of my misery.* He leaned in. "It's a joke, Selah. Perhaps you do need that second glass."

I sipped at the spiced liquor. "How is she?" I asked.

"Well. Thanks to you," Nix replied. "Andren's healer was quite impressed at your treatment and said he couldn't have done a better job." I allowed myself to smile, aided by the second round of whiskey.

"Glad to hear it," I said, though I maintained my guard. I seriously doubted he came to update me on Andren's servant. Nix crossed his ankle over his knee, sprawling out of the delicate chair, and flashed a wide grin.

"I see why Andren is so smitten with you. That was some show you put on." He studied me, his bottomless eyes drinking me in. Whether it was the whiskey, or the intensity of his stare, I grew lightheaded. He'd said Andren was *smitten* with me, but I couldn't clear my mind long enough to absorb it. I squirmed, grateful for the respite when he finally looked away.

"Did he send you?" I asked once my vision quit swimming. Nix planted both his feet on the floor, the wooden planks groaning beneath his boots. I couldn't make out the look that flashed across his face before it vanished.

"He did. He told me to tell you he's sorry he hasn't called on you and that he's been busy with work." Nix recited it like a report.

"Work?" I asked. The corner of Nix's mouth twitched.

"He's a very busy man, Selah. I'm sure you expected that, given his position." Nix's voice was gentle, but it stung nonetheless. A rational person would have expected that, but clearly I hadn't. "But at least you'll always have me to keep you company while he's off doing *govern-*

mental things." Nix waggled his shoulders and straightened an invisible necktie. I couldn't help but laugh.

"That's quite a perk," I said. "But aren't you leaving soon? To the Trials?" Nix's face settled, the humor evaporating.

"I am," he replied.

"Are you ready?"

"I'll take that drink after all," he said without blinking. The Trials must have been unimaginably awful if someone like Nix was nervous about them. I poured the amber liquid with a finger more than usual—he looked like he needed it—then handed the tumbler to Nix. He polished off the glass as I had done, then winked. He was good company.

"That bad, huh?" Nix chucked me the glass and nudged his long, straight nose toward the decanter. I refilled his drink before handing it back. "I'll take that as a yes." Nix chuckled before clinking the emptied tumbler on the table.

"This whole ordeal is...a lot." Nix gestured around the parlor. Nothing seemed out of the ordinary to me. "Working for a Governor is one thing, but joining all *this* is pretty overwhelming to someone like me." He wasn't worried about the Trials; he was worried about being Casted. God, I could be so dense sometimes.

"That's understandable," I replied. *Real supportive, Selah.*

"The question is—are *you* ready to be a Governess?" Nix pulled back one side of his mouth in a lopsided grin, revealing sharp canines. I coughed on the burning liquid, then took another sip to wash it away. "I'll take that as a no," he teased.

"I guess I hadn't really put a label like that on it. *Governess* sounds so stuffy, doesn't it?" Just saying the word out loud felt heavy and awkward, but the humor and the alcohol helped lighten it a little.

"Oooh, yeah," he said with a low whistle. "That's far worse than *Lord.*"

"Guess we better get used to it though." I took the remnants of my glass and clinked it to his empty one. Nix wrapped his fingers around mine, the heat of his palms firing all the way to my chest where the whiskey had pooled, and lifted my glass and my hand. He took a drink, then released me.

"Cheers to that," he said. I laughed away my nerves and finished off the rest. Nix stood from the chair, sending it back with a loud scrape across the floor. "I should get going. Andren wanted me to let you know he's made your courtship public, and that he'll see you at the next event."

I gulped hard. "Public?"

"That's the next step in a courtship, isn't it? I don't really know how these things work, but I do know Andren has to play by the rules given his title." Nix paused, seeing I hadn't moved past the *public* part. "This is what you wanted, right?"

"Yes," I said tentatively. Nothing public on Oberin had ever worked out in my favor, but there probably weren't many secrets when you courted a Governor. *What did I get myself into?*

Nix left me to my thoughts, and whatever was left in the decanter. He held onto the doorway and gave me a tight smile before vanishing from the room.

Public.

"Will he be escorting you to the next event?"

"Yes."

"Will he be presenting you at Palladria?"

"Hopefully."

"Should we call upon his parents to discuss logistics?"

"Not yet."

"Can we expect a betrothal soon?"

"I really haven't thought that far."

Given both of our statuses, we could wed in as little as a month if everything fell into place, but we had to make it through the rest of the Debut season. All he had left to do was propose. We were the only ones in Oberin who hadn't discussed that minute detail yet, even finding Martock shooting curious glances at us whenever we were out. The other participants flitted around like moths to a candle, never coming out to chat, but instead, scrounging for a morsel they could devour with their friends behind closed doors.

Myran made me drink with her in celebration, gushing her approval then sharing that she was standing her ground with the rest of these "sad sacks". She elbowed her brothers, who I could now tell apart. Willem smiled at her banter and joined in, but his attempts were flat. I'd never seriously considered a courtship with him, and assumed he hadn't either, but perhaps I'd been wrong. Myran, on the other hand, seemed completely unbothered at the idea of closing out Debut without a match.

It was hard to worry about the fate of my new friends when the amnesia of my other classmates was suddenly lifted. They flocked to me, kissing my cheeks, holding my fingers in theirs, pawing at Andren's jacket sleeve, all to get a closer peek at us. Under any other circumstance, I would have been crushed beneath the debilitating attention, but the confidence wafting from Andren was contagious. I wasn't here as the curious red-haired Lady. I was here with Andren. I belonged to him and the whole crowd knew it. That thrill alone kept me buoyant through the residual parties until we had nothing left but Palladria.

Two evenings prior to the ball, I went to dinner at my usual time, finding my parents already in their places. Their chairs had been scooted a little bit closer to one another, something undetectable to an outsider, but something I noticed as soon as I sat down. Beneath the table, I could see their hands joined together in Mother's lap.

"Selah." Father began his preamble as I took my seat. "Your mother and I are so proud of you."

I flushed.

"You stand on the brink of womanhood and I hope we have prepared you well," Mother chimed in with a seamless transition, as if they had rehearsed this many times.

"You have." I curled my intonation into a question.

"This afternoon, Governor Whit came to call. The Fifth Governor." He said, as if I needed the additional clarification.

"He has asked us to commit to a betrothal between you two." My ears rang to hear it spoken aloud. I'd run them through my brain over a million times like a woman obsessed. *Me*, the permanent loner, had drawn this card in life. Andren had chosen *me*. It had been brewing for weeks but the moment was no less fantastic to actually chew on those words. It was really happening. I had my very own love story to add to my father's chronicles. My heart would've danced on the table if it hadn't been locked tight in my chest.

My parents slid to the edge of their chairs, waiting for a response I couldn't give. But how could I respond to something so monumental? *Yes* just didn't measure up to the brimming energy inside me.

"Before we signed a commitment," Father said when I didn't answer. "We wanted to ensure you agreed to this betrothal. It is a high honor in the Caste, but it will come with great responsibility. You will be one of the matriarchs to our people." His eyes glistened in the candle-light. "Have you considered all of this?"

"I have." *Only every second of every day for the past week.* "At least I think I have."

"And do you wish for us to accept this offer?" All three of us sat unmoving, frozen in the enormity of the moment.

"*Yes.*"

The morning of Palladria was conspicuously silent in the house. There was a vibration thrumming through the walls, as if they reflected the energy squirming inside me, but no other sounds from the residents. I took the opportunity to walk to the dam, strolling idly along the cobble road and soaking in its familiarity. I wouldn't get these moments to escape for much longer. The warmth of the sun and the smell of the saltwater was a stern reminder that in spite of their consistency, I would not be spared from change.

I knew Corinna would be furious if I didn't allow her ample time to complete her crowning piece, and rushed home long before I was ready to part with my hiding place. The preparation for Palladria had been her focus since my betrothal was announced. Even I was an active, willing participant this time around. I relished in the way she rolled and fastened my hair, admiring her skill as she brushed rouge over my cheeks and blotted my lids with a golden powder. I was going to be on display tonight no matter what, so I might as well look good.

Hours later, I raked my hands down my waist, smoothing the emerald material that hugged my hips before falling to the floor. I extended my dainty slipper to expose my scandalously bare leg beneath the skirt, rotating my ankle to view the detail from every angle.

"Thank you, Corinna." I kissed my Lady-in-Wait's cheeks before tip-toeing down the staircase. Mother and Father were poised at the bottom, hands clasped and eyes wide. Father touched his hand to his forehead as if he was shielding his eyes, and my mother sucked in a long, loud breath I could hear from the landing.

Andren's carriage had already arrived, complete with two footmen in tow. I hung in the doorway with my parents behind me, watching him unfold from the carriage. Once he planted his feet on the ground, he froze. Bright blue eyes locked with mine. His mouth went slack. *This is mine, actually mine.* I wouldn't process it until I could actually put my hands on him, and they itched to be *all* over him.

"Selah," he said, catching his foot in the carriage door. "You're *magnificent.*" Andren hung back as the footmen helped me climb into the carriage, never peeling his eyes from me. He opened his mouth and picked up his hand like he was about to speak several times on the ride over, but settled into the crumbling gravel beneath the carriage wheels. Governor Andren Whit was speechless. He was never without words, but his reaction was far more than I'd ever dreamt. And it was genuine. No Casted Lady was lurking in the corner to deliver the punchline that typically followed any compliment given to me.

Palladria was held inside the courthouse, a space deceivingly large for its purpose. The circular drive around the lawn was lined with carriages, and the arching entrance swarmed with servants dressed in tailcoats and top hats, poised to greet every guest. Hundreds of Casted filtered through the doors, under the domed ceilings of the courtroom, and then spilled out onto the rear terrace. It was a sea of travertine and marble, bronze and crystal, with people in every corner. The entire Caste was present tonight.

Andren gripped my fingers in his, pulling me close to avoid the throng of bodies, all dressed to the nines in extravagant formal attire. Every head swiveled to watch us together, and the politest few waited until we passed before they turned to whisper to one another. I was quite accustomed to their snide comments, but there were no outward insults tonight. Not to my face at least. No one would touch me when I was with him.

"This is the Council table," he said, pulling out a chair for me. *It's reserved for* us. The act of being Governess had already begun. I surveyed the vast room of people swirling about in an uproar of commotion. Andren sat next to me and together we watched the crowd while they all watched us. I couldn't run and hide in the corner; we were an exhibit on display. Fortunately they looked like a writhing ant hill from this vantage, no bigger than insects, allowing me to stay far detached from their chaos. Is this what Andren felt like on a regular basis? Perhaps he chose me because I was someone who also didn't belong in the mass, just like him.

"It's okay to be nervous." Andren squeezed my knee under the table. I shoved my racing thoughts into the farthest corner of my mind, focusing on Andren's warm, golden face. His touch softened my core into liquid metal. If I closed my eyes and focused, I could spread it over the rest of my body.

The rest of the council filed in behind us. The other Governors and their spouses were older, and quite at ease at the head table, carrying on with cordial greetings. One in particular caught my attention. He was nearly as large as Nix, but far more weathered. His face was marred with angry scars, and his white hair was gathered at the base of his head. When Andren introduced him as Governor Gregor, the man raked over me with a sharp, examining eye instead of a formal greeting. It left me stinging from the aftermath. Hopefully we wouldn't have to attend many events with him.

The room fell silent and every guest faced the entrance expectantly. A slow, rhythmic *click, clack, click, clack* echoed off the vaulted ceiling. The Chancellor had his wife on his arm, the statuesque pair making their way to the head table. He leaned into a cane as he walked with a canted gait. I squinted to get a better look at the odd, white apparatus, then realized it was carved from bleached bone. A trophy from his time as commander in the War of the Scrolls. I shivered, envisioning the face-less Alloyed soldier who'd been the unfortunate donor.

The entire room stood. I sprang to my feet, adjusting my dress from the hasty change in position. The First Madame sat down in her chair, but the rest of the hall remained standing, including the Chancellor. He cleared his throat.

"Lords and Ladies of the Caste, loyal servants, and distinguished guests." He waved his cane out over the crowd. "Your presence here tonight is a mark of the vitality of our beloved society." His voice crackled like dry leaves. Now that he was nearer, I could see the deep crevices of time overtaking his face. If the accounts of him battling the Alloyed in my history books weren't telling, his ancient countenance was clear evidence of his age. He was at least 750 years old, the patriarch of the Original Bloodline.

"I invite you all to celebrate the betrothals that signify the future of our generations, perpetuating the purity of our Bloodline, which has been cleansed through the Scrolls of our people. Through this diligence, we will be blessed with years of enduring health and power." I shifted from foot to foot, anxious for the support of my chair. "It is my honor to give blessings to those who uphold the duty of our people." He flicked his cane in a downward motion to indicate it was time to sit. Once he was in his place, at least a hundred servants began scurrying around the room with hors d'oeuvres and drinks. The hum of conversation ensued.

Andren turned to face the rest of the table. "Chancellor." He dipped his head. "Please let me introduce Lady Selah Sharpe." The Chancellor drank me in with eyes so pale they were creamy, but too sharp to be cataracts. And only lesser classmen got cataracts.

"This is our Chancellor, Rudolph Adelfried and our First Madame, Zelda." The pair remained in their positions. I backed my chair from the table and stood to render a formal curtsy, just as I was taught.

"Lady Selah," the Chancellor said, as if my name had a hidden meaning only he knew. "What a unique specimen you are." I cut a quick look to Andren, then back to the Chancellor, opting to curtsy instead of respond. "But you are Casted born?" I flinched, but Andren squeezed my hand under the table.

"Yes, your Grace."

"Daughter of Lord Danby Sharpe?" The Chancellor pressed on.

"Yes, your Grace." His jaw worked from side to side, measuring up my answers. I'd somehow fooled myself into believing I was good enough for Andren, but the Chancellor saw straight through me. Andren should be with a direct descendent of the Original Bloodline, not some fiery-haired anomaly.

"Splendid," the Chancellor said, taking one last look at me before turning to the other distinguished guests. I released a gush of air, but the scratchy, nagging sensation persisted. I rubbed my arm in effort to focus on anything else, looking down to see I'd made a bright red patch on my skin. The night had just started and I'd already caused bodily harm; there was no chance I'd survive the rest.

"For the toast," Andren said when a champagne flute was dropped in front of me. I looked from the glass to him. The fading willpower on my face giving me away, but I nodded anyway. The hall grew quiet as the Chancellor stood once again, raised his glass, and spoke.

"To the Scrolls!" His voice crackled over the room, and he took a single sip of his glass. The guests echoed the toast at him. "To the Bloodline!" They all dutifully mirrored his movement. I barely let the liquid brim my tongue for fear of gulping the rest down. "To the Caste!" He tipped back the champagne and emptied the glass in one swallow, so I did the same.

The Chancellor deposited his empty champagne glass on the table and lowered himself into his seat with the bone cane. A smartly dressed servant parked himself at the corner of our table, and unrolled a crisp piece of parchment.

"Lord Quincy Fritzhand!" The servant yelled into the crowd. *This is it. This is the moment my humiliation peaks.* Everything had been building to the cherry on top of my tragic existence.

Lord Quincy took choppy, short steps to the head table with a mousy Casted Lady at his side. She was as forgettable as he was—just another Lady who'd slung insults at me with her dainty mouth, now pursed in perfect gentility. I'd kill to be forgettable, to have the upper hand. Lord Fritzhand and his intended knelt to the ground in front of the Chancellor, just as she'd rehearsed her whole life. She always knew this moment was promised. "Lady Ada Riddle and I humbly ask your blessing on our betrothal."

"Lord Quincy and Lady Ada," the Chancellor said. "I grant my blessings to your union." The pair rose, bowed to the Chancellor, and retreated back into the crowd. It was simple enough, but the cold, heavy rock inside me grew larger and larger with each Lord called to the front. *It's never that simple.*

"Lord Martin Hamerstock!" Martock made his way through the rows of people, with his betrothed in tow. I expected to see Ophida's diminutive stature at his side, but the girl with him was tall, with thick, sandy hair. Martock was holding Myran's hand. Even though they were now standing directly in front of the Chancellor, asking for a blessing with the scripted delivery, my mind reeled. *How? When?*

"Lord Martin and Lady Myran," the Chancellor said. "I grant my blessings to your union." Martock beamed and Myran mirrored his expression, exuding a brightness behind it. She was happy, and I'd been too distracted with Andren to share that with her. Her smile sent a dagger of guilt directly to my chest, as if I needed further proof on why I'd always be alone.

"Lord Percival Frier!" I was still watching Myran and Martock when the timid young Lord made his way forward. I failed to register the tiny girl with stick-straight hair as his pairing until she turned in my direction. *Ophida.* Ophida had lost out on Martock, but she'd still managed a pairing. Her face didn't reveal anything other than engineered determination as she approached the Chancellor, and Lord Frier's was frozen with sheer terror.

"Lord Percival Frier p-presents to your G-Grace," Lord Frier said. "Miss Ophida Brown and I h-humbly ask your blessing on our b-b-betrothal."

"Lord Percival and Miss Ophida," the Chancellor said. "I grant a provision to your betrothal, pending the Cleansing of Miss Ophida to join our Bloodline. At that time, I will bestow upon you my full blessing to your union." Lord Frier and Ophida bowed before marching stiffly back to their places. Myran clapped for their quasi-betrothal, but Ophida cut her a scathing glower. She was nasty and spiteful, but I understood why she was guarded. I had been balancing between excitement and utter dread, but her situation was much more daunting.

Lord after Lord was called up to receive their blessings, returning with their newly-betrothed Lady in hand. Notably absent from the list of names were Wiles and Willem, just as they said they'd be. Myran took the stage for her family, but there was a tremor in a dusty corner of my heart that tapped faintly when I pictured Willem's confident smirk.

"Governor Andren Whit!" The name startled me, and the soaring ceilings plummeted down on me. Why were there so many people? Before I could dart for the doors, Andren wove his arm through mine and pulled me from my seat. I reached for the string of pearls around my neck, spinning each smooth bead until it grew hot in my fingers. Andren tapped my back and let out a subtle *ahem,* so I let them drop against my chest. I locked my fingers in my dress to keep my hands at my side and marched in front of the Chancellor. Thankfully, I only had to stand there while Andren did the work, but staying on my feet proved to be quite the challenge. I sighed in relief when he guided me to my knees in front of our ruler.

"Governor Andren Whit presents to your Grace," he said with such smoothness it took my breath away. Everything about this man was so refined, while I had to string my limbs to keep from falling to pieces. "Lady Selah Sharpe and I humbly ask your blessing on our betrothal."

"Governor Andren and Lady Selah." The Chancellor spoke over us to the guests. "I grant my blessing to your betrothal." Dumbstruck, I was nothing more than a marionette that Andren was puppeteering. He pulled me to my feet and took the lead on a very deep bow. My body responded purely from muscle memory, because my entire head had been wiped clean. Nothing but white noise and echoes.

"Selah!" A body careened into me. "That was *fantastic!*" Myran bounced up and down with excitement, waves of hair dancing with the motion. "You're going to be a Governess!" I blinked, then blinked again, finally regaining control of my thoughts.

"I am. But you're betrothed! To Martock!" I needed to redirect the conversation. "When did that happen?" Martock waltzed up behind Myran, grinning until his mouth practically touched his earlobes.

"We connected over our mutual love for academia and dislike for stuffy societal nonsense," he said, but he was just as springy as Myran. They fused together, such an obvious unit that I'd overlooked. Andren had consumed every inch of my life, but now I was officially his and life could resume. I should've been relieved, but I couldn't replicate the same effortless posture of Myran and Martock. Why couldn't I accept this was happening? That there would be no punchline?

"But mostly I saved him from Ophida," Myran said, reading the pang in my features. "Which wasn't easy. That girl had her claws buried very deep." Martock bulged his eyes for emphasis.

"Lord Frier is undoubtedly thrilled with the assistance."

Myran and Martock cackled devilishly. He draped his arm around her shoulder and she leaned into it. I looked up to Andren, who was laughing along with the group, but paused to gather me up and pull me in. I melted into the moment, when he planted a soft kiss on the back of my head. Tucking deeper into the pocket of his shoulder, I allowed myself to relax. Just a little.

Chapter Seven

As the time approached, our family home grew to feel larger and colder–practically institutional. *Since when did the hallway echo so much? And when did everyone get so busy?* The servants swarmed the property like drones in preparation for the wedding, but I had no desire to be the queen bee. When I walked into my room after breakfast, finding Corinna waist-deep in my wardrobe, pressure slammed into my skull. The array of belongings pulsed in my vision. *My head might explode if one more person asks me something.* I rubbed my temples, trying to dull the persistent ache.

"I hope you don't mind, my Lady," she started. "I'm going through your wardrobe to select what to pack. Some of these will not be fitting for a Governess." As my Lady-in-Wait, Corinna was the only servant who would accompany me to Andren's estate. She'd already sorted out my belongings into "take" and "keep" piles, neatly sorting my future on my behalf. Corinna hummed as she worked, while I started to drown on dry air.

"Thank you, Corinna," I managed, then wiped my nose. All of the contents from my head seemed to be leaking through my sinuses. *Great, my head is actually overflowing.*

It was more than I could withstand. The never-ending list to plan. The endless discussions over painful details. The constant interrogations. I may have been bigger and stronger than other Casted girls, but that all ended with my physical appearance. Internally, I was sloshing around whichever way the world pulled me, trying not to get swallowed by my own life. Nobody else seemed to recognize my turmoil either, because they just kept hitting me with more. Everyone wanted *more.*

"Governor Andren is here to call on you." The butler appeared at the threshold, eyeing me warily, pursing his lips while he awaited my response. I was still in my robes, laying on my side on the settee. Evidently it was well past morning time. "I will tell him you will be down momentarily," he said.

I didn't wait for Corinna to break from her current tasks, and threw the robe off myself. I ran down the marble staircase, but slowed as I rounded the corner, coming into view of the doorway. Andren stood silhouetted by the morning sunlight, decked out in a riding coat and clutching a crop in his left hand. He dropped it against the wall and raced to the stairs the second he saw me, then hugged me so tightly my toes lifted from the ground. The weightlessness was bliss. There were no questions, and no extra layer of skirts between us.

Andren planted a kiss on my forehead before setting me back down. "My Lady."

"Sire."

"*Madame,*" he said into my ear, the title by which Governesses were called. It felt bulky and foreign, but I needed to start acclimating to its sound.

"Please tell me you're here to help me plan this ceremony." Andren chuckled as I led him into the sitting room. The servant followed us in with tea and almond biscuits, then closed the door behind him to leave us alone.

"I wish," he said. "I came to let you know I am being pulled away for another trip to the mainland and won't be able to call on you for a little while." My heart dropped. I couldn't do this without him.

"The Alloyed again?" Andren had been filling me in on the growing situation. Though the Casted had defeated the savage clansmen in the War of the Scrolls centuries prior, they were hellbent on stealing them back. If they could get their hands on the ancient document, they could potentially create their own faction–longevity, health, cohesion–all the attributes we'd cultivated in the Caste. And if we lost them... well, it would end our society. The diseases that plagued Lower Oberin alone were only a sampling of why the threat kept me up at night. Andren emphasized how disorganized they were, so their attacks were usually small and ineffective, but I hadn't missed their increase in frequency.

"But I will be back for your Scrolling," Andren said. "I would let the entire Alloyed militia overtake all of the Dominion before I allowed that to happen." *Is that a possibility?* "Besides, I hear I have big plans shortly after." The fluttery nerves returned, but he'd successfully washed some of the dread away. Andren had a talent for that.

"Not if I can't work out these details." I laid my teacup on the side table with an unceremonious *clunk*.

"Please don't stress yourself over details. I fear all this is starting to take a toll on you." Andren ran his hand along my cheek. "You could wear nothing but a tablecloth and I would marry you just the same." He flashed a diabolical grin. "In fact, I'd prefer it." He lowered his voice to a suggestive hum. My heart leapt into my throat. I kept waiting for this seesaw of emotions to settle, but I suspected that wouldn't happen for quite some time. Judging by the smirk on his face, Andren was keenly aware of how he affected me, too.

"Sire, you embarrass me." I bit my lower lip and let it fall into a full, moist pout. I then clutched my hand to my breast dramatically. If he could flirt, so could I. Andren's eyes flared.

"My dear," he said. "That is only the start of what I will do to you." He said this as a threat to all of my sensibilities, and my body quivered in response. Hiding the flush from my face, I took a long drink of my tea, oblivious to the scalding heat.

"I am truly sorry I won't be here to help you," he said after letting me cool back down. "I hope this life never grows weary to you. I've been hesitant to take a wife because I fear the resentment and the callousness I see from the other Governesses, but you don't seem bothered by the usual things that trouble other women."

"Thank you?"

"I suppose I should thank *you*," Andren said. His eyes were like sea glass staring back at me, so intensely bright as they darted their focus between my eyes. Once again I had the urge to reach out and touch him, but this time I didn't stop myself. I let my hand drift to his face and caressed his smooth, high cheekbone. Andren gently tipped his head towards the motion.

"I don't deserve you," he said. But the feeling was mutual.

Before we walked out of the sitting room, Andren wrapped his arms around me and closed his lips over mine. His kiss was nowhere near long enough, but neither of us wanted the consequences from being caught. He let his fingers linger on my bare skin, sending tiny shockwaves up and down my spine.

"I will see you soon, my love." I vibrated with the heat of his breath and the sound of his words in my ear. *My love.*

I would never grow tired of hearing that.

Andren strutted from our house and mounted his steed in one swift motion, his limbs long and graceful as he kicked the sides of his mount. He looked every part the distinguished Governor trotting down the hill, golden hair bouncing against his head. I didn't care who saw me staring because I was savoring the vision, committing all of Andren's finite details to memory.

Alone again, I paced so many laps around the parlor I left a ring of tracks in the piled wool rug. Maybe if I walked enough, I could force the ringing in my ears to dissipate. The butler periodically popped his head in to refresh my beverage and confirm I hadn't worried myself into a pit of destruction, eyeing the rug every time he reappeared. He was too polite to ever say anything, though I knew he didn't appreciate my impromptu artwork.

Just past four, I heard our oak doors crash against the walls as if they were kicked open, and the scrape of a heavy trunk being dragged across the marble floor. *Lilah.* My sister was the epitome of the youngest child, buoyant, outspoken, and half-feral, but she was the apple of my parents' eye. And of mine. I rushed into the hall to greet her, but was intercepted by a flying mound of curls.

Lilah was what I should have looked like, with her perfectly creamy complexion and wheaten locks. We had the same unruly curls, however. She was at least four inches shorter than I was, and a fraction of my mass. But what she lacked in size, Lilah made up for in noise.

"Selah!" She bellowed into my ear, even though her face was close enough I could smell her breakfast. Her cheeks were bright pink and her eyes danced as she clung to my midsection. "I've missed all of the excitement! You have to give me every detail!" Lilah bounced up and down, her curls striking her shoulders with each launch. She grabbed me by the arm and dragged me into the parlor where she perched like a parakeet.

"Wouldn't you like to unpack and relax a little?" The journey from the school was half a day or more. Any other person would be exhausted, but my sister didn't know how to rest. I had years of late nights and early mornings to show for it.

"Not a chance," she said. "My sister is about to be a Governess. Everything else can wait!"

I threw my hands up and sighed in resignation, assuming my place on the opposite settee. The butler brought in a tray that contained a pitcher of water, sweet bread, dried meat, hard cheese, and sliced strawberries. He always had a soft spot for Lilah.

"I don't know where to start," I said as I inventoried all of the moments with Andren that led to this point, struggling with a way to capture it all in words.

"Start at the beginning! What's his name? What does he look like? How did you swing a courtship with a senior government official?" She rattled the questions off as if she had them jotted down on a notepad somewhere. Considering it was Lilah, she probably did.

"His name is Andren Whit and his brother, Amon, is also a Governor. He's very handsome." I listed off his attributes.

"So is every other Casted Lord," Lilah said. "What does he *actually* look like?"

I sighed. "Well, he's tall and rather... trim." I tried to find the appropriate descriptor for *unbelievably attractive*. "We actually met in the market."

"The market?" Lilah's eyes widened to the point her irises looked comically small. "You're still going down there?"

"Yes," I said.

Lilah shrugged her shoulders as she popped a strawberry into her mouth. I explained our chance meeting and subsequent courtship in sequence, skimming over the juiciest moments alone with him. Those were just for me to savor. "You make it sound so sterile."

"I'm sorry. Most of the time I don't even know how I feel, let alone how to describe it. I'm still in shock this is even happening." I dumped everything in a string for Lilah to unravel.

"Well it *is* happening and I'm here to help you!" she said. "Just in time, too. You look like a wreck!"

I swiped my forehead. I did feel pretty ragged, but was it that obvious? "I am a wreck. I have no idea how to plan a marriage ceremony."

"Well lucky for you, I have been preparing for this my whole life."

I believed her.

"Lilah," I said to my little sister as she stood to head to dinner. I laid my palm over the back of her hand. "Thank you."

On the night before my Scrolling, we finally had everything in place. And by *we*, I really meant Lilah. I was boiled down to a gelatinous sludge from all the arrangements. Details were never my thing. Andren barreled through the door late in the evening, looking road worn and ragged, but he greeted me with a hearty embrace. I held him tight around the neck, breathing in the smell of mellowed sun and dust, and his familiar stormy musk. When he let go, he handed me a loaf of spiced bread, a bag of fine candies, and a small box. I set the food aside and opened it, finding a gold charm in the shape of a circle with a straight bar passing through the middle. I marveled at the glimmer of the fine metal.

"It was forged from the gold mined in the Andalls," he said as he fastened it around my neck. "I thought you could wear it for your Scrolling tomorrow." Stepping back to admire the final look, he gave me the widest, dimpled smile before kissing the tip of my ear. The charm had a satisfying weight against my breastbone, a reminder I belonged to him. Something tangible, real.

"Beautiful." He drew me in closer to him. Mumbling about privacy, my sister politely excused herself from the room. The second she was out of sight, Andren locked his mouth to mine. I wanted to speed up time, to get him back to me sooner, to be his wife sooner, but above all else, I wanted to suspend myself in that moment forever. But he pulled away all too soon, leaving me breathless and a little chilled. I watched the back of his head vanish through the doorway as I clutched the pendant between my fingers and sniffled.

Chapter Eight

The Scrolls were not only the founding document of our society, they were the source of our good health, longevity, distinguished traits, and everything that made us Casted. The Prophecy had been scripted by the Ancient Ones when the Scrolls were given to the Casted, delegating us to rule over the rest of the lands and thus, gifting us with all the traits to keep us in power.

Though it was written in a language no longer spoken, we'd all recited the translation of the Prophecy from the time we could speak. We knew our places, and we knew our obligation to the Dominion. By signing the Scrolls, we were publicly identifying our Original Bloodline and pledging to protect it at all costs. Signing meant swearing our allegiance to its calling, and fulfilling our societal duty. Though I knew all this, I'd never actually seen the Scrolls before, and their nearness permeated my flesh and vibrated into my bones. Or perhaps it was just my nerves.

We were back in the courtroom, all signs of festivity from Palladria removed. I was mashed in a gaggle of young Casted men and women, draped in long black robes that grazed the floor as we walked. They were meant to be representative of the actual Casted Court, mimicking the flowing velvet robes worn by our leaders, but they looked like fancy tripping hazards to me. I raised my hand, letting the wide cuff drift around at my waist in hopes of catching some air into the heavy fabric. How did Andren wear these for hours on end?

Sweat formed on my palms that had nothing to do with the stuffy heat of the crowded courtroom. Andren would be here any second, not just as an observer in the stands like my family, but as one of the facilitators of my ceremony. *My* betrothed was going to preside over *my* ceremony, in front of everyone. The hard part was over, and this was the final formality before I could wed Andren, but the publicity of it all shook me. I had nothing to worry about, but I couldn't swallow away the sour taste of nervousness.

I palmed the blade sheathed in my pocket under the robe, a gift from my Father just for this occasion. We all carried them beneath the layers of heavy, suffocating fabric. I ran my finger up the rough sides of the hilt, visualizing how I was supposed to hold it when my name was called. The coolness of the steel helped soothe the panicked scorch bearing down on me, and the weight of the weapon grounded me. I took a large breath and the irritation in the back of my throat increased. I opened my mouth and let out a loud sneeze just as the Court paraded into the large, domed room. Several heads turned my way, but I stood as still as a statue to blend into the other candidates. I never sneezed; my nerves had a death grip even on my nasal passages.

I craned my neck to find Andren in the mix of moving bodies, everyone shuffling to find their places, then finally spied the Governors walking in a row toward the front of the room. He was last to file in, but his gold hair shimmered like a beacon. My heart somersaulted at the sight of him, his lithe movements silhouetted in his dark robes.

If I needed any further proof of the Scrolls' magic, Andren was a walking showcase of their capabilities. When the warriors first used the Prophecy housed in the pages to cleanse the Bloodline, they'd created the perfect ruling class, and the Whits had to be direct descendants. Despite my grandfather being cleansed after he'd passed the Trials, I still had the misfortune of wearing my separation from the Bloodline on constant display. Yet every dreadful second in this stagnant, stewing courtroom brought me a little closer to being Andren's wife in spite of that anomaly. Forever a mismatched pairing–the underdog story of my life.

The Chancellor walked in several beats later, carrying his cane and making the same, steady *click, clack* as he moved. The bleached bone of the handle illuminated bright white from the afternoon sun pouring into the courtroom. Everything else went blurry around him. I had to get used to this, to tuning all this out, but the Chancellor's voice cut through my concentration.

"Ordained by the ancient, borne from flame...." The words were familiar, imprinted in my brain from daily recitation. We'd read the preamble to the Prophecy at the beginning of each class, as was customary for all Casted children.

"Today we welcome the Seven Hundred and Twenty First cohort of Casted," he said. "Signing the Scrolls is not only a duty to the Original Bloodline of our ancestors, it's an honor to enter their ranks. It's a tribute to those who fought to preserve our sacred mission, granted to us by the Prophecy housed in these very pages. Many of those warriors stand here today." The Chancellor paused to scan the room, his eyes holding just above my head. The hairs on the back of my neck pricked to attention.

"You will join those who have gone before and take your place in our great society. You will sign the Scrolls with the very life force that ordains us with the obligation to rule. You will emerge as leaders of our time."

He quieted, leaving a charged cloud of silence in the packed courtroom. I peeked at my parents' position, trying to catch their eyes. I wanted reassurance, permission even. I wanted someone to tell me this was real, and that I was fit to be here, regardless of my silly hair. It was just hair. I was Casted after all, and I was going to be Andren's Governess. But I still wanted someone to validate all that, because I was doing a terrible job convincing myself to believe it.

Gregor sauntered to the center of the room and unrolled the faded parchment, winding until he came to a blank space at the end. My lungs squeezed at the sound of him hammering a tack into the wooden stand. The Scrolls were proudly displayed in front of the room to give the best vantage. I couldn't make out the signatures, but I could discern the browned, dried blood of the others who had already signed. The dagger grew heavier against my side.

Gregor swung around, moving the air in a startling gush. I jerked with the sudden movement, then clamped my jaw when he opened his mouth, and roared the first name. Rilla Abbington marched the rehearsed path to the mounted Scrolls. She reached into her robe and recovered a small dagger, which she used to draw a thin, red line into her forearm. *See?* There was nothing to worry about. If she hesitated, no one saw. There was no time to analyze her movements before she scrawled her name and replaced the quill in its dry well. *How anticlimactic.*

The hoods continued to file through for over an hour before I crept close enough to see the altar-like display in detail. I rolled onto the balls of my feet to keep my legs from falling asleep. The last thing I needed was to trip from the lack of sensation. When Gregor finally reached my name, I stepped out with as much confidence as I could manage. A twinge of nerves danced along my sternum when he called my name across the courtroom, but they were numbed along with my feet after the monotony of the ceremony. *Finally.*

I unsheathed my dagger and peeled back the sleeve of my robe. Pain was no issue, and I'd had far more serious injuries before, but every ounce of self-preservation actively pushed back. My knuckles were bright white as I drew my right hand up and hovered over my bare flesh. A sheen of sweat formed and I feared the blade would slip right off. As quickly as possible, I snuck a glance to the golden-haired ray only a few feet away from me. Andren met me with a warm smile and my head spun. It wasn't from the ceremony at all; it was from him. Why hadn't I connected everything sooner? I didn't care about this stupid ceremony or these ridiculous robes. Being Casted wasn't anything special and the Scrolls were just old paper. Being with Andren was special. And all I cared about was living up to his expectation.

The blade shone menacingly back at me but I pushed it into my arm. I splayed my fingers out wide, gritted my teeth, and dragged the edge across my forearm diagonally. It took a second for the pang of pierced skin to register, but the thin trail of crimson forming at the bottom of the cut affirmed I had succeeded. The worst part was over. Letting the blood pool a little bit more, I reached for the bone quill and then dipped its tip into the well I just made. Once the chamber was filled, I reached the quill to the Scrolls, trying to ignore the throbbing sensation pounding in my arm. It echoed in my ears, but I wasn't falling for my body's nonsense. This ceremony was just for show. I hovered my hand above the yellowed fibrous material and angled the quill to let loose the bloody ink. As steadily as I could, I curled my name onto the waxy surface.

But something wasn't right. The ink started to run off the paper, my blood landing in droplets on the stone ground. Why would the ink run? Had it done that with other candidates? *Why didn't I pay better attention?* The sound of blood tumbling to the floor cut through my growing dread like the blade of my dagger. *Drip, drip, drip.*

My signature had completely run off, as if I never signed at all. I raised my hand to try again, now trembling with the quill in my fingers, but I was jerked away from the Scrolls. Hands pawed at my arms and back, and the air completely disappeared. I spun in a daze, but a sea of hooded figures grabbed hold of me, lifting me off my feet like a rolled rug. I kicked and pulled against them, demanding they put me down. *Let me go!* The bone quill fell from my hand, but the faceless captors never regarded me when I begged them to let me pick it up. *They aren't listening to me. I have to sign the Scrolls.* Sweat streamed along my spine, then froze and splintered as I was carried farther away from the Scrolls.

"Andren! Please!" He had to intervene, to right this situation. There was no way he'd sit by and let this happen. I screamed again, his name scratching my vocal cords as I cawed like a caged animal. *Just look at me!* I searched the crowd for his face but only saw an angry blur. He had to be there somewhere. He had to fix this. They just needed to let me sign my name, fix this mistake. But no one was listening. I screamed louder. *Why aren't they listening?*

Still expecting them to put me down, for Andren to order them away, my rage blinded what little senses I had left. They were moving me, their rough, invasive hands gripping my body, forcing me to comply. I couldn't see where they were taking me, but I knew I was moving. I sensed the change in air pressure, shifting into something closed and stagnant, like a hallway or small room.

I smashed into a hard chair back, my shoulder blades cracking against the wood, and the legs tipping from the ground. I kicked my feet to the stone floor and anchored myself to keep from pitching back. The black sea of robes dissipated without so much as a word of explanation, abandoning me in an empty room with exposed walls and risers, as if it was an unfinished space in the courtroom. I bolted to the door and jiggled the handle, but they'd locked it from the outside. There were no windows to be found and the only light came from an oil lamp by the door. They'd dumped me into a forgotten space, and they intended to keep me there.

"Andren! Father! Please, help me!" I banged my fists against the door. I yelled at the worn wood until my throat was hoarse and my voice faded out. When my hands were scraped and splintered, I resigned myself to the chair. Nobody was coming. Andren, my father, the other Governors—all of them had watched the injustice play out, but no one had come to my rescue. The longer I sat in the filmy, dusty room, the more I seethed.

My back screamed in pain from the stiff, unyielding chair, so I tried walking circles until exhaustion won over. I plopped back down and hugged my arms as tight as possible around my midsection. My mind raced but none of the thoughts made sense. They had to let me sign the Scrolls, and they were wasting too much time by holding me back here.

I crossed my feet over each other, then uncrossed them, dragging them around in patterns to pass the time. *How long are they going to keep me locked up?* They owed me an explanation at the very least for this. Wearily, I finally let my legs flop outward after so much time passed. It felt like hours had crept by but there was no way of knowing for sure without some sort of reference. It was the middle of the night for all I knew.

Startling me from my stupor, I heard voices in the hall. Familiar voices. My father burst through the door with my mother hanging from his arm, and Andren filling the space right behind him. After the three of them tried to squeeze through the wooden frame at once, several other cloaked figures marched in. I recognized the brutish face of Gregor, and instantly boiled with white-hot anger. I had no proof, but I knew he had to be behind this madness.

"You've kept her locked in here this whole time?" My father yelled at the ring of men. I expected Andren to grovel to him, to me, but he stood erect without speaking.

"We had to complete the Scrolling ceremony," Donorio said.

"The ceremony has been over for two hours." My mother's shrill voice bounced off the exposed walls. The hooded man barely reacted, giving her a lazy nod.

"We also had to evaluate the...information."

"You should have updated them," Andren said.

Donorio reached out and touched his arm. "Let them do their job. They are with her now and we can proceed with the information we have. And investigate what we still need to learn." His words were given like a report, but they curled in sinister threats. I wanted someone to answer for this immediately. Andren broke away from Donorio's grasp and took two swift paces to kneel in front of me. He looked at me for the first time since my ill-fated ceremony.

"Are you alright, Selah?" His eyes bounced around from my face to my body, searching for any signs of injury.

"Does it look like I'm fine?" *Whose side is he on?* "Someone needs to tell me what's going on." I stomped my foot like an insolent child, but I didn't care at this point.

"Of course. We all want to sort this out." Andren's tone was soft, patronizing, and it filled me with the urge to smack his golden face.

"What exactly is *this*?" I jumped from the chair, forcing him to leap back.

Andren coughed into his fist, keeping a wide berth from my erratic movements. "That is what we need to determine." He turned to Donorio and then Gregor. The three men exchanged glances before settling their gaze on my father.

"You need to tell her." Gregor's grating voice rubbed against my raw nubs of nerves, though it was the first sensible thing I'd heard. Andren fidgeted with his thumbs behind him, apparently playing deaf and dumb. He knew something he wasn't telling me.

"What's going on?" I threw my hands on my hips.

"Selah, the Scrolls appear to have...rejected...your blood." Andren exhaled.

"They *what*?" *How could the Scrolls* reject *me*? If this was Andren's idea of a sick joke, I was far from amused.

"It means you are not of the Original Bloodline, or not fully,"

Donorio said through his thick accent. I whipped my face around the semi-circle they'd formed. My mother balled her hands and brought them to her chest. Distracted by the color draining from her face, I didn't hear my father's next question.

"Though it is rare, the Scrolls have been known to reject impure bloodlines. We have done well to weed most unknown factors out of the Caste but it appears this has slipped through the cracks."

"By *this*, you mean my daughter?" Father said. The panic beginning to filter into his speech snaked into my chest, making it difficult to draw in air.

"She's not your daughter," Gregor said so abruptly, it felt like he had physically struck me.

"That's the most absurd thing I've ever heard!" Father's face went purple with rage. "There has to be another explanation for this and you need to figure it out!"

My mother stood motionless in the corner.

"He's right." Her voice was so small, she wouldn't have been heard otherwise. But everyone halted. My ears played twisted games, and obviously I was exhausted.

"Imogen, I've had enough of–"

"He is right, Danby." My mother spoke to her feet. "I'm so sorry." The floor fell from underneath me. My ears hadn't lied and I had heard what I thought, but I didn't believe it. How cruel would a mother have to be to say something so wildly wrong?

"What the bloody hell are you trying to say?" It was the first time I had ever heard my father speak to my mother with anything but affection and admiration. Everyone in the room was suspended in air, only moving their eyes from my mother to my father. No one spoke, and no one breathed.

"There was a man, years ago," she said, wringing her hands in her skirts. My father looked like he wanted to yell again, but stood motionless, face cemented with disbelief. *No.* I refused to listen to this. I had to tune her out. *Think of anything else. This isn't real.*

"He was a strange man who looked like no one I had ever seen before. He told me he was a traveler. He...pursued me. I told him I was betrothed, I tried telling him I couldn't go with him, but he was so *forceful*." Her face twisted at the memory.

"Did he hurt you?" My father grabbed her arm and tried to pivot her towards him. Mother shrugged his hand away, eyes fixed on one spot. Hurt *her? Doesn't she see what this is doing to him? To* me?

"No. He did not hurt me. Somehow he *compelled* me. I knew it was wrong, I didn't want to, but my body wouldn't resist. Couldn't resist." I was compelled to make a run for the door. Maybe take her down on the way.

Donorio and Gregor flashed a look to one another.

"And you laid with him?" My father was suspended in animation, yelling in barely a whisper. His eyes paled with each word that left his mouth as the light drained from his face. I wanted to hold him, but then it would be real. I refused to acknowledge this.

"Yes." She rubbed her forehead with the back of her hand. "It was long before we had Selah, longer than it should have been, when we were just courting. I never thought there could be a possibility she..." Mother's eyes glazed over, lost in a faded memory. "He was just so *strange*."

My head spun from the 20 year-old confession she'd just released. There was no reason for my mother to lie, but my brain rejected every word she said. It was impossible. But the Scrolls didn't lie.

My father isn't my father.

The man who held my hand walking down the giant staircase, the man who paraded me around town to all his friends, the man who always took my side. That man was not my father. I did not carry the Original Bloodline on my paternal side. I was not Casted born. My head spun so rapidly I had trouble focusing on any point in front of me. A hot wave of nausea rose from my guts and burned ominously against my tongue, and at that moment I was grateful for having an empty stomach.

"Selah." I felt Andren's hand on my shoulder and startled. Every touch, every look, every *smell* was alien, like I was occupying someone else's skin. "Selah," he said again. "Are you alright?"

My eyes sharpened to meet his. That had to be a joke. A twisted, sick joke.

"Am I *alright*? Are *you* alright? You keep asking me that asinine question!" My voice cracked on the last word. I was trembling and knew Andren could see, but that was the least of my worries.

"Of course you're not alright," he said. "It's a lot to consider right now but we're going to make this right." His attempts at consolation were about as effective as a raft on the ocean, and if he couldn't see that, he must be a miserable politician.

"*How?* How can you make this right?" I couldn't look at my father, or the man I had thought was my father, because I was so shamed with the burden of my mother's indiscretion. I had no trouble glaring at her, however.

"I'm not Casted," I spat at her. "My whole life has been a lie." She didn't say anything back, but I saw her eyes redden.

"And if I'm not Casted, then *this*–" I motioned by hand back and forth between Andren and me. "–is a lie."

"There are options," Donorio said. I didn't possess the wherewithal to consider what he was suggesting, but I wanted him to shut up. I couldn't move past this moment in time, where the earth just opened up and swallowed me whole, and all the extraneous chatter made me want to scream.

"It has been a long and trying day," Andren said. "Let's get you home to rest. I will call on you in the morning and we will work this situation out."

Situation. I scoffed, ripping my hand away from his embrace. My world was capsizing but somehow this was just a situation to be dealt with. Completely incapacitated with the sourest, foulest rage, I clamped my jaw and let them lead me out.

Chapter Nine

I had no clue what time it was when I came back to life the next morning; I didn't even recall falling asleep after Corinna deposited a sleeping draught on my nightstand. The curtains were still drawn and my lamp oil had burnt out, but seeing everything in daylight was more than I could bear. Then this godawful nightmare would be real—not just something contained to the dark.

I felt around for a robe and peeked through the drapery to find it was past midday. My eyes were filled with sand, and my head pulsed at my temples. It was not unlike indulging in too much wine, but with none of the merriment. I was positive I'd never feel merriment again. I couldn't go downstairs and face everyone, but I couldn't stay here forever. *I don't belong here anymore.*

Detecting my bare feet on the wooden floors, Corinna entered my room carting a steaming cup of tea and a sweet roll. She set the tray down on my dresser and went to work filling the basin with the pitcher of water that accompanied the tea, and pulling out a gown from my wardrobe. She plaited my hair in a loose braid down my back, as if she knew my head couldn't handle any additional pressure from my hair.

"Thank you." My vocal cords were shredded grit. I didn't deserve her kindness, and I didn't want her sympathy. How could she feel bad for me when I was no different than she was?

"Think nothing of it, my Lady." The use of my former title fired a fresh streak of nausea, spoiling the few bites of sweet roll.

Finally out of options and as refreshed as I could be, I gritted my teeth and walked downstairs. Each room I passed was deserted, void of any servants. Something was going on–the house was refusing to greet me already. Noises drew me to the back study–soft murmurings just out of earshot. I could hear my father and mother arguing, though I couldn't quite decipher what was being said. Creeping to the corner and looming outside the doorway, I leaned in to hear, but my movement caught Andren's attention.

"Selah," he said, the room as silent as a tomb. *My tomb.* Nervousness bubbled inside me like a boiling pot. I knew it was coming, I thought he'd at least give me a day to digest yesterday's events before he did it though. I padded into the study and took a seat in a wingback chair in the corner. The velvet material scratched against my skin and the horsehair padding did little to cushion against the springs in the seat, but it was preferable to the tension stringing in the air.

"Drink?" Andren raised a crystal decanter. It still felt like morning but I accepted the hefty pour, welcoming the amber burn. There wasn't much point to decorum now. The numbing effect was instant, and when I slammed the heavy tumbler to the table, Andren refilled it. It would take more than a few glasses of whiskey to recover from the news he was about to deliver. I knew better than to let my guard down. I knew it couldn't be that good for me, but why did he have to let me catch a glimpse of it?

"How long have you been here?" I asked, noticing the scattering of plates and cups throughout the room, as if they had been holed up in here for hours.

"A while," Andren said. "There was a lot to sort through."

"Well I certainly hope I'm not intruding while you *sort through* my life." Hadn't he manipulated me enough? I'd be damned if he thought I'd just overlook his inaction yesterday, and *now* he wanted to do something?

"That's not what I meant, Selah. There is a lot to process and we wanted to have all the options on the table."

I finished the second glass but the spirits could only do so much.

"What exactly do you mean by *we*, Andren? There isn't a *we* any longer." My mother flinched, but I ignored her. Andren was the easy target, though. Her sins had roots too deep to pull.

"Andren is here to ask us to honor the betrothal," Father said. His voice was so stern it jarred me. I choked on the whiskey, sending the liquid up my nostrils until I could breathe fire.

"How? I'm not Casted. I'm not permitted to wed a Casted Lord, let alone a *Governor*." He was trying to save his perfect, golden, Governor face but I was going to make it as difficult on him as I could. I didn't need false hope on top of everything else. He'd given me too much of that.

"You can still be made." Mother's voice was thin and thready, as if it was being crushed into a flat line. *I can still be* made *Casted*. It sounded so simple that I was surprised the thought hadn't struck me before, and for a very brief millisecond, relief grazed my fingertips. But I wasn't about to believe a word from her mouth.

I remembered everything I had learned of the process to become Casted. That cursed day in the market when Andren stumbled into my life should have been foreshadowing. The Sponsorship broker had detailed the abysmal pass rate of the Trials, and the unspeakable cost to get in. Even if Andren and my mother *were* serious about pursuing an alternative, I'd never be able to pass. And I definitely wouldn't find a *Blood Sponsor*. I clutched my arms to my torso and shivered hard.

"No. I can't...." I wouldn't entertain the idea knowing I couldn't pay the price of entrance.

"We have a Sponsor."

I slammed the glass down, making Mother jump. "Who?" I said. Father and Andren exchanged looks, but didn't answer. "*Who?!*"

"It's nothing to concern yourself with right now, but it was voluntary to meet the conditions of the Sponsorship." Father sounded hollow but I laughed anyway. *Nothing to concern myself with?* I was several shades past *concern*.

"I can't accept that." I wasn't bringing anyone else into this mix, no matter how handsomely Andren *was* paying them or how desperate my mother looked. Her face could have frozen solid with that look of dismay and I'd relish the image forever. She's done all of this to me—to us. She didn't get to sweep in and be the hero to her own fucked up tragedy.

"Of course you can, Selah." Andren's clear blue eyes rimmed with moisture. The tightest thread inside me snapped.

"But there's no way I could pass the Trials," I said, letting the sharpness in my voice dull. People like Nix went to the Trials, not me. I couldn't begin to guess what they entailed, but I didn't need to be a scholar to realize they were bordering on impossible. The Sponsorship broker had all but said so in his legal jargon. What good would a former Lady do there, when I was raised to be soft and didn't know if I had enough of the Original Bloodline to keep me healthy? "Even if I wanted to."

"Of course you can." Mother sounded stronger, edgier, and it cut into me. "You are still my daughter in spite of everything. You are still Casted, destined to rule just as the Prophecy has said. That part of you hasn't changed." She breathed in sharp gasps as she spoke. It was convenient that she'd left out the unknown half of me. "You will pass the Trials and cleanse my indiscretions because you have to."

"I've already worked with Donorio and the Chancellor. We can get you into the upcoming Trials. The Chancellor still holds his blessing on our betrothal. We could be wed by the end of the year, Selah," Andren said so perfunctorily, the rest of my fight evaporated into the air.

"We have everything in order if you're still willing to marry me." The boiling pot poured over, the flame far too hot. If this was a ploy to maintain his reputation, the lengths he was willing to go were unnerving at best.

I fingered the charm hanging from my neck, thumbing the circular pendant. The gold line aimed back at Andren. He was waiting for an answer I didn't have. I looked to Father, who watched me with a silent intensity that didn't fit his face. I didn't care about helping Andren's reputation, and I definitely didn't care about Mother's, but I would do anything to take that look away from my father.

"When do I leave?"

Chapter Ten

I had one week to prepare for the Trials–not enough time to flee, and hardly enough time to pack. My body was a piece of glass so thin, the tiniest touch would've shattered me into millions of pieces. The smallest mercy was the limited amount of time to fret over things well beyond my control. Andren had set this into motion, and I was as powerless against the momentum as I was against my mother's sordid history.

"Need some help?" A thundering sound crackled around me as I huddled by the fireplace in the study. Even the wild blaze wasn't enough to thaw the bone-gnawing chill that blanketed my body. Nix propped himself against the wall, consuming the entire doorway. Andren's visits set me on edge, a golden reminder of all that I'd lost. But the sight of Nix elevated my body temperature just a hair. My subconscious warred on whether I should be attracted to him, or deathly afraid of him.

I opened my mouth then closed it immediately. "Andren had to work but he sent me to help you prep," he said. There was no way I could be ready for the Trials in a few short days–I wasn't even prepared to pack my trunk–but Nix traipsed into the room with a stack of books nearly as tall as I was. I threw my bare feet onto the floor, tucking them under my skirts as I straightened my posture. Nix plopped into the wingback chair next to me, his knees colliding with mine as he sat. He was even bigger up close.

The muscles around my ribcage contracted, the atmosphere suddenly thin between us. "Where do I start?" Nix smirked before winging a book in my lap. The heavy leather hit me in the sternum, making oxygen even more of a scarcity, but I managed to catch it. The cover was a faded emerald green with black embossed script. *Hanover Hall: A History of the Caste's Proving Grounds.* I raised my eyebrows at him but cracked open the book. It couldn't make things worse.

"I've been there a few times," Nix said, propping himself up by his elbows. "With Andren. It's an old fortress from the War, where they used to train our Armies." I thumbed through pages with sketches of the stone castle, encompassed by acres of greenery and mountain peaks. I knew it was in the foothills of the Andalls, but I couldn't bring the black and white sketches to life in my mind. Everything outside of Oberin didn't exist to me yet. *Yet.* "Might be good to see where we're going."

"Maybe I'd prefer for my death to be a surprise. I'm getting pretty good at those." The corner of Nix's mouth twitched. At least someone appreciated my dark humor around here.

"You'll be with me, and even Death stays out of my way," he said. "Besides, Andren would level the whole fortress before he let that happen." He'd intended it to be hyperbole, a joke even, but his face hardened. Despite my excellent marks in class, I could be really obtuse. I was getting a ticket into the Trials just because of my fiancé. Nix had been a servant his whole life and had to earn his way into this, and only one of us was likely to actually succeed. He knew it as well as I did, and yet he was still here trying to help me. *Because Andren told him to.*

"Sorry," I said under my breath, then closed the book. I was such a selfish mule, and willfully oblivious to everything outside of my little bubble. Nix had every physical advantage, but I had somehow swiped the upper-hand from him, and from countless others, just because of who my future husband was. I would hate me if I was in his shoes. Guilt wrapped its bony fingers around my neck.

He rested his hands over mine, sandwiching them between the book cover. "What are you sorry for?" The heat and heaviness of him on me, even just his hands, sent tiny stars into my vision. Casted rarely touched one another, but Nix was far from being Casted. I peered up at him, studying the angle of his cheekbone, and the way his waves of midnight hair hung over his eyes of the exact same hue. The combination was so striking, the light seemed to disappear when it reached his features. He didn't meet their standard of appearance, but the thought of Nix in any other form, washed into another bland Lord, nipped at my insides. Casted or otherwise, I had to appreciate his organic beauty.

"This," I said, pulling a hand free so I could gesture to the stack of books. "Everything happening I guess." Now it was Nix's turn to study me. Heat crept up my neck and I pried my other hand loose.

He sighed loudly and crossed his arms over his chest. "Selah, when are you going to stop letting things happen to you?"

I choked on my own saliva. "What is that supposed to mean?" I'd always been cordial, if not friendly, with Nix, but there was an unmissable edge in my tone. He ran his hands through his hair and it reminded me of Andren, but far more untamed. Black orbs stared at me from under a half-moon of dark lashes. I shifted in the chair, tucking my legs back underneath me as a shield. I certainly hoped he didn't blame me for my mother's choices before I was even born. How had I *let* that happen to me? Who would choose that for themselves?

"Somewhere under that shiny, Casted shell is an actual person. I've seen her." Nix leaned closer, and I pressed my back into the chair. "You're not just another mindless Lady, Selah, so why do you keep pretending to be?"

My chin fell to my lap. Of all the vile things I'd been called, no one had ever told me I was *mindless*. Pretending or otherwise, the insinuation boiled the blood inside my veins. I leapt from my chair like it was on fire, ready to push or swing or kick, or *something*.

"Easy," he said, which only made my vision go deeper red. *How dare he?*

"I'm not mindless nor have I ever pretended to be." The words slithered from my lips in a dangerous hiss. Nix had the decency to recoil slightly.

"No." His jaw tightened under the scruff of his beard. "You're not. Apologies my Lady." My anger fizzled, and I dropped my hands to my side. Nix certainly knew how to head off an argument, but hundreds of unspoken words still pressed against my lips. He'd planted a seed, and he knew it. It was in the slight upturn of his mouth, not smugness, but another shade of satisfaction. If I said he was clever, exceptionally smart for a servant, I'd be proving his point. *Bastard.*

He stacked the other books on the drawing desk in front of me. "I should be going." When he stood from the chair, my muscles tightened. "Those should keep you busy until Andren returns but I'll be back to check on you tomorrow." With one more glance from the books to me, Nix stalled in the doorway. His face was soft and underscored with heaviness; it made it hard to stay mad at him.

Just as he promised, Nix came by each morning to check on me. He was on his best behavior the entire time, never venturing back into our conversation, and always coming with text sections tabbed and outlined for easy reference. By the end of the second day, the tension between us dissipated and I was able to focus more on the Trials. Nix's readily-available knowledge and worldly experience drowned me in the perspective of what I didn't know, but the sessions were helpful. I gained an idea of what to expect when we traveled out, about how many candidates attended, and what the proving grounds contained as possibilities within each Trial. Nix had even drawn an intricate overlay of the training site, marking known obstacles and training courses with scaled renderings of each.

By the time Andren returned from his trip, I'd made my way through a dozen different texts and was swimming in information overload. I could identify the poisonous plants native to the Andalls, and recite the strategies used in each key battle of the War, but my internal organs still threatened to shut down every time I thought about leaving the island. Andren's golden, smooth face should've been a relief, but it only reminded me of what I was truly leaving behind.

"I won't be able to see you again until after your Cleansing, so I need to take in as much of you as I can," he said. I resisted his affection, standing several feet away from him in the study, but Andren was persistent as he closed in on me. My cheeks flushed with a fevered heat when he pressed the hard outlines of his body against mine. But all the security his arms offered was still just a temporary stronghold. When he released me, the chilly air penetrated my crocheted shawl.

"Will you take a walk with me?" He tipped my chin up to his face. I stifled a shiver, already dreading leaving the grand fireplace of the study. Andren's ice blue eyes danced with the movement of the orange flames, giving him a monochromatic illusion. "Please."

I exhaled my secession and followed him outside, clutching my shawl tightly around my shoulders. Nights on the island were crisp with the impending cold season, made more frigid by the damp, salty air blowing from the north. Summer was over, as if I needed another reminder. Andren wrapped his fingers around mine, but even his skin was cold against mine.

We meandered down the walkway, towards the forest at the end of the hill. The trees were already forming a glorious canopy of burnt umber and goldenrod under the midday sun. Everything was fragrant with the spice of damp leaves, cedar, and pine, and for a brief moment, I got lost in it. I was walking through a living mural with Andren and it was too magical not to surrender to it.

"You have the same look you did the first time I saw you." Andren stopped walking to examine my face, still holding me by the hand.

"What look is that?" I frowned at him, certain *that* wasn't the look in question.

"Like you're completely relaxed. You have such a natural peace whenever you're outdoors."

I couldn't help but smile a little. He was right after all. "It's the outdoors. It's where I feel most at home." Perhaps Andren had considered me more than I realized. While the island created natural confinement, the open air here rejuvenated me. I craved the outdoors like a decadent treat. The sun and wind greeted me regardless of who my actual father was.

"You. Here. It's the most majestic sight any man could lay eyes on." Andren's voice lowered, drawing the hairs on my arm to a point. He tugged at the hem of my shawl.

"You're quite remarkable, you know." His warm breath moved around my cheek and hair. *I have to keep my distance.* But the way he looked at me spiked my hopes.

"I have no idea what you're talking about." I tried to shake it all away. The other shoe was bound to drop, and the longer it took, the more it cinched my anticipation.

He chuckled. "You have a quiet strength no one else does. I've never wanted something more." Andren inched closer, waiting for me to stop him, but when I didn't, he pressed me against his body, lips grazing my forehead.

"Do you want me, too?" He ran his hands down my sides. I was paralyzed, too afraid to acknowledge the longing now drumming at my insides.

"Of course." I gave a tiny nod. "But how could you want me? This whole plan is never going to work." I would've kept going, letting all the trepidation tumble out, but Andren clamped his lips over mine. I gasped into his mouth, but then he kissed me. He kissed me slow, and hard, and I kissed him back with a need that terrified me. All of my defenses crumbled with his mouth on mine. My thoughts blurred together, and I could no longer recall why I'd been holding back. The Trials were still so far away, separated by hundreds and hundreds of miles, but Andren was right here in front of me.

"Selah," he said, pulling away. I gasped for air. "I want to do something if you'll permit me. A bit of a...ceremony."

"Ceremony?" The Casted were big on public ceremonies, and I had no intention of going anywhere near one after my miserable Scrolling.

"Yes." Red, searing energy wafted from him as he stared at me. I tasted salt on the tip of my tongue. "I will not let you go to the Trials alone. I want to go in with you."

"But you can't...." Andren really had some nerve. I didn't deserve to jump ahead in the long line of Sponsorship, and I certainly didn't deserve whatever else he had arranged.

"I can—at least in spirit. As your Sewn Soul."

"Sewn Soul?" I asked. "I've never heard of that."

Andren rocked on his heels. "It's not something the uh, Casted do. But it's an old ritual a lot of the serving class conduct—like an incantation to bind lovers."

I sucked in, debating if I should laugh. But his crystal blue eyes glowed in the fading light with a fierce intensity. He was serious.

The way Andren described this ceremony made it sound like *magic*, and the mere mention of anything supernatural had been banned. We had to stay focused on the power of the Scrolls alone. They'd gone so far as to destroy all records of old practices from before the War. Even if this was heavy on the ceremony and light on the magic, Casted had no need for bonding rituals since they paired out of utility. Anything to perpetuate the Bloodline.

"But...it's against the Caste law." I still wasn't sure if this was all in jest. Surely a Governor wouldn't risk something illegal for me.

"Selah, you're not Casted." He hadn't intended for it to land so hard, but the blow hit me in the face.

"I don't know," I said, rubbing the invisible wound on my cheek. "How do we even do something like that?"

"Nix has an acquaintance in Lower Oberin who can conduct the ritual. I figured it was worth a try, even if that old stuff doesn't actually work."

The silence between us roared in my ears. It was taboo at best, but would likely be the scandal of the century if a Governor got caught in such a compromised position. I wasn't Casted, no matter how nice my house or my clothes were. It was a farce. Andren wouldn't risk his position for the off chance a fairytale might work. Would he?

"Are...are you sure?" I asked him once again. Andren grabbed a rogue curl from my temple and let it fall over his fingers.

"Selah, I've never been surer of anything else. Please let me show you." There wasn't much else I could lose. I raised my chin in a single nod.

"Let's go, then." He tugged at my hand, running off into the woods. I dug my feet into the earth and yanked him back.

"Now?"

"It has to be tonight. Nix is already waiting."

Andren guided me through the woods around the edge of the little town, using the trees' dense foliage to guard from prying eyes. After a trek to the very outskirts of a shanty village in Lower Oberin, I spied Nix waiting for us at a clearing.

"This way," was all Nix said in greeting, but he shot me a cryptic look, letting his onyx eyes linger on me. An involuntary shiver raced from my crown to my calves–my body trying to loosen the vise of his stare. It was a bad idea. Nix had it printed all over his face. We could get caught and risk not only my future, but his.

Andren trotted after him without looking back at me. My feet clung to the dirt, but I ripped them away. He was so determined to do this, and I didn't have the reserves to say no to him. Nix knew the risk as much as Andren, and of three of us, Andren had the most to lose. Pocketing the residual hesitation, I followed the two men through several alleys lined with dingy linens and trash. Everything appeared to be some shade of gray as we approached a dilapidated door of the same color.

"She's inside," Nix said, gesturing to the door. Andren pushed it open, the rusted hinges protesting noisily against his weight, then turned back to me.

"Wait here while I ensure everything is ready for us." He kissed my cheek then vanished inside, leaving me in the heavy silence of Nix's grim expression. I dragged my toe through the dirt in a circle, trying not to meet his eye again.

"You don't have to do this, you know." His voice startled me, and I swung my head up to face him.

"Excuse me?" I understood his concern, but I didn't need his commentary. "It's a bit too late." Nix blinked slowly, then rolled his shoulders back.

"It may feel like it is, but you don't have to go through with this if you don't want to."

"I want to," I said before he could continue. What had gotten into him? I readjusted to stand at my full height, though it was an empty action given Nix's size. The look I shot him made up for my lack of stature, however, and Nix raised his hands in surrender. He quickly stowed them at his sides when Andren popped his head of the door.

"She's ready for us."

Nix had to crouch, bending in half to clear the entrance. I ducked behind him, letting my eyes adjust to the dim light.

The room was too cramped for all three of us, but I followed them into the back where an old woman perched on a wooden stool. Her skin was paper-thin against her jet black hair streaked with silver. Her giant orb eyes were the same inky color as her hair and void of any discernible pupils, giving her a ghostly appearance in the candlelight.

Her nails also shone black as she raised a bony finger to indicate where we should stand. Nix crept to the corner and sat on the floor, something that seemed so natural to him but would have been unacceptable in a typical Casted estate. But I was closer to Nix's status than I was to any Casted. Nix caught my eye for a beat, frowning before turning his attention to the woman. *I want to do this*, I projected to him wordlessly.

"Thank you for seeing us, Noala." Andren greeted.

"Did you bring the articles?" she asked in a voice that settled like dust.

Andren pulled a velvet coin purse from his pocket and emptied its contents into the woman's hands. There was a thin handkerchief, stained yellow with age, a needle and thread, and two pieces of silver. She inspected them before returning each piece to the bag.

"A vessel to bring your souls together, tools to bind them, and an offering to the Ancient Ones to watch over your Sewing," she croaked at the objects, arranging them just so. "Come, give me your hands."

I blinked, waiting for Andren to move first. He extended his palm to her without hesitation, so I mirrored him, letting Noala take us by the hands. Her fingers felt like dried twigs I could easily snap in two, and her skin was rough against mine. I reached for Andren's free hand with mine, and the three of us formed a small circle.

"Sewn Souls are the oldest union of my people," she began, focusing somewhere behind us. "They extend beyond any human commitment and will last until one of the Souls are broken, usually by deep betrayal or death, though I cannot say for sure how the Sewing will take to someone like you."

My body rocked with chills; even the serving classes rejected me. But Noala didn't appear to be looking at me, though it was hard to tell with just round orbs. She was looking at Andren.

"If the Ancient Ones are willing and your bodies accept it, you will leave here tonight with a connection that runs deeper than the ocean and stronger than any metal or stone. You will know each other on a level unreachable to any other life form."

I sensed Andren's gaze, watching me. A week ago, we were on an entirely different trajectory, ready for a marriage ceremony to legally bind us, but fate was funny. Now we were about to be connected in an arguably more profound way—bound by a forbidden secret. *If this works.*

"If you are sure of your decision, we can proceed with the Sewing," she said.

I looked at Andren and met his eye before we both turned back to Noala.

"We're ready," he said, and released my hand.

Noala pulled a satchel from behind her. She unraveled the braided leather with her skeletal fingers, then retrieved a dusty silver mirror from inside. She placed it at our feet and motioned for us to sit next to it. Andren and I both obliged and sat cross-legged on the bare, dirt floor.

"Tonight we will ask the Ancient Ones to reflect one soul into the other." Noala spoke monotonously, drawing her words up every fifth syllable as if chanting. She pulled a piece of silver from Andren's coin purse and placed it on the mirror. She then placed my left hand on top of the silver, palm down.

"Selah, you will commit every corner of your soul to Andren." She continued chanting without pausing for any response, then rested Andren's hand on top of mine. His fingers were cooler than usual, but the piece of silver burned hot underneath. I shivered at the contrast.

"Andren, you will be charged with guarding not just your soul, but Selah's as well."

The air shifted between us as he nodded his approval. *Why does this sound so final?* It was as if Noala knew I'd been doing a poor job caring for my soul on my own.

"Finix, you will stand witness to the promise made by Selah and Andren tonight." I couldn't see Nix's face from behind me but assumed he had agreed. Noala pressed on, digging her onyx nails into the dirt beneath her and scooping a handful on top of Andren's hand. Tiny clumps peppered the side of my hand as it spilled over his.

"As organic as the earth, you will be made into Sewn Souls," she sang. "You will return to the earth together."

The dirt and soot in the air clumped in my sinuses. I tried to steady the shake in my hand as Noala advanced in the ritual, pulling a candle and small blade from her satchel. *I don't actually believe in old magic, do I? It's just fairytales and myths.* She lit the candle using the one nearest her and let it flicker over the blade's edge until it glowed red hot from point to hilt.

But what if this works? I pulled back when she reached for our hands, but she yielded an unexpected force against my resistance. Between Noala and Andren, I had no choice but to let my hand move with theirs, giving it over. She held us in something resembling a double handshake, then turned both our wrists face up. I coughed a muffled yelp when she brought the knife blade towards our flesh. It was the Scrolling all over. I yanked back, but the two held me steady. *No. I don't want to do this anymore.* My muscles tightened to force out a scream, but Noala had already made a small incision. The cut was only a few millimeters long and approximately the same depth, just enough to draw blood. Still reeling, I watched her do the same to Andren. He was so confident, so sure; why was I panicking all of a sudden?

"A thread from your strongest steed," she said as she took what I now recognized as horsehair and deftly looped it through the eye of the needle. Noala brought the candle to the needlepoint and annealed its metal in the flame. Pulling our wrists as one unit back toward her body, she took the needle and stitched a crisscross pattern over Andren's wound. Without tying off the stitch, she kept the thread's length and did the same to me. The needle burned more than the blade, and I felt every inch of the horsehair pass through my flesh. Something close to bewilderment filled me from the ground up, like an overflowing glass.

Once she was finished sewing, I turned my wrist over as far as the thread would allow me. Andren and I were quite literally stitched together with only a few inches of lead between us. Noala pulled the handkerchief from the satchel and tied it snugly over the stitches, our hands still stacked on top of each other. She closed her eyes and began to mumble a garbled, haunted song. Each word tapped at my vertebrae, one by one. I didn't recognize any of her words, but they landed somewhere deep inside me. *What did we do?* When her voice came to rest and her eyes swept back open, the whites of her eyes were visible.

"I have done everything required of me to sew you, and you must complete the rest of the ritual on your own. If you fulfill your bodily duties this eve, you will both awaken as Sewn Souls." My midsection wound into a tight spiral. *Bodily duties?* "Whatever you do," she said. "Do not sever the threads until the Sewing is complete." Cold sweat prickled across the small of my back. I was no longer standing in my own body as I listened to Noala explain the final steps.

Andren pulled me to my feet, while keeping the thread safe. He thanked Noala and left the last silver as payment for her service. Nix stalked out of the shack behind us, stretching dramatically as we reached the fresh air outside. The gust smacked my face and cooled me in a rapid rush, reconnecting my mind to my body. It was fully dark now, and I really needed to get home before someone realized I was gone. It was the smart thing to do, the safe thing.

"Selah, it's alright," Andren said, rubbing his thumb against mine. *What* exactly was alright? Sneaking about at all hours of the night with a Governor and his henchman? Being a lesser classman myself, about to complete *bodily duties* for whatever the hell happened in there?

"But what about my parents?" I asked. "You heard her—we have to stay tied together, and–and...." My face burned brilliant red just at the thought. I couldn't bring myself to say the words.

He brushed my hair back with his free hand. "I have all the arrangements under control. I'm sure you heard but there's uh, one final step to the process," Andren said sheepishly. "If you're not comfortable with it, I understand. I want to see you through the Trials, but I am a gentleman and will take you straight home if you wish." Nix whistled in the background, but Andren shot him a warning glare.

"I have a room at an inn. It's nothing special, by no means worthy of a Governess, but it's discreet." He tried to assure me, but quickly amended his statement. "That sounds so much seedier than I intended." Tiny birds let loose inside me, fluttering madly as he spoke.

"Yes, it did," I agreed with a tight laugh. Andren tucked his hand in his pocket as he swayed back and forth on the balls of his feet.

"Selah, I want to hold you all night before I have to hand you over in the morning. I will leave the rest up to you." My knees melted like butter as my body flared from Andren's suggestion. I wasn't ready for proposals like these. The very idea of spending the night with Andren, bound to him, and the open-endedness of *the rest* punched me in the gut.

I swallowed hard and rested a hand on my hip. "So where is this inn?" My own recklessness took me by surprise, but my body wasn't waiting for my brain to rationalize anything. Since my failed Scrolling, nothing in my life was rational. It would be wiser to distance myself from Andren, even if he'd been truthful about his motives for sending me to the Trials, because I'd never be able to have him. I wasn't going to pass, and we both knew it. *But I can have him tonight.*

"Come with me." His tone turned dangerous. "I'll show you."

He walked off into the night, and I had no choice but to follow the tug of the thread at my wrist. I looked over my shoulder one last time, finding Nix looming on the edge of the road. He stood rigid, hands straight down at his side, before turning away, leaving me alone with Andren.

Chapter Eleven

Seedy was an accurate description for the inn, but so was discreet. It was a few blocks from Noala's shack and tucked behind stacks of other wood-framed homes and stores, in a part of town I'd never dared to go. Standing two stories, it had a ragged A-frame roof peeking above the tops of the others. The sign out front hung by one chain and was so faded the name of the establishment was left a mystery. I paused outside to stare up at it, bringing Andren to a stop with our thread. He looked over his shoulder, waiting without speaking.

Without stopping to speak to the innkeeper, Andren led me directly to a steep, winding staircase with treads so small, I had to turn to the side to climb them. The landing was in the very peak of the roof, giving the impression that both walls were closing in on us like a book. I crept down the narrow hall, waiting for both sides to shut on me. Andren continued on to a door at the end, tugging me along by the very thin thread keeping me from bolting.

Inside the tiny square room, the area was just large enough for a four poster bed and nightstand. Everything looked distorted under the dim oil light flickering from the corner. Though the bed was once a grand piece of craftsmanship, it had since been worn and chipped away into a shadow of its former glory. The quilts were faded and threadbare, and the mattress itself looked like it was stuffed with straw, judging by the lumps spread throughout. It was such an unassuming bedroom, drab even, but the bed leered at me like a shrine to all the unbelievable things that had happened in the last week.

"You deserve so much more than this." Andren stomped into the room.

"It's perfectly fine." I lied, but couldn't stand the look on Andren's face. Of course I would do this for him. I grazed his hand with mine. "Charming, actually."

"It was the only place I knew that could accommodate us," he said. "And the uh, Sewing." He shot me an impish smile. "If you still wish to proceed with it."

"I do," I said, but the quaver in my voice betrayed me. I left out the part about getting used to these surroundings, and the living conditions in Lower Oberin in general. My lavish Casted lifestyle was nearly over. *This* was my destiny, whether I embraced that tonight or after I failed the Trials.

He wheeled me into him and held my free hand in his. "That's what I was hoping you'd say."

His mouth danced against the tip of my nose. Lingering there for a few seconds, he planted the softest kiss before moving away. As if by magnetic force, my body ached for his contact again and I tugged at his tunic. It was just a gentle, shy tug, but Andren was already there, ready to meet me. He pressed his lips to mine and kissed me so deeply he pulled the gasp straight from my throat. The room tilted and spiraled around us, but I anchored myself to him.

Andren explored my mouth, my lips, my teeth, and I followed his example. Though he'd kissed me several times before, this time was different. Everything was intensified with a sense of urgency, or maybe even a sense of purpose. Andren touched me like he was on a mission. He cupped my hand, keeping us together as a single unit, and ran my palm across his chest and down his taut abdomen. Through the tunic, I could feel the twitch of his muscles as I grazed them. He kept going, leading my hand farther down, ratcheting the tension between each of my ribs. He brought my fingers low on his waist, skimming the edge of his trousers and the crest of his hips. We worked his shirt loose until our hands slid underneath, making contact with his bare flesh.

It burned like a stone in the sun, but I pushed harder, lower to seek out that delicious heat. Is this what two bodies together always felt like? Andren gasped, breaking away from my mouth. He gaped at me, lips still parted, but he read the fervor on my face and proceeded to inch his lips down my jawline to my neck. The blaze of his mouth and the blast of cool moisture left a trail of devastation as he moved. But then Andren traced his finger in the pathway, from my jaw to my breastbone, and a forceful shudder rocked through me.

"Too much?" Andren rested his forehead on mine.

"No." I knew he felt my chest heaving against his, but I was too flustered to slow it. Andren watched my bosom rise and fall before dragging his gaze up to my eyes. The air between us was alive, a serpent in the grass that caressed me as it wound around my limbs. It was maddening. If I let his mouth pull me all the way under, this would become a reality. And tomorrow my reality would slip through my fingers like sand. If I played it safe, ran home now, I'd never have to know what I'd lost. I held my breath, bracing myself for whichever way I decided to go, but Andren chose for me. He ripped his tunic over his head, leaving it in a ball at our wrists. I scanned over the perfection of him, letting my free fingers wander up and down his side.

"I want you so badly." He hummed against my ear. The feel of his breath and mouth, the sound of his desire, rushed between my thighs. No text book, no romance novel, and no murmurings from servants in the corners adequately captured the ache I felt for him. I jutted my hips in attempt to curb it, letting a pure animalistic instinct take over.

"*Selah*." Andren jerked his head back, leaving a chilly void where his warmth had been. After a painful pause, Andren once again took my mouth and completely engulfed me. His free hand cascaded down my chest, cupping my breast in his frenzy. I ground into him, summoning an unrestrained groan. I'd unhinged whatever control he'd been maintaining.

"Bloody hell," Andren pushed his forehead into mine. The pressure of our bodies together, of his hardness against my palm, made me seize in shock. Every cell wanted to give into him, so why was I hesitant? I felt a moan escape my lips, and Andren echoed in reply.

"Selah, I want you to fully understand the decision to Sew ourselves, and what that will require of you tonight."

"I know what needs to happen." My words were stippled from my mutinous lungs. *Breathe, Selah.*

"But is that what you *want*?" He jerked me back into reality, out of my stupid, overthinking head. Of course, it was what I wanted.

"Yes," I said, my own voice hardening. Because I did. I'd craved affection from my earliest memory, when all I received from others was indifference at best. And in the cruelest moments, when their interactions became physical, I accepted I would never know a pleasurable touch. But Andren was here, offering me the one thing I never believed I could have.

"Remember," he said, the tension in his face subsiding. "You're in control."

The sheer magnitude of his words had my pulse clanging through my veins chaotically. *I'm in control.* Nix had told me to quit letting things happen to me, but I doubted this was what he had in mind. Smirking to myself, I pushed him hard, yanking his bound hand with mine. Andren moved with my momentum and pulled me on top of him, landing us both on the bed. He was cautious to keep our bound hands safely to the side as he sat me on his lap. Resting his head back on the pillows, Andren looked up deferentially at me.

"You're the most beautiful creature I've ever seen." I turned my head sideways, my burst of confidence fading. Andren caught my chin with his free hand and brought my face back towards his. His eyes blazed, clear and crystal blue, totally transparent to his intention. If he wanted permission, I was going to grant it. How could I say no?

I planted my hand into the mattress next to his head and leaned in. The tips of my breasts grazed him, tingling everywhere they made contact. Andren seized the opportunity to push my sleeves over my shoulders, then continued on his journey to my bodice laces. Even single-handed, he managed to loosen it until it hung around my waist, leaving nothing but my thin undergarments. With one swift motion, Andren yanked the bodice free from its bindings and tossed it across the room.

A slithering tension wound deep in my pelvis as he directed his focus on the skirts, unfastening buttons and untying ribbons in a single sweep. He shifted my weight and freed me from the layers of fabric around my waist, exposing me completely to him. Andren's breath hitched, and his hand faltered when he reached to touch me. It made me bold, and I craved more. I straddled him, delighting in the way his eyes widened. I was in control, just as he'd promised.

"Selah–" I rocked, giving into the snaking desire. His hands flew to my hips, taking mine with it. He raked over my curvature, leading me to feel the smoothness of my own skin. "Keep going," he commanded, and I did.

We outlined my form with his fingertips beneath mine. My abdomen twitched, and the serpent livened when he reached the underside of my breasts. I sucked in sharply as he tugged at my nipple, his fingers woven through mine to reach the tender peaks. He drew tantalizing circles, coiling the energy building, bringing it all deep inside. I wanted him to touch me, to keep touching me. When I was ready to shatter, Andren flicked over my nipple with his tongue. Everything around me spun while he sucked with a sweet, hot pressure. Andren groaned into my breast, the vibrations nearly sending me over the edge.

"*Please*," I begged. He dragged his teeth over my flesh and I arched my back, grinding into the hardness beneath me again. "I don't know what else we need to do to complete the ritual, but I'm about to improvise."

Andren released my nipple from his mouth, the cold air hardening it more, and grinned.

"Say no more," he said as he rolled me onto my back. Our tied hands were now planted overhead, my undergarments still dangling with his tunic around our wrists.

"I can't wait to make all of this mine," he said into my neck. The serpent wound itself into knots of anticipation, and I drank in the sight of him above me. His body was kissed with a bronze tone, the lean muscle accented by the oil light in the corner. I dragged my fingertips down the small patch of hair descending from his navel until I reached his belt buckle. He watched from under his lashes, urging me to continue. The heavy clasp was awkward with only one hand, but Andren held the leather tight while I pulled it free. The two of us used our functioning hands to unfasten the buttons of his trousers until they barely hung from his hips, exposing the most delectable V.

With one quick motion, Andren pivoted and pushed his trousers down around his knees. I heard the thump of his boots against the floorboards. The sound reverberated through my body, a warning of what was to come. Andren lowered himself on top of me, skin meeting skin. My mind raced from the unimaginable sear of his touch *everywhere.*

He pushed my legs apart with his, and I eagerly opened up to him. My breaths quickened until I verged on hyperventilation, and my pulse thrummed so hard I could feel it everywhere. Could he feel it, too? He nudged me with his tip, coming dangerously close to the writhing, twisting beast in me. *Please.* I needed him closer, impossibly close.

"Are you sure this is what you want?" His question grated me, and I was already too raw. I shook my head up and down, clawing at his back to ensure he got the message. *Quit stalling.*

"It will hurt," he said. "I'll go slow, but there will be pain."

Andren had done this before. I was plainly inexperienced laying under him, meeting the expectations of a fine Casted Lady, but not *those* expectations. My midsection clenched and my throat tightened, sending a tiny squeak into Andren's ear. I was ready, or at least I thought I was. But I needed him to stop talking before I lost my nerve.

"It will be okay." Using my free hand, I tugged at his hair and reeled him into me. His kiss was harder, hurried. We didn't speak. There were no more questions from either of us. Andren threaded his hand between our bodies, moving downward, hitting a line of demarcation that tensed my whole person into a rigid board–the point of no return. I choked on my own breath when he crossed it, and finally touched me.

Andren slid a finger inside of me and I gasped, but the sound fizzled into a languid sigh, and my body eased into his intrusion. He stroked against the slickness, slow, calculated, plunging a little farther with each pass. When I thought it couldn't get better, he dragged his finger up, gliding against the electrified nerve bundle. I arched my hips into his hand, and Andren began a rhythmic massage at my peak. I tried to focus on his face, his brow furrowed with an intense concentration, but my vision was narrowing into small tunnels.

"I want you nice and ready for me," he said from somewhere in the distance. The urgency swiftly mounting inside me stood between us, demanding my attention. I heard myself cry out for him into the dim room, but I didn't recognize my own voice. When he pulled his hand away, I slammed my hands against the bed, yanking at the thread holding us together. Andren chided me with a single eyebrow but I didn't care, so long as it brought him back. I pawed at his back with my other hand, squirming underneath him to fill that insatiable demand.

After an eternity, Andren widened my legs impossibly far with his. I was totally opened to him, panting like a maniac. He inched forward, leaning on his elbows and making contact with my opening. *Bloody hell.* The velvety smoothness of him was ecstasy, and yet so torturous as he leaned in with more pressure, but releasing it within seconds. Andren pushed against me and pulled back, leaving me damp and writhing, and manic to have *more*. I jumped when he kissed me, his teeth clashing with mine, letting the hunger ring through both of us. He pressed harder against my mouth while he continued to rock against me. Then he clamped his fingers around mine beneath his shirt, and he thrust.

The burning was unbearable. He collided into me, his length filling me, stretching me. I dug my nails into his hand and breathed through the pain. Andren stilled inside me, pausing for the shock to subside.

"Are you alright?" I followed a bead of sweat rolling down his face, starting at his tousled hair and meandering downward until it dropped from his cheek. He was so beautiful, and I had him at my mercy, at my control if I said the word. The pain throbbed between my legs, but I let loose of his hand, taking note to apologize to him for the damage later. My spine steadily curved back into the mattress, my limbs regained control, and the familiar serpentine hunger reignited. His muscles trembled under the strain of holding himself steady.

"Yes."

Andren slowly slid back out, gliding with my wetness as he passed. I shivered, clamping my thighs around him. That was the only cue he needed. Andren descended once again, this time pressing everything into me. His breath shook as he exhaled roughly into my shoulder, pulling back out in a tantalizing draw. When Andren pushed into me again, every inch of me livened. I was ravenous, more beast than human, to fill the void I didn't know I had. I grabbed the meat of Andren's backside and pushed him against me, raising my hips to meet him in his descent.

He rolled his eyes back into his head and groaned. Dropping his head to mine, he began to move his hips at a faster pace, still cautious, but giving into the carnal desperation enveloping both of us. I was fevered in sultry, damp passes, each growing deeper and deeper until he buried himself to the hilt. *Fuck.* It was taboo to think like this, and completely illicit to act on these impulses, but I never wanted to be a Lady again if this was the alternative. Andren's flesh melded with mine when he let his body pin me to the bed, his arms shaking around me. The wildness in his breath and the wetness of my response pushed me into a feral state.

Desperately trying to drive him as far into me as I could, to mold myself even closer into him, I wrapped my legs around his waist and linked my ankles in the small of his back. My hips angled to meet him squarely at his base, and he slammed into me. It knocked the air from my lungs, but I locked my legs to hang on tighter. Shocks of pain jerked through me, and I yelped. Andren hesitated, but that hurt even more. I needed the friction more than I needed comfort, blinding me in white-hot desperation to regain it.

"*Don't stop.*" I grasped handfuls of the quilt to ready myself for more.

Andren fastened his movement. He drove into me forcefully, grunting between each thrust. Tears sprang to my eyes, but I clamped down around him. My wetness surged, now dripping down me to the bedding below. Andren shuddered. On his next pass, he grabbed my bound hand and shoved it over my head, stretching me into a long line that left my body tight, and my nipples hard. He braced our bodies against the rails of the four-poster bed with his free hand, creating a magnificent counterforce as he continued to devour me until I was ready to boil over like a whistling tea kettle.

"Andren!" I was desperate to release the turbulence swirling through my whole body. He spoke my name back into my mouth, and I let go. My head careened backwards and my hips jerked. His hardness swept against my swollen, tender tissue and I lurched with a ravaging bolt of pleasure. Andren plummeted deep into me, using both our hands to brace my hips. With a guttural noise, Andren slammed against me with a powerful surge. Ripples of electricity pulsed through me in waves, squeezing my temples and tugging my belly button.

He cursed before collapsing on top of me, salty and slick with sweat from both our bodies. The room was perfectly still, nothing moving except the rise and fall of our chests and the flicker of the lamp. A soft hum hung around us as we laid side-by-side. It purred in my ear with a sense of satiety I'd never experienced, willing me to fill the space between us. To rejoin our flesh. The sound tempted me to give in to it, to Andren, and to only feel complete with him. I shooed it away and rested my head on Andren's chest. This was good enough; it had to be. After quite a while, I felt Andren stir.

"Well, we're still connected." He smirked, raising our hands as evidence. "I'm not quite sure how." God, if he only knew what that actually did to me. What it meant. Even I didn't fully know, but it was something I'd never get over. I nestled into the worn quilts and his chest, letting my eyes drift shut. I didn't want to think about when, or if, I would be able to share a bed with Andren again, or what tomorrow would hold for me. Tonight, I was happy.

Chapter Twelve

I woke to a filmy light filtering through shabby drapes, the bed creaking and rustling under my weight. Confused, I attempted to focus and refocus the image, something unfamiliar from my normal bed chambers. The events of last night slammed down on me, as if I was pinned against the crags of the strait, the wild sea pulling me under. *Andren.*

I pawed around the quilts near me, finding nothing but the warmth Andren had left behind. He wasn't here, but I swore he was still laying next to me. There was that vague sensation of mass, of air being breathed by more than one body–that sensation from being close to someone. My skin tingled but I flipped around to confirm no one was in bed behind me. Raising my hand to sharpen my sleep-weary eyesight, I gasped at the dangling thread from my wrist. The horsehair was clipped neatly and knotted off. Andren was no longer connected, but when I moved my arm, the thread tugged with an invisible force.

Closing my eyes, I focused on my other senses. There were wafts of something sweet and rich in the air, with a fine layer of saltiness. The smell reminded me of caramel. Inhaling deeper, I detected notes of amber so strong I could taste them, as if I was finishing a sip of whiskey, letting it hit the right spots on my tongue. I recognized it as Andren's scent, but he was nowhere to be seen. I *knew* he was close though.

Pushing harder to tune out my surroundings, I honed in on the sensation nagging me. The tiniest tug at my bellybutton caught my attention, guiding me in his direction. It pulled harder and harder as the scent grew stronger. Then Andren appeared in the doorway, and I nearly passed out from the visceral jerk of his presence.

"You rang?" He squeezed himself through the threshold with a serving tray in hand. His voice caressed my ear and cheek. I could *feel* the sound. The tray contained a tea set, a loaf of bread, and a jar of jam, which set my stomach into an anticipatory somersault. Andren set it down on the dresser before joining me on the bed. I scooted to the edge, overwhelmed by his presence. One touch from his fingertip would cause me to implode on myself.

"I tried to get back before you woke up, but I felt you calling me," he said.

"You felt me calling you?" I hadn't called him, had I?

"I certainly did. I felt you next to me when I woke up, not just your body but your mood. I could feel you dreaming peacefully. The Sewing was successful," Andren said. "Do you feel it, too?"

"I–I *smelled* it." In fact, the smell was so close and intoxicating, I wasn't sure I had actually woken up. Maybe the golden amber glow was still a dream.

"You smelled it?" Andren's lip curled around his teeth, and I flushed like I was meeting him all over again. I'd never get used to him in my space.

"I-I could smell you nearby, almost *taste* you," I said. The words were ridiculous, but his eyes danced at my struggle.

"I like the sound of that," he said. "Tell me, what do I taste like?"

I shoved against his arm, but there was no hiding the blaze across my cheeks. His taste still lingered on my tongue from the night before, vanilla and amber muddled with the char of my embarrassment. There was no way I was telling him that bit of information. I'd die of mortification before the Trials could have their go at me.

"We should head back." I swallowed hard and grabbed the quilt underneath me. I needed proof I was actually here in this room with Andren. Even if this wasn't actually reality, the repercussions of being caught certainly were.

"I brought you some breakfast before we head back," he said, offering a piece of bread. I accepted the slice of crusty bread and smeared what appeared to be strawberry preserves on it. "I also brought you this."

Andren reached into his pocket and produced a folded piece of paper. He unraveled it, revealing dried herbs inside. "I'm going to mix it with your tea. It will uh, prevent any mishaps from last night. We can't have you going into the Trials with child."

Why hadn't I considered that? And even worse, why had he? The bread turned to sawdust in my mouth as I imagined Andren with other Ladies, giving them the same morning-after service I was receiving.

"Oh," I said.

"I told you." Andren draped his arm around my shoulders. "I had it covered. Your priority is to complete the Trials, and now I will be with you the entire time." I nodded, but the vision wouldn't vacate my brain.

After we ate, I took in the shabby inn room, memorizing each detail before Andren dropped me back off in my reality. The rumpled sheets where we'd made love. The flat pillows where he'd nestled his head next to mine. The dent in the mattress where he'd held me all night. If I didn't show up today, would they come looking for me? Would my parents know to find me here? What if Andren and I stayed here together and let the rest of the Caste move on without us?

Exactly as Andren described, he delivered me to my door before anyone noticed. We parted with a long kiss that trickled through the hollowness where he'd been inside me. The shadow of his touch stayed on my lips long after I was back in my bed chambers, hastily changing my outfit before Corinna came in to catch me in the act. Just as the iciness filtered back in and I lost the remnants of Andren, the tug at my bellybutton resurfaced and I knew he was on the other end.

The rest of the day was spent packing my trunk full of clothing, text books, my favorite fountain pen, and anything else potentially useful for the Trials. *And anything I want with me in case I don't return.* I topped everything with a small oil portrait of our family, neatly securing it amongst my clothing. With everything packed and ready, I stared down at the trunk to find my entire life fit into a single box. There was no time to mourn the loss of my title, but I sat atop the trunk and let the hot tears well anyway. Sniffling, I wiped my face when the door to my chambers swung open.

"I-I came to see you off," Mother said, hanging in the doorway. "I have to call upon a close friend later and will not be here when your carriage leaves." She watched me for a beat while I straightened my back.

"Come in," I said. She rushed toward me, sliding onto the trunk at my side before halting. Mother extended her hand but let it hang in the air between us, her face dark and clouded. I recoiled from her touch involuntarily, and she backed away. Funny she could still find disappointment in something I had done. Her eyes were just as red as mine, with purple rings beneath them. My mother looked old, in a way a commoner would age instead of a Casted Lady. In a way I likely would without the influence of the Original Bloodline on my paternal side.

"I will never forgive myself for the burden you've been made to carry. Because of my transgressions." Mother bowed her head.

I touched her hand. "I don't blame you." But I did blame her. Even with the evidence of her own torment painted across her face, weighing her shoulders down until she was a shadow of the proud Lady I'd known my whole life, I still seethed. Father didn't deserve this, and neither did I, but the bitterness in my belly wouldn't do anything to change the situation. "I will be okay."

"I know you will," she said. "But you need to know about the man that sired you. Your birth father."

My heart thumped out of rhythm, and I tasted blood. I would never *ever* refer to some stranger as my father. Danby Sharpe was my father and nothing in my mother's sordid past would alter that, Original Bloodline or not. I shook my head and crossed my arms over my chest.

"You need to hear it." Mother balled her fists, as if she was convincing herself as much as she was me. "He was not just any ordinary man. He was a force, so *vivid,* with an aura that consumed me. I still remember everything like it was yesterday, but I never believed he was real." She paused to lick her lips. "And then you were born, with hair like his and that same strength. I should have known, but I didn't want to. And you and Danby were always so close...." Her eyes were glassy as she spoke my father's name.

I sat motionless, trying not to listen, but she pressed on.

"I never knew his name, but he was the first man I'd ever laid with. Danby and I were betrothed, but this man was relentless, as if he'd put me under his spell," she said. I swiveled to face her, arching my eyebrow to ask the question hanging between us. "No, it wasn't like that. He wasn't forceful–he was gentle actually." I glowered at her, and she at least had the decency to look away as she continued. She could have spared me some of the details; this was already hard enough to hear. "I don't know enough about the world to tell you who or what he was, but I do know he was not a mere man."

"I'm not sure I understand," I said, still letting her talk to my side. Nausea rolled across me, making the room seem off-balance. She made no sense, not that any of this did. But what exactly could she mean–*not a mere man?* Obviously this stranger wasn't Casted, otherwise I wouldn't be in this predicament. And I supposed he wasn't a mere man. He was the man who destroyed my family and my future.

"I don't either but I felt it was important to tell you. I don't know what the Trials will entail, but I want you to go into them with all the armor I can give you. You *are* Casted. You have been your whole life, as you've carried my blood in you. But you also have his. You have something more." She forced the statement from deep within her chest, making herself breathless as she spoke. Before I could ask anything else, she rose from the bed and rested her hand on my shoulder. I tensed under her touch.

"Please forgive me for this." Then she slipped out of my room, leaving me with a hollowness even Andren couldn't fill. The notes of amber and vanilla were flat, almost sickeningly sweet in my state, and the tug at my abdomen only flared the queasiness churning within me.

Hours later, under the pale, full moon, Father and Andren stood at my side as Nix loaded my trunk into a small carriage. Corinna and the other servants lingered in the entryway, watching everything from the cracked door, though most of them were no longer on duty. It was well past dinner, but we needed to reach the mainland before dawn in order to find my escort to the training camps in time. Nix and I would travel to the port across the island, where we'd catch the last ferry of the day to cart me across the Mar Sea. It was going to be a very long journey into the Andalls, but the first leg felt like the longest.

Father took me into his arms. I was taller than he was, but he pulled my head against his chest. His heart pounded into my ear, and I inhaled the wool of his jacket, saturated with tobacco smoke and traces of brandy. This man was my father, and nothing could take that away from us. I wrapped my arms around his waist and squeezed him as tight as I could.

"Selah, your blood is no matter to me. I love you and am proud to be your father." He kissed my cheek. "Be safe." His eyes were the same, familiar navy, and he looked at me exactly as he did when I was a toddler on his knee. *His daughter.* Such simple words but they ripped a hole straight through my chest. Maybe I deserved this, but he didn't.

Andren stepped in front of me and held me at arm's length, though I'd been resisting coming close to him again. How could I let him go now? My legs turned to tree stumps and I fought to stay upright. Whatever strength that had carried me through packing and preparing to leave leeched out of me. How was I going to say these words to him?

"You don't have to tell me goodbye," Andren said. He squeezed my shoulders for emphasis. When he leaned in close, my knees buckled, but he caught me. "I will be with you the whole time." He ran his thumb over the scar on my wrist, setting it ablaze under his touch. "And for the moments when you need something more, here's this." He tapped the pendant draped around my neck.

"Goodbye, Selah." Andren kissed my cheek, then stepped away. The pit of hollowness opened even further, sucking me into its depths. He looped his fingers in mine and led me to the carriage door where Nix stood. In a ceremonious fashion, he placed my arm on Nix's—relinquishing his responsibility to him. Nix helped me into the carriage, and shut the door on the only home I'd known.

"Ready?" Nix asked after several hours of silence. He'd graciously tucked his head in the corner and slept, or at least pretended to sleep, so I could let my tears flow without an audience.

The carriage rolled to a stop and one of the footman held the door open for Nix to unfold himself from the tight quarters. Nix offered me his arm, and I stepped out into the cool night air. The Mar Sea was much angrier from this part of the island, where it flowed without its restraints. A ferry was tethered to the dock, rocking in wide swings as Nix and I tiptoed up the ramp to board.

"Cabin seven," he said, trailing behind me to stow my trunk with the crew. I shuffled toward the rear of the ship, careful to maintain my balance against the movement of the boat, examining the markings on each faded door down the aisle. They counted down, all odd numbers painted in bleached, peeling lacquer. Locating the appropriate door close to the end of the row, I pushed it open to find nothing but stale darkness. The waterlogged boards groaned under our weight, and I waited for my eyes to adjust before proceeding into the pitch-black cabin.

Nix didn't wait for an invitation and vanished beyond the threshold. His oversized form bled into the darkness, making it impossible to tell where he ended and the cabin began. I hesitated, not keen on leaping into an unknown void when there was a confirmed monster lurking inside.

"Better get comfortable. There's no turning back now," he said. *As if I need the obvious stated.* His arm appeared into the moonlight, where it connected with mine and yanked me through the doorway. Holding my breath, I plopped into the corner, hoping to land in the empty space and not on his lap.

Nix shifted his weight to make room, but our legs still ran together. The space was barely big enough for two typical-sized Casted adults, not large and... *Nix.* The air was stuffy and tight, but the restrictiveness was strangely comforting. At least I wasn't alone in this.

"I'm still shocked Andren actually let you go," he said after I settled into the wooden bench. I cocked my head but I doubted he could see it. If Andren *let* me go?

"Honestly, so am I," I admitted. "He's kept me so...wrapped up I didn't think I'd make it either."

"Wrapped up is what we're calling it?" I resisted kicking him in the shins. It was the middle of the night and I knew Andren was sound asleep, but my wrist burned where we'd been sewn together. Nix had witnessed the whole thing. Well, *most* of it. "Don't worry, Andren made sure I wouldn't forget about you." My stomach flipped, and it wasn't the rocking of the boat. *Why does that sound so ominous?*

"So you're here to monitor me, but might get cleansed as a consolation prize?" I said, massaging the raw spot with my forefinger.

"I am a man of requirement." Nix chuckled to himself, and I eased my own back into the wall.

"Well, it's nice to have a friend," I said. "Even a required one."

"Yes, it is," he replied, then settled into the calm quiet. Whether it was voluntary or not, I was thankful for a guardian through this. Maybe it was an unfair advantage, and maybe I was using my situation to get ahead, but I needed all the help I could get. What little I knew about the Trials was enough to know how unprepared I really was. The air around me rippled from Nix's soft snores, already dozing from the sway of the boat. There were far worse allies.

"Selah," Nix stirred me back to consciousness some time later. "We're here." The motion and noise had all ceased and Nix was already at the door, ready to disembark the ferry as soon as the shipmen rolled out the catwalk.

"Let's get going," he said. His tone was so stern by default, and I wasn't about to argue with him. Instead I got to my feet, straightened my skirts, and followed Nix off the boat. He found my trunk in a pile and hoisted it onto his back. And then he took off at a pace impossible to mankind, trunk and all.

"Do you know where we're going?" I said between pants. How was he so damn fast lugging all that weight around?

"I have an idea." Of course he did. He'd been preparing for years, and had traveled to Esson many times before. Meanwhile, I was just floating from moment to moment in survival mode. Nix had his work cut out for him if he was charged with chaperoning me.

"Do you need a break?" Nix called after we'd covered what I thought was a long distance.

"No." *I would kill for a break.* But I wasn't going to admit that to Nix. We weren't even to the Trials yet and he was already questioning my ability to get there.

"You're not on trial yet," he said with a shrug and then pressed on, though at a slower rate. *Great.* Now I had *two* men reading my mind.

We walked along the ocean to a boardwalk that hugged the expansive pebbled beaches glowing under the moonlight. Oberin had just one beach on its north side, which was so densely forested no one visited. While the ocean smelled familiar, it looked like a different creature altogether, wafting in foamy bursts on the sand instead of angry crashes against stony cliffs. Even in the dark, the beaches were breathtaking.

I can't afford to lose any more breath. By the time Nix slowed down, the sun peeked over the rooftops, revealing a foreign world all around me. We really weren't on Oberin any longer. Nix cast me a sideways glance as he approached a fawn-colored building with red terracotta shingles. If I'd had the energy, I would've analyzed his expression further, but I was too tired and too absorbed in the scenery. Even the door was more intricate than anything at home, with its deep brown stain and brass knob.

"This is the Navigator?" I asked, soaking in the craftsmanship of the building. Nix nodded. "I always thought the Trials were hard but maybe most candidates just couldn't find them."

"If only we could be that lucky," Nix said before knocking on the door. It creaked open almost immediately.

"More candidates?" The small, thin voice registered as neither male nor female. As the door widened, a frail figure with snow white hair bound in a ponytail appeared.

"Yes, Candidates Emrys and Sharpe," Nix said.

The figure sized us both up before stepping back to allow us to enter. It was odd to hear a working classman's last name. Family titles were irrelevant among anyone outside the Caste. *Finix Emrys.* I tested it out in my head, curious of his heritage. Where did the Dominion store men that large and *wild?*

"Welcome to Esson, Candidates Emrys and Sharpe," the figure said. "I am Gaine, the appointed Navigator of the Casted Trials. My duties are to help the candidates through their challenges, offering direction and guidance." While it was a nice gesture to offer direction and guidance, I strongly doubted Gaine's ability to help much. If he was as old as he looked, he likely wasn't even Casted, though I couldn't fully rule out that possibility from his nondescript features.

"I am not a Proctor and will have no influence on your standings during the Trials, but I will see you through until either completion or disqualification. Whichever path you take." He swiveled his eyes over us, making wide sweeps from the height difference between Nix and me, then pushed open another door to a room that looked like a cellar above ground. The stucco was exposed on the outer walls and the interior were nothing more than wooden shelves. The floor was simple, unpolished stone coated in a layer of sand and dust. Gaine retrieved two large satchels and handed us each one.

"Your provisions for the duration of your time," he said. "You will leave the rest of your personal effects here." Nix and I both looked at the trunk on his shoulder scornfully, but likely for different reasons. A fresh wash of sadness gutted me at the realization I wouldn't see my family for weeks—even their portrait I'd packed. Gaine gestured to an empty shelf in the corner and Nix silently stacked my trunk against the wall. My lip twitched in amusement when he plopped his single bag next to mine. If I had packed less, there wouldn't be as much to miss right now.

"You will be able to reclaim your belongings when you finish," Gaine explained. "Everything you need will be provided to you." I shook the satchel, feeling the thump and swish of its contents. My entire body was flipped inside out with emotions, but doubt managed to overshadow the others. The bag was suspiciously light compared to the notoriety of the Trials.

"We will wait until noon before we depart, in case other candidates show. In the meantime, there is breakfast ready in the next room. I do suggest spending this time fueling your bodies and minds, because the Sponsorship will be the first occurrence upon arrival. It is known to be quite... taxing." The word cracked at me like a lightning bolt despite my best effort to dance around it amidst all the logistics of getting here. But the Sponsorship broker had laid it all out for me long before his contract had become my reality. Slimy, icy dread balled deep in me, then used my spine to crawl upwards until it reached the top of my head.

Unfazed, Nix didn't need any further invitation and raced off to the adjacent room. He'd let his purist instincts take over if he could focus on eating right now, because nothing could be more distant in my brain. I dragged myself after him, hoping there was something hot to sip since my stomach was in no state for solids. When the spiced aroma reached me, the fog in my head preemptively lifted and I rushed to the table.

"Here,' Nix said without looking at me. He slid a thick clay mug with the side of his hand, tea ball already steeping in the hot liquid. *I could hug him right now.* I brought the hefty cup to my lips, then jolted when an invisible thread tugged at my navel. Andren really was watching out for me, even if it was through his Hand.

Tiny footsteps sounded behind us, followed by a sharp *ahem.* Abandoning my mug before my first sip, I wheeled around to find mousy hair and an unamused expression to match her flat complexion. Ophida's eyes darted rapidly around the room, from Nix, to me, to the spread of food. She looked suspicious of all three.

"Rough trip?" Nix tossed a biscuit in her direction, which fell to the floor after she made no attempt to catch it. Ophida gave a half-hearted glare, the weariness of travel muffling her usual snappiness. Her hair was just as stick straight as it had been during Debut, but the sea air pulled the fine strands in tufts around her face, and her cheeks were bright pink from sun exposure.

"Considering I didn't have anyone to carry my luggage, yes. It was a rough trip." She dropped her bag to the ground. "I didn't realize we could bring our own servants to this."

Nix kicked his boot over the chair to face her square on. "Oh, well which candidate brought you?" The little color she had drained from Ophida's face under the ferocity of Nix's stare. I tilted back to stay far out of the crossfire, though a spark of admiration kept me from changing seats altogether. Ophida's snark was nothing compared to

Nix's, a trait he'd apparently watered down around Andren and the others.

"You might be less cranky if you ate breakfast," he said between bites of biscuit. Ophida's face was plastered with objection, but she obeyed without argument. Perhaps even she had a limit to her petulance.

The three of us picked at the food in silence as more candidates began to trickle in. Two young females in particular caught my eye—one with her shock of black hair that rivaled Nix's, and the other with the looks of a tabby cat. Neither looked familiar from Debut, or any of my other interactions on Oberin, though I only really knew my own servants. *And Andren's.* The girls kept their elbows interlocked as they whispered conspiratorially to one another, apparently already acquainted. I stole a glance at Ophida, who was in the middle of the same routine she had presented to me at Debut. She and I weren't going to be on that level of kinship any time soon.

The rest of the candidates were men of various ages and backgrounds. Dozens of them poured into the building, flooding the corners, doorways, and halls. Seeing them en masse, all lithe and muscular, resurrected the pit of impending doom. Did they all have to make Nix look...*average? Okay, Nix will never look average.*

"The wagons have arrived and are lined up outside." Gaine appeared in the doorway. The gaggle of candidates shuffled through the back entrance but I lingered close to Nix.

"You ready for this?" His words danced in my hair as he leaned in to speak.

I squeezed my eyes shut to keep the flutter inside my chest from knocking me over. "No, but I'm going to do it anyway." Even Nix couldn't release the shackles of unpreparedness I had chained to my ankle. Why had I thought I could do something like this? I'd never even dressed myself, but somehow I was supposed to trudge up a mountain *before* the Trials even started? It would be a miracle if I just made it out alive—forget passing these things—and if I didn't take Nix down with me.

His side vibrated as he laughed to himself. "Let's get going then." He pushed through the crowd, out the backdoor, and I followed at his heels.

My jaw dropped to my chest at the six uncovered wagons towering in front of me, each hooked to the unimaginable colossal beasts. They had sets of horns larger than my legs, with reins so thick I doubted I could lift one. Even the coachmen steering these creatures were every bit as large as Nix, if not bigger.

"What *are* those?" The horizon teetered in front of me, giving me the dizzy sensation that came from processing something expansive in front of me. *The courthouse rotunda. The ocean. Andren's estate.*

"They're oxen," Nix said. "You've never seen an ox?"

Oxen. "I've read about them, but nothing said they looked like *that.* I thought they were just...large horses." All of Nix's teeth were visible as he beamed at me. My face bloomed into deeper and deeper shades of red.

"I forget how sheltered most of you live sometimes," he said, shaking his head. I'd been teased plenty, but something about Nix calling me sheltered struck a different note.

"Sheltered?" I grabbed his sleeve, as if that would stop him. He paused out of politeness, his smile still lingering. Everything about him flashed *untamed,* from the point of his canines to the width of his jaw, but his teasing didn't feel threatening. Not like the others. I still didn't like being called *sheltered* though.

"Yes, sheltered. Next you're going to tell me you've never seen a goat." Without thinking, I shoved at Nix's arm playfully, only to be met with utterly immovable stone. Nix didn't even swat me away like a pesky gnat. So this was how friends joked around.

We boarded an empty wagon and climbed all the way to the back. Ophida must have been trailing closely because she got on immediately after, but sat all the way at the front without making eye contact. I sighed, too tired to be irritable at our stowaway. She didn't have anyone here. The two other girls from breakfast filled in the space, followed by three more men.

The girl with the black hair was the first to speak. "I'm Rashel," she said. "And this is Della. We both have served the Dunkirk family since we were young girls." She raised her chin, obviously proud of this distinction. I didn't know the Dunkirk family, but smiled politely anyway.

"I am Selah and this is Nix." My finishing as a Casted Lady was my default, even here. Rashel waited for more information but I wasn't about to offer that up, formalities or otherwise. Nix waved two of his fingers in greeting. I caught Rashel's eyes lingering on him longer than necessary, and swallowed back the urge to shove her backwards over the side of the cart. Nix was Andren's Hand, so by proxy, he was mine.

"I'm Ophida." Her voice was shrill, and almost as piercing as Rashel's. Was that what the other Casted girls had thought about me? I adjusted my seat and worked a neutral expression on my face, doing my very best to let her speak without reacting. I could do better than what was done to me, if nothing else. "I've been a Lady-in-Wait and will be marrying Lord Frier after my Cleansing," Ophida said. Rashel's face twitched, but smoothed before anyone could notice. But I noticed.

"Well, good afternoon ladies," a stocky, red-faced man slurred as he leered at us. The tone of his voice reminded me of oil—smooth and greasy. "This here is Bodney." His companion raised a single eyebrow beneath disheveled brown hair, turned darker just from the layers of grime. He picked at his teeth then sucked the morsel before nodding. "And I'm Rior. We don't serve no one." Rashel was far less discreet with her repugnance, screwing up her face at the pair.

"And who are you?" Della turned to an older man with deep, leathered skin and salt-and-pepper hair. He looked at her with hauntingly hollow eyes for some time before answering.

"Tomas." He didn't offer anything additional and nobody asked. Tomas was wiry, with a look of age that came from both a hard life and a long one. He hardly seemed like Casted material, but it didn't appear he'd let us in on why he was pursuing it anytime soon.

"Are you betrothed, Selah?" Rashel asked. Her voice was razor-sharp and calculated. I'd recognize it anywhere; it was the same voice that had called me a common trollop and red witch while pushing me to the ground. "Or are you planning on holding a role in the Caste? Della and I are going to be tutors for the Dunkirk children."

"I am betrothed," I said. Hopefully that would be enough to satisfy her.

"To a Governor." I snapped my head toward the high, tinny voice. Ophida looked quite pleased with her contribution to the conversation.

All my patience had been a waste because I would bully her right back to the island if she didn't stop talking.

"A Governor?" Rior was a dog with a bone. "Well, you must be pretty important."

"She's a *Lady*," Ophida said. My nostrils flared. Lord Frier was going to have to repeat Debut, because Ophida wasn't going to make it off this cart.

"I am not a Lady," I said. "Not anymore." My spine stiffened as four pairs of eyes pelted me. Even Tomas's interest had been piqued.

"The Scrolls rejected her." Ophida *kept going*. My blood boiled until it turned to steam in my veins. Alone here or not, I was going to kill her in front of all these witnesses. I could shut her up with one swift blow.

"You're certainly the most... vocal... Lady-in-Wait I've ever encountered," Nix said. My rage diffused long enough for me to register his words. Ophida shot him a venomous look but clamped her mouth closed. God, the silence was so gratifying. Della and Rashel snickered openly this time and I couldn't find it anywhere in my shriveled heart to feel bad about it.

The land curled into a ribbon of hills, the oxen leaning into the roadways as they marched along the inclines with their cargo. As the cart angled more and more with our ascent, gravity pulled me against Nix's broad side. The sun dipped behind the foliage, and I clutched my shawl tighter. I sank into Nix, letting my head go slack against his shoulder and my lids drift shut.

Sometime after dusk Nix rustled me awake. "You're missing them." I rubbed my eyes and followed the direction he pointed. The landscape came into focus with a crescendo of white peaks. A thick cloud of fog hung at the base, giving the Andalls a ghostly vibrance. They appeared to float away from the earth, blocking us in from the east like an advancing army. My mouth dropped. Their magnitude was unbelievable—*nothing* like the bland renderings in portraits and text books.

"Amazing, huh?" Nix eyes were on me and my reaction instead of the scenery.

"They're magnificent." I reminded myself to take a breath, too awestruck to bother with pesky bodily functions. Even in this wretched situation, I housed a hum of excitement. Excitement and the marked epiphany that the world was so much bigger than I knew, never stepping foot off my island before today. For the first time I felt small, though having Nix next to me didn't help matters.

The mountains grew closer and closer until they surrounded us from all angles, too large to make out their silhouette from our position. The train of wagons slowed to a halt, flint and gravel crunching under the hefty wheels. The oxen snuffed and stomped at the ground, and I echoed their sentiment. My knees crackled under my weight and my hips protested every move as I stretched. Whatever dread had built up over the past week had been absorbed in my aching bones. I just wanted off this stupid wagon.

"I gotta piss so bad my eyeballs are floating." Rior crudely adjusted his crotch, leaping over the side of the wagon. Ophida scrunched her nose in revulsion, and for once I didn't disagree with her. As soon as Rior's feet hit the ground, he took two steps off the path before unbuttoning his trousers. I did an about-face as quickly as I could and moved to the other side of the cart, where people were starting to gather around Gaine.

"Candidates," he said, his voice even quieter in the vast expanse of land. "We must walk the last portion of the journey. I will lead, but please keep to a single file. The paths can get quite narrow." I got in line, diligent to keep close to Nix in the shuffle. I wasn't about to crawl up a mountain at night without my escort.

Between the darkness and the wall of people in front of me, I couldn't see ahead, but I sensed my balance shift with the steady incline and huffed against the thinning air. I collided into Tomas's back, then felt Nix's hands on my shoulders to steady me as the line came to a screeching stop. Gaine's thready voice wasn't audible this far back, so I stood waiting. My boots chewed at my heels, but there was nowhere to sit for a second of relief.

Sure enough, the line picked back up at half the cadence we had been moving and I realized we were now traversing on a level plane. *Finally.* Clutching my side as my ribcage expanded, I passed under a stone archway with two lanterns suspended. The path opened up to a large courtyard, allowing the candidates to disperse so I could see ahead. What could only be described as a fortress constructed from slate gray stone rose from the snow, complete with turrets in each corner. Rows of iron bars lined the perimeter and each of the windows, either to keep something out, or to keep us all in. My teeth clanked together from the cold, though the menacing security did nothing to help. It wasn't an island, but this was my new prison.

"You will now enter Hanover Hall and proceed directly to the Sponsorship." My stomach wrenched hard, folding me in half. Whoever was waiting in there for me was about to die at my hands. Even if I didn't hold the weapon, the blood would be on me. Streams of sweat rolled from the base of my neck, down my spine, despite the chill, and there was no attachment between my brain and my body, but I traipsed forward with the crowd.

Chapter Thirteen

G aine led us into a vast entryway with spiral staircases on either end. Our boots thumped against the stone floor, reverberating off the slate as we marched into a large arena. The ceiling was at least three stories high, with enormous stone pillars supporting it. Rows and rows of stone benches filled in between the pillars, circling around a raised stage. An empty marble table stood in the center, glowing stark-white under the torches.

I grew dizzy from the flickering light bouncing off the heads of other candidates, casting distorted shadows on the walls of the auditorium. Their patterns looked like wild birds clawing to get out. Nix sat down next to me, brushing against my arm with his. The contact snapped my focus back to the white table, then to Nix. He looked so calm, unruffled, while I was ready to climb the walls, too. They'd made the Sponsorship venue rich and polished with lavish carvings and fixtures, but the truth was as cold and hard as the stone. People were going to die tonight. Real people who had families and lives beyond the Caste. And yet they were dying for this facade of refinement, even though they'd never taste it themselves.

"I–I can't." I pawed at Nix's arm, shooting up from the bench. "I'm going to be sick." I was desperate for fresh air, and to be anywhere but here. I never should have come in the first place, not with so many other deserving people waiting their turn.

"You have to keep it together," Nix whispered, yanking me back down and holding me in place. I whimpered, holding my head in my palm. If only the room would stop spinning. Those stupid birds were still trying to get out, but they were as hopeless as I was.

"Candidates of the Caste," a clear, commanding voice spoke. "As the Commissioner of your Trials, I welcome you to Hanover Hall. Your mere presence here is an honor most will never have in their lifetimes, and tonight you will participate in the most hallowed ceremony."

I shifted against the hard bench to see the source of the speech. I didn't want to, but I had to. He was broad-shouldered under his black robe. The man's smooth, pastel complexion was a stark contrast to his angular proportions and harshly clipped hair. He looked over his nose at us in spite of the stadium seating placing us over his head.

"Our society began over seven centuries ago, erected from conflict and fire in the War of Scrolls. Our founders recovered the Scrolls of the Ancient Ones from the hands of our enemies, unearthing the Prophecy that ordained the Original Bloodline. And so, from the blood of those spilled in the war, the first collateral was paid.

"To continue to fulfill our ordained Right of Blood, all candidates petitioning the Scrolls must, too, pay their collateral as a willing offering to the Ancient Ones. With this ultimate sacrifice, the candidate can trial and cleanse as our Original Bloodline once did." My stomach threatened to empty its contents right on the floor but Nix held his hand over my legs to keep me from bolting out of the room. I focused on the spread of his fingers in my lap, the way they overlapped both of my legs and gently curved with the contour of my thigh. Relaxed, but powerful. Working hands. Hands that would carry him through this flawlessly.

"Just as you will be born into the Bloodline, tonight you will earn your Sponsorship in birth order. Please come forward as you are summoned."

The dread should have lessened knowing I'd be one of the last to go, but it only compounded. Prolonging the inevitable did nothing to get me out of this moment any faster, and I spent every other second convincing myself not to run. I just wanted this over so I could focus on the Trials.

"Tomas Offler!" I shuddered at the clang of the Commissioner's voice over the slick surfaces. In my periphery, the lanky, graying man rose from the crowd. Tomas took smooth, long strides as he made his way down to the platform. I jerked to watch the platform, where two other men in black robes escorted a woman to the table. Her skin was weathered and loose, making it hard to tell how old she might be. Tomas stuttered, his arms flailing, but he didn't stop.

"Welma Offler," the Commissioner said. *The same name.* The woman kept her focus locked on Tomas with an intimacy that only came from decades of shared moments. "You have committed to the consecration of Sponsorship for Tomas. Do you do so willingly and freely?" Welma nodded with unmoving eyes. Tomas remained a statue, his expression as blank and pale as fresh parchment.

The Commissioner nodded to the two robed men, who maneuvered Welma onto the stone table in a supine position. They crossed her arms across her chest, her exposed skin paper-thin as it rose and fell with each breath she took. One of the men dropped to his knees on the other side of the table, hidden from the spectators' vantage. The other kept his back to the crowd and reached into his robe. I strained to see, morbid curiosity taking over. She was so frail–they couldn't actually hurt her. Not like this.

The static in the air charged as the first man raised his hands high above Welma, the glint of a blade shimmering against the flames. *Not like this.* He drove downward, connecting with her concave chest with a *thud* that reverberated against my own sternum. A wounded bay echoed from the stone walls, like the whole auditorium cried out in agony. I cupped my ears, the pain too raw and searing to bear. When I focused on Welma, the only animation in her body was the trail of crimson dripping onto the table. Tomas fell to the floor and screamed until the grating noise ran out, leaving him to choke on his own despair.

Horrified, I waited for someone to move, for anyone to move. Where was the outrage for this woman's life? Tomas was frozen in place, his hands tearing at his face. He was trying to escape, too. Trying to flee his reality. The two robed men remained huddled around Welma, sliding her up the table by her armpits, carrying on in spite of the man gasping behind them.

Welma's feet dragged and her head lulled around in an unnatural manner. Her body left a vivid streak of red in its wake. Where she had been was alive just seconds ago. It glowed against the blanched marble, eternally burned into my retinas. I squeezed my eyes shut but the vision wouldn't fade. I knew this would happen. *I knew it.* But actually seeing it, witnessing death so close, rippled through me like a poison, rotting everything it its path until there was nothing untouched. There was nothing left of my old self to return to after that scene, and it wasn't over yet.

One of the hooded figures held up a glass vial, which he corked and handed to Tomas. He fingered the vial, turning it over in his hands. The torture looming in the creases of his face dripped away, leaving just the stains of trauma behind. Tomas stilled into an uneasy stoicism.

"You have been sponsored, Tomas," the Commissioner said. "You may now enter the Trials." Tomas pocketed the vial, careful to keep his hand over it before returning to his seat. His face stayed as blank as the granite encircling us. No hint of what brought him here. Of what it took to keep walking back to his seat after that grisly display. *What would justify another human's life?* My mind thrummed with the desperation to know, as if that would be some sick measuring stick for my own reason.

"Cecil Holliday!" A brown-haired man with freckles walked down to the stage. I scooted to the edge of my seat when the hooded forms reappeared with another young man in tow. Not a young man, a *boy*. He couldn't have been more than fourteen, judging by the thin arms and unformed pectorals. I gripped the edge of the stone until my fingernail bent to the quick. *A fucking boy.*

Cecil was unaffected when he reached for the vial, the Commissioner giving him the same speech. It was all so well-rehearsed, so routine. Even when everyone expected it, including the victim, I teetered between comprehension and chaos. *What are we all doing this for?* I'd lived as Casted for two decades, and nothing in my life was worth *this.*

I jumped. The jolt to my core was another shock through me, but then it dulled and steadied into a gentle pulse. Andren must have sensed my turmoil and was attempting to tether me back to everything I lost. Most importantly, back to him. He was the only thing that kept me from sprinting from this hell and straight down the mountain. That, and the girth of Nix's arm across my legs. I wiped the sweat from my temple and inched back into the bench, trying to thwart the nausea gripping my throat.

The next few men were called forward and continued in the same manner. I recalled the contract in the brokerage, and the figure that had been outlined as compensation. The Sponsors were paid handsomely, and all marched forward with their pockets all but jingling. *They want this.* Tomas and Welma had been the exception. The eagerness in each Sponsor didn't soften the impact of each dagger, but I'd formed a callous over the unending line of blood. Vial after vial was handed over, and the candidates returned to their seats holding their golden ticket.

"Finix Emrys." the Commissioner's voice echoed through the stone. Finix pursed his lips and stiffened, reverting to his hardened, beastly state. His eyes turned to ice in an instant, but he squeezed my hand with the tips of his fingers as he stood, then marched to the stage. I wanted to reel him back in, to tuck him under my arm as if he wasn't twice my size, but he was already out of reach. This time the hooded duo led an older man, so feeble that he crouched forward as he walked. He raised his head and pulled his mouth into a wide smile when Nix approached, revealing several missing teeth. From the distance to the stage, I thought I saw Nix's lips twitch and...*his eyes glisten*? In the low light it was impossible to tell.

"Ephraim Heaton." The ceremony commenced. The dullness of the routine was gone, and each syllable was sharper than ever. I scooted to the edge of my seat, rubbing my fingertips raw with my vise grip on the stone. Ephraim's voice was nothing but feathers and dust when he answered the Commissioner. He laid on the table, unable to completely flatten against the curvature of his spine. Nix pitched forward, as if the kinetic energy was ready to overtake him and thrust him into action. His fingers opened and closed, biceps flexing with each squeeze of his hand.

Nix turned away. His shoulders fell, his chest caved inward, and his chin slumped towards his clavicles. All the power deflated from him, and in that moment, Nix looked so *fragile.* He was the impenetrable wall behind Andren in every scene, the light-hearted smart ass who stole Lady Helena's chair at dinner. But this wasn't the same Nix, and it ripped my heart into shreds.

"You have been sponsored, Finix."

He slipped into his seat like a specter in the frigid air. I placed my hand on his forearm, trying not to move too quickly in case he'd evaporate under my touch. The muscles in Nix's arm tensed and I held my breath, but they softened seconds later. He exhaled into his palms before lifting his head back up to watch the remainder of the candidates and their Sponsors. To anyone else observing, he had completed his routine, but I saw his pupils go vacant. He was far away from this dreadful place.

"Selah Sharpe!" The Commissioner's voice slammed into me. It couldn't be my turn, not yet. My knees rocked as if made of paper under my body weight. Andren squeezed me hard over the invisible thread, holding me from the safety of our island. I would do anything to be back there right now, to take back all those times I wished I could leave it. The steady tug was the single source of strength allowing me to put one foot in front of the other. I had to do this for Andren. It was the only way.

The other Sponsors had all been willing, even eager, in their participation, but I still dreaded having to look mine in their face. I was afraid to disappoint them, to waste their gift to me, to take their life in vain and simultaneously lose mine. The Trials were challenging to the best of candidates, and I was wholly unprepared, undeserving. The rest of the people here had earned their spots, but I was merely a product of luck, attaining something overnight that most could only dream to have.

But it was too late to turn back. My head spun in wild circles as I descended to the stage where the Commissioner stood. It was much larger up close. I peeled my tongue from the roof of my mouth, as the two hooded men appeared once again. I swore they'd slowed to half their speed, inching forward painfully. My temples throbbed in agony, blinding me from the pressure. Finally, the men emerged completely, and I caught a glimpse of my Sponsor.

"*Mother!*"

Piercing screams jolted me, rattling my bones against each other. *My screams.* The sound of my voice was distant and unrecognizable, but it choked me as it tore out of my mouth. There was no stranger behind the Casted men, no faceless servant. It was my *mother*. She was cloaked as the others had been, free of any of the makeup she normally bore, with her hair tied in a knot at the top of her head. My beautiful, sophisticated mother was in a robe and nothing more. I couldn't process anything my eyes were reporting. It was the most surreal, disturbing dream. No, it was a fucking nightmare.

"No, you can't do this!" My screams echoed in the chamber. Mother shushed me from behind the men. How the hell could she chastise my behavior here, *now*?

"Selah," she pleaded. "You have to move forward. You have to let me do this."

I shook my head violently. I wouldn't let her do this. I would never move past this, *could never,* move past this. "I can't!" I didn't care about the ceremony anymore. Andren tugged harder and harder, but I didn't care about him right now. I just needed to get to her, to get her out of those awful robes and back home to Father.

"You have to. It's the only way. I want to do this, Selah. I *need* to do this." Her face was soft but persistent, beseeching me to keep moving forward. Her beautiful, smooth face. She was young and virile, the matriarch of our family's prestige. She had hundreds of years ahead of her. Thousands. This was my burden to bear, not hers. She had to live.

"You have to," she said again. "Please, trust me."

"Candidate Sharpe, you must complete the Sponsorship to continue with the Trials," the Commissioner said. "Your Sponsor is willing and ready." He didn't wait for me to reply before he started reciting the same line. He spoke louder to drown out my protests. It had to stop. *He had to stop.*

"You have committed to the consecration of Sponsorship for Selah. Do you do so willingly and freely?"

"No, no, *no!*" I shrieked.

"Yes," Mother spoke over me. The men helped her onto the table as she laid down flat.

I wanted to lunge forward to shield her, but my feet were plastered to the floor, and the men blocked my path from her. Still, I tumbled forward and pulled at them, but they elbowed me away. I couldn't get to her, and she refused to get up. The reality of the situation was so far out of my reach everything appeared to be under water.

"It's the only way," my mother called from the table. "You have to do this for me." Her words stole a piece of me I didn't know was there, but I was certain I'd spend the remainder of my abysmal life missing it.

"Please do this for me," she implored over and over. The men assumed their position, and a cold, dreadful sweat prickled at my hairline. I felt so nauseous I couldn't move even a fraction of an inch.

"I love you," Mother whispered before the dagger pierced her chest. I didn't know I was on the floor, until I felt strong hands slinging me under my arms. Andren was pulling as hard as he could, compelling me to stand.

"You have been sponsored, Candidate Sharpe."

Chapter Fourteen

"**C**ome on, it's over." The faceless figure walked me to my seat, not pausing to address the other candidates gawking at me. I vaguely noticed familiar hands around my waist. *Nix.* He had gathered me from the floor, scooped me in his arms, and carried me away from *that.* I was too numb to absorb anything happening. The ceremony could have ended or it could have gone on for hours. Noises echoed all around me but the sounds were all garbled. I wasn't going back to the outside world. I'd stay inside this delirium forever.

A *tink, tink, tink* sounded in my head, like metal clanging. Andren called for me but I was too far away to respond. All of Noala's magic couldn't hold us together, and I watched the frayed ends of the golden thread flop around on the back of my eyelids. If the dagger into my mother's chest hadn't severed our bond, I would have torn it apart with my teeth. Beneath the tidal wave of losing my mother, worse than the incapacitating loss, I had been *betrayed.*

Everyone must have known, my mother, my father, *and Andren.* They'd all been in on this but no one had told me. *None of them.* They'd planned my life like I was nothing but a puppet in a dress, and Andren had pulled all the strings. The gentle taps and tugs from him trying to reconnect us raked over my nerves as I sat in the hallway, seething.

"Did you know?" I bellowed the second we were outside in the cool air and I had a few of my bearings back.

"No," Nix said. "I didn't know."

"But Andren knew."

Nix's temple flexed. "He likely knew."

"He had to know," I insisted. "They all knew. They let this happen." Panic crept up my vocal cords. I'd been betrayed by every person that mattered to me, but the pity on Nix's face incited murder. Not sadness. Not loss, not yet at least. Just white-hot rage.

"Yes." I wilted under Nix's stare. Maybe it wasn't pity. "But you can't blame Andren. Sponsors have to be willing." His hair was wild, and his own eyes were bleary and bloodshot. *Empathy*. Not pity. "Your mother wanted to do this."

"But *I* didn't want this!" My voice cracked, betraying everything just beneath the surface. Even Nix was complicit, standing by their decision on my behalf. I was not only not Casted, I was barely my own person after having all my autonomy snatched from my fingers.

"Of course, you didn't. But what other choice did you have? Living outside the Caste is not what you think, no matter how quaint your strolls around the market are." I clamped my lips together and stared up at him. He'd ripped open a cut that had barely grown together, but the tone of his voice tugged the last ounce of compassion from my chest. I fizzled as he looked over the top of my head for what to say next.

"It's ugly and dirty and hard. Working for the Caste, living in their presence, is a mere shadow of a life. I am a *servant*, even as the Hand to a Governor. And you, as a woman? You definitely wouldn't be a Governess. You would be lucky if you were permitted to clean a Governor's house. What mother would want that life for her child?"

I had no good argument to fire back. I never thought of Nix as a servant, but everything about him declared that's precisely what he was. Andren may have favored him and treated him well, even afforded him some of the luxuries of being Casted, but he wasn't. He was Andren's pet, allowed to serve him and reside in his estate. I couldn't guess at what his life had been like, all while someone dressed me, and fed me, and *served me*.

"Sponsors don't just pop up," he said, the frost in his tone biting at my open wounds. "The ones you saw tonight? Their Casted families have been saving for years. Most Lords will never be able to afford the price of one. Even Andren wouldn't be able to buy you a Sponsor, not for several years at least."

I flushed with heat. God, I was abysmally out of touch with his reality, and the reality of everyone else here. Money seemed simple to me because I'd always had it. He had to think I was such a spoiled twat.

"Selah, your mother saved your life. At least, your life as you know it." Nix glared down at me with such ferocity I didn't dare suck in a breath. I nodded, smearing the saltiness clinging to my face with my sleeve. He was right, but that didn't make the tearing in my chest dull at all. "I am sorry," he whispered. Nix pulled me against him and held me, his mass like a fortress from the madness circling around us. I closed my eyes and blocked out everything except the sound of Nix's heartbeat against my ear. Strong, steady, alive.

"Come on, they have dinner for us." Nix grabbed my arm to drag me to my feet. My legs were tingly and mostly deadweight, but he held on to keep me steady. My insides flickered, trying to warm despite the barren cold surrounding me. *Gratitude.* In the gritty mess of everything, I was grateful Nix was here with me.

Food sounded trivial, and the thought of something in my stomach turned it into knots. The dining hall forked off one of the corridors, with a long, low ceiling and rows of heavy wooden tables. Each table was lined with bowls and platters, goblets and carafes. Under any other circumstance, I would have salivated at the smell, but right now it roiled in my bowels. The echoes of raucous laughter and chatter pressed on my shoulders, my head, my neck. I dragged my feet along the stony floor to follow Nix to a table without really looking where I was going. All of my fight was gone, replaced with static.

"Why aren't you eating?" Ophida's voice was shrill and assaulting in my cloud of misery.

"I'm not hungry." *Can't she shut up, just once?*

"You'll regret it tomorrow during the Trials," she said, as if she knew the entire itinerary already. As far as I was concerned, tomorrow didn't exist.

"I already regret it."

That silenced her momentarily. Nix, however, seized the opportunity to elbow me sharply in the upper arm. I took a few nibbles of a roll, more to occupy my mouth and avoid conversation than for any sort of nourishment. The bread tasted like paste, but I forced it down with a swig of wine.

Following dinner, Gaine met the group at the door and headed off down the same corridor, lamp bouncing back and forth in his hand as he stepped. He walked us to a single oak door centered on the wall at the very end of the hall.

"This is it," Gaine said as he pushed the door open. If I could pinpoint a single moment when I really understood how far from home I was, it was right then. The room was an open bay with two columns of bunks lining the sides of the walls. There was a set of trunks shoved together between each bunk and a few knobby hooks on the raw wood walls. Except for a fireplace in the very back of the room, the only light was a torch posted by the door. No frills, no comfort, and no privacy.

"This will be your home away from home for the next few weeks." Gaine gestured around the room. It smelled of wet pine, not entirely unpleasant but heavy and overpowering. I wrinkled my nose at the assault.

"Where are the female quarters?" Rashel clutched her pack to her chest, holding it like a shield.

"Right here," Gaine, said with a flick of his wrist.

"Here? With the *men*?" Della stomped her foot and leaned over Rashel's shoulder. The quarters were dreary, sure, but dreary was an improvement for me.

Rior didn't wait for confirmation and strutted off to pick his bunk, settling on one in the center of the room. Bodney followed him, ever the devoted sidekick. Rashel and Della stood frozen in the entrance while the other candidates pushed past to claim their beds.

"Come on." Nix pulled me along until he stopped at a bunk near the fireplace, and threw his bag down. Nix pivoted to face me, but I leapt back with a start.

"Top or bottom?" *He wants me to share a bunk—with him?*

I gulped. Maybe Rashel had a point—the accommodations were far from decent. "Um–." I licked my suddenly dry lips. The notion of Nix sleeping above me made my head spin. His eyes danced with amusement as he waited for my reply. "I've never slept in beds stacked like this, so whichever you prefer." Only one man had ever been in such close proximity, and that was just two nights ago. Now his much larger, much more dangerous Hand was asking me how I wanted to share a bed. Was this what Andren had in mind when he asked Nix to watch over me? *And does Andren care that I* want *to be close to him?*

My intestines fluttered. *God.* The Sewing had been disconnected since... well, since before dinner. If Andren was still with me, I'd never felt him like that. But there was no other logical explanation for the twisting deep in my abdomen. It had to be Andren's response, redirecting me to where my head *should* be at. I tightened my muscles to lull the feeling. I'd be damned if I forgave him that easily, though.

"I'll take the bottom then." He shrugged, then flopped down, rattling the wooden posts against the stone floor. I scaled the heavy wooden ladder to make my way to the top rack, carting my bag with me. I attempted to fluff the mattress's straw stuffing, and the bed groaned under my weight. Nix made the right selection. The fireplace crackled at our backs, and radiated a soft warmth to help with the flimsy quilt. The mountains were much colder than Oberin, and the ice churning in my veins didn't react to heat. Finally alone, or as alone as I could be, I drew my knees to my chest until I was just a ball, taking up the least amount of space possible. Maybe I could make myself disappear altogether.

But my thoughts found me anyway. Not only was I mourning the loss of my father, the idea of the man who had raised me suddenly becoming a stranger, the only person to blame was gone. In every sense of the word, she was *gone.* Maybe her guilt had washed away, and she was finally at peace, but I would never be, so long as I carried her burden. *And now I'm stuck in this place.* Pretending like I wasn't vibrating with putrid rage for what she did. *What kind of fucked up oxymoron of emotions are these?*

"Selah." Dark eyes peeked over the side of the mattress. "Are you going to be alright?" Nix's brow furrowed and he chewed at his lower lip.

"I'm fine." I flinched when Nix grazed the side of my face with his hand. It was surprisingly soft, and wet. I jerked my own hand to my cheek and felt the sticky dampness covering it. Aware of my sniffling, I gulped down a breath and swiped the tears with my sleeve.

"Ephraim is the man that raised me." Nix focused on the fireplace behind my head, orange flickers reflecting off his glassy eyes. I hastily stole the chance to clean my face up. His voice lowered until the modulations nearly separated. "I don't remember my actual parents. Ephraim found me alone in the mountains when I was four or five. He was accompanying the Lord he served on a trek through the Outer Andalls, not far from here, actually. Ephraim threw me on his horse and brought me home to his wife. They raised me like their own son."

"So your Sponsor...." I stumbled through the words. "He was your *father?*"

"Essentially, yes. The closest thing I had," Nix said. "He worked for Lords his whole life, never had a son of his own, and wanted better for me. He got me connected to the Whit family so I could avoid being a laborer. His wife, my mother, passed away years ago and his daughters are grown and married off now, so I'm all he has—*had* left."

Nix lost a parent tonight, too. I studied the servant, Andren's Hand, and the closest thing to a friend I had. His jaw tensed but his eyes were wide in the low light, his pupils indiscernible from his irises. Even though he still towered over me in my bunk, his shoulders slouched. Nix looked *small.* As fragile as I was.

"I'm so sorry." I touched the back of his hand with mine, afraid I might actually break him. The muscle in his forearm twitched.

"It's okay," he said with a small smile. "It's what Ephraim wanted. I just need to make sure I do my part to carry his wishes out. And you need to do the same for your mother." This time I felt the tear escape down the slope of my face. "Besides, Andren will kill me if I don't get you through this." The mention of Andren revived the nervous fluttering—not *over* him, but rather from the anxiety I'd brought upon myself. Andren was supposed to be my reason for being here, yet I hadn't once thought of him while Nix and I talked.

Nix drummed the side of the bed lightly before disappearing back to his bunk. Once he was out of sight, I fell backwards against the worn pillow and smacked straight into the rail. I yanked the threadbare quilt over my shoulders but its mismatched edges barely covered me. The chill sank its claws into any exposed part, penetrating the skirts and bodice I still wore, but I didn't actually feel it. My body was already ice cold as I succumbed to pure exhaustion.

Chapter Fifteen

"Candidates!" A voice echoed through the dormitory walls and I shot straight up, trying to orient myself in the unfamiliar setting. The quilt felt wrong, the mattress moved wrong, and the air smelled *wrong*. "Move along! Let's go!" I clawed the flimsy blankets away from my face to find the Commissioner looming in the doorway.

"Selah." Nix's face materialized in the tiny window of quilt I'd created. Shoving away the material, I rubbed my eyes to focus on him, realizing he was pulling on his pants. I flushed from my cheeks to my chest, then quickly drew the covers back over my head to shield the bright red display.

"You need to get dressed," Nix said, all business despite his compromised position. "There are clothes in your bag." The pack still sat in the corner of my bunk where I had abandoned it last night, neglecting to unpack its contents like everyone else. I had no idea what it contained but reached for it anyway, keeping my eye on the Commissioner. And trying to avoid watching Nix.

Turning it upside down unceremoniously, I found linen tunics and trousers, several pairs of wool socks, a belt, and heavy leather boots. Noticeably missing were any undergarments, bodices, or skirts. Instead, I retrieved a single, sleeveless white garment. I held it up, finding it wouldn't even cover my midriff and was as thin as gauze. Scrounging around to the bottom as my breathing quickened, I came up empty handed.

"Come on. We need to hurry." Nix tucked his tunic into his trousers and ran his hands through his tousled black hair. Immediately I pictured Andren, the motion so familiar. On cue, a tingling spread through my abdomen and sharpened at my navel. A faint scent of vanilla lingered in my sinuses, and it made my stomach grumble in hunger. So the thread between us hadn't completely snapped, though Andren was far more distant than before.

I picked up the pace, facing the back of the room to hastily tug the undergarment over my head and wiggle out of my skirts. They'd be completely useless with trousers. Frosty air nipped at my exposed skin, and the scratchy linen of the tunic and pants weren't any better. But they would have to do.

I jumped from the bunk, landing at Nix's hip. He raised a single eyebrow and smirked.

"I know," I said, heading him off. I felt ridiculous in the ill fitted getup, so I could only imagine what I looked like.

"Hurry up," Nix called, but his smile lingered. I shoved the tunic into the pants and stepped into the leather boots. They were heavy and clunky under my feet, weighing me down with each step. Nix sat watching me intently while I tied my hair at the base of my head. It had been years since I braided it myself, so I didn't have time to attempt it right now. Not without Corinna.

The Commissioner led our group back to the dining hall where a spread of eggs, biscuits, and ham waited on us. Sliding into a bench, I reached for the mug and carafe amidst the food. Expecting hot water, I was bewildered by the dark liquid pouring from the spout. Worried the carafe was dirty, I lifted the lid and looked inside, swirling the liquid around. A rich, inviting aroma met my nostrils and livened my salivary glads.

"Coffee," Nix said. "Try it."

I picked up the mug, inhaling the warm, intoxicating scent one more time before taking a tiny sip. It was more bitter than tea, but also more layered. At first I didn't like the way it hit the tip of my tongue, but then I swallowed it down and got a smooth, chocolatey flavor. I sipped again.

"We don't import it on Oberin because the Casted prefer tea, even though coffee beans are harder to find. Tea is more expensive and therefore more *desirable*." He rolled his eyes.

I tilted the carafe to fill my mug completely before offering it to Nix.

"It's wonderful," I said. "Where do you get it?" Nix poured a mug for himself and then spooned several heaps of eggs on his plate.

"In Torred, south of the mountains in the tropic region. They're shipped up the river and roasted by coffee distributors here on the mainland. You can find the beans in pretty much any market." I'd been missing so much of the world. "Andren doesn't prefer it, but I'll make sure he brings plenty back for you when he travels." Even if it was an empty gesture knowing I stood no chance of seeing Andren, or Nix, after this, I appreciated the sentiment nonetheless.

I didn't have long to enjoy the drink before Rashel and Della flopped onto the bench across from us. Their prattling formed a cloud that followed them wherever they went. Even while slathering their biscuits with jam, they talked in hushed voices, eyes darting around conspiratorially. Rashel poured the coffee into her own mug and brought it up to her mouth.

She spat out the drink. "What *is* that?"

Nix repeated the information about coffee but Rashel stopped listening after she heard the Casted didn't favor it.

"No wonder they don't ship it to the island," she said as she pushed the mug away. I proceeded to pour a second cup and rearrange bits of biscuit around my plate.

"What do you think the first Trial will be?" Rashel rambled on with food in her mouth. Nix gave her a noncommittal shrug but Della chimed in with her theories of Alloyed tracking in the mountains and wild game hunting.

"Ridiculous," Rashel said. "Everyone knows the first Trial is a puzzle or something."

Ophida appeared at the end of the table, sullenly leaning over her plate. I was very familiar with the look of loneliness. It didn't take much analysis to see it wafting from her. But before I could rouse the energy to tolerate her in a moment of weakness, the Commissioner spoke.

"I congratulate you on your entrance to the Casted Trials. Your presence in these halls is a privilege and your continued participation in the Trials is an honor." The dining hall was so quiet, no one dared scrape a fork over a plate. "Momentarily, you will begin the Scholarship Trial. You will work both as a team and an individual to earn a place in the Dominion's elite society, being evaluated over the Tenets of the Caste: Scholarship, Leadership, and Creed. You must display a superior competency in each of these areas, even when you are not being assessed. Many of you will not make it." The Commissioner paused as he scanned the room. "First Officer Pickham will lead you each day. Good luck." He vanished through the exit but the noise of the hall didn't return. *Scholarship.* The first Trial would be something academic, so perhaps I did stand a chance. At least I knew it wouldn't be wild game hunting.

Another man with a shiny, bald head nodded. "Follow me," he said.

The silence broke with benches scraping, boots shuffling, and low murmurs of anticipation as we funneled behind Officer Pickham into the corridor. Every sound gnawed at my insides. My stomach growled, chastising me for not eating more, but it was too late now. Officer Pickham led us to the other wing of the fortress, opposite of the dormitory. The halls were narrow and domed, as if the stone was swallowing us the farther we walked. I wished they would. The crowd turned behind the Officer, heading through a low arch into the fortress's basement.

"This is the Candidate Library." Behind Officer Pickham stood rows of shelves, all filled from top to bottom with books. We gathered around him in the back of the library, where six round tables were arranged in a row. Each one had rolls of parchment, inkwells, and quills laid out neatly. It would have looked quaint, like an inviting study, if it wasn't the stage for the first Trial. Unease soaked through every turn of my head as I surveyed the library.

"You will have everything you need to prepare here. As the Commissioner mentioned, you will complete your Trials in groups of eight but you will also be assessed for your individual merits as you work with your team. Please select a team and take your seats."

My worst nightmare reared its ugly head in the biggest trial of my life–being picked last. I peered around nervously, not wanting to draw attention to myself but also, not *not* wanting to draw attention. I'd better do this now before it was too late, else I stood no chance at all.

"Can I be on your team?" I fixed my stare on Nix's boots as I spoke. While he was obligated to Andren, I really didn't know how far that extended when it came to his own chances in the Trials. No doubt I'd be a liability for him, coming here without a drop of training to my name. Bracing myself for refusal, I was met with a roar of laughter.

"I'm not letting you do this alone," he chuckled as he spoke. He shoved my shoulder in jest, though it nearly knocked my feet out from under me. I exhaled, and even let a small laugh creep out.

"I'm sorry you're stuck with me," I teased, testing out my humor. It turned out that hadn't died yesterday, too. "I'll try not to hold you back."

"I am sure we can manage," he said. "Besides, this is Scholarship. You have the most schooling of any candidate here. You'll be my secret weapon." He winked, and the damn spot deep in my abdomen squirmed.

"Shouldn't we pick the rest of our team?" I swiveled my head around, not really seeing any faces, just a blur of bulk and color. Nix was on my team; that's all that mattered, but it wouldn't hurt to stack the cards in our favor wherever we could.

He lowered himself into a velvet chair and crossed his foot over his knee. "We'll just let them come to us." The way he could just *relax* was maddening, but his easy manner won me over and I bit back my skepticism.

Sure enough, a man I recognized from the Sponsorship approached our table. He was shorter and not especially athletic looking, with more freckles just on his nose than I had over my whole face. *Cecil Holliday*, I recalled.

"Can I join your team?" He picked at his cuticles, but he straightened his back as he spoke. "I'm not the sharpest, but I served for a very renowned Professor. I could help." He wasn't the strongest either, but we really didn't need muscle in Scholarship.

"Pull up a chair." Nix patted the seat next to him.

"Thank you." Cecil accepted the invitation. Across the table, Ophida slid into a chair. She glared at us, daring someone to voice opposition. Rolling my eyes wasn't very ladylike, but then again, I wasn't a Lady and I'd rather go through the Trial alone than deal with her more than absolutely necessary. I turned to Nix, waiting for him to turn her away, but he simply nodded his head. Either I'd severely miscalculated his desire to win, or I had underestimated his confidence in his own capabilities. *Or mine.*

"You look like you need a few more." Rashel rubbed against Nix's arm like a cat. She and Della didn't wait for an invitation before they sat down on his other side, leaning closer than I preferred. Nix didn't seem to mind though. First Ophida, and now these two. The odds were becoming more grim by the second. Even if I stood a chance at passing this Trial, I'd have to make it out without maiming one of my teammates. That probably wouldn't be very Casted of me. I kicked Nix's shin under the table, but he shot me an impish grin. That bastard. *He's enjoying the attention.*

We had six total candidates around our table, and only two more spots to fill. I searched the remaining potentials still standing, growing anxious to find someone to balance our roster. The Commissioner said our Trials covered Scholarship, Leadership, and Creed. Nothing sounded exceptionally physical, but it would be down to Nix if it came to that. Sifting through the stragglers, I spied Tomas. Sure, he wasn't the most fit, but he had a quiet strength about him, and a composure that might come in handy.

Springing from my seat, I hurried to the older man.

"Do you need a team? We have a few spots left." I pointed to our table. Tomas cut me a wary glance, his physical aversion to joining any team painted on his face. The look of a loner–as if I was seeing my own reflection. He turned to the other tables, fully occupied, and the resignation flashed in his pupils before he locked eyes with me.

"Yes," he said.

Nix surveyed me from his vantage, his attention tingling my skin as I prowled for the remaining member. He leaned his head to the right, gesturing to get my attention across the room. I moved my eyes in the direction he was pointing and saw a young man I hadn't noticed before.

He appeared to be about my age and my height, with an average build and dark skin. I wasn't surprised I had overlooked him before.

"Do you have a team yet?" I asked as I approached. The man's already-brown complexion managed to redden as he looked at his boots. The laces were untied but he'd made no effort to fix them.

"No," he said without looking up. "I uh, don't know too many people." I'd wanted someone in Nix's league to help strengthen our numbers, but instead had found his polar opposite. The timid dog to our feral beast.

"Well, we have one more spot if you would like to join us," I said, worried I would scare him away if I moved too quickly. Whatever Nix saw in him was a mystery, but we had little other choice as the candidates matched with other groups.

"Oh-okay."

I bent over and tied his laces, patting the toe of his boot as I stood up. "I'm Selah," I said, extending my hand to him. "What's your name?"

He rocked backward but accepted my hand in a loose grip. "A-Abernathy." His face burned brighter. "But I go by Abe."

"Very nice to meet you, Abe."

"I hope you have chosen your teams wisely, candidates." Officer Pickham's voice interrupted our introductions as Abe took the final seat at the table. "This will be your team for the remainder of the Trials."

"That's it?" Della squawked. "What the hell are we supposed to do with this? Where's the actual Trial?" Abe flinched at her outburst.

"Looks like we start studying," Nix said. Della looked at him wide-eyed but Nix swatted the air lazily. "It's a library, right?"

"Well, yes," she said. "But what are we studying *for*?" I'd almost asked the same question, but thanked myself for withholding it after hearing how petulant it sounded.

Nix shuffled the parchments around, and instead of answering Della, placed them neatly in stacks and grabbed a quill. His fingers were surprisingly light and nimble despite their size, moving adeptly over the papers. *Mathematics, literature, history.*

"I am pretty keen with literature," I jumped in, trying to fill the silence with something constructive. "It was my favorite subject and I've always been an avid reader." Nix smiled at me.

"Excellent start." He tapped the quill on the empty page, leaving a small blot under the nib. "Any other strengths in the group?"

"Well, no one else grew up with private tutors." Ophida's voice could have cut glass, and oddly enough, I could've cut her. Six pairs of eyes raked over me, but I glared back at the sullen blonde target.

"Then you're quite lucky you chose to be on Selah's team." Nix tapped my hand, more as a restraint than a comfort. My chest squeezed at the compliment, or possibly at the physical contact, but I couldn't dissect that just then. Ophida crossed her arms in a dramatic *hmph* and pressed her back against the velvet chair.

"What about you, Ophida?" Nix pressed on. "A Lady-in-Wait should have quite the experience living in an estate. Perhaps one with a library?"

"I never had access to tutoring," she said. "But my Lady did have me read to her nightly. I suppose I could help with literature." *Lovely.*

"Excellent," Nix said. "Well, I'm not the best student, but I have picked up a lot of history piecing the boundary lines of the Dominion together. Maps are kind of my thing." A wide, sheepish grin spread across his face. The youthful innocence reflected on the brutish frame was uncanny, and I had to chuckle to myself a bit as I recalled his tackle in the marketplace. He did love his maps.

"We can do mathematics," Rashel said. "We're not trained tutors, but we've helped the Dunkirk children with their lessons for years. They're all quite horrid with numbers, so Della and I had to practically finish their schooling for them."

"That would be very helpful," Nix said. Della beamed under his attention. "Tomas." Nix turned to the graying man sitting quietly. "How's your history?"

Tomas peered at Nix. "Are you asking because I'm old?" Up until now, I hadn't known Tomas knew what humor was.

"Well that would be convenient." Nix slapped him on the back, propelling Tomas off balance. Tomas's face moved, almost in the shape of a smile.

"I'm not much of an academic," Cecil said. He looked over Nix's list with wide eyes. "I'm sorry. Put me wherever I can do the least amount of damage."

"I'm sure you will be just fine," Nix said, but the expression on Cecil's face didn't evoke much confidence on my part.

"So what do we do now?" Rashel queried the group.

"We study." Nix chucked empty quills at each of us. "We have a week to brush up with all the knowledge we can. Let's split up and take notes, then meet back at noon to check our progress." Rashel looked nonplussed at the idea of Nix breaking away from the group, but she agreed. I wasn't thrilled to spend time with Ophida but Nix's plan was solid; there was much more at stake than my comfort.

We all grabbed the quills and extra parchment, then took off to various sections of the library. Ophida trailed after me, following me to the fiction section. Her mouth was agape as she walked past the towering shelves lined with colorful bindings and worn leather spines. There were thousands and thousands of novels to review, but we only had a week to sift through the necessary information. I had to find a way to narrow down our search, which was far easier said than done. There were enough books in here to last two lifetimes.

"What do you like to read?" I asked Ophida, primed for an icy reaction to my prying. But she didn't come at me with her usual bite for a change.

"I read whatever my Lady preferred," she said. "I never read anything for myself." I frowned at her admission, taking in the way her face flickered with embarrassment.

"And what was that?" I asked quickly, trying to smooth over the moment for her sake.

"Mysteries, mostly." She fingered a few titles at eye level. "And epic adventures. She liked action, even though it would keep her up far past her bedtime." I swore I detected a hint of sentiment as Ophida recounted her Lady. The fountain of emotions that spouted from such a tiny body were exhausting, but I couldn't help the urge to comfort her.

"I do like a good adventure," I said. "But I will always love romances the most."

"Is that what we should look for?" she asked, staring up at me. I was at least two heads taller than she was and she looked like a wide-eyed child from her vantage, waiting for my guidance.

"No," I said. "We should review the ones we have the least familiarity with."

"Oh," Ophida replied, her tone completely mellowed. "I guess that makes sense." Even her features had shifted now that she was away from the others, losing the sharp angles usually present. I'd managed to get her to lower her defenses, which in turn allowed me to relax in her presence.

"If this is a Trial of Scholarship, we should probably start with the classics." I gave her a wink and a conspiratorial smile.

"Classics?" She wrinkled her nose at me.

"Yes," I said. "We have to consider what information they'd find most valuable. And we never read contemporary work in school."

"Classics." She mulled my theory over. "Okay." It was as if the admission physically pained her, but her usual sarcasm was absent.

"Let's get going then."

Ophida and I tackled opposite ends of one of the aisles, each piling book upon book in stacks all around us. I indexed titles, authors, and publication years on my parchment to keep everything straight. Once I had a solid sampling, I carted the books to an empty leather chair tucked in the corner of the library and cracked the covers.

A Widow's Winter, The Journey East, The Courage Well, Warrior of the Scrolls, Crystal Ridges.

All of the titles centered around the War of the Scrolls. It had been the turning point that formed the Dominion as we knew it, and ultimately the Caste, so authors tended to romanticize the war when it came to novel writing. Epic battles against the Alloyed. Heroic acts of valor in the snowy mountains. Long lost lovers reunited with their warriors, Cleansing themselves together with the Scrolls. Now that I thought about it, most of our books had something to do with the Scrolls in some fashion.

Shuffling through the stack, I examined their faded covers, the leather patinated and pages yellowed. I had read almost all of them before completing primary school, so this was mainly a refresher to capture the highlights. I flipped open a faded black book without any title, its gold embossed pages still perfectly intact despite the appearance of the cover.

The Geomancer. I had never seen that title before. The letters were inscribed with large, looping calligraphy but there was no author listed. I shifted its weight back and forth in my hands, marveling at how heavy it felt. The pages, however, were soft and thin, as if they'd crumble with too much handling. As I turned each one over, I smelled the heavy musk unique to an old book. Something whispered to close the cover, return the novel, and keep moving through my stack, but the curiosity was overpowering.

I skimmed the first page, and before I could return to consciousness, I had completed the first chapter. It outlined several neighboring clans, likely fictitious though the setting was reminiscent of the Dominion with its mountains and plains, even an island up north. Each area was occupied by a different clan and named accordingly. They all cohabitated the land peacefully. As the chapters stacked up and I lost myself in the pages, I started to believe the book had some basis of truth, possibly just written far before the other novels, in a time preceding the war and the Caste. The descriptions felt so specific. But then it started to morph into obvious fantasy as the story progressed.

Beyond puberty, the young men of the Mountain would develop a talent. They began to connect with the earth and learn to manipulate it in new ways, to hear the soil and sense the vibrations in the mountains. The strongest among them could fertilize the ground to grow supple crops for their people, open caves in the cliffside to shelter them from the harsh winters, and even rebirth their dead and wounded from the fertile soil. These talents were unique only to the great guardians of the Mountain, and soon the other clans grew jealous of the clan's prosperity. Shielding their abilities from outsiders, these men grew into myth, even among their own people–the Geomancers.

I was enthralled. The Caste didn't permit books about magic, and even the old lore from before the War was scarce. The Scrolls were the only power we learned about, and it was the only driving force we needed. Or that's what they told us, at least. This book depicted themes that surely would be banned on Oberin, if not all of the Dominion. The leather burned my hands as I devoured illicit pages as fast as I could, terrified someone would catch me.

"*Selah!*" A high-pitched voice drew me from the story and back into the library. I looked up to find Ophida's face, hot with annoyance.

"I've been calling you." She threw her hands on her hips, face pink. "It's time to go back." I nodded and reached for my stack of books, careful to leave *The Geomancer* on the bottom to prevent her from asking too many questions. I had to keep the book to myself. Even though it was here in the library for anyone to access, it had to have been misplaced, and no matter how docile Ophida was at the moment, I didn't fully trust her. This book was something special. Something *un-Casted.* I returned the other books to the shelf but paused when I got to the forbidden cover. Hastily, I gulped down all reason and tucked it under my tunic.

"I'm worried." Nix popped over the side of my bunk once we were back in the dormitory, coming within inches of my face. The torch was already out and the room was dark, but I could see his profile reflected by the fireplace and feel the air move from his nearness.

"I am, too," I said.

"Do you think we should do anything?" He was so close I could smell hints of cedar in his hair. My stomach fluttered involuntarily. *My damn nerves will kill me before the Trials do.* It had to be my nerves. There was a lot of mounting pressure for our team to perform, and none of it had anything to do with the proximity of Nix to my bed.

"I guess we could study more," I said. *Focus.* The Trials. Math. *Not Nix.*

"We could, yes," Nix said. "I'm just hopeful the rest of the candidates might struggle, too. None of us have ever seen a classroom except you, Selah."

I sighed. "But neither has anyone else here."

"See?" He rested his hands on my crossed knees. "I knew you were smart." I beamed back at him with the first genuine smile I'd had since my Sponsorship. The fluttering persisted until I worried Nix could actually hear it through my bedding. My nerves were worn down to frazzled nubs and my emotions were all over the place. *Nix is your friend and all this seriousness is starting to get to you.* Nix patiently waited for me to settle whatever conversation was running through my head, a twist of amusement tugging at the corner of his lips, as if he could read my inner monologue. As long as he couldn't read my body's reaction–I wasn't ready to forfeit all my modesty yet.

"Good night, Nix."

He winked at me, then disappeared to his bunk.

As soon as the room was completely silent, I pulled *The Geomancer* out of my pillowcase and dove back into the story. The protagonist was having his first baby and the migrant River Clan was coming to meet with the Mountain Clan leaders to trade goods. Despite the Geos managing to grow crops among the rocky cliffs where the soil should have been barren, they were in need of fish, nets and traps, and other items the River Clan could supply. In return, they could give precious gems and wool, rare commodities to the clans living in the lowlands.

On the eve of the second moon, the River Clan Chief arrived with his lieges. The River Chief was highly polished compared to the gruff men of the Mountain. Their horses were even smaller and more refined than the hardy beasts beneath the Mountain men, with eyes that swiveled wildly. The soil beneath their hooves tensed and the mountains leaned in suspiciously. The Geos circled the party, opening themselves to the cues hidden to all but them.

I read until my eyelids became too heavy and my better judgment kicked in. I needed to be sharp for the others, especially knowing I'd have to help pick up some of the slack. All of our livelihoods were dependent on our performance, and as Nix pointed out, I had the best vantage to help everyone. I needed to stay sharp for myself and my team; they all depended on me in this Trial. As I settled in with that thought heavy in my head, Andren's touch thrummed over the thread, gently caressing me until I let my eyes close.

Chapter Sixteen

A piercing shriek roused me from a deep sleep. I sat straight up, catching fragments of yelling across the dormitory.

"That's cheating!" A woman yelled. "I'm turning you in!"

"Don't be ridiculous." A man's voice. "You really gonna snitch on me, girl?"

My eyes were still foggy from sleep, refusing to focus on any of the figures in the dim light.

"Shut the hell up!" Another male voice called.

"Try and fuckin' make me!" The first man yelled back.

I rubbed away the sleep and sat fully upright in my bunk. Nix kicked his bare feet onto the stone floor, leaning over to sit on the edge of his bed. He peered up at me with a look mirroring my confusion, eyes baggy and red-rimmed. I had no idea what time it was but judging by the other candidates' state of half-sleep, it was still the middle of the night.

"Can you all just give it a rest?" someone else called. "Go back to sleep!"

"He's cheating though! His team is going to have an unfair advantage!" The tinny pitch and telltale whine was undeniable, especially when it drummed across my skull like a xylophone. *Rashel*. For the love–it was the middle of the night and she was carrying on at full volume. Wiping the trail of drool from my chin, I grumbled and squinted toward the noise. I could make out her shape in the center of the room, pointing at the bunk in front of her. Not her bunk though– Rior's. Frowning, I sat upright and tried to get a better look. *What the hell is she doing?*

"Won't you calm the hell down?" Rior bellowed, rustling the attention of several other sleeping candidates.

"No!" She screeched. "I'm going to get the Officer." Before she could storm off, Rior snagged her by her arm and threw her to the floor. The vibrations of her knees striking the stone traversed up the posts of my bunk.

"You crazy bitch, sit the hell down."

Nix leapt to his feet and made it across the room in two strides. He snatched Rior with both hands, lifting him off the ground before shoving him into his bunk. Rior flopped back like a rag doll, fuming against the stone wall, but too smart to make a move with Nix hovering over him.

"Don't touch her," Nix ordered through gritted teeth. "And hand over the book." He didn't wait for Rior to respond before he snatched a small item from Rior's bed.

"I'll take this back to the library. If you have any desire to get out of here with a job that doesn't involve wiping some fat Lord's ass, you better never pull that shit again." He turned to walk back to bed but Rashel scrambled to her feet, clinging to his arm as he passed.

"Are you going to turn him in?" She looked like an insolent child hanging from Nix. When he shook her off, I had to stifle my smirk in the darkness. It was way too late for me to pretend I didn't find deep pleasure in the way he pushed her back to her bunk without a second glance. At least he shared in my sentiment.

"No. It's a math book, not a war crime."

Rashel opened her mouth to argue. "But–"

"But nothing," Nix shrugged her off. "Go to bed, Rashel."

She stomped off without another word, climbing back into her bed. Nix padded back towards me and tossed a book on top of my quilt. I froze as panic iced over my gut. *Intermediate Arithmetic.* Not my book. Rior was getting in extra study time. While it wasn't explicitly forbidden, Officer Pickham had made it clear all the materials had to stay in the library. We couldn't have any unfair advantages over other candidates. Which meant I now had two illicit texts in my bed.

I laid my head down on the sunken pillow and tried to capture whatever sleep was left to be had before daylight. It was a fruitless effort, as my mind shot from one thought to the next. Somehow I needed to sneak *both* books back into the library. It wasn't safe to keep my contraband much longer with Rashel and the others sniffing around, but the gold leafed pages kept sucking me back in. The book had a grip on me I was far too weak to shake.

Just as anticipated, the sun crept through the dormitory like a serpent hours before my body was ready to wake. Every ounce of my skin felt three times its density, fusing me to the mattress with invisible force. I stared up at the dusty, stone ceiling, attempting to sharpen and focus my vision.

"Selah, you need to get up," Nix said from over the side. I shifted my eyes to him without moving any other part of my body. The sound of his voice hit my eardrums but the words failed to permeate my brain.

"Selah." Nix took up my entire line of sight. His even, dark complexion was backlit by the grimy light of the windows, making his eyes look bottomless. I sat upright in my bed, then crossed my arms over my chest when I realized how flimsy my garments were.

"I'm up," I said, face flushed. I felt Nix's eyes dart down then back up before he turned his back toward me. A wildfire blaze struck me in the deepest part of my core, somewhere brought to life only once before. *Nix just checked me out and* this *is how I react? Dear god, we haven't been here* that *long.* Clearly the distance from Andren and the damaged Sewing had messed with my head, because I could *not* permit those kinds of thoughts about *Nix* of all people.

Trying to get my mind right, I scrambled to find my thicker tunic, then fed each leg through my pants as quickly as I could manage. I still didn't have the dexterity in my fingers to braid my hair in a hurry, so I opted for another low ponytail tied with the leather strand. Once semi-decent, I tossed myself over the side of the bed. Nix reached an enormous hand towards my face and pulled a rogue curl off my forehead, then tucked it behind my ear.

"You are a mess." He snapped his hand to his side. I wanted to be irritated at his brusk command, but he had a point. My own body was running itself today, and it had an agenda *far* different than mine. "Let's go." Dismissing the fluttering feeling that masked Andren's persistent pulls in my chest, I scurried along behind Nix. I didn't have time for *any* men right now. As we reached the door, I stopped in my tracks. *The books.*

Nix looked over his shoulder; comprehension washed over his face. We both peered around the dormitory to ensure it was empty before heading back to the bunks. How the hell was I going to dig out the math book without exposing my own infraction? Nix, however, didn't give me the time to consider my approach before he swooped down on my bunk and tossed the pillow aside.

"Selah!" His disappointment struck my rib cage. "What is this?" He held up the copy of *The Geomancer.*

"A book?"

His large, black eyes narrowed. "Obviously," Nix said. "*Were you cheating?*" He scolded me in a harsh whisper, eyebrows nearly touching his scalp.

"No!"

"Then what were you doing? Do you know what this looks like?"

I swirled my thumb against the inside of my palm, pressing my nail into the meat. "I... I just wanted to read it," I said, looking at my boots. "It was never covered in any of my schooling." It was the truth, but it sounded ridiculous saying it out loud.

"You just wanted to... read it?"

"Yes," I said. "I couldn't put it down in the library and just wanted to finish reading it."

Nix examined the cover as if it was a living creature, trying to analyze what was so unique about this particular book that would cause me to risk the Trials. Clearly, nothing stood out to him because he looked back at me for more information.

"It's fantasy." I started to explain the book's contents. "At least, I think it is. It's about some land long ago with different clans, and people with powers of some sort."

"Powers?" Nix eyed me dubiously. "*Like magic?*" He cut his eyes back and forth—Casted were strictly forbidden from talking about any magic other than the Scrolls.

"Like *abilities*. They called them Geomancers," I whispered.

"Geomancers?" he asked.

"Yes. They were men from the Mountain Clan that could connect to the earth, understand it, even regenerate from it."

"Regenerate...." The wheels turning inside his head were nearly audible.

"Yes, but we really need to go," I said. Nix nodded absentmindedly, his wheels still churning. I gestured down to the book.

"We'll return it tomorrow," Nix said. "We need to get this one back, though."

I paused for his face to relax before I tucked the book into my pants, then fluffed the loose tunic into the perfect camouflage. His face was unnaturally taut, making it unreadable. I winked, trying to get a reaction from him. The deep-rooted drive for people pleasing didn't make an exception for Nix; I *needed* him to not be angry with me for my transgression. Nix grinned at my parlor trick, finding no trace of the book, and I let out a forceful *whoosh* of air. At least I had the advantage of ill-fitting clothing. Meanwhile, I couldn't ignore the way his tunic hugged his biceps and tapered waist far too closely to disguise anything more than a knitting needle.

"Let's go."

Once in the library, our team dispatched to our respective areas. Somehow, I had to find a way to dispose of a math book in the classical literature without being caught. As lunchtime approached, my avenue of opportunity to dump the evidence opened. Ophida was nose-deep in the post-war transformative era and hadn't looked up in a while. Everyone else was tucked in aisles or sitting in random chairs dispersed through the area. Like a flash, I pulled the book from my waist and tucked it into my pile of novels, spine facing towards me. Waiting for the same trays of food to arrive, I joined my team with the stack of books in hand and nonchalantly set them on the team's table.

I looked up to see Rashel eyeing the book before turning to me. I stared back at her, keeping my face lax and refusing to let it betray me. I wanted to keep peace between our team and Rior, but I was equally complicit, if not more so since *The Geomancer* was still tucked under my pillow at that very moment.

"We only have a few days of studying and I don't feel like we're making it very far," Ophida said over her plate of cheese and bread. She picked the bread into tiny crumbs before placing one morsel on her tongue.

"Well, extra studying isn't exactly an option, so what do you suggest we do?" Rashel eyed her venomously. Everyone sat in silence, pretending to chew their food or read over their notes, making no attempt to answer her. I pushed a square of yellowed cheese back and forth on the polished silver plate, fixating on the dullness it left in its tracks.

"There's no way we can know everything," Della said. The others nodded in agreement.

"You're right, but we have to know how to make the smartest guess." I spoke before the thought had fully formed in my head. It was a line one of my favorite tutors used to say whenever I prepared for an exam.

"So you want us to guess?" Rashel asked, still sharp.

"An educated guess," I replied. "It's a game of odds."

"So helpful." Della rolled her eyes. I ground my teeth together to keep silent. Arguing with them was a waste of my waning energy. "Anyone else?"

"But Selah's right," Nix said. "We need to prepare to play the game." I lifted my chin and met his gaze. Whatever expression he wore had too many layers to itemize, but they each melted me into a worthless puddle. Being praised by a peer—publicly—was now on my list of crowning achievements. *Especially by Nix.*

"Do you really think we'll be okay?" Nix called to me from under the bed that night. I stared up at the ceiling, making the water stains form animals in my mind. "Guessing and all?"

"Yes," I said. "I do." If it was a lie, my body didn't register it as such. My pulse clicked away steadily, allowing a grain of confidence to settle within me.

"How are you so sure?" Nix's confidence, however, had evaded him. The twinge of his words stabbed at me. Nix didn't strike me as someone who was afraid of much. I leaned over the side of the bunk, letting my loose hair hang wildly.

"Because we have to be," I said, blood rushing to my face. His smile was small, and upside down, but it was there. "Goodnight, Nix."

The bunk rocked as he turned on his side. I righted myself and slithered under my quilt, too tired to risk another reading session. Instead, I stared into the fireplace and tried to pull against the connection with Andren, wanting him to pull back, to reiterate my pep talk. I called out to the empty space, failing to reach my target. He must have been busy, or even asleep. Curling my knees close to my chest, I looped my arms around my legs and hugged myself into a tight ball.

I hoped I was right.

For the next three days we studied, we outlined, we mapped, we plotted, we practiced, and we categorized all of the information as succinctly as possible. It was grueling and tedious but I felt like we had covered everything possible to prepare us for the upcoming Trial. There wasn't enough time for bickering or cattiness, either. We resembled a team, albeit an exhausted one.

"I'd rather just go home than spend any more time studying." Ophida slumped into her palm. "How much longer?" I hated when she whined, but I couldn't bring myself to be annoyed. It *had* been dragging on. Either we were prepared or not, so long as we came out ahead of the others.

My brain had spent hours absorbing the deep red walls behind the shelves of books, burning the port color into my retinas so I still saw it when I closed my eyes. Ophida had finally settled into more books, albeit at protest, and the other candidates were too preoccupied to pay much attention to anything else around them. I was able to sneak a few more chapters of *the Geomancer*, stuffing behind another title to avoid drawing attention. I was nearly to the end and determined to finish it before this Trial was over and we were no longer permitted in the library.

In the throes of its plot, with the two clans coming together, the tension was palpable through the thin pages of the book. The powerful men detected the mountains' pleas of caution with the River Clan's intentions, but the men had no choice but to proceed with the transactions. They remained vigilant as the day of the visit faded into night. I flipped each page furiously, devouring every word.

At the end of the visit, the River Chief and the Mountain Chief came to an agreement on their bartered goods. The Mountain Clan would haul pounds of grain and loaves of stoneground bread down the mountain, and exchange it for all the fresh river fish and strings of net their horses could cart back up. The Geos felt the earth trembling with unrest as the Chiefs bowed to one another, sealing a pledge between clans.

Seven days later, the Mountain Chief and all of his able-bodied clansmen loaded their broad beasts with sacks of grains and breads, until the animals' backs swayed under the weight. After a day on the trail, the splintering streams tumbling through the rocks converged into sharp, foaming tributaries, falling to the greenery below. The Geomancers all froze in their tracks, pausing the line of Mountain clansmen. The horses pricked their ears in nervous anticipation. Two of the oldest Geos transmitted a silent message. The warning came too late.

My heart pounded furiously as I flipped page after page, crinkling the frail paper in my haste. The River Clan ambushed the Mountain Clan, stealing their goods and trapping the men in nets. The mysterious narrator laid out the action in painstaking detail, down to the cry of the hillside at the disturbance. The story was alive in vivid color in my brain, not just words on a page, and I furiously flipped pages to reach the ending.

"Secure the Geomancers." The River Chief stood in the center of the chaos, screams and bellows of defiance and rage booming across the clearing. "And drown the rest so they can't come back."

"This betrayal will score the earth and taint your descendants with a black plague that will not be forgotten." The ancient Mountain Chief spat his curse to the opposing Chieftain.

"So much pride, even as your people fall." The River Chief stood over his opponent, sword in hand.

"I have nothing in my heart but pity for you," The Mountain Chief replied. *Even in his bindings, as his men were slaughtered all around him, he refused to bend.*

"I need no pity from a man who led his warriors to extinction," the River Chief said, crouching over the wounded man. *"Without your warriors, your village will be ours by morning. We will dispose of your children and take your wives to breed our own new race. Your precious Scrolls will give us the power to do so and the blood of your Geomancers will supply the fuel."*

I gasped and slammed the leather cover closed, trying to will my pulse to slow. I looked around the library, ensuring my outburst had not alerted the others. Everything was still—except the percussion of my own heart against my ribcage. Was it possible the Scrolls referenced could be the same Scrolls the Casted used today? Although the content of the novel seemed fantastical, something about the plain, pastoral narrative read as nonfiction. But that was impossible. The Scrolls belonged to the Caste, gifted to our people by the Ancient ones so we could rule over the Dominion. It only made sense someone would try to steal them from us, inciting the whole War to win them back.

"You ought to be studying." *That voice.* So smooth and rich, and one I hadn't heard in days. I tore my head to face the sound, and saw golden blonde hair gleaming back at me.

"H–how did you get here?" I rubbed my eyes, positive I was imagining the sight before me.

"You called me," Andren said. "And it looks like I made it just in time." He wriggled his slender finger at me chidingly. "You need to focus on the Trials." I nodded, jaw slack. How was he here? This was impossible.

"I will." *I'm hallucinating.* Between the Trials and the mysterious book, I officially was losing touch with reality.

"Good girl." Andren's lips curled in a cat-like grin. That damn dimple. Whether he was real or not, my chest still lurched at the sight of him.

"Take me home with you." My voice sounded like it was coming from someone else, someone sad and desperate. It definitely couldn't be me. And Andren was too icy to be him.

"Then you know what you need to do." He curled each word with his mouth, enunciating every syllable.

"I'm trying my best." I reached for him, but he stepped back. I just needed to touch him one more time.

"Now get up." *Why is he being mean?* Even before the Sewing had been damaged, it had never worked like this. Yet I couldn't actually feel him, or his emotions, like before. I had to be hallucinating.

"Huh?" I cocked my head at him. He was so stern, so hard. Nothing like the Andren I was used to. Real Andren or fake, *I* should be the one mad; he'd sent me here on false pretenses, conspired on my mother's murder, and left me with his aggressively good-looking Hand to get me through this *mess.*

"Get up," he ordered once again. I had no idea what he was talking about. He repeated himself, moving inches from my face, but I *was* up. "Get up." He punctuated his command with a light kiss to my forehead. *"Get up, Selah."*

"Selah, you need to get up." I snapped my eyes open to find Nix's dark eyes in startling contrast where Andren's had been. I reached to my forehead, Andren's kiss still tingling my flesh. *What a bizarre dream.* Without anything left to read, I *had* to get better rest tonight.

"Selah." Nix crossed his arms and bent over me. I shrank into my chair as his body eclipsed mine. He was particularly domineering from this angle, and my brain wasn't ready to process what he was saying. "Are you still sleeping?"

"No, I'm up." I started scurrying around to gather the books spilled across my lap.

"You must have been having one hell of a dream," Nix said, but I didn't respond. *If he only knew.*

Nix drew out a chair at the table where the rest of the team sat. Cecil droned on about pre-war trading and bartering, but my mind was still stuck on those bright eyes, and that dimple. The rest of the team continued on with their conversation, while I wrapped my arms around myself and squeezed, trying to simulate being in Andren's arms. Clearly my subconscious was trying to tell me to rearrange my priorities and focus, Sewing or otherwise.

"You know, I'm a bit relieved to see you finally look stressed." Nix jerked me back into reality, and I scowled at him. Of all the times I'd been caught revealing too much on my face, this wasn't the most opportune. Everything here was stressful, but a fake visit from my fiancé wasn't something I was keen on sharing with Nix. "You've been making this look easy so far. I wondered when you were going to crack." His mouth spread into a wide, toothy smile glimmering brightly against his dark skin. His teeth were unusually straight for a working classman, though his canines jutted into sharp points standing out from the rest. Everything about Nix looked lithe, almost feral, and potentially dangerous.

"I'm fine," I said. *Priorities.*

Rather than arguing, Nix just shook his head, letting his shaggy black hair fall across his forehead. I watched him sweep it back in place with one hand. "Of course you are." He rested his hand on my shoulder and held it there. The weight of it was heavy but not unwelcome, satiating some of my body's starvation for touch. It wanted Andren, but Nix's contact soothed away the angst and allowed my muscles to unclench. He must have sensed me slacken because his smile shifted into something gentler, more familiar. But it was gone before I could put my finger on it. Nix was already lost in conversation with Cecil and Tomas.

Chapter Seventeen

The biscuits at breakfast were flavorless, just a filler to get me through the day. Even the coffee was starting to taste the same, though I embraced the jolt it sent to my nervous system. All the studying numbed my brain, and the days blurred together over the course of the week. At least I thought it had been a week. We were all stuck in an endless loop of meal, study, meal, study, meal, sleep. Repeat until I would've rather cleaned sewers for the rest of my life if it meant seeing something new. *Or tasting something new.*

Without a word, Nix nodded to the others before pushing away from the table. As was customary, I followed him like an obedient dog. We all did. Nix was the only one that had the gumption to keep showing up, and pressing on. Today was no different, with his half-smirk and seamless forehead. If this mental warfare bothered him, he didn't let any of us see that. He paraded back to the dorms with his back straight and shoulders high, though I couldn't quite lift mine to mirror him.

But if we actually made it to the dormitory, I wasn't sure. Somewhere in the length of the corridor, my shoulders slumped, but then the weight grew to be more than my dreary outlook. My head became too heavy for my neck, and my hands and feet went numb. Even my tongue began to tingle as my vision narrowed into pinpoints. Nix called my name but it was so far away, he must have been in a different room. I had to get to him, but my body wouldn't respond to my commands. Something was seriously wrong. And then everything went black.

⚜

I blinked once, cringing at the dry sand that raked over my eyeballs. I tried it again, prying the crust from my lids. When the relentless, penetrating light struck the sensitive surface, my head squeezed like it was in a vise, and I slammed my eyes shut again. *What the hell happened?* The last thing I remembered was eating breakfast with Nix, and then....

Nix. Where was he? Where was I for that matter? I forced my eyes open, crying out at the searing pain of the light. My temples pulsed so hard I could see the red flashes of each beat, like little blotchy lightning bolts. Rolling to my hands and knees, I let my head hang towards the floor until everything stopped spinning. The ground was hard and cool under my fingers, giving me something to focus on. *Don't vomit. Don't vomit.* I heaved, tasting sharp acid, but I willed my stomach to settle. The coffee was even worse the second time around.

Bending all the way over, I pressed my forehead to the cold ground. If there were others around, they had made it clear no one was coming to help me, and the relief the floor provided was too sweet to deny myself.

"*Nix.*" My voice clawed against my throat, bringing a well of tears to my eyes. The moisture wasn't unwelcome, however, and I used it to blink again, and then again. Finally the white marble beneath my hands came into focus, and I picked my head up to look around. "Nix!"

Black and white tiles lined the floor. I looked up a little higher, finding they also lined the wall in my immediate line of sight. The contrast shifted my vision to an odd purple and green tone, giving everything a fantastical tinge. Perhaps it was a fantasy. My body still didn't feel attached to my head, so I hadn't ruled out the possibility I was dreaming. Squeezing my eyes shut to steady myself, I pushed against the marble, finding the floor hard and unmoving. The density and the temperature were very real.

"Nix!" I tried again, patting around my immediate area with my hands. I gasped when they struck something soft and warm, and *hairy*. The object squirmed under my palm, and I shrieked.

"Selah." Hoarse and gravelly, but familiar. I knew that voice. "Selah!" He coughed. I ripped my eyelids apart and pushed my body upright with all my strength. My limbs were unwieldy and sluggish to respond to my demands. But I sat unsupported and managed to stay that way. There were two of him in my vision–wild, midnight hair and darkened onyx eyes. His skin was more gray than brown, but it was still him.

"Nix!" I clambered across the slick floor and fell into his arms. He winced but smiled through it. "What happened?"

"I don't kn–" Nix's eyes focused somewhere behind me. I veered around, but the room failed to move with me, and tilted until I feared I would fall into the ceiling. Then I spotted it, or him, rather. Tomas was slumped against the wall, tucking his knees to his chest. Nix lifted me away from him and bear-crawled to the old man. A groan rang behind me. Shuffles. *A cry.*

A fresh wave of nausea swept across my midsection, but I hoisted myself to my feet. The pulsing in my head refused to ease, and the tiles danced in time with the beat. My joints creaked and protested, but I was standing. Swaying, but still standing. Ophida materialized in front of me, curled into a tiny ball on her side. Next to her, Rashel slouched against Della's shoulder. Nix knelt over Abe, who groaned groggily on the ground. When I turned back to Tomas, he'd managed to pull himself upright, using the tiled wall for balance. Our entire team was here, but that was the only answer I had, with too many questions to process in my state. *What the hell is happening?*

"We were drugged." Tomas navigated his way to my position.

"Well, no shit." The sound of Rashel blared in my ears. It sliced through the lobes of my brain, delaying the connections I needed to process this scene. The persistent foggy ache was reminiscent of the times I had indulged too much in my father's stock of wine.

"Where are we?" Ophida squeaked, taking the words from my cottony mouth. I shook my head, sending myself off kilter, but it seemed to help regain some coherence. I realized the large checkered tiles carried into the ceiling. There was no discernible exit, but we had to have gotten in here somehow. Others were catching onto the same train of thought, and had started feeling along the marble squares. *We need a way out.*

The sense of being trapped was a tripwire to my heart's explosion. Cecil and Abe worked a circle around the room, accounting for each square until they could no longer reach. Tomas pushed random places in the wall, while Nix stomped across the floor. The ceiling was too high even for him to reach, but he eyed it suspiciously.

"Selah, come here." He motioned for me without looking away from the pattern on the ceiling. The rest of our team watched as I let Nix hoist my legs over his head. He wrapped his hands around my thighs and anchored me to his shoulders, and I gulped. I had no choice but to grab hold of his face to keep from pitching backward, trying not to block his eyesight. Looking down at the others, I felt a funny twinge in my gut. It wasn't Andren, but it was some residual Casted reflex. If other Lords and Ladies saw me in such a compromised position, with a servant practically fondling me in public, I'd be outcasted beyond a doubt. Yet here I was, forced into this position by the Trials to become Casted.

The Trials. This was a Trial. My cheeks flamed from the realization I was probably the last to figure that out. Although Nix's palms so high on my legs weren't helping. I laced my fingers into his thick hair, which was surprisingly silky despite its constant unruly state. Following the lead of the others, I extended one hand in the air and made contact with the ceiling. I pushed my fingertips against the cold stone, but it didn't budge. Nix shifted from spot to spot, but everything was mortared and locked tight. We were trapped in this horrific room.

"What do we do?" Ophida's tone had shifted from groggy to panicked. "They can't just leave us in here."

"How is this supposed to be about Scholarship?" I asked, clambering to hold onto Nix's arms as he lowered me down. It was much more of an effort for me than him. Ophida's face went completely colorless. For a second, I worried she'd keel over right there. Maybe I wasn't the last to figure it out.

"You think this is the Trial?" Rashel snorted, which triggered a fit of giggles from Della. I scowled back at her through my haze.

"What else would it be?" Tomas interrupted their antics. Rashel clamped her mouth shut and took on a color similar to Ophida's. Abe scratched his head and Cecil's eyes went wide. Apparently I was far from the last to figure it out. Everyone stood frozen, seven sets of eyes all on me. A chilly stream of sweat worked its way from the nape of my neck down my back. Or maybe I was way off.

"So... this is a test of... knowledge." Abe's statement registered as a question. He placed his hands on his hips and scanned the room again, as if seeing it for the first time. "And we have to solve it."

"Thanks for your insight." Rashel narrowed her eyes until she looked like an angry cat. We were caged after all.

"He's right." My nerves were wearing thin, and if this was a Trial, I doubted our time was unlimited. "Keep looking." The acid in my voice was enough to shut her up, and the resulting silence from the rest of them was just an added benefit. My head bubbled with relief when the chatter finally silenced. They resumed their methodical search, going back over each black and white square. I watched from the center of the room, floating above my body. The frenzy of people moving flashed in and out of the black and white, skewing their motions into mechanical jerks. Black, white. Black, white. Black, white. Black, black.

Black, black. My pupils screeched to a halt over two particular tiles, where the pattern broke. I ran over to the corner, my sudden movement drawing the attention of the others. Nix knelt beside me, and I was vaguely aware of people hovering over my shoulder as I inspected the anomaly. Nothing about it was unusual at first glance. Dejected, I turned to Nix for help. He nodded at the tile, and I picked up my hand to start again. This time I dragged my fingers from corner to corner, forming an X before I traced the perimeter.

On first pass, they weren't detectable. But when my fingertips made a second lap, I felt the grooves. They were too small to seem meaningful, but the variation in the surface nagged at me to go back over them. Nix's lips fell apart as he waited, and Cecil breathed so heavily in my ear I couldn't tell whose exhale was whose. My only options were to let loose the scream building, or tune them all out, so I gritted my teeth and pushed my finger harder into the tile. *Straight lines. Curves. Angles. And, a period?* There was writing etched into the black tile.

"Here!" I turned to face them. "It says something!" I traced the lines again but they were so tiny, and my skin was growing clammier by the second.

"Well, what is it?" Della pushed Cecil out the way, and the distraction caused me to lose my placement. I slammed my fist into the tile. The unforgiving wall struck back, shooting a burst of pain up my wrist.

"I don't know!" My outburst forced her back, and for a brief second, I suffocated on all the commotion. "It's too small."

"Here." Tomas held his hand out, and instinctively I opened my palm to receive a rolled piece of parchment. I stared at it for several seconds before looking into his deep green eyes. The color was very uncommon on Oberin, but I wasn't on Oberin and I didn't have any spare time to ponder working class genetics. The only thing that mattered was that writing on the wall, and whatever Tomas had in mind for the piece of parchment.

He tipped his chin, asking for permission to squat down next to me. Nix shifted over to allow room. I handed the parchment back and rocked on my haunches as Tomas unrolled the paper. There was already writing on it, but he hastily flipped it over and smoothed it against the wall. The old man turned back to me, but I could only offer him a confused glance. I had no idea what he was trying to do, but he seemed to be mulling it over himself.

After several seconds, Tomas handed me the parchment, careful to keep the writing face down, then reached for the buttons on his tunic. The pressure must have been getting to him, too; my own tunic had started to cling to my flesh in all the wrong places from overheating, and I strongly considered tearing it away, modesty be damned. But he grabbed hold of the top button and brought it to his mouth, then he chewed at the threads until the button came loose. He'd lost it. The old man had been driven crazy before we really started, but I was too stunned to interrupt him.

Tomas laid the parchment over the etchings again, careful to line it up just right, then he rubbed the edge of the button over top of the paper. He worked it up and down for several passes before accomplishing whatever he was trying to do. Without a warning, Tomas shot up. My heart skipped no less than two beats. Tomas held the paper up to the single chandelier hanging in the center of the ceiling.

"*But before I am reduced to the belly of the river, I will meet the ocean with a willing...*" he read. My chin hit my chest with each word out of his mouth. Maybe the old man did have a few tricks up his sleeve.

"With a willing *what*?" Ophida bounced from foot to foot.

"That's all there is," Tomas said. Ophida stomped louder in frustration. Couldn't she shut up for just one second? *I need to think.* I recited the phrase over and over in my head.

"What are we supposed to do with that?" Nix jerked the paper from Tomas's hand. He had a point; the words were largely unhelpful, but the more I replayed them, the more they resonated. It was as if someone turned a key to a rusted lock long forgotten. *I know them from somewhere.* I had read them before.

"But before I am reduced to the belly of the river, I will meet the ocean with a willing *jump.*" I recited the poem excerpt under my breath, the words spilling from my subconscious. Tomas held his arm up, silencing the room. The hyper-focus aimed at me made the arches of my feet itch.

"What did you say?" Rashel called from behind Nix.

"Jump," I repeated, smoothing my voice as much as possible. "It's from a poem called the Island." But nobody seemed to care about my explanation. A bubble of chaos bounded to the center of the room, with Rashel leading the charge.

"Get up!" She grabbed at the remaining team members and dragged them to their feet. "We have to jump," she yelled at them. Ophida rolled her eyes but crawled to her feet.

"This is never going to work."

"Worth a shot," Nix said before swinging his arms until his feet left the ground—slowly at first, but then he picked up his pace. The vibrations of his heavy boots danced up my legs. *What the hell?* We didn't have any other options and it was as good of a guess as any. My hair flung around my face as I sprang into the air with the others.

But nothing happened. My temple sopped with sweat, and the vicious pulsating crept back into my skull.

"This isn't working," I said. Everyone slowed, realizing to their dismay that I was right. There had to be more to the clue, if it meant anything at all. But this room was too deliberate for it to be totally meaningless, with its hidden writing and extra black tile. *This is a Scholarship Trial, Selah. So* think *damnit.*

"The black tiles." I blurted the words out before my brain caught up. "Try the black tiles." Nix stared at me for a beat before maneuvering his boots onto a large black square. Everyone followed suit. But again, nothing happened. If I had something to throw into the stupid checkered wall, I would have. Nothing was working and the longer I hopped up and down on these gaudy tiles, the more ridiculous I felt.

"There are sixteen black tiles and eight of us," Cecil said. I whirled around to face him, and he shrank instantly. "We can try one foot on each." He whispered, the bridge of his nose blazing with heat. "Or not. It's a bad idea." Before he could go back to looking at his shoes, Nix caught him by the arm.

"That's a great idea," he said to Cecil, but he looked directly at me, as if no one else was present. There was that annoying flutter again. I swallowed it away and turned back to Cecil. His freckles practically danced off his face from Nix's validation.

We waited for the cue, then took our places on our respective tiles until every one on the floor was covered.

"On three." Nix raised his fist into the air, pointing with his index finger. "*One, two, three!*" We leapt into the air as a group, falling back to the floor on our black tiles.

I squeezed my fists and braced myself for the impact of the hard marble, but it never came. Instead, I was jolted by the sensation of falling—the unexpected drop when nothing connected beneath me. The floor was gone. One second it was there, and the next we were plummeting into empty, black space as if it had never existed at all. My stomach leapt into my throat, the relentless tug of gravity making it impossible to form a coherent thought. Milliseconds became millennia as I fell through cool, damp air, unable to see anything but black. In that suspension of time, I flailed around to touch anything solid. Perhaps I had died. That was the only corner of my mind I could reach, and the only feasible conclusion.

But then my boots collided with solid rock, and my knees buckled beneath my weight. I hit the ground hard, sending a coppery rush of blood into my mouth. Blue and pink stars danced in my vision, and my chest felt like it was permanently flattened. By the time the pain registered, I was on the brink of consciousness.

"Selah," someone said, shaking me. I groaned and rolled over. *Just let me die in peace.* But the intruder shook me again, and I snapped my eyes open. I was face down in something wet, and though the darkness was still opaque, I could make out gray silhouettes moving in the emptiness. If this was death, it was no wonder the Casted opted to stave it off as long as possible. I'd always thought the act of dying would be the worst part, but this was misery. My bones ached and the throbbing had intensified to a point that the figures in front of me shifted in and out of view. Sticky wetness clung to my face when I moved away from the ground. It smelled sickeningly sweet and metallic. *Blood.*

I was covered in blood. My face was starting to dry and flake where the air had begun to oxidize it, and it clumped on my tunic. The linen material clung to my form when I sat up. *Is it mine?* Frantically I patted myself, finding just a dull ache and tender bruises, but no lacerations, and all my limbs intact. Nothing that would have caused this amount of blood loss. I sighed a dramatic gust of air. *But where the hell did it come from?* Though it was dark and I couldn't properly see the color, there was no mistaking the texture. I'd seen my fair share of blood. And that *smell.*

"You okay?" Burly arms wrapped around me and pulled me to my feet. I wasn't ready to stand, but the arms held me steady until the ground ceased to quake. He really needed a new way of waking me up. Nix kept both his hands firmly on my waist and let me lean back against him. I caught whiffs of cedar, wet leaves, and sweat, and I inhaled until it skimmed the darkness that had built up inside me. The scent was a much welcomed respite from the assaulting iron and rot.

"I–I think so," I said, trying to rub some of the sticky blood from my face. "What happened?"

"We solved the puzzle, or at least I think we did. You landed pretty hard when we fell." He wheeled me around and gave me a once over. His face was noticeably clean.

"Whose blood is this?" My pulse quickened as I rubbed furiously at my cheek, turning it raw and angry. Even in the low light I could see his expression darken. We simultaneously inspected the spot on the floor where I'd landed. Coagulated blood puddled in an oblong circle, then streaked several feet away. I doubled over but Nix hoisted me back upright. Whoever had fallen here probably hadn't survived.

"I don't know." He brought his forearm to my face, then helped wipe my face with his clean tunic. The dried patches refused to budge, but Nix had managed to clear the layer from my eyes. *Just breathe. Don't panic. Breathe, Selah.* I wanted to fold inside myself and disintegrate, anything to be free of the tightness closing in on me, but I couldn't. I had no time to panic. *Breathe*, I quieted myself, deliberately drawing the air in and out of my lungs.

With my vision and my soul blackened, I surveyed our new hell. We were in a tunnel of some sort. It looked similar to the basement of the fortress, but with a lot more neglect over the years. I scanned over the gawking faces of the other candidates staggered around me. Stuck somewhere between the impulse to run and hide, and the mounting desire to come out swinging, I rocked onto the toes of my boots. Everything down here reeked of uneasiness, and I would've done almost anything to get their attention away from me. Della moved her mouth to speak but was interrupted by a curdling howl behind her.

"*Help!*"

The voice harpooned me with fright, and I stumbled when Nix released me, but I was on his tail half a second later. Abe writhed on the floor, with an arrow protruding from his upper arm. *Oh, god.* Terror exploded in my chest, but my instincts yelled at me through the fog of chaos. *He's not our main concern right now.* That arrow had to come from somewhere, and I didn't want to be anywhere near its path when we found where.

Whoosh.

Wood and metal hurtled through the air, missing Nix by inches. My throat constricted as it carried a piece of his hair on the wind. He dropped to the floor. *Whoosh, whoosh.* More flew overhead, followed by the *clank* of each striking the ground. I flinched as the weapons broke the still air surrounding us. They were coming from everywhere–high, low–but I couldn't pinpoint a source. Following Nix, I threw myself to the floor for safety then craned my neck to find the shooter. The onslaught of arrows had us pinned down like a battle straight out of the books Nix had brought me. I was far from a warrior, but even I knew we had to get out of here. *Quickly.*

"We have to move!" I yelled at my team, half of whom had frozen in confusion with the whirling barrage of arrows. "*Go!*" Gritting my teeth, I took off running toward the end of the tunnel.

Nix and Tomas grabbed Abe by his arms and dragged him backwards while the rest of us sprinted. We hit a rough, rounded wall, and I quickly realized there was nowhere else to go. More arrows whizzed into the tunnel, but they all seemed to be contained to the other side. At least I hoped they were. I pressed my back into the rock as hard as I could, shoulder to shoulder with Tomas and Ophida. Nix stayed at our feet with Abe. After a minute or two, the arrows stopped completely, but my heart rate kept up the same pace.

"Can we make it across?" Cecil asked. Nobody dared to move. The air passing in and out of my nostrils echoed off the wall of the tunnel. *We clearly can't stay here.* But I couldn't see through the dark to determine what, if anything, was beyond the choke point. As if on cue, the whooshing of metal tips started again. The breeze rippled over the crusted blood on my face. One, two, three. They kept going and then paused again.

"I'm making a run for it," Cecil said. He sprang forward but Nix hooked him by his sleeve and yanked him back. Cecil tumbled backward, a wounded expression painted on his face. "I can do it," he said indignantly.

"I know," Nix replied. "But an arrow won't kill me." Cecil clamped his mouth shut. The declaration would've been cocky from anyone else, but I believed it from Nix.

At the next pause, Nix pushed off the wall and sprinted with a power that pushed me back several steps. I gritted my teeth, trying to peel my eyes away but failing. *Run, Nix.* I pushed him with my words, but it wasn't enough. The arrows resumed, and Nix's silhouette vanished as he landed on the floor. My fingernails carved holes in my palms the entire time Nix low-crawled back to our spot. He stood up and dusted himself off, and I punched him square in the stomach.

"What was that for?" He didn't have the decency to flinch.

"Don't do that again!" I screamed, ready to swing at him again. How could he laugh?

"You shouldn't worry about me." I crossed my arms, squaring my shoulders as I stared him down. He had some nerve being that big while I tried to scold him.

"Maybe a few arrows to the chest would be good for you." I shoved him again, meeting only rock and perspiration.

"Oh, Selah," he said as he pulled me near him. My breath caught and the other candidates faded away. He'd funneled me somewhere far away from the Trial—and away from their stares—as he whispered into my ear. "You can't get rid of me that easily."

I shivered as the arrows stopped once again. I counted the seconds until my heart started beating again.

Twenty-four seconds passed, and then a single arrow flew, followed by nine more. *One second, two seconds, three....* I counted ten seconds and before the *whoosh* of two, *no three*, more arrows. This time I tracked the sound of fifteen arrows. Several of the candidates murmured among themselves, but I didn't hear what they were actually saying. I was too focused on the forty-five seconds that had passed.

"It's a pattern!" That shushed them all. Rashel rolled her eyes, but Nix stood up and stared at me, features sharpened. "Listen," I said. *Two arrows at the beginning—twelve total.* "They'll start again in twenty-four seconds."

"How the–" Nix clamped his hand over Rashel's mouth before she could finish her sentence. Sure enough, the arrows began firing in under half a minute. Nix's eyes widened, and Abe craned to see me from his spot on the ground.

"How did you know?" he asked. I explained my theory as fast as I could, then counted seconds and arrows to confirm. It definitely was a pattern, and it was repeating.

"So we have forty-five seconds to make it across," Tomas said.

"When we hear three arrows at the beginning, we run." I sounded more confident than I felt, though. That wasn't much time, and the tunnel looked endless.

Abe caught me eyeing him. "I can make it," he said, pulling himself to his feet with his good arm. His face was as pale as Cecil's but he looked no worse for wear. I had no time to argue as three arrows fired into the tunnel. *No time like the present.* Every intrusive thought beat the side of my skull. I had years of bullying to thank for my fine-tuned fight or flight instinct.

"Go!"

Nix laced his arm under Abe's and dragged the man with lightning speed. I pumped my arms and legs as hard as I could, trying to count the seconds down while keeping my dizziness from overtaking me. Ophida started ahead of me, but quickly dropped behind the pack.

I yelled for her over my shoulder. "Run, Ophida!" She didn't seem to hear me. "Hurry, Phi!" I tried the nickname she had given to Martock what felt like centuries ago at Debut. She'd never offered it to me, but I took it anyway. She jerked her head up and pedaled her legs faster, almost keeping pace with me. "You can make it, Phi." She sputtered, and we sprinted until we slammed into the wall. The arrows resumed their cadence in the space behind us, but they were several yards away. I pressed my body against the wall and clenched my eyes shut until the sound stopped, and the last arrow clattered into the ground. We made it.

Abe and Nix hunkered down next to me, Nix's body leaning over the injured man for protection. A feathery feeling flittered in my chest—near my heart—but it was gone on my next gasp for air. A quick inventory confirmed our whole team had made it. If we all were here, and I'd counted twice to make sure, why didn't I feel safe?

"Look," Ophida said, pointing. "There's a hallway." She tiptoed to the mouth of the blackened opening, then disappeared into it. Apparently the pet name had been *too* effective. I stumbled to catch her, but my feet screeched to a halt at the shadowy barrier. I should have kept going, chased her into the abyss like a selfless heroine, but I hit my own imaginary wall. My own self-preservation. The hair on my arms stood on end seconds before the dull thud reverberated in the hall, followed by a shrill cry.

"Phi!" I shouted but was only met with her muffled screams, drifting farther away into the darkness. *Shit.* Even I couldn't ignore her cries for help, no matter how insufferable she could be. I rubbed the sweat and blood from my forehead and bolted after her, self-preservation be damned. Judging from the echoes of boots on rock behind me, the others had done the same. We shouted and ran, my arms pumping to speed up, but her screams vanished in the darkness.

My foot collided into something on the ground, interrupting my stride and throwing me over my legs. It was dense, but with an odd give as I struck it. I fell, landing on my knees and elbows overtop whatever was on the floor. Pain shot up and down my bones, but I could hardly feel it over the sickening knot forming in my gut. *Hair. Skin. Blood.* Vacant eyes stared at me, with a dark ring of lips, slackened into a grotesque expression.

I shrieked, scrambling to push away from the body tangled around me, but I got caught on the shaft of the arrow lodged in its chest. I froze, lost in the gaping pits of pupils. The first dead person I'd seen was at our Sponsorship, and I'd never be able to purge those images. But this was death up close. A violent, unprovoked death. My hands began to shake uncontrollably, and every cell in my body repelled me from the dead man. I flung myself backwards, slamming hard into the wall of the cave.

"Selah, we need to go." I startled, ratcheting my nervous system to critical failure before I eased into strong arms. Nix seemed to have a habit of picking me up, like I was just a small piece of luggage to him. "We have to find her."

I took one more look at the candidate, someone I had seen in the dormitory but couldn't place. The man who was dead at my feet. A deep, bone cracking tremble coursed up my limbs, but I took off running to shake it loose. I didn't want to leave him, but I had to get out of here, and quickly. There was a candidate dead and Phi was a sitting duck.

Chapter Eighteen

The route was less of a hall and more of a maze, with twists and turns, odd corners, and several forks. Nix and I chased after Ophida until her trail went completely cold. Ophida was gone, we'd lost our group in this wasted search, and I was already nauseous from sucking in the musty air down here. If we didn't stop running soon, I was going to be the next candidate dead on the ground. But that wasn't an option with Phi out there alone.

"What do we do?" I asked. My hands trembled but I managed to grab hold of Nix's arm. He flexed under my grip and stared out over my head, his face as sober as the bare, gray walls. He was so...calm. Nix had seen death before. *Of course he has.* The man exuded violence, and only allowed Andren to tame him because he wanted to. From his seat at the dinner table, to the way he handled affairs among the most elite Casted, Nix belonged there. He belonged *here*, and I had the ultimate advantage because he was on my side. If my cynicism hadn't convinced me long ago the Ancients were nothing more than a fairytale, I would have thanked them for such a fierce, handsome, gift.

Nix knelt to the ground and placed both his palms flat on the cobbled walkway. I fixated on his liquid movements, too distracted to question what he was doing. At this point, nothing could make the situation worse. He held perfectly still, looking like a panther in the filmy lighting. When he stood, he brought his hands to his face and *sniffed.*

"She's this way," he said, and pointed to another fork in the passages. When he saw me gaping at him, he added, "It's a long story."

Nix dragged me along, leaving me hurdling over my own feet. *What was that?* I made mental note to drill him about it later, if we ever made it out of here. I hustled to stay close, attempting to mirror his pace, but his strides were far too long. My muscles burned and my knees throbbed with every pound of my boot into the unforgiving ground, but losing Nix would hurt worse. I pushed harder to keep him in my line of sight.

There! I spied her just ahead of us, blonde head turned away. I'd know that doll-like stature anywhere. Warm, sweeping relief filled me. Whatever odd tactic Nix had employed had worked.

"Phi!"

She whipped around and rushed toward us, but threw her hands out in front of her. She stopped. Something was off. Ophida moved her hands around, feeling at nothing in the air. My mind conjured old scenes of mimes at festivals in Oberin, servants painted in odd makeup to entertain the little Lords and Ladies. I had been terrified of their unnatural movements and always begged not to go, but my mother wanted me to socialize. She *always* wanted me to socialize. That same pit of fear chewed away my brief moment of hope.

A loud *thwack* shook the stale air, sending me back on my heels. I couldn't place where the sound came from. Nix cursed and rubbed his arm before dropping to one knee. He, too, raised his palms, looking like Ophida's reflection in a twisted mirror. *What the—* He pressed his monstrous hands against a pane of *glass.* They'd trapped Ophida inside a glass cage. Her mouth moved and her face crinkled in effort, but the sound was muffled and distant.

"Stay calm," I shouted. "We're coming for you!" This time I pulled Nix, which was about as effective as moving a whole carriage on my own, but he humored me and stood. We rushed to the side, scaling the glass to find any opening. Sweat pilled on my brow–I'd seen their idea of games in this Trial, and none of this bode well. I wasn't about to leave Ophida alone in that tank, probably scared out of her wits. Although I did appreciate the buffer between me and her mouth.

Something creaked over our head and I grabbed for Nix's arm out of reflex. Too many things had been shot at me today. The noise surrounded us, and the air grew unnaturally still. Nix dragged me with him to keep moving, but a glass wall lowered in front of us. There weren't any ropes or levers to move it, but another wall formed behind us in the same manner, sucking away any outside sound. I twisted around in a tailspin to get away from the floating panes. But everywhere I turned, I ran into glass.

I pounded on the glass and screamed until my voice cracked. Nix touched my shoulder, and the sound caught in my throat in a choking sob. There had to be a way out of this. I banged my fists harder. When the room brightened, illuminating from the floor up to the cavernous ceiling, I froze. The sides of my hands throbbed. Something was happening. Given the course of things, it probably wasn't good.

Nix launched to the corner, but my attention lingered at a speck of movement. Red and gray streaks. Tomas and Abe stared back at me, Abe still hunched over, favoring the side of his injury. We needed to get him treated, but so far we'd only managed to trap the rest of our team. *And ourselves.* The look on Tomas's face sent an eerie chill down the nape of my neck. *How can he be so still right now?* He was practically unresponsive to everything around him. Despite his appearance, the old man terrified me just as much as Nix.

The fog cleared from my senses, and I surveyed the rest of the space. Someone quite masterful had designed it, and even in this situation, I had to tip my hat to them. There were *rows* of cages, all glass-faced and stacked like boxes down the row. From our spot, I saw the various stages of panic on the faces of other candidates, dozens of them. The entire class looked to be here, but I couldn't tell for certain. Rior jeered at me from the top right corner, peering directly down into my cage with a lecherous quirk to his lip. Thank the Ancient Ones I was trapped with Nix and not him. But we were trapped all the same. This was a torture chamber, not a test of Scholarship. I should have been scared—I *was* scared—but a sulfurous rage brewed in its place. This place had stolen my mother and now it was trying to take me.

"This is horseshit," I said. Nix's lips parted briefly before he clamped them shut again. He wasn't accustomed to hearing that kind of language from me, and neither was I. But I overflowed with fury. "They've tricked us all, Nix." He lifted one shoulder noncommittally, but his warm brown eyes told me all I needed to know. *Why isn't he mad, too?* He could've at least pretended to look ruffled.

"The Trials aren't known for their stellar pass rate," he said. But were they meant to be impossible?

"*Paper.*" The muffled male voice rippled through the glass, followed by a *tap, tap.* Cecil had his nose pressed against the transparent wall, distorting his features as he talked. He tapped again, pointing to something on the ground. Nix dropped to his knee and retrieved a parchment roll from the floor. Cecil held up a matching one on his side. Nix shrugged, and they both unrolled the papers without further attempts at communication.

Nix's jaw flexed, but he kept his mouth sealed shut. Whatever was housed in that paper had better be our ticket out, and not a vessel for more torture. No Casted Lord or Lady would ever need to run through arrows, and yet I had. My skin crawled with anticipation, and I secured my hands in my pockets to keep from ripping the item out of Nix's fingers. He moved so slow it hurt. So I moved to him and leaned against his side to read over his shoulder.

"*Name the five first cities of the Dominion to earn your way out.*" Nix rumbled against me as he read the parchment out loud. I still had to scan over the words several times before they made sense.

"Another quiz?" They really liked riddles here. Icy water surged just beneath my skin. I barely knew anything of the Dominion outside of Oberin, let alone the ancient cities. My fancy tutelage wasn't getting us very far in the one Trial I was supposed to ace.

"Asa Ha'i, Esson, Lasso, Swyft, and Dua Merno." His eyebrows furrowed, and his jaw still worked fervently, but Nix radiated a coolness as he spoke.

"How di–" First the sniffing thing, and now this tidbit of knowledge. *What else is he hiding from me?*

The ground rolled underneath us, like an enormous snake just under the stone. It quaked and rolled past, making its way down the row of cages. The glass walls shuddered and a cracking sound lurched ominously over the panes. Nix and I raced to the window when the sound dissipated, craning hard to see. I thought I heard screaming, but the faint noise was overpowered by the blast of rushing water. Not the roar of an ocean wave, the cacophony of thousands of gallons ravaging through a small space—closer to a waterfall. It came from the other direction, but there was no sign of water gushing between cages.

"*Ophida!*" I tilted my head to hear Cecil through the glass. He knocked furiously in front of him, attempting to catch Ophida's attention. Wedged in the corner, straddled between Cecil and Ophida's cages, I swung my head from left to right to make sense of the conversation. Fragments of words bounced through glass chambers, but Cecil was coaching his teammate to find her parchment as he had with us. Not that it had done much good; I assumed Nix was correct, but we were still stuck in the cage, and nothing else had transpired.

"Look." Nix pointed to the opposing glass window, caddy corner to Tomas. A shimmer from the bright torches sent sparkling dots around the chamber. They moved rapidly, and the fragments of light started to rise within the candidate's cube. The two men within it thumped against the front pane, eyes as wide as their whole face. There was no mistaking the sound of sweaty palms squeaking across the glass as crystal pieces flooded around their ankles, and then their knees.

Oh god. Their cage pooled with glass shards, and they were about to be completely swallowed. Even the thickest window pane couldn't suppress their splitting cries of agony. I turned my head from the grisly sight, not wanting to see the outcome of such an attack. Cecil stared down at me, shaking his head in small sweeps. He wiped his forehead with the sleeve of his tunic, then turned back to Ophida, resuming his charade.

"The questions," Nix said. "They come with consequences." A thin, blue vein crept from his temple to his neck, bulging against the stretch of his flesh over his skull. It hadn't been there before. I loathed the word *consequences.* My mother used it whenever I disobeyed her. All of my tutors used it for unruly children. But it was never about a natural occurrence of events; it was always about compliance.

"What happens if you get them right?" My tongue was thick and awkward in my mouth. *Did you get the question right?* If we were about to get pummeled with rocks or glass, I wanted to know now so I could get my mind ready. I'm sure I had some apologies to make in reconciliation before the Ancient Ones had their way with me.

"Looks like nothing," he said, peeling his stare from me to continue his observation of the action. So if Nix was accurate, a wrong answer resulted in some unthinkable physical punishment, and a right answer gave us a pass. If ever there was a time for him to be correct, this was it. Cecil's urgency smacked me in the face, drawing tears in the process. *Our teammates are in grave danger.*

"Rashel! Della!" I kicked and banged on the pane facing the two girls, but they watched something above me. I didn't want to know what was happening in the other cages but I needed them to focus on mine, otherwise they would be the next victims. "Get the paper!" Cecil and Nix joined in, alternating their calls from one cage to the other. Tomas and Cecil leaned against the corner, hopefully safe and sound.

Finally Ophida pivoted in the center of her own entrapment, retrieved her parchment from the floor, and leaned over the tiny piece of paper for several beats. Rashel and Della scrambled around, so I picked my own parchment and pressed it against the window. *Please get them right. Please get them right.* My eyes darted back to Ophida. She kept her back turned, deliberating over her question. *Oh no.* We'd only studied literature, and the question Nix and I received was the exact opposite. I'd failed her. I should have studied more, focused on helping more instead of reading that stupid book.

Ophida whipped around and sprinted to the glass. I squeezed my lids shut until my eyes burned from the strain.

"Selah." Nix didn't tap my shoulder so much as he fell into it, getting as close to the clear wall as he could with me wedged in between. His heart pounded so hard into my back, I could hear the reverberations traversing into the large sheet of glass. What would she get? Fire? Buried alive? Her cage remained empty, seconds ticking by like lashings on my skin, until the slight figure raised her fist. *Oh no.* She gave a thumb's up.

"No." Nix shouted at the blank window. "Nooo!" His yelling was unnecessary–didn't he see she was fine? But Cecil began his pounding again, too. They looked ahead, somewhere in front of me, and it wasn't at Ophida.

Rashel and Della contorted into unnatural movements, elbows

bending at impossible angles, knees flailing forward, sideways, to the ground. They swung their hands around their face, trying to get our attention. *No.* Trying to swat the air. The girls desperately attempted to shield themselves from something, but from what, I couldn't tell. Nix stiffened behind me, still leaning into my back as we both gaped out our front wall, helpless against the growing fear. The thrumming grew louder, and Rashel's dark hair started to blend into a hazy cloud filling their chamber. The buzzing came from *their chamber.* Black, gray, and *yellow* blazed in shifting, pulsing clouds. And the clouds *buzzed.*

Their cage was filled with bees.

Chapter Nineteen

"Congratulations, candidates." The Commissioner greeted us in the same arena from our Sponsorship. Seeing it again, the stone wasn't grand or impressive; it was crowded and constricting–just another cage. "You have successfully completed the Scholarship Trial." I flinched at every syllable. There was nothing congratulatory about this. At least a third of the candidates were missing from the sterile marble benches, and the scent of death still lingered in my nostrils.

Officer Pickham stood behind the Commissioner as he droned on about our performance, but his words were garbled. I couldn't look at that stage without seeing my mother, even though the stone platform was long gone. Her absence was clearer than ever, sharpened by our missing team members. Rashel and Della had been scooped from their cage on stretchers, and then we were ripped away ourselves, ushered into this room like we had been the first night. The chances of their survival seemed smaller than my chances of getting my old life back, but they wouldn't give any information, no matter how much I demanded it from the faceless robes that pushed us through the halls. Not knowing was worse than the alternative, because it left room for hope. And hope was what had landed me here in the first place.

"While this is a test of individual worthiness and aptitude, you must rely on your team for our great Society to prosper." The Commissioner kept going, but my mind was a continuous loop of their angry, swollen faces. The redness that flared against Rashel's deep chestnut hair. The way Della's hand hung limply across the stretcher as they loaded her. "Therefore, you must have seven candidates remaining to proceed to the second Trial." Nix went rigid next to me.

We need seven candidates. Just in case I was still disoriented from the first Trial, I did a mental headcount of our remaining members. *Nix. Ophida. Tomas. Cecil. Me.* We had five without Abe, Rashel and Della. None of us could proceed unless one of the girls survived.

"Nix...." I wrapped my hand around his forearm.

When he looked at me, his eyes were bloodshot and clouded. He shushed me as the Commissioner dismissed us to breakfast.

"Let's go eat." I'd originally thought he just liked to eat, but perhaps food was his comfort. It was the only physical evidence I could find of him processing everything. I needed Nix; Nix needed food. *Fitting.*

Fragments of teams were seated at their tables when we entered the dining hall. Rior and his rowdy crew boasted loudly about the obstacles they'd conquered, each candidate trying to upstage the other with the role they played.

"Shame they fucked up their questions when they already lost one." His voice rubbed my frayed nerves raw, but Rior's stupid face kept gloating. "He sure made an excellent shield though." My boot caught on the seam in the slate floor. *The candidate in the hall.* That's how Rior got across the arrow field. He cackled with his cronies, Bodney's guttural laughs ricocheting off my temples. The table across from them had two vacant seats at their benches, and so did ours.

The dense biscuits couldn't fill the hollowness festering just under my navel, growing by the second. I had to admit, however, the coffee came close. Steam twisted from the spout of the carafe, spelling out the nagging thought in the dewy morning air. *Andren wasn't there.* Sure, I'd torn apart our thread, but he'd made a promise. We'd likely lost two of our teammates, our standing in the Trials dire, and we probably weren't progressing. *Rior is capable of killing someone to get through this.* But the heaviest rock on my soul was Andren's absence through all of it.

I reached for another biscuit from the center of the table and ate it dry. Then I grabbed a second, and a third. Nix side-eyed me as I started in on a serving of eggs. My skin pinched against the waistband of my trousers, but I kept going with the cured meat. Perhaps it was my body's way of pushing through all of this madness and ensuring it had the nutrients it needed. Or perhaps I was trying to fill a bottomless hole. Ophida watched me warily, but she remained subdued in front of her untouched plate.

The energy shifted from restlessness to downright dread after the time kept ticking away. We had nowhere to go except back to the dorm, but there was no chance I could sleep right now. The remaining candidates must have shared that sentiment, because breakfast dragged on and on. Finally, the clicking of boots against polished stone dragged our attention toward the doors, where Officer Pickham appeared.

"Congratulations on your completion of the Scholarship Trials." His crackling voice filled the empty spaces of the hall, where the other candidates should have been sitting. "Many of you will advance to the second Trial, though we are still awaiting final results." He scanned the room for our reactions, settling on our table before licking his lips.

"Right now, I will offer you my candor. I do not want you to lose your ambition in the breaking wave of the aftermath. Our candidates must be tried and proven in all of the tenants of the Caste. We cannot risk inducting anything less into the Bloodline we hold sacredly in our custody." His voice rattled each syllable, folding it between his teeth. "Most will not make it."

A stitch formed low in my ribs, making it painful to sit fully upright.

"With that in mind, you will start preparing for the Trial of Leadership until all results are in. By the end of the night, a Proctor will be around to notify you on your status. Those eliminated will depart in the morning." Several gasps sounded across the dining hall. *I can't go home. I'd die in those tunnels before I'd face my father after everything.*

"Unlike the first Trial, there is nothing to prepare you for Leadership. It is something you must tap into on your own. We will provide you the environment to do so." Pickham continued without any transition, speaking to the listless crowd. Across the table, Cecil clanked his fork against his plate. Ophida jumped, and a handful of the candidates in the hall turned their heads to find the source of the commotion. Cecil's face fired brightly.

"I suggest you all get some rest. The Trial begins tomorrow." With that, Pickham turned and stomped back through the double doors. Tomorrow. *Tomorrow.* Every damn thing was tomorrow, but I still had to live through today.

"Let's go," I said in a hushed voice to Nix. If I had to look at Cecil's hopeful face any longer, I'd go crazy.

"You're hurt." Nix touched my side and I flinched. Though I'd grown accustomed to the new modesty standards after a week in the dormitory, Nix's fingers on my bare flesh were something that would never feel routine.

I contorted my neck to see what Nix pointed to, my damp tunic still stuck around my elbows as I stripped it away. A large red mark curved around my ribs, angry against my olive complexion. My flimsy undergarments were plastered to my breasts and my midriff was completely uncovered. I had also run off without belting my trousers this morning, which now slumped below my hip bone. I pushed the material down farther to find splotches of blue and purple forming. The fall had been worse than I realized.

"We need to get you cleaned up," he said, more to himself than to me. He appeared concerned, and a little distracted, all spiraled together and painted on his earthy, brown skin. His eyes were murkier than usual, and they traversed my body with such intensity I shriveled. Nix bombarded my space, trampled whatever shred of comfort I had left, and stifled me with something so intimate, I couldn't form the proper words to describe it. I couldn't form *any* words while he stared at me like that.

"Put these on," he said, handing me garments he'd retrieved from my bunk. "I'll be right back." Then he vanished down the dormitory hallway, leaving me cold and breathless. *It's just Nix. He's just trying to take care of me, like he's supposed to.* The tattered remnants of Andren's thread drifted around inside me.

I turned toward the wall and stripped the rest of my soiled clothing, piling it in a wilted ball on the floor. I doubted any of it was salvageable, but the discarded mound glared at me as if I'd betrayed it. I'd let a great many things down today, so the dirty clothes would just have to get in line. Wincing, I pulled a clean tunic over my head, the rough fabric grating against my tender flesh. Too haggard to climb into my own bunk, I eased myself onto Nix's and retrieved my brush from my trunk. My arms cried in agony as I forced them overhead, raking the bristles through the tangled madness of my hair.

Even my scalp throbbed and ached now that the rush of the Trial had dissipated, only a temporary analgesic. But the repetitive motion was both distracting and cathartic, and it was far more productive than obsessing over all the things I didn't know, so I kept going. By the time Nix returned, I had most of the knots tamed and was working the bulk of curls into a loose braid down my back. He faltered for a split second as he approached, but then sat a basin of water on the ground and knelt beside me.

"They didn't have any antiseptic but this is better than nothing," he said, locking his eyes on mine. "May I?" He reached toward the clean tunic and raised it to my rib cage, letting a blast of cool air onto my tender skin. I hissed in pain when he made contact, but gritted my teeth to let him continue. Within seconds, the stark cold faded into heat, and his feathery touch settled the roar of the pain. Nix was gentle, soothing. I could actually relax around him, even in my compromised state.

"Thank you," I said, holding back the blasphemous heat that continued to build. Trauma affected us all differently, but my wretched body tugged in excitement when the man was merely cleaning my wounds. *Can't get much more sterile than that—god.*

Nix issued a half-smile before turning his attention to my partially-finished hair. He raised his eyebrows. *Now what?* I shrugged, curious to see what he had in mind. Nix swiveled to my side and leaned close, depressing the mattress until I nearly fell into him. He lifted my hair from my shoulder then separated the pieces to continue plaiting where I left off. Andren's Hand was *braiding my hair.*

Was there anything this man couldn't do? I flashed back to the tunnel—Nix tracking Ophida with an impossible precision.

"Nix—" I said. He gave me a dreamy *hmm?*

"In the tunnel, you did something." His hands went still, but only for a second. He carried on braiding in silence. "You know what I'm talking about," I said. I wasn't letting him off that easily.

Nix swallowed, his Adam's apple bobbing just beneath his beard. "I could tell you, but you wouldn't believe me anyway."

"Why wouldn't I believe you?" I asked. He gazed at me under dark lashes. They were so delicate against the chiseled cut of his face.

"Because I don't even believe it most days," he replied. His full lips stilled—that's all I was getting from him. And really, that was more than he actually owed me. I was the one who'd convinced myself we were friends here, and that our relationship was open enough to share secrets. But clearly Nix didn't reciprocate. I was a ward—a task given to him by his master. I knew that, but couldn't figure out why it sent a lump to my throat.

When Nix got to the end, I handed him my leather strap so he could tie it off. He laid my hair on my shoulder to admire his handiwork, his eyes dancing against the flicker of the dormitory fireplace. I traced my fingers up and down the folds to inspect it.

"Impressive," I whispered. Because it *was* impressive. He'd put Corinna to shame in half the time. "Where did you learn that?"

Nix stood from the bed, which I took as an indication the conversation was over. I'd pushed his patience with my invasive questions. He may have braided like my Lady-in-Wait, but he wasn't going to fulfill my demands like she had.

To my chagrin, he pulled his dirty tunic over his head instead of answering, revealing deep grooves of chiseled muscles that tightened and released as he moved. He bowed into his trunk to unearth a clean shirt, lingering next to me for a beat. I held my breath, trying not to inhale the scent from his naked skin, but warmth still radiated from it. If this wasn't intentional, he had to be the most naive bastard in the Dominion. Nix's head disappeared above my bed once again, and I marveled at the immaculate specimen before me. Even as the woman betrothed to his Governor and master, the sheer sight of him stroked the most primitive parts of me. I told myself nobody was immune to biology and turned to face the wall.

"Ephraim had six daughters. I was the closest thing he had to a son, but I helped him care for the girls after his wife got sick." Nix spoke to my back. I twisted to see him in my periphery.

"Oh." My voice was tight, fighting against my constricting rib cage.

I clenched my thighs together as Nix proceeded to drop his trousers. I feared he'd see my cheeks reflecting off the walls. My mutinous eyes cut back to the thickness of his quads, the cut of his calves, the enthralling dip of his lean hips peeking out from his undergarments. I gulped. *He has to know the effect he has.* Hell, he could probably *feel* my stare plastered to his flesh. Nix lifted his foot to pull it free from a wool sock, setting his bare foot down on the stone. *Oh hell.* He repeated the motion with the other. He was so damn magnetizing, nothing like any man I'd ever seen. *Quit staring, quit staring, qui–*

A forceful tug ripped through my abdomen.

Andren.

I yipped out loud, then slapped my hands over my mouth. Nix peeked at me from over his shoulder, eyebrows raised in curiosity. Steaming, stinking guilt oozed over me, subduing the unrestrained approbation I'd been soaking in. Andren's timing was impeccable, suspecting his aim was to make me as uncomfortable as possible. I deserved it, too.

I pushed myself off the bed with my tail tucked between my legs, but it put me mere inches from a pants-less Nix. He made no move to distance himself, or to even attempt to cover his backside. Pure panic shuttled me upward, but I bumped into his bare legs in the process. He *fucking smiled*—a maddening, coquettish grin at my discomfort. A jumbled mess of words meant to be an apology fell from my mouth as I attempted to hoist myself out of that corner as fast as possible.

In my haste to flee, I forgot about my side, but the tearing, crunching sensation quickly reminded me of the injuries I'd sustained. White-hot agony flung me backwards, but I fell into a cage of strength, warmth, and a hint of cedar. My chest was too tight to breathe a sigh of relief. *Please have pants on.* Between the gnawing in my gut and the flutter everywhere else, I was on the verge of unraveling completely.

"You shouldn't be moving that much." He backed away, thankfully revealing pants, but kept his hand on my waist. For stability, not for my enjoyment. *Relax, Selah.* "Why don't you just lay in my bed." My lips opened and closed like a fish. Andren poked at my navel again, and I folded over to try and muffle the feeling multiplying my pain and embarrassment. *I can't lay in his bed.* Hell, I couldn't even form coherent words.

"I'll move to yours," he said. "You need to get some rest." Slinging my mouth shut, I nodded and disappeared under the bunk as fast as my body would allow. My side burned, but it was much more tolerable than trying to hoist myself up the rickety bunk ladder. Nix pulled back the covers while I eased down on my good side, then he tucked me in like a small child. His scent was everywhere on the linens, overtaking every sense. The possibility of me ever falling asleep in a nest of Nix was slim to none.

"Good night, Selah," he called from the bunk above me. I curled into a ball as the frame creaked under his weight. I forced my eyes shut in spite of the threat of imminent collapse; if I died from a bunk bed, then so be it. There were certainly worse ways to go.

Sleep had been less restorative and more comatose, as if I'd spent the night with a ton of bricks over my body. I'd gone still out of pure exhaustion, all while my brain wound and wound until it expended the last stockpile of energy I had in me. Finally, hours into the night, it had collapsed, too.

I smacked my lips and peeled the cotton back from my tongue. The thick fog in my head shrouded my train of thought. The surroundings were alien, unfamiliar and murky. But I blinked the sand under my lids away, and the walls of the dormitory came into focus. Still in Nix's bed, I looked across the dormitory to see Rashel and Della's beds empty. Last night's events smacked me fully into consciousness. *Andren.* I pawed around the invisible connection with my sluggish brain, but I found only the hollow void where he should have been. Everything ached. *Please don't be upset with me. Please don't be upset with me.*

"There you are," Nix called from the corner of his bunk. I rubbed my eyes, feeling his stare on me through the haze. "I was about to wake you up for dinner but alas, you're alive."

Dinner? There was no clock to check, but the growl in my stomach confirmed the time.

"I'm alive," I said, patting my hair to find Nix's braid held strong through my sleepless battles in his bed. He tracked my hands with his dark eyes, and I flushed. *I must look like a disaster.* I certainly felt like it, at least. "Let's go." I eased myself from the bed, the pain dulled but replaced with crippling stiffness that screamed at me to lay back down.

Nix grabbed my elbow to help me sit up, then placed my boots in front of me. Before I could lean forward, already bracing myself for the eruption of pain, he knelt in front of me and took my ankle in his hand. I never looked small in Oberin, but my ankle was as fragile as a baby bird in his hands. I opened my mouth to protest–I was fully capable of putting on my own boots–but he'd already maneuvered both shoes on my feet. When he'd knotted off the last lace, Nix patted my knee. Did he have to be so damn charming *all* the time? I had enough to contend with, and the depth of commitment Andren's servant was giving me was in a heated war over the lack of connection I'd had with my betrothed. *What a fucking mess.*

We shuffled down the dark hallways that were all but deserted, the rest of the candidates already gathered around their dinner plates. The remnants of our team slid on the benches to make room for Nix and me, asking how I felt and if I got rest. We exchanged formalities as I dished my food, now lukewarm but still filling. I supposed discussing my misplaced attraction to our teammate all because I'd driven a wedge in my actual relationship wasn't appropriate dinner conversation.

"You ready for tomorrow? You missed the Proctors coming by while you were asleep." Cecil caught me up while I chewed. I gulped down my roll in one swallow. Nobody wanted to acknowledge the elephant in the room, but Cecil's question kicked me in the chest. *Am I even ready for today?*

"No." I shoveled a heap of tepid potatoes in my mouth as punctuation. The first Trial happened so fast, without any closure. How was I supposed to be ready for another one?

"You can't be worried about this Trial," he said. My head throbbed with his incessant talking. "This should be a piece of cake for you." *Piece of cake?* I let the fork fall, still loaded with more potatoes.

"For *me*?" The Trials were rough on all of us yesterday, and I'd barely been aware of my own feet, but Cecil must have been somewhere else entirely to think it was easy for me. "I only squeaked out because of Nix." The giant man flashed me a cryptic look, but then reached for another biscuit. It had to have been his sixth at least.

"Yes, you. You were brilliant with all the patterns and the puzzles and th-the things." Cecil's face was ghostly, eyes wide and haunted.

I swallowed hard. Nix watched me with his eyebrow raised, but I was still unraveling the hidden meaning in Cecil's words. It had to be there. This was some kind of setup. If I hadn't chased after Ophida, maybe we wouldn't have separated from Rashel and Della. *Is this the part where they turn on me?* It was bound to happen sooner or later. But Cecil didn't blink as he stared like an owl, no hint of malice hiding in his freckles. The *thump* in my brain picked up speed.

"Do you mean that?" I couldn't feign composure. Cecil's eyes were as round as my plate as he shook his head up and down. Nobody else moved to say anything. Cecil cocked his head at me.

"Of course. We all saw it." He looked down the table. My heart leapt into my mouth as Tomas nodded back. Even Ophida gave one curt movement of her head, her mouth still uncharacteristically quiet since yesterday.

"Um, thank you," I said, more as a question than a statement. My abdominal muscles had been bracing for impact, but I allowed myself to settle into my seat. There wasn't a punchline. I wasn't the butt of the joke. I'd actually been *complimented*, and it was like wearing clothing far too big. "I appreciate that."

"But who knows if we'll get to move on." Ophida had regained her voice.

"We'll advance," Tomas said without looking up. Her milky cheeks went red, but she clamped her mouth shut, nostrils flaring as she chewed. It was beneath me to enjoy the scene, I knew that, but it tasted better than my dinner. At least someone on our team knew how to silence her.

Swiping gravy with the last bite of my biscuit, I missed my mouth as the hall doors clanged open. Officer Pickham paraded into the center of the dining hall and coughed into his hand. Heads jerked and forks clanged against tables. I wiped the drop of gravy away with my sleeve. Couldn't I enjoy one meal without him?

"Good evening, candidates," he yelled a little too loudly across the dining hall. "Once you are finished, you will make your way to the armory to draw your supplies for the morning. We will load out before dawn, so make sure you are packed and rested." Our speculation about the next Trial hadn't covered anything that would include an armory, or packing. *Where could they be taking us?*

The little inflation of confidence I'd gotten from Cecil fizzled away as Pickham's words clanged; the second Trial was offsite somewhere, and we needed armament. My side throbbed in time with my racing pulse, a physical reminder of how awful the first Trial had been. Hell, we still hadn't heard an update on Rashel or Della to even know if we were going to the second round, but nobody had kicked us out yet. That had to be a good sign, at least I assumed it was.

"What about the other candidates?" My voice was sharper than a dagger against the dead silence of the room. Pickham veered around to stare at me, apparently unaccustomed to questions in his role. He cocked his head to the side. "Our injured teammates?"

"They are all in the medical ward," he replied, venom dripping from his words. He definitely didn't appreciate the outburst from a candidate.

"But how do we proceed without them?" *Stop talking, Selah.* I struggled with speaking to people, except in completely inappropriate settings, apparently. Pickham's eyelid twitched under the torchlight, but I held his stare. It was far too late to back down now. But instead of retaliation, he whipped the sleeve of his robe and marched out of the room. My mouth slackened as I turned to the rest of team.

"What do we do?" I hated how rattled I sounded.

"Well," Nix said, arms crossed as he hovered near me. "I suppose we should go pack."

The armory was close to the library in the basement, though the walk seemed twice as long as it usually did. A short, squat man with a shock of black hair stood behind a counter in the middle of the room. He was definitely not Casted. Rows of shelving lined the walls behind him, and stacks of odds and ends threatened to collapse down on him at any second. We shuffled through in a single file to receive the load of provisions. If I had to figure out how to use any of that stuff, we'd have no hope of making it through the next round.

The compact man shoved the backpack at me as I approached him, grunting with each movement. He then dumped a satchel onto the counter and slid it over to make room for the next person in line, already done with our transaction. I hoisted the backpack onto my uninjured side and reached for my satchel, but Nix intercepted. He pulled the backpack off of me and threw it over his other shoulder, then piled my second bag on top of his.

"One of these days I'll let you cart your own gear," he teased. "But not tonight." My aching side squeezed in gratitude, and we headed back to the dormitory. Trailing behind him, I watched the packs on his back bob with each step he took. I should've been used to servants doing things for me, but Nix wasn't a servant here. Hell, it would've probably been easier if I kept him in that role, but how could I? Andren had sent me off with Nix to look after me, but I was certain that expectation didn't extend to dressing my wounds and carrying my bags. *Or braiding my hair.* I shivered in the damp air of the hallway. Finix Emrys confused me more than anything I'd ever experienced.

Nix laid the bags across his bed, then proceeded to take inventory of everything inside.

"From the looks of it, we're going to be outside for a while," Nix said.

"A while?" The squeak in my voice betrayed me. "How long is *a while?*"

"No telling. The last Trial lasted over a week, and that was in a library." He held up a heavy down jacket.

My mind raced with the possibilities, lost in the mountains with nothing but a few trinkets. At least the jacket looked warm. But there were so many things that could go wrong. I'd never slept anywhere but a bed, let alone outdoors. I could barely find my way across an island if we had to navigate this terrain. Miles and miles of mountains and snow. My upbringing had barely given me an edge in the first Trial, but it was going to hold all of us back in this one.

"You'll survive." Nix interpreted the dread on my face. "I'll take care of you." He offered his assistance like it was second nature, and I realized it likely was second nature to him. Guilt grabbed hold of me and refused to let go. Nix had been carrying me through everything, and if I was perfectly honest with myself, I *enjoyed* his closeness. As if I wasn't screwed up enough. I *should* have felt guilty over ignoring Andren, and somehow reversing our *irreversible* Sewing, but all I felt was remorse for something that hadn't happened yet. I was going to destroy Nix's chance at Cleansing if he kept this up.

"If you say so," I said. I couldn't let him shoulder my weight and his through this. *And I really need to sort out my emotions. Soon.*

I didn't bother straightening the bag like everyone else, and instead climbed into bed. My head grazed the pillow before I shot right back up.

Shit.

The Geomancer was still concealed underneath, beating into the back of my head like it had a pulse of its own. I couldn't just leave it there while we were gone, especially since I had no idea how long it would be until we came back. Nix sat up in his bed as I climbed down from the bunk, tiptoeing barefoot. He hissed words at me but I shot him a look warning him to stay silent, concealing the book against my side.

"You're taking it?" he mouthed at me while I rifled through my pack, burying the leather beneath my clothes.

"I can't risk leaving it here," I whispered. "And someone is bound to see me if I try to take it back."

"It must be a hell of a book," Nix replied.

"You have no idea."

Chapter Twenty

I dreamt of Andren, his golden hair and dimple framed by a façade of disappointment. I had let him down, both in reality and in my dreams.

"You need to be careful." His words were sharp and dangerous. I wasn't sure if he was referencing the illicit thoughts I'd been having about his Hand, or the harboring of contraband literature. Probably both. The guilt drowned me, filling my airways and pouring from my nostrils like sludge. My head seized and my lungs burned for oxygen. Andren's ice cold eyes bore into me, intensifying my desperation as I spiraled under a sea of sorrow.

I snapped up, sputtering and choking on the free-flowing air in the dormitory. It was still dark, all the other candidates sleeping peacefully in their bunks. I flipped to my other side, wincing when the tender skin struck the lumpy mattress. *Just close your eyes. Go back to sleep.* My mind refused to cooperate, scrambling to make sense of my dream. I really needed to reconcile with Andren before this escalated. He had to understand why I was upset. But when I called out to him into the night, pulling on the remnants of the invisible thread, I got nothing but dead air.

I flopped again, flailing my arms across the mattress in search of a more comfortable position when I heard a faint *swish, swish, swish.* I froze to listen. The sound repeated over and over in a steady tempo until I couldn't block it out. My sleep cycle had become nothing but one giant interruption since coming here. I sat up, clawing at the hair stuck in my face, and leaned over to the source of the noise. Nix crouched at the side of his bunk, bare back glowing in the moonlight.

He wore nothing but his unbuckled trousers, and was swiping one of the hunting knives on a strap of leather, sharpening the blade to a lethal point. I watched him from my perch, soaking in the way his muscles flexed with each movement. I traced the path of vasculature spotlighted on his arms, transfixed by the raw power of him.

The scraping stopped and Nix froze, then reared around with dilated, turbulent eyes. I shivered at the chilling inhuman expression.

"S-sorry," I said. "I didn't mean to scare you." Several long seconds later, his face drifted into something more recognizable, something softer. His pupils narrowed.

"Selah." Nix's voice cracked, thick and husky in the dark.

"Why aren't you asleep?" I asked.

"Why aren't you?"

He had a point. I shimmied down the side of the bunk as gracefully as I could, still nursing my injuries, then took a seat on the edge of the bed.

"Can I help?" Other than the dagger at my Scrolling, which I actively tried not to remember, I had never held anything but a dinner knife before, let alone yielded one as a weapon. Nix shifted the polished hilt into my hands. It was ivory, a material coveted in Oberin, smooth and creamy. The steel blade extended over ten inches and felt imbalanced in my grasp. I passed it from palm to palm, getting accustomed to its weight.

"Here." Nix handed me the leather strap. "Hold it like this." He positioned it between my fingers then tucked the other end between my knees. I clamped down to hold it in place. Reaching across my lap, Nix curled his long fingers around mine, closing my grip on the knife. Desire rushed over me. *For the love—now I'm aroused by a fucking knife?* My dream swam in my head, sloshing like a dingy on the ocean; it wasn't the knife.

Nix guided my hand to the strap and I grappled to maintain focus.

He dragged the blade at a precise angle over the material, his fingers flexing over mine. After a few passes, he released my hand to try on my own. The repetitive movement sucked me in, offering just the distraction I needed.

"Were you dreaming again?" Nix's question caught me off guard.

My hand froze. "I uh, didn't know you heard." *How much did he hear?* I'd stab myself if I'd spoken any of that out loud—if he knew the way I ran from my fiancé's judgment just to be near him.

"It's hard not to when you toss and turn over my head," he said. I flushed.

"I'm nervous about the Trial," I said. I *was* nervous about the Trial, so maybe it hadn't *really* been a lie.

"If you think for a second you made it through today without the skill to get you through another one, you're crazier than I imagined." Nix's white teeth flashed in the dark.

"Crazy?" I gripped the helm of the knife as I swiped down the leather strap with a satisfying *swoosh*. Nix smirked.

"Not crazy. But certainly not the subdued little Lady at her Governor's table." My cheeks twisted into a smile in spite of my best efforts to resist. Those words would've nipped at me before, immediately set me on the defensive, but not from Nix. I didn't want him to see me as a subdued Lady. The irony that I couldn't let Andren see this part of me —that I saved different pieces for each of them—sat heavy and unmoving inside me.

"I could say the same of you, *Lord* Finix."

He slapped his knees and leaned forward. "I'll never get used to that," he said, cheeks wide in a smile. An actual laugh fell from my lips before my humor dimmed again. I didn't want to get used to that. A cleansed Nix was an abomination to nature.

"Do you really think I'll make it?" I asked, too uncomfortable in the silence between us.

Nix narrowed his eyes at the seriousness in my tone. "I do," he said. "Andren believed in you when he sent you here, but even he would never believe the way you performed." I twitched involuntarily, gripping the knife to keep from dropping it.

"He shouldn't." Bringing up Andren stung more than I anticipated.

Nix really was just following orders and getting me out of here as promised, even at his own expense. I toyed with the dagger, running my thumb over the side of the blade. So much for not talking about Andren. Nix dipped his chin so subtly, I didn't think he actually moved.

"Andren is a Governor," he said. "A young Governor. That comes with a certain level of pride, and you will learn Andren values that pride, protects it." He paused, running the tip of his tongue over his lower lip. "He bears a lot of responsibility as a Governor, but he shoulders it all." I cocked my head. Nix had a very peculiar method for describing his boss. "It's the source of his pride. You need to understand that." He stared at me, waiting for me to catch up. My own lips had gone bone dry. "And when you return to him, you'll hold a piece of that pride, too. And he will protect that."

"You make it sound like I'm a prized possession." Unease roiled in my intestines, filling the space where Andren should have been. Nix blinked at me several times, face perfectly still. *He is Andren's possession. Fuck, Selah.*

Nix pursed his lips. "He's a good man. He will take care of you." He turned away from me, studying something in the night. I swallowed the lump in my throat, trying to wash away the taste of salt and regret. I shouldn't have mentioned Andren.

I glanced down at the knife in my hands, the blade sharp enough to split hairs. Nix half-nodded in approval before retrieving it from my hands.

"Good work, little Lady." He sheathed the dagger. I bristled at the jab but he shoved me playfully, toppling me over. "Now time for some rest."

He was right; I did need rest. Sharpening a knife had been a brief distraction, but it hadn't kept my monsters at bay. My dreams had failed me, too, but my body yearned for sleep. Punching the flat pillow, I rolled onto my side and let my eyelids close, praying for a dreamless remainder of the night. The heat from the fireplace kissed my skin and I drifted, but I stood no chance at peace tonight. The door slammed open and the sound of shuffling feet filled the dormitory.

"Shhh!"

"You're causing the commotion."

"I'm never going to sleep tonight with this miserable itching."

"Be quiet, Della!"

I sat up in my bed. The frame shifted as Nix did the same beneath me. He craned his head out and peered up at me, one eyebrow arched.

"They're okay!" I rolled from the bed in a ball of blankets. *Rashel and Della are okay.* I sprinted to their bunks, sensing Nix right behind me. Rashel stumbled backward at our sudden appearance in the dark, but I didn't care. I embraced her in a tight hug, smelling the hints of antiseptic clinging to her hair.

"You're okay," I said, holding her at arm's length to inspect her. Della perched over her shoulder. Both girls were covered in red spots, but Rashel's skin was mottled with angry blotches. They didn't look okay, but they were alive.

"I don't think I'll ever be okay again," Rashel said, peeling my hands away from her. "That healer was horrid." Della's eyes went wide in emphasis. *Horrid?* That healer was downright magical to bring them back from an attack like that, with only a few welts to show for it.

"But you're here. You're alive." I clutched the sides of my trousers to keep from touching her, just to make sure she was actually standing here. Rashel snorted.

"Is that the baseline?" Della picked at one of the scabs on her arms.

"Are you still able to compete?" I asked. There was no point in making small talk at this hour of the night.

"I'd rather hide under my bed and sleep for a month," Rashel said. "But yes, we're cleared to compete." *We have enough.* My head swam as if the whole room was under water. The second Trial wasn't some notional thing in the distance—we were leaving tomorrow. Sure, I'd prepared, but hearing the words spoken sealed everything in stone. I needed to step up, to clear my head, and most importantly, not drag Nix or the others down. I had to do better.

"What about Abe?" Nix nudged me aside.

"Still there," Della said. We waited for her to embellish more, but it became apparent that was the only update we would get. We'd be moving forward, but likely without our whole team. Not only would we be degraded from other teams, we'd also lost one of our own along the way. Nix grunted, then grabbed my tunic and pulled me back to our bunk.

"You need to rest before we leave," Nix said. The jovial air he'd had only a few minutes prior was gone. Reality must have gotten to him, too. Every now and then he left me little fragments of proof Nix was actually human and not a wild beast clawing his way through these Trials. *But he could be both.*

Hours later, the candidates scurried about in the dormitory, strapping weapons to their bodies and heaving their packs high onto their backs. The more experienced outdoorsmen coached the others, cinching straps and tying ends with an artful mastery. Nix gave me a once-over after I wiggled my equipment into place, but he was distant after our early-morning exchange. I coached myself through the mountain of doubt, but my bones felt brittle under all the weight. First I'd driven a wedge between Andren and me, and now I feared I'd overstepped Nix's boundaries, too.

The rest of our group was staged in the corridor, packed to the brim with all of their gear. In that moment, they all seemed so fragile. Rashel and Della stood erect next to Cecil, hoisting their packs on their shoulders and fidgeting uncomfortably under the bulk. Cecil, however, beamed from ear to ear when he saw me, and I didn't have the heart to dissuade his eagerness. I conjured the most authentic smile I could reciprocate, finding it easier the closer I got to the center of my team. Their energy was electrified, a steady current of what I had originally thought to be nerves. But in the thick of it, I realized it was more nuanced.

I spun around to see the others, and there, harnessed in a muslin sling, was Abe. "I packed away all the leftover biscuits from this morning," he said before I could choke out a greeting over my astonishment. *Biscuits?* Abe cracked his bag conspiratorially to show me a mound of baked goods wrapped in a towel, along with other odds and ends. He'd even secured a cheese wheel. For the second time since my Sponsorship, a genuine smile cracked the shell across my face. Though we were a little battered and bruised, we still had our whole team together going into the Trial. *We're still in this.*

"Already dead. The rest of you should start packing." Rior pushed past in the corridor, sneering directly at me before ramming me hard with his elbow. Bodney was right behind him, waiting for me to wince, but I refused to give them the satisfaction. The injuries on my side flared while I stared them down without flinching.

Rior turned over his shoulder. "I give it two days before you come begging for your mansion and servants. Good thing your master loaned you the big one." Flipping his unkempt hair over his forehead, he raced off with a putrid gust of air. My vision went red and I coiled my thighs to lunge at him. A heavy hand on my shoulder pulled me back.

"It's not worth it," Nix said. I blew steam from my nostrils, the murderous urge still sharp in my fingertips.

"Oskar was the butcher's oldest son. I knew his family," Tomas said as the pair disappeared out of sight. Their scent lingered in the dewy air, dissipating with my rage. "The boy he killed yesterday. His team got sent home. Probably should steer clear of that one."

Those empty eyes staring back at me, the limp weight of his body on the floor, and the odd angle of his joints all pounded the back of my head. A cold sweat filtered over me. That could be us. Rior had already shown his capabilities and the lengths he would go, and the stakes were even higher now. Tomas nodded to Nix in an expressionless gesture.

"We should get outside," Nix said, holding Tomas's gaze. The old man waited a few more beats until Rior's head was well out of sight, then trodded out to the fortress lawn.

Officer Pickham stood on a round platform at the end of the court-yard, the candidates fanning around the grassy area beneath him. Distaste dripped from his face as he eyed the crowd, like he was visual-izing our inevitable failure, and how he would play a part. The Commis-sioner was nowhere to be seen, likely the reason there was an extra puff to Pickham's chest this morning. I did catch a glimpse of Gaine lurking in the back of the crowd, apparently less of a benefit to us and more of a spy to the Proctors.

Officer Pickham began. "In a few moments, we will provide you all maps with your starting points. You will need to make your way to these points using the tools you have, relying on the strengths in your teams. At each point, there will be an object of value you must locate and secure. Once secured, you will make your way back to Hanover Hall with your object." He licked his lips with a short flick of his tongue, reminding me of a viper.

"But–" His voice greased the air, shooting goosebumps down the backside of my arms. "You must also bring an object from another team to pass." The breeze dancing around the grounds ceased completely. We had to do *what?* A collective gasp rang out, then the frantic murmuring began. Ophida's eyes bugged out of her head. Mine were probably doing the same, but I was suspended in disbelief.

We had to bring our object, plus an object from another team to pass, with no indication of what these objects were. There were five teams remaining...five objects.... Over half of the groups would be eliminated before the end of the Trial. I swallowed back the breakfast threatening to make a reappearance.

"Silence, please." Pickham relished in the frenzy he'd just created. "As the Commissioner has previously explained, only the best candidates can carry on the Original Bloodline. You should also know only the best...canvases will be able to handle the Cleansing. We must weed out those...unqualified... for the protection of the Caste and for the protection of themselves."

"I can't go back," Ophida wailed. "This is all I've got!" I felt like doing the same, but pride wouldn't allow me to forfeit that much constraint. Well, pride or shock.

Della and Rashel were ghostly pale, the red patches fiery in the daylight, and Abe had staggered a few paces away from everyone, lost in his own thoughts. Tomas and Nix, however, retained their same stoicism as they marched up to Pickham to receive the map on our behalf, the image of iron and grit standing side-by-side. Nix had seen something in Tomas, and now I could see it, too. His aura whispered secrets of darkness that made this Trial just another bump in his road. It felt like a staggering cliff to me.

"You will have one week to make it to your point and back." Pickham scanned the tousled crowd of candidates. "Begin."

We looked from one to the other like prey, frozen and vulnerable. Rior jetted off, the rest of his team sprinting to catch up, snapping Nix into action. He unfolded the map and smoothed it over the marble ledge of the courtyard wall. Tomas plopped a round, metallic object next to it. Nix balanced the compass between his thumbs, angling the golden arrow bobbing around. Nobody else existed to him when he was in that form. Nix pointed into the mountains.

"We're headed that way," he said, and started walking.

"I think they need a break," I pleaded, trying to disguise my own panting. Nix looked over his shoulder and grunted, but grudgingly slowed to a stroll. Ophida hopped through the brush before dropping to her knees, her face redder than Cecil's hair.

"How much farther?" she wheezed.

"Far." Nix clipped the word without looking at her. His brow hung low over his eyes, creased into a harsh V that wasn't usually there. "Especially at this pace."

"This is what they want, you know?" I yanked on his tunic sleeve. He glared at me, but I kept hold of him. He was in this mood because of me, and I was going to fix it. "To break us from the inside." My voice quavered, but it did the trick. Everyone's head reared to look at me.

"They want us to fail," Cecil echoed, igniting theatrical brooding from Ophida as she slung her arms over her chest. Della rolled her eyes, and I couldn't fault her for the sophomoric gesture, but even I had to admit a good tantrum sounded medicinal.

"Yes," I said. "That's exactly what they *told* us they wanted. But we're going to fail together before we fail because of another team." Abe screwed his features, muddling through what I was trying to say. *What am I trying to say?*

"Only two teams are going to get through. That's a fact we know to be true, and it's something we have to navigate. Everyone else has the same odds, so we have to find a way to increase ours." I paused while I curated my thoughts into the precise words I wanted, inhaling the crisp pine air.

"They're stressing us on purpose, pitting us against each other. It's breaking us down—we all feel it—and it's going to break them down, too." Lights flashed on Abe's face. I hit the mark.

"We can't let them break us." Cecil hooked his thumbs through the strap of his pack. I could feel their well of motivation rising as we huddled around with red cheeks and sweaty brows, a well *I* tapped. If Nix wouldn't let me make up for last night, I could at least bolster the others. A little less misery would lighten the load.

"We need a strategy," Nix conceded, letting some of the edge in his tone dissipate. He laid the map across a fallen tree trunk, dried from the harsh winter weather, and pointed to our destination in the corner. I pursed my lips and gave him a soft smile. The crease in his brow melted into his usual smooth skin, then he cleared his throat.

"We're headed down the valley, following the river," he said. "We're in the thick of it right now but the terrain starts to clear once we make it into the foothills. It should take us..." He muttered something I couldn't make out, likely calculating the lag with everyone in tow. "About two days, if we push through the night." For the dozenth time that day, Ophida erupted in a diatribe of complaints. Despite her bark and limited bite, she dotted a few of her words with perfunctory curses. Though I'd abandoned the expected Ladylike demeanor the second my blood dripped off the damned Scrolls, I'd never seen Ophida draw back the curtain to her real personality before–the messy pieces that were behind the layers of the Caste.

"You know we only need seven people to complete this." Rashel shot a poisonous jab at the bleary-eyed girl. Even I flinched at the harshness, but Ophida fell into a quiet bout of sniffles. Progress was progress, though it would take some time for the team to fully embrace the concept of cohesion. Ignoring the exchange, Nix continued.

"We have at least eight more hours of daylight, so if we keep moving, we'll be in the river basin by midday tomorrow. From what I can tell, we're headed to a tributary in the eastern corridor. Pretty remote space, but I've been to that region before." He turned down to Ophida. "We can make it." She chuffed at him but didn't argue.

"What about the other teams?" Abe asked.

"Right now we need to hurry and secure whatever is out there. Then we find a way to draw an alliance." Nix's eyes brightened. I scowled at him for keeping us in the dark for so long when he had clearly been brewing a plan all along. He shrugged.

"Increase the odds," Cecil said.

Chapter Twenty-One

Nix had not exaggerated when he said we were crossing rough terrain; in fact, he had undersold it. Coming from the north-west to Hanover Hall when we first journeyed in had not given us a proper visual of the mountains, particularly how massive and piercing they were up close. We traversed to the southwest, straight down the ridge where we would pick up the river. It would lead us the rest of the way and offer a reliable navigation point, as Nix had explained to us all. I trusted him implicitly, but the journey seeped into my bones.

"This was the smoothest path," Nix promised. I glared at him as sweat beaded on my forehead. Okay, I *mostly* trusted him.

The oranges and reds of daylight faded to black in front of us, a breathtaking sight against the granites and greens of the Andalls. I chuckled to myself as I recalled all the times I had wished to see the mountains in person, and now I stood in their heart, reaching out and touching them with each passing step. None of this was ever part of my daydreams. In the unfiltered truth of the situation, the mountains were treacherous and unyielding, resisting our mere presence. It filled me with a wistful pang that tasted of bitter anise and the nostalgia lost. I should've been used to that flavor by now.

I couldn't tell if we were moving faster because the ground was unencumbered by rock, or if it was an illusion in the darkness. The cold air whipped at my face, along with the occasional tree limb, but it was keeping me awake so I did my best to embrace it. The rest of the team was just as focused, because we descended with minimal conversation. Even Ophida had ceased her crying, aside from a single outburst when she met a possum darting across the unlit path.

In the dark I had little frame of reference for time, but it felt like hours had passed when Nix held his hand up. He signaled for us to halt, shushing everyone as we shuffled to a stop.

"Water," he said. I strained to listen for whatever he detected in the distance, but came back with just crickets chirping. Swallowing my breath to listen closer, I heard a faint but familiar *whoosh* several hundred feet away. After all the time I had spent on the dam, I recognized the sound of moving water instantly.

Nix beckoned for us to follow him towards the source. The ground softened and the land curved inward to reveal the broad sides of the River Fulde. The little blue line on Nix's map had given no credit to its overwhelming magnitude. We stood at the bank in awe, hypnotized by the rushing water extending almost as wide as the Dargon Strait separating Oberin from the rest of the mainland. The other bank was an eternity away, but I could make out the spotted tree line against the filmy moonlight. It wasn't salty, and the movement was all wrong, but the closeness of water catapulted me back home.

"We can rest in a few hours," Nix said. His voice was muffled against the roar of the river. Ophida didn't wait for an invitation and plopped to the ground, pack and all.

Nix ran his eyes over her before addressing the rest of the group. "I want to make it as far down the mountain as we can tonight." He was concerned with securing our object in time, the slump of his shoulders and static creases around his eyes evidence enough, but I knew he didn't want that to bleed over to the rest of the team. There was plenty of worry to go around, but Ophida clearly wasn't on board with his rest cycle. My own legs rubbed raw with each stride, and the blisters had grown their own blisters within my heavy boots, but the longer our object was out there in the riverlands, it was free for the taking.

Just as I expected, Ophida whimpered when Nix gestured for us to move out. I had to admit, her whining had faded–a bit. With the winding banks stepping in as the navigator for our expedition, and with the ground leaner on obstacles, we were able to cover a significant distance before the birds started chiming in the treetops. The sun was still just a murmur beyond the hills, but Nix guided the wilting group to a temporary resting place.

"We can make camp here," Tomas said after several hours, pointing to the tree line.

The thought of laying down among the soil and brush never sounded more welcoming. I didn't need the camp or any of the gear, I was so exhausted. But Tomas flitted into a strange ritual amongst the trees, dropping his pack to the earth and staring into it for several seconds. He produced one of his wool blankets from its depths and started draping it artfully through the limbs, letting one side hang longer. He took the second issued blanket and laid it on the forest floor, followed by his thick down parka.

The rest of the team observed in fascination, catching on to his example. They burrowed for supplies in their bags, retrieving blankets and coats before weaving them around the birch limbs. Any predator within a fifty foot radius knew we were there from the flurry of movement, swishing and cracking in the clear night. I sat on my haunches and watched Della and Rashel join their blankets together to make a larger tent, then Abe and Cecil followed suit. For a brief second, I considered inviting Ophida but abandoned the idea when I spied a clear piece of ground beckoning to me. No tent was worth forfeiting my sanity.

"Up for company?" Nix said from behind, sending goosebumps across my torso. I spun towards him, caught off balance as he married his blanket up with mine, forming a tidy square pocket. Judging from the expert shelter he constructed before I could even form an answer, Nix had clearly forgiven me for my comment. And he apparently saw no issue with any blurred lines between us.

It really was all in my head. Admittedly, having Nix nearby with a forest full of stalking, creeping wildlife felt too good to pass up. *Strictly for security.* Andren was still keeping his distance, but I rationalized the repentant fiancé would have to take a seat for the pure survivalist out here. I could keep it all business.

"Sure," I said with a flip of my hand, trying to ensure I kept every-thing cordial, or as cordial as possible when sharing a sleeping space with my future husband's right-hand man. *As cordial as possible with my heart pounding loud enough for the entire campsite to hear.* I shook my head, willing my body to behave, and rushed to give Nix a hand.

I stood with my hands in my pockets, watching helplessly as he worked. Nix was doing fine without my help. When the makeshift shelter was complete, I hesitated at the threshold. Nix, however, didn't need an invitation and wiggled in comically, ducking his head to clear the tiny space. A strange, tickling sensation filled my chest. A bubble of laughter. Of humor. And a shit ton of nerves. Nix patted the ground next to him, and I crawled into the space on my hands and knees.

The air evaporated around me, transforming my chuckles into gasps for oxygen. He was so close I could feel the heat from his body on my cheeks. Or maybe that was my own flush. Now that we were both scrunched inside, I realized two blankets were overkill. In fact, I wished for a gust of the cool night air to regulate my body temperature. *It's just Nix.* I had no reason to be this flustered, and yet a bead of sweat trailed down my temple as a single act of rebellion.

"You need to take your boots and coat off," he said as he yanked off one of his own oversized boots. His arm brushed against mine as he moved, and he didn't break the contact when he sat back down. I tried to focus on his actions, observing how he unfolded his socks from his feet and balled them into the boots, but I was ready to spontaneously combust. *Why is it so hot?*

"Keeps the critters out." Nix flashed a devilish grin, and my insides went straight to mush. *What am I doing?* There was no corner of reality where I could, *or should,* have thoughts like this about Nix. Sure, he had an uncommon attractiveness, a drastic change from the sea of Casted I normally saw. But I was drawn to his protection, his friendship. *And his fucking charm.* Nix was kind to me, and that alone was enough to send my mind into overdrive. I needed to nip those thoughts in the bud, and hastily mimicked his actions with my own feet. There was nothing remotely sexy about dirty boots.

"You're lucky you didn't overheat," he said, tugging the coat from over my shoulders. *He has no idea.* The rush of icy air stabbed at me like needles, but it was the shock I needed to regain my composure. I looked down at the sweat-plastered tunics I had piled under my jacket, clinging to my form. Nix shook his head. My clothes needed changed, but every joint I had seized at the thought of undressing around him.

Still, the threat of hypothermia was stronger than my concern, so I pressed my eyes together and hoped the darkness could offer some privacy. As fast as I could manage, I stripped away both layers down to my undergarments, then draped the shirts across my boots to dry out. While fumbling with my bag to find a new one, cursing myself for not doing that first, Nix grabbed my arm.

"You're going to have to trust me on this," he said, eyes reflecting the shreds of moonlight from outside. "But you'll be better off sleeping with fewer layers." I gawked at him, his broad, and *very bare* pectorals staring back at me. *When did he take his shirt off?* Nix was in my space, breathing the same air, and we both were shirtless. If I hadn't died in the first Trial, this one was about to do me in. "Respectfully." He let loose a clipped, baritone chuckle that struck me in all my indecent places.

"Respectfully, I'm going to bed," I said, turning away from him. The ground tilted a little less when I couldn't see him. Ever the gentleman, and *my fiancé's faithful servant,* Nix rolled to face the other direction so we were back-to-back. His skin grazed mine and I was acutely aware of every point where the arch of his spine came in contact, producing a current of electricity between us. Curling into a tight ball, I held as still as possible and counted blades of grass in front of me. Just a few hours ago, I worried about staying warm. Now I was on the verge of heat exhaustion. But eventually the actual exhaustion won and I drifted to sleep.

When I woke sometime later, I found the tent void of anything but ruthless daylight infiltrating the blanket. I heaved on my boots and one of the tunics from yesterday, dense with morning dew, and emerged from the tent like a cave animal. Judging by the stares awaiting me outside, I must have looked the part, too.

"Looks like you slept well," Nix said as I shook the remnants of my braid loose. His eyes lingered too long, and heat flashed across my chest. I had to get that under control. Abe continued talking with Cecil, but Nix tracked my fingers as I plaited my hair into a tight braid. He could probably do better, but I'd sooner shave my head bald than ask him to do my hair again.

"I did," I replied once I put myself back together. Ophida sat just beyond us, sprawled on a large, flat rock with her bare feet propped in the sunlight. It was much warmer at this elevation than in the caps of the mountains, and the gentle kiss of rays felt good on my cheeks. I hadn't seen daylight since arriving at Hanover over a week ago, and I greeted the sun like an old friend, taking a seat next to Ophida.

"So what now?" Rashel asked as she stuffed a large corner of bread into her mouth, not bothering to seal her lips when she chewed. "More walking?"

"More walking," Tomas said. He picked at a piece of dried apricot, lost miles away to his own thoughts.

"We need to send a few scouts," Nix said. Tomas didn't look up, but the rest of the team hovered, the idea capturing their interest.

"Scouts?" Della repeated.

"Yes," Nix said. "Scouts."

Tomas reemerged back into our reality from wherever he had just been. "The likelihood others are somewhere out here is high," he said. "We're exposed in the daylight so it would be wise to send two people ahead. Someone who can move faster and recon our path before the rest of us walk into...." He trailed off. I didn't need to hear the rest.

"Problems." Nix eyed Tomas, placing his hands across his chest with an ease far too casual for the state of my nerves. "The scouts will stay ahead of the group and ensure the path is clear, then we'll link back up at the objective."

"What if the p-path isn't clear?" Abe battled against his stammer, his anxiousness moving in tandem with mine.

"The scouts will rush back to warn the group. With just two of them, they should be able to move under cover, and at a much faster pace."

"Brilliant," Cecil whispered under his breath.

"So who are the scouts?" Rashel asked. "Nix and Tomas?"

"Tomas will escort the main group. You'll need someone to keep you on pace and on track." Nix tipped his head to Tomas, appointing him the honor. "I'll take Selah."

"*Me?*" I scanned the crowd for some indication of what Nix had just said, because I clearly had misheard him. But Nix stared directly at me. There was no way I could keep up with his preternaturally long stride over mountains and rivers, and whatever else was lurking out there. Had he lost his mind in the altitude?

"We need to move quickly and you can do that." He held his voice perfectly even. *Where's the joke, Nix?* I flipped my head from person to person, waiting for one of them to object. Surely Rashel or Ophida had something snarky to say, but everyone just looked at me with *reassurance?* Not a single argument. Not even a raised brow. *They can't possibly trust me to do this, can they?*

"W- when do we leave?" I asked, wondering how much time I had to get my bearings together. Apparently Nix was serious about this.

"As soon as we pack up." I stared at him as he spoke, watching my pulse pound into my vision to distort his face. He really wasn't going to give me the proper amount of time needed to panic, was he?

I dragged my feet but Nix had the camp packed up in spite of my stalling. We pushed out into the brush before I could process the fact we were separating from our group. Their faces faded into the distance behind us as Nix kicked his pace into gear. I made sure I kept my parka and extra tunics rolled into my bag, and topped my canteen off in the river before we took off. The metal clanged and bounced against my hip, gnawing at the bruised and tender flesh underneath. I made a quick note to tie it to the other side as soon as we stopped. If we stopped.

Nix prowled through the woods, taking long, loping steps that cleared logs and brush without demanding so much as a glance in their direction. He glided as he moved, his tanned forehead glistening in the streaks of light lacing through the trees. I, on the other hand, clambered just beneath a sprint, sopped with sweat after the first hour. I also discovered my uncanny talent for attracting every thorn bush or rogue tree branch.

By the time we paused for the evening, I barely had the energy to replace my soaked tunic with a dry one. Nix and I didn't bother with a campsite, and instead, situated ourselves back-to-back deep in the brush. I was far too ragged to worry about the multitude of things that might stalk us in the night, and far too comfortable against the warmth of

Nix's body. I never felt the sleep hit me, but woke sometime just before dawn with my head on Nix's lap.

My chest constricted when he flashed a lopsided smile down at me, already awake. *He's watching me sleep.* I squirmed under his stare, but I was too out of sorts to explain away my excited energy. Any normal female would react to being cradled by someone like Nix. *Just look at him.* I'd never understand how the Casted had established their standard of beauty when *this* existed. Andren had been silent since we left Hanover Hall, but drowning in guilt for recognizing a simple fact wouldn't change the way my heart malfunctioned every time he smiled at me like that.

"You ready?" he asked, offering me a fruit leather and piece of cheese from his bag. As I sat up to eat, he freed his legs from under me, then stood to stretch. I followed his lead, dusting my rumpled clothing and hoisting my pack back onto my shoulders.

"Shhh." Nix hissed, careening into me and yanking me to the ground. I tasted the soil and jousted my elbow into Nix's ribs, but he didn't flinch. His eyes were fixed somewhere into the distance, scanning like a wolf on the hunt. I followed his gaze, finding nothing but rows upon rows of firs. But then, the scenery shifted. I sharpened my focus to spot a figure walking several hundred feet away along the tree line. Not sure of our next move but too afraid to give away our position, I froze, drawing in shallow breaths to still my chest against the ground. We stayed like statues as the figure wandered closer, its mannerisms jerky and disoriented. Whoever was out there looked to be alone.

"They don't know we're here," I whispered. Nix flexed his temple in acknowledgement.

"And they won't see us coming." He swiveled his eyes to me, locking me into his intense dark stare that made me feel like the prey and not the huntress. On the precipice of melting me into the earth, Nix turned back to his target.

"What do we do?" I searched Nix's face for any traceable clue. We couldn't just ignore them. They could be hurt, or worse–they could hurt *us.* I tracked the movement again, but the odd, uneven gait didn't come across as threatening. Nix was steely and silent, nothing in his visage betraying his intentions. Over the last few days, I had grown to both loathe and appreciate that quality.

"We catch them."

"Say again?" I choked on the fresh forest air.

"We need an ally, and they just delivered one," he said without breaking his sites from his target. Nix readjusted himself, brushing the pine needles from his tunic. He raised his eyebrow at me, asking if I was ready. *Absolutely not.* But I inhaled and shifted my pack on my back. Without any other warning, Nix took off running. *Shit.*

I sprinted as fast as I could in his wake. Slinking through the undergrowth, it didn't take us long to flank the figure and surround it before it knew we were there. *It* was a male with hair as black as Nix's, but a stature a quarter of the size. Once we moved in on him, I recognized his face. We weren't acquainted, but I registered his name from the first Trial. *Maher.*

The man's complexion went stark white as we approached him. He dropped to his knees and raised his palms to face us. I faltered in my tracks, stumbling over the pure terror seeping from his pores. He was clearly defenseless, and I hoped Nix took that into account with whatever plan he was brewing, but Nix descended on him.

"Please don't hurt me." Maher clamped his hands together and flung himself forward. He revealed stripes of scratches across his back, and blotches of bruising poking through his shredded clothing. My stomach sank low. Something bad had happened to him. Something far worse than crossing paths with us.

"Where's the rest of your group?" Nix tugged him up by the remnants of his shirt. Maher recoiled, shielding his face like a beaten dog.

"They're gone," he said. "We were attacked and everyone scattered. I fled." He kept his head angled away, but lowered his hands.

"Attacked by what?" I asked, not waiting for Nix. What kind of animal could do this to him?

"Rior."

My mouth went completely dry, and a prickling frost crept up my neck. No translation was needed to register everything hanging in the grave look Nix gave me. He crouched down by Maher. The man risked raising his head to face us, revealing haunted shadows in his eyes. Rior was dangerous–that was quite clear after the first Trial–but the sheer terror clinging to Maher made my blood run cold.

"He–his group attacked us, took our map, and…" He clawed at the side of his face, leaving angry streaks against the bruising. I knelt on his other side while Maher collected his words.

"It was horrible." His whole body heaved. "They ambushed us in a pass. We had nowhere to run. I only got away because I was in the very back. I heard the screams, saw Rior cut them off. And Deona…" Maher broke into a sob, disappearing into the safety of his arms. Nix raised his eyebrows, the desire to quiet the man displayed in his expression, but he let it go. The two of us sat in silence while Maher cried.

"She had the map." He sniffled. "I don't think she made it out. None of them did." I couldn't bear his unfiltered anguish, not when it was this close to my own.

"Come with us," I said. Nix glared at my outburst, but I didn't care about our plan at the moment. What plan would actually dig us out of this? Get us away from Rior? The only plan was surviving each second, and Maher's were numbered if we didn't help him. "We can at least get you back to the trails."

"You-you would do that?" Maher smeared the wetness on his face with his sleeve.

"Of course," I said. Nix turned away, propping his hands on his hips. He could brood all he wanted. This was *not* the time to think about how much I liked seeing Nix brood, and knowing I'd gotten to him. Wasn't he the one who told me to quit letting things happen? Well, I was taking charge, and I wasn't about to let anything else happen to Maher.

"Do you remember where your object was?" I asked. Nix swung around. Was it so surprising I could multitask?

"I think I could point it out on a map," Maher said as he righted himself. "But Rior will be headed that way."

"Correct," Nix said, finally accepting the turn of events and rejoining the conversation. Maybe I wasn't so bad at taking charge. "And we need to stop him."

Maher stood bleary eyed, mulling over Nix's declaration. Before he had a chance to oppose, Nix was already jogging away with a pace even more intense than yesterday's. I gave Maher a half-smile then took off after him. Without a better option on the table, Maher followed after us.

"We've got to make it back to the group and get our object before Rior moves on. Then we need to catch him." Nix explained like he was telling me what he ate for breakfast.

"But they already took off," I said, trying to disguise my breathlessness. Nix didn't respond. Either he had no answer or he knew I wouldn't like it.

Skirting the rocky banks of the river, we eventually hit a sharp bend that cornered us with its angular formation. Nix steered us perpendicular to the point and parked in the safety of the camouflage. I shuffled next to him and took a sip from my canteen, welcoming the cold water sloshing out of the sides of my mouth and streaming down my neck. It didn't take me as long to catch my breath, a momentary triumph in all this. Maher crept up several minutes later, still following our trail. He swabbed at his damp face with his sleeve, and I offered him my canteen.

"They should be close," Nix said, scanning the horizon. I joined him, standing arm to arm and watching the light move through the trees for any sign of our group.

"There." Nix pointed several hundred feet away. Sure enough, the remnants of the sun glinted off Cecil's bright orange hair. I gathered up Maher, letting him keep the canteen, and trotted toward our team.

"Did you see anything?" Cecil called the second he spied us, sending the others in a swarm to head us off. Cecil stopped dead in his tracks just over halfway. "Who's that?"

"Maher." Nix tilted his head at the man hunched behind me.

"His group was attacked by Rior and got...separated," I said, censoring the details for Maher's sake. "We found him roaming the woods alone."

"Let me get this straight." Rashel's voice gnawed at my patience. "You found an opponent out there and brought him back?" Her pitch rose higher as she kept going. "While we go traipsing around the wilderness for some unidentified *object*?"

"We couldn't just leave him," I said with a shrug. I snuck a glance at

Maher, who cowered behind us as we discussed him. The sight ripped at my chest, unable to imagine what horrors he had seen. "And he knows where his group's object is. We needed an ally, right?"

Nix cut in. "Rior isn't going to make this easy on us, but we can beat him to the second object. If we find ours." The others eyed Maher. Clearly this wasn't what they had in mind when Nix said we needed to partner with another group, but no one dared to argue.

"Well, he can help search the area." Tomas's gray-blue eyes scanned the hunched man without a drop of pity. While it wasn't a warm look, it was receptive. Firm. Tomas knew the value the other candidate could offer, and something told me he also knew the terror he had seen, too.

"How will we know what we're looking for?" Ophida asked, kicking a rock around with her boot. The sun kissed the tips of the trees, rendering everyone as dark silhouettes against the fiery sky. Her whining was somewhat justified, if I continued to be frank with myself. Officer Pickham hadn't given any indication of what we were looking for, and our daylight waned as fast as our motivation.

"I guess we're about to find out." Abe shrugged at her, not lingering for more questions. He and Tomas circled the group, then assigned us each an area to search. We fanned out, turning tree branches and leaves over, searching for a needle in the haystack in the low light. A wordless Maher went in his own direction and combed the shrubbery along his sector. I caught Abe watching him from the corner of his eye, but he went about his business once he was satisfied with Maher's performance.

An hour into the search, I had covered close to a mile with nothing to show but a dead mouse and what I hoped wasn't poison ivy. The rest of my team was no longer in my line of sight, so I figured it was safest to head back in hopes someone else had better luck finding whatever it was hiding out here. I envisioned some nebulous item concealed in a tree, stalking us while we hunted in vain.

"I-I think I found it," Abe called. My heart rate doubled its cadence and I ran toward the commotion, finding Abe crouched over a spot on the ground. At his feet was a small shield, cut from steel and lined with gold filigree. He picked it up and flipped it over, catching a crimson inscription in the moonlight. When he turned it back, I recognized the seal of Hanover Hall embossed in the center. *This has to be it.*

"How the hell do we keep that safe?" Rashel crossed her arms, popping her hip to one side. Ophida may have been coming around, but Rashel's petulance held strong.

"Guess we'll have to take turns guarding it," Cecil said. She shot daggers at him with her eyes, daring him to volunteer her for watch duty. Part of me wished he would, just to see her head spin. "I'll take the first shift," he conceded.

With Cecil securing the shield, the rest of us bedded down. I stood by while Nix set up camp, half-afraid to ask if it was, in fact, *our* camp-site or if I was just making assumptions. Nix unfolded the blanket from his pack, then reached a hand for mine. Sheepishly, I handed him the second wool blanket. To my surprise, he didn't string it into a tent like he had the first night. Instead, he tossed it to Maher before turning back to me.

"Hope you don't mind sharing," he said. I glowed so hot I didn't need a blanket at all. Nix didn't wait for me to nod, and I wasn't sure if I actually moved my head or not. He laid out his parka before kicking off his boots, then yanked away his tunic. He balled up the garment and tucked it behind his head, propping himself up to meet my gaze. All at once, my skin felt far too tight. The moonlight bounced off the perfect lines of his chest and abdomen, drawing a path for me. *Oh, god*—the way I *salivated.*

"Selah, it's getting cold." Nix patted the ground next to him with his free arm, summoning me next to him. It was a small miracle my knees didn't give out, and instead, carried me to his side. The second I was within range, Nix hooked me around my shoulders and pulled me against his bare chest. I sucked in small gasps of air, petrified Nix would feel me panting against him. Surely he could detect the clanging along my ribs, but he swallowed me with his arms and tucked us under the single blanket.

In the stillness of the night, I was anything but. How could I sleep with Nix invading every inch of my space? He smelled like the deepest woods, wild and green, and his skin sizzled everywhere it made contact with my body. The cold air wafted around us, but Nix tightened his grip. He rested his chin on top of my head, rustling my hair with his breathing.

He has to know. The truth blazed as hot as Nix's flesh on mine—he had to feel it, too. Perhaps I was letting things happen to me–the emotion of this place shoving me into corners I couldn't acknowledge before and doing all the things Nix told me not to. But did it count if I wanted them to happen? *Does he want them to happen?* Just bringing that thought to the surface was forbidden. I couldn't think like this, and I certainly couldn't give into these thoughts. But *damn*.

"We can't let Rior pull this off," Nix whispered into my hair, his lips brushing the strands. We let the words hang between us without saying anything else, and I slept soundly for the first time in weeks.

Chapter
Twenty-Two

"It was over here." Maher said, his finger hovering over a spot on Nix's map.

Nix circled the point. "That's north, back in the mountains," he said, pressing his lips together. My heart sank low in my chest. We'd just faced them, and now we had to trek back without much of a respite. "It will take at least a day to get there, but we can pick up the tributary and follow it. Then we can cut south to get back to Hanover. If we go straight over the ridge."

The others lurked behind him to visualize his plan on paper, munching on the remnants of Cecil's snacks. The path he outlined was hatched with thin lines that converged until they appeared to be gray splotches in some areas. An icicle stabbed me through the middle in spite of the warm temperature. Those were elevation marks. Nix planned on taking us along the spine of the Andalls' western range instead of the foothill passages we used to get here. There was no way we could scale *that*.

"Can-can we make that?" Abe echoed the questions in my own head.

Nix didn't answer right away. That was all the answer I needed.

"Yes," he said finally. The curve of his pecs rose up and down, and I pictured them shirtless against me. *Focus.* "We have to make up time and that's the shortest route."

I nibbled on a fruit leather, but it turned rancid in my mouth. Our dried meat was rationed to one slice in the evening, but even that wouldn't have satiated me. Nix's ambition needed way more fuel than the sad provisions we had, and the wilting energy from days in the elements. He gathered us up anyway, and led us back into the mountains.

Our newfound companion stayed with our group in spite of his short stature, keeping pace with Tomas for miles across the prairies circling the base of the Andalls. I trotted along, too exhausted to do much more, and far too distracted by the changing scenery. The expanse of grassy reeds was disorienting after spending a lifetime on an island, and I actually found myself yearning for the walls of the Andalls. Walking through the chilly, open air reminded me I no longer had the safety of Nix's arms around me. In the daylight and the silence of my own mind, prickly guilt crept in.

Does Andren know? Ever since my Sponsorship, our connection had been strained. But in the last few days, I hadn't sensed him near me at all. It could have been a coincidence, and perhaps he was busy, but there were too many parallels between the silence and the blaring draw toward his Hand. Doubt nagged at my heels as my boots rubbed raw spots with each step. I had no logical reason to be conflicted–the Trials had one simple objective. I was here to get my life back, to return to Andren, and to live out my days *happy.* But the farther from the island I got, the more I realized happiness might not be gold and polished.

Ophida's head caught my eye as she tripped over the gravel, cursing out loud. The line came to a halt, yanking me from my daze. *Ophida's really milking this.* But I quickly realized she was upright and silent. Maher, however stood frozen on the rocky path, clutching his sides and crying out with such a tormented pain, its residue reached me. Tomas pulled the young man back to his feet by his wrist. He didn't appear to be injured, but Maher dropped to his knees, fighting battles none of us could see. Nix's dark, shaggy head came into view, his face riddled with concern. The wind itself ceased as we all stood around the man, watching him crumble apart before our eyes.

Finally Nix broke the silence. "This is a good place to rest for a minute," he said. "We're nearly there." Tomas looked to the man on the ground, resting his hand on his shoulder as Nix left to update the rest of the group. Tomas didn't try to interrupt Maher, to quiet him. I hovered a few feet away, letting Maher take his time. When he finally emerged from behind his hands, his face was red and blotchy. The crimson hue deepened when he saw all of us standing by.

"S-sorry," Maher whispered.

"Let's sit," Tomas said, taking him under his arm. The others slowly disappeared from the scene, leaving me awkwardly behind the pair of men, intruding on the private moment. Maher made eye contact with me, and I gave him a small smile before planting myself several feet down the hill. I leaned against a burly pine, listening to their quiet murmurs behind me. The wind whisked past my ears, and their whispers carried. It was voyeuristic, and I would have been much smarter to take a nap, but their conversation roused my interest, and I wasn't strong enough to resist.

"I just can't believe she's gone." Maher's voice danced in my ear. "Deona and I were going to finish this together." I pictured the only female in their group: a short, stocky girl with golden brown hair down her back. She wasn't conventionally pretty, but there was something appealing in her features. The same argument could be made about me, I supposed.

"I-I loved her." He sobbed again, pausing for big gulps of air. "Nobody knew about us. But we were supposed to be together." There was silence for a long time, and I assumed the conversation was over.

"I lost someone I loved, too." Tomas's weather-worn voice wound through the darkness, pricking the hairs on my arm at the lilt in his speech. Tomas had pulled back the curtain on a side he kept closely guarded. I held my breath to listen closer.

"Who?" Maher asked. There was shuffling and another pause.

"My daughter," Tomas said at long last. "Menifee. She was nine."

"What happened to her?"

"My...former...Lord stole her from me," Tomas said. "I served in his household for over ten years. My wife did as well. Our Lord forbade his servants from having children, said it was a distraction to their work."

The older man's sigh cut into the wind, tangling in my hair. In the cold, crisp air, it sounded like he was right behind me.

"But that was the one thing that would bring joy to my wife and we were not as careful as we should have been. She was with child and we had to hide it. The other servants helped us, knowing what could happen if our Lord or Lady discovered the baby. They even faked an illness for her when she delivered." I thought of my own servants, who'd mended my cuts and bruises without a single complaint, caring for me more than my own mother had. Not once did I ask them about their lives, their families. The mounting guilt caged me like a wild animal.

"I knew we couldn't stay there, so I started doing odd jobs after my work in the house. I found a carpenter who was willing to take me on as an apprentice, even with my restricted hours. I had my very own job and moved us out in the middle of the night.

"We tried to lay low since we had not been released from our servitude, and it worked for a long time. The Casted tend to not notice people like us. My wife and I had a humble life with Menifee, but it was a happy life." There was silence again. I couldn't picture Tomas as a servant, or as anything other than the controlled, dignified man leading us through this mess. We were equals here, but *I* had been on the villainous side of Tomas's story. When he spoke again, his voice was strained and paper-thin.

"Oberin is a small place, and the Lord saw my wife in town, walking with our daughter. He recognized her. A week later, he sent his sons to return us to the family house, like property. The young Lords dragged Menifee back with us. They... No one stopped them. No one cared about the servants' daughter. And they discarded her like trash."

I clamped my hands over my mouth to stifle my horror, but nothing more came from Tomas. My whole body lurched with unease and the compulsion to run to him. To apologize on behalf of all Casted, for being complicit in this horrid system. But what use would that do? I was sitting here in the frigid mountains, trying to claw my way back to that life.

God—how can he even look me in the eye? How can Nix?

"So why would you want to be one of them?" Maher asked. I froze, leaning closer to their direction as slowly as possible.

"To make them pay."

Shivers racked through my bones, chilled by much more than the temperature.

"Better go," Tomas said, the stony distance returned to his voice. I turned to see him dust off his trousers, then walk up the hill to rustle up the rest of the group. Wordlessly, he pressed on into the night, side-by-side with Nix, and the rest of us followed as if nothing had just happened.

We advanced as the river delivered its serpentine curves back to us, revealing great silver cliffs lining the path of the river. The foliage was all but gone, replaced with a few barren pines poking through severe shards in the earth. It was an endless chasm of stone that made my stomach lurch as we crested it. Why did everything about the mountains have to be so threatening? And yet, they offered a protection unmatched by any place I'd ever been. *Some metaphor, Selah.*

"There's an opening in the rock down there," Abe said, gesturing to a spot about halfway down the cliffs on the opposite side of the river. "D–do you think that's it?" he asked, his confidence waning.

"I think it's worth a shot," Nix replied. He kept the hole in the cliff wall in his sights, even as he addressed Abe. *That has to be it.* "But getting there will be tricky."

I shifted my own gaze from the opening to the water, watching it dubiously in the moonlight. The current was so strong, I could hear it from my distance, and it stretched to the horizon with no sign of a way around. The impossibility of finding it only confirmed that's where it was hiding. I was starting to acclimate to the tempo of these Trials, but after living almost all my life as Casted, I failed to see the correlation from one to the other. Mastering the Trials was the opposite of being Casted, yet they'd thrown us out here to cut each other out of the running.

"We could cross there." Nix pointed to a black patch in the river. He really was part feline, if not canine, because I couldn't make out anything but a blob. I advanced to the edge of the cliff to get a better vantage, backing away a few inches when the tug of gravity threatened to throw me into the rocky, churning abyss. Squinting where Nix referenced, I found a patch of white on the inky water, a few slick rocks reflecting back at me in the moonlight. *That?* That's where he wanted us to cross? The air moved behind me, and I wheeled around to find Nix had materialized at my shoulder.

"This way," he whispered, drawing a trail of goosebumps over my arms. I sucked in deeply, holding the air in my lungs as Nix hovered near. There was that deep forest scent again–undertones of cedar and balsam after a snow storm.

"Don't fall," I yelled.

He shot me a quick grin. "Don't worry—the mountain would spit me back out." Nix winked before vanishing beyond the side of the cliff. My heart clawed its way into my throat but I couldn't bring my feet to move. Instead, my gut clenched, waiting for the *splash*, but it never came.

"Come on!" Nix called from below. This was crazy. I couldn't scale a cliff, but there I was–swinging my legs over to follow after Nix. The tug of the quick elevation change jerked at my midsection, almost as if Andren was pulling on the shredded Sewing. I reached for the frayed ends of the thread as I climbed downward, but found nothing. My imagination was trying to keep my conscience in check.

Before I could analyze my aptitude to chase after Nix while having an existential crisis on the cliff wall, I connected with a solid surface, and let my biceps loosen. The sides of the ravine were eroded into jagged ledges, leaving several inches of clearance to maneuver downward. I rearranged my pack to my front and pressed my back against the rock, running my palms next to me as I trailed behind Nix, careful to follow his exact footing.

We reached the canyon floor unscathed, and I said a silent prayer to the Ancient Ones in gratitude. I'd never been a big prayer, or one for the Casted pomp and ceremony when it came to religion, but it couldn't hurt. Not when we still had to cross the river and climb *up* the other side. Nix shouted at me but I couldn't hear him over the roar of the water echoing off the rocky walls sandwiching us in. Rather than bark instructions, Nix stepped out onto the glistening wet boulders. The water foamed and slapped around his feet but didn't sway him from his perch.

For the thousandth time in the last hour, my heart froze while I watched from the bank. He threw his arms out to his sides to balance, creating a perfect silhouette of his form against the moonlit cliff. The rocks fell farther apart now that we were up close, shiny and slick with the water rushing over them. My heart restarted with an odd fluttering when Nix leapt to the opposite shore. He amped up the theatrics by twirling to face us, then flashed a wide smile. Did he have to look at me like that?

I hung in the back of the line while the candidates crossed the rocky avenue one at a time. Ophida navigated the obstacle on all fours, crawling her way to safety. As ridiculous as she looked, the maneuver was pretty clever. But I couldn't avoid the trek any longer; I was the last one standing while all the others watched from the bank. I straightened my back and approached the first rock. If Ophida could do it, so could I.

Attempting to keep my knees from quaking, I planted my foot on the first rock. The water crested the toe of my boot, sneaking in through the eyelets. I had to hurry if I wanted to make it in one piece. Pushing the last of my trepidation from my brain, I locked eyes with Nix, who stood cross-armed directly in front of me, and I leapt from stone to stone. The final one was partially submerged, and my heel just missed the landing. I pitched forward, my stomach rolling over with the sudden momentum, but Nix snagged my forearm and plucked me from the water. I stood next to him with my hands on my waist, waiting for the ground to quit shaking beneath me. Hopefully Nix attributed my disheveled state to the near miss, and not the way my body trembled under his hand on my side.

Fortunately, the climb up the cave was far easier than the one to get to the bottom. The slope had a much gentler rise, with a narrow path that had been formed over the years. It led straight to the mouth, worn into a smooth avenue to greet us. Someone had clearly climbed the cliff wall many times. This landmark had been deliberately chosen, of that I was sure. What I still feared, however, was if Rior had made the same discovery first.

Chapter Twenty-Three

Wasting no time, Nix disappeared into the cave mouth, ducking his head under the low rock formations. I stepped inside and was struck with a moist wave of musty air, tinged with fish and decay. The smell was stifling. I yearned for the fresh, earthy scent of Nix, but he was long gone, leading the others deep into the cave. Only the echoes of their movements still lingered. *How can he even see through this dark?* I should have been used to his prowess by now, but everything about Nix was remarkable. Meanwhile, I bumbled along with Maher just ahead, managing to lose him in the darkness, too. Cave exploring clearly wasn't a hidden talent of mine.

The moisture grew thicker, melding together with the dense blanket of black around us. The must became a wall, and I had to force my way through the air to keep walking. *How far back does this go?* There was little chance I'd see any object back here; I could barely see my own feet. On my next step forward, I proved my own point when I bumped into Maher, unable to see the back of his head.

"What's happening?" I whispered. I wasn't trying to be quiet, but the air around us hung so heavy, it was the only sound I could squeak out.

"I'm not sure," he replied. "But we've stopped moving."

"Hello?" I called to the emptiness ahead of us, but nobody

answered. *Why can't they hear me?* I yelled again, louder this time. The noise should have bounced back against the rock walls, but it was absorbed into the dullness of the moisture. My pulse quickened with each passing second of silence. They *had* to hear me. I skirted around Maher and flailed my hands in front of me, finding only rocky walls and void. *They're gone.* Maher and I were separated. My mouth filled with a bitter taste, and my spine jolted me with static electricity.

"They're not here!" I yelled to Maher. "What do we do?" The shrillness leaked into my voice, and I sensed Maher's unease even without seeing his face.

"I–I don't know," Maher replied. Trails of cold sweat streamed down my sides now, my heart moving so fast it was halfway out of my chest. Between the pitch-black cavern and the surge of fear churning in my gut, I held onto my consciousness by a thread.

The putrid musk filled the corners of the cave until it overpowered my other senses. Frantically, I tried to snuff out the odor, feeling my way around the walls blindly, but it just grew stronger until it invaded the space around me.

"Do you smell that?" Maher asked. It wasn't just me. The smell was intensifying, and it smelled familiar. Rotten eggs and gas. It singed my nostrils as it wafted through the cave. I racked a cough from my chest, the stench clinging to my sinuses, restricting any air from moving. The black turned to bright red panic, complete with stars shooting across my vision from my pounding temples. I smelled sulfur.

Frenzy took hold of me, and I clambered for any indication of what was happening. I needed fresh air before my lungs ignited. *Or worse.* Dread brewed all around me but I couldn't think through that *awful smell*. I only knew I had to find Nix, and I had to move quickly.

My surroundings shifted—a hint of something else infiltrated the air. Something very distinct, sharp and sweet—like Father. *Whiskey.* The hairs on the back of my neck stood on end.

"Maher–we need to go." Maher's face came to light in a shock of brilliant, blinding orange, his features frozen in terror. Before either of us could react, the blast of heat struck us. Large flames pranced along the side, highlighting a fork in the passageway I'd failed to see before. The line of fire tearing past made the decision to run easy.

Maher darted toward the newly revealed opening, but in the brightness of the fire, I spied a rope running along the cave wall. Its fresh, taupe braid was out of place in the murky rock enclosure. The flames paralleled his movement, spreading down the fibers with an alarming speed. The rope erupted the second the orange and red licked over it, rushing in a stream of angry flames. *Dear god, the alcohol.* The rope had been soaked in whiskey. The fire was no accident.

"Maher, run!" I choked on my words.

He sprinted down the cavern and I pumped my arms to catch him. Just as I reached the fork, the cave thundered with an ear-splitting *boom.* Maher skidded to a stop and I careened into him. The opening to the second passageway was nothing but a blazing wall of flames, completely blocking the path forward. Piles of branches had been stacked meticulously on either side to close off the entrance, their carcasses burning before our eyes. *We're trapped.* The whole thing was a setup. From the very inception of this plan, we'd been walking into a trap.

"We have to get to the others!" I screamed, but I sputtered on the billows of black smoke filling the small space. Gritting my teeth, I prepared myself to make the leap through our only egress, but the fire scorched my skin before I could even make contact. *Shit.* It was the kind of heat that could melt flesh off bones. Doom billowed deep within me.

I coughed and gasped, edging myself as close as I could until I couldn't bear the daggers shooting up my arm. *Nix is in there. Our team is in there.* But I couldn't do it. The heat was too much to bear. Defeated and quickly unraveling, I tried to scream again, but the smoke out-willed me into submission. I dropped to my knees, tears blinding my vision. Nix's warm smile and coal black eyes sparked into my head. His hands braiding my hair, mending my wounds. The way he'd cared for me at my lowest. *And I failed him.*

"We can't stay here," Maher yelled over the roar of the burn. He grabbed at my arm but I fought back. How could he expect me to just *leave*? "Selah!" He shouted again, then yanked me harder. The fibers of my clothing bit into my skin, but he managed to get me to my feet despite our size disparity. Standing upright again, I smelled the burning hair–*my* hair–from the encroaching fire. *I didn't come all this way just to be incinerated in some cave.* Maher and I zig-zagged in the direction we came, leaping over the wall of fire, until the mouth reappeared.

Piercing cold rushed into my lungs as soon as we exited the cave. I gulped giant swallows of it as fast as I could. Sweet, wintery air. If I hadn't been suspended from the ledge of a cliff, I would have collapsed in relief. Instead, I ran as fast as I could down the side, hugging the wall of the cliff's narrow path. But my eyes still burned and my limbs were unsteady. I slipped on the damp stone, my insides halting in place while the rest of my body plummeted to the bottom of the canyon. The ground rose quickly, too quickly. When I landed, I felt nothing, and heard nothing but the sickening thud of meat on rock, and a deafening ring.

The fog of the impact cleared and the ringing was replaced with a white hot pain radiating to every nerve ending. *Fuck.* My side, my shoulder, *everything* roared in agony. Death would have been far gentler. I gripped the dirt with my nails, trying to return my soul to my body, but waves of nausea pelted me. And then I was hit with another shocking blow to my ribs.

"*Little bitch thought she'd get away.*" The voice was distant, far from the wrenching ache in my bones, but it sounded familiar. Another crack struck me in the back and my vision went black. *Please stop.* But the words were only in my head. I wheezed, writhing about on the ground like a defenseless animal, desperate to draw air back into my lungs. *Please.*

"Get the hell off of her!" Maher screamed, yanking me firmly back into consciousness. I pried my eyes open, rolling to my hands and knees to stabilize myself. The world pitched violently on a plane, sending me forward onto my face. My skin tore, and I tasted blood and dirt amidst the mouthful of grit in my teeth. Instinctively, I knew the threat hadn't gone. I had to get up. Had to fight back. Maher called again, and I curled upright to face the sound of his voice.

I lifted my head up and took in the scene. Maher was hanging from Rior's back, the stocky man swinging him around like a sack of flour. Maher's feet flailed wildly in a spiral behind him. Rior managed to break away, then struck Maher hard with a blow to the face. My own stomach knotted as if he'd hit me, too. *No!* I had to help him. I had to do something. My muscles flared as hot as the fire when I pushed off the ground, blinding me for several seconds as I swayed against the consuming pain. I was up, but Rior had thrown Maher down. *Move, Selah!* But I wasn't fast enough. Rior pounced on the smaller man, kicking him in the side like he had done to me moments before.

"Leave him alone!" I yelled, rushing to Rior as fast as my legs would allow. There was no plan, and I didn't know what I'd do when I reached him, but I couldn't sit by and watch. I'd lost my team, *lost Nix*, and I sure as hell wasn't going to lose Maher, too.

I hurled myself at Rior, cranking on his neck as hard as I could. He stumbled to the side before he dropped to his back, driving me hard into the ground. The rock stabbed into my spine and I struggled against Rior's dense body. I couldn't breathe, could barely move, but I hung onto his filthy neck like my life depended on it. The combination of sweat and grime weakened my grip, and he broke free of my hold. I grappled to regain dominance, but he swung back to me, landing another powerful kick to my side. His boot sent a *crunch* I both felt and heard, thrusting me to the edge of consciousness. My vision pinpointed, and I couldn't see him lunge again and again. I rolled my knees into my chest to protect what I could while he continued to rain kicks upon me.

A dull *thud* paused Rior's advances, leaving me bracing for an impact that didn't come. This was my chance to get away from the ruthless assault. Numb to the damage, my only hope was to get up again. I found Maher standing over Rior with a rock in his palm, a spidery trail of blood trickling from the side of Rior's head. When Rior twitched and attempted to roll over, I tasted a hint of disappointment knowing he wasn't dead. What kind of monster had I become out here? *The kind who survives.* I kicked the bloodied man hard with my boot, embracing my own pain from the force I'd used.

"Let's get out of here," I said to Maher. If I didn't start moving, my limbs were going to shut down and pin me here forever. With one heavy boot in front of the other, I forced myself away from the carnage in a delirious scramble to distance myself from the assault, with Maher right behind me. I blinked. I blinked again. *Focus, Selah.* I felt the *thump* on the ground before I heard it. Dull but deafening. Begging the world to stop spinning, I wheeled around and squinted to make out the shapeless mound.

Sick, hot dread writhed in my intestines. I didn't want to look but it was already too late. Maher's vacant eyes stared up at the sky, and a black, slick liquid seeped from his neck. Rior was on his knees, ripping his dagger from Maher's lifeless body before wiping the blood away on his trousers. He stood and turned to me. *No. Oh god, no.*

I lurched upward and threw my arms out to steady myself, each passing second giving me a drop of my strength back. Scraping my knees across the gravel, I forced mobility back into my joints. My heart pumped furiously, but I needed the rest of my body to catch up, and *fast.* Rior smirked at Maher's lifeless body, then charged at me.

"Not so high and mighty now, are you *Madame,*" he said, mouth snarled into a twisted grin. He had a rogue drop of blood on his cheek. *Maher's blood.* I swallowed back a gag. "Where's your oversized servant to save you?" The blow stung worse than his kicks. *Nix.* I stumbled back, putting as much space between us as the narrow river bed would allow, but Rior stalked forward.

"For someone with such a fancy education, you sure aren't bright," he continued. "You think I'd let that pathetic maggot escape? I let him get away. And sure enough, he found you." He kicked dirt toward Maher, sending a shower of dust over his face. Uncontrollable rage replaced the nausea in my abdomen, quickly overflowing into my torso and down my appendages. My fingers tingled with anticipation. He set us up. He trapped my team. He killed Maher.

And now I'm going to kill him.

I chewed on the salty resolve, using it to numb the searing pain in my sides. *Come get me you bastard.* I paused for Rior to lunge, forcing him to show his hand, before I made my move. When he rushed me again, I side-stepped his attack and pivoted into his back, then kneed him as hard as I could in his flank. My chest expanded with satisfaction, watching the squatty man pitch face-first into the ground. I wanted to crush his face into the dirt until it disappeared. But he got back up and retrieved his dagger, madder than ever.

Rior jumped and I narrowly dodged the kiss of his steel, but he managed to reel his other hand into an uppercut that blasted me in the chin. My teeth bit into my tongue and copper gushed into my mouth. The pain cracked through me. *God. Gods. Ancient Ones. Whoever the fuck I need to pray to–just take me anywhere but here.* I barely moved away from his reach so I could get my ears to stop ringing. He rushed, and I swung. I had to stop him. Rior ducked out of my reach, but I was ready.

I kicked at his knees as hard as I could, making a solid connection. He buckled and hit the ground again. Triumph pulsed through my veins, and this time I didn't hesitate to attack. I drove my boot into his windpipe, relishing the crunch that rang out. He screamed an airy, scratchy caw. Before he could crawl away, I straddled him. Being tall had its advantages after all. Rior bucked, but I pinned his arms to his sides with my knees. I was probably the first woman to willingly climb on top of that revolting pig, but I was going to make sure I'd be the last.

Squeezing my hand into a fist, I punched him. And I punched him again. Over and over, I struck at his face while my knuckles cracked and split on his bones. The sound was blissful, and watching him flinch was an aphrodisiac. I squeezed my eyes as I pelted him, instantly back in primary school with the Casted boys surrounding me, taunting me, poking me with sticks and showering me with rocks. In that moment, all the lessons from my servants came flooding back–how to make my hits count so I wasn't the victim. My mind shot backward a decade until it found pure, electric, survival mode.

Rior's nose poured blood and his eyes were already swelling shut under my barrage of strikes, but my restraint was trapped with Nix in that cave. *Burned away at this point.* I didn't notice my leg had come loose, and that my grip on Rior's waist faltered until it was too late. He yanked his arm free and drove his blade into my bicep, sending a jolt of disorienting pain down my arm. I shrieked and clutched the torn flesh, fearing my whole arm was going to tear off. With my defenses down, Rior worked the rest of his body from my hold and scrambled to his feet. The thrumming in my neck nearly choked me, but I pushed away with my good arm. *Get up. Fight him. You have to fight.* But he didn't advance on me.

"You're not worth it," he said, then spat blood into the dirt. "By now your whole team is dead and my group is already on their way back with two items. Seeing you grovel is just an added bonus." His black eyes burned into me, leaving me feeling violated.

Then he turned and ran.

In the hole where relief should have been, there was only an emptiness tugging relentlessly. A sob escaped my throat as I sank into the gravity of the situation. *I'm alone. They're gone.* Sweat dripped into my eyes, but I was impervious to the burn. Nothing could hurt worse than this tearing inside me, as if my navel had been tethered to a sinking pit of desolation. So fast. It had happened before I blinked. My team was here, Maher was here, and Nix was leading us through this fucked up Trial. And now they were all gone in one sweep.

Nix is gone. I retched onto the bank, clamping my hands down into the gravel in an attempt to stop the world from spiraling around me. Every heave brought an agonizing sear to the tear in my flesh, and my ribs crunched threateningly, but it was nothing compared to the turmoil in my mind. I'd failed my team. For the first time, I had tasted what it was like to be on the inside, to have someone notice me, even care about me, and I'd let it all slip through my fingers.

I vomited until nothing came up. Utterly empty, I collapsed on the bank. There was nothing left to do but weep, so I cried until my face felt detached from my skull. Maybe if I kept going, I could detach from this place. When I had nothing left to cry, I laid on the frozen ground, clinging to a fragile existence, barely vibrating with life.

Either dying came with tremors, or the vibrations were growing. I pressed my cheek to the loose sediment, confirming I could feel the snag of the gravel against my skin. *Still alive.* I held my breath and listened– the rumbling was coming from the earth, and it was getting louder. *What the hell is that?* A thundering crash of stone meeting stone rattled my teeth together. Maybe I really was dying, because it sounded like the apocalypse coming for me–the Ancient One of Death careening down the side of the cliffs to gather me up. I rolled over as quickly as my ragged body would allow.

Boulders poured from the mouth of the cave, spitting flames and plumes of black in their wake. Giant cracks splintered across the surface, forcing shale to slide away as a rainfall of debris peppered me. I propped myself up on my elbow to get a better view of the commotion. The cliffside was caving in on itself. *Get the hell out of here!* My injuries held me in place, weighted down by the paralyzing knowledge that my friends were inside. Dead or alive, they were in there and any hopes of reaching them were crumbling apart like the stone.

A silhouette appeared in the curtain of silt. A very large silhouette. I had to be hallucinating. The raw adrenaline and horror of everything was skewing my sense of reality. I was seeing things that weren't there–seeing ghosts.

Nix. No ghost moved like that. That was meticulous construction of pure, organic muscle and bone. Nix was *alive.*

The relief was so strong it burned. A fresh swirl of nausea struck me, and I swallowed hard to hold myself together. *This is impossible.* But there he was, tall and broad, and a little dirty from all the soot, as he scaled the remnants of the cliff. There was something on his back, some-thing limp and unmoving. *A body.* I gasped, surprising myself that I could still process any emotion at all. Seconds ago, they'd all been lost. But dread pulsed through me when I realized Nix had *two* bodies strewn across his shoulders, making his way to the base of the ravine with both in tow. He locked eyes with me and I didn't attempt to hold back the fresh tears streaming down my face. It was really him. This was no hallu-cination. The look in his eyes was far too real for that.

Using my discarded pack for leverage, I teetered to my feet and limped to him as fast as I could. As soon as I was within arm's distance, I snagged his face in my hands, clutching him in a vise between my palms. Nix's eyes widened, the bottomless onyx shining back at me, but I had to touch him. My mind wasn't firing any coherent signals, only a single compulsion to feel something tangible. Something alive. Nix laid the two forms gently on the ground without breaking contact. Only when I registered the blank faces of Ophida and Cecil at my feet did I let go. My soul bottomed out, with far more force than any of Rior's strikes. *I just got them back.*

I'd been horrible to Ophida when she'd only needed understanding. She knew the Trials were stacked against her, that life was stacked against her, and I never gave her that grace. It was too late to apologize, but I knelt at her side anyway. Her hand was fragile in mine, so tiny. I should have protected her. I should have done more to spare her from this. But her delicate fingers curled, wrapping around mine, and then they jerked away. Ophida sat up, coughing and spitting thick mucus. My heart leapt into my mouth. Cecil's eyelashes fluttered against his freckled cheeks. His face was caked in dark ash, making his amber irises glow bright in contrast. *Thank god.* I hugged Ophida's tiny form to my chest, inhaling the piercing scent of singed hair and smoke, the remnants of how close I'd come to losing her. She squirmed weakly in my grip, but I didn't care.

Nix 's eyes cut to Maher's body before I had a chance to fully celebrate the moment. Ophida and Cecil were still disoriented and hadn't noticed, but Nix honed in on the lifeless body before turning to me. I let Ophida loose and stared into the sea of rock over her head, ashamed to meet his gaze. I'd gotten Maher killed, and every line on Nix's face suggested he knew all the grisly details without asking. Nothing, no injury or explosion, or even death, stung worse than the flash of disappointment in Nix's face. I'd let him down, and I had let Maher down when we'd been his last hope.

"The others?" I asked, my voice strained. I had to do something to redirect his focus. Nix looked up from his trance and settled on me. His brow was soft, no sign of anger, but he stared for several seconds, as if translating my words into something understandable. The air grew thicker, and my mouth went dry the longer the silence floated between us. Finally, he gestured back to the hole in the cave wall. Crouching low to maneuver through the obstacles was Tomas, his face as unruffled as ever. More and more weight lifted from me as Rashel and Della followed him out, with Abe trailing in back. An involuntary sob clawed in my throat. "How?"

"I don't know," Nix said, shaking his head. His hair curled into waves on his forehead from sweat and smoke, and I wanted to run each curl through my fingers. The ringlets were so delicate in comparison to the rest of him, an understated softness in the way he'd carried everyone out. My heart squeezed, and I dropped back down to the bank, exhausted from the pendulum of events. The bleak lows tugging me down while I reconciled Maher's death made it impossible for me to trust my own feelings. Of course seeing Nix alive would affect me; it was perfectly natural to marvel at him like this, when he'd been lost forever only a few seconds earlier.

"It got... bad. But then the cave collapsed, and we were able to escape." He paused while the others rejoined our group, dirty and winded, but unharmed. "The falling rocks suffocated the flames and we were able to crawl out." He shrugged to Tomas, as if looking for another explanation, but everyone seemed to be in agreement with Nix's version. Whatever miracle had occurred, they were safe.

I flung myself at Nix, standing on my tiptoes to wrap my arms around his neck. The movement split open the dagger wound in my arm, leaving a trail of blood across my clothing, and his. I hissed, but Nix's embrace was the best remedy the world could offer, so I squeezed tighter.

"Selah, you're hurt!" Nix peeled me back to inspect me from head to toe. I shivered under his scrutiny. *It's just Nix,* I reminded myself again. His mouth fell open when he reached the gash in my upper arm, and then closed when he landed on Maher over my shoulder. I sighed, having avoided this conversation amidst our joyous reunion, but Nix folded deep creases in his brow. "What happened?" He lowered his voice, keeping his hands on my shoulders to brace me.

"Rior," I whispered, afraid of alarming the others. Nix narrowed his eyes. His hands squeezed tighter around my arms until I squirmed under the pressure. "He set us up." My voice broke just speaking about the awful events. "He used Maher as bait to lure us here and... we got separated when the cave caught fire. We made a run for it, but he was waiting. I should have known."

A fresh supply of tears arrived in spite of my best effort to keep them at bay. We'd walked right into a trap. I'd fled when Nix and the others were lost, and I'd let Maher die–right in front of me while I did nothing to stop it. Once again, I'd allowed this to happen to me–*to us.* Nix drew me back into his chest and held me. I clung to his tunic and breathed through the smoky scent, finding the traces of cedar and dew. Safety was such a novel concept out here, and yet I held a piece of it. Andren had Sewn himself to me in some ancient unbreakable bond, but even that crumbled away in all this destruction. Nix was my only true sanctuary.

"Where is he now?" Nix asked. The vibrations in his chest reminded me of the quaking earth before the cave collapsed.

"He ran off. They have the second item."

Nix didn't respond, but the race of his heart told me all I needed to know. We had to head him off, but not yet. I wanted to cling to the respite of Nix for just a few seconds longer, and Nix obliged.

Chapter
Twenty-Four

With no immediate plan and a river at our disposal, we washed the soot from our bodies in the bitter current. I chanced washing my hair, knowing I'd regret it later that night, but drowning the blood and grime in the river was the reset I needed to climb back out of the ravine. After Nix bandaged my arm with one of the cravats from the first aid pouch, he worked my wet locks into a loose braid, then tucked it under one of the caps from my bag.

"What do we do about him?" Rashel pointed to Maher, still laying in a pool of blood where he had fallen.

"We send him to the Halls of Dead." Tomas's solemn guidance knocked at my tender rib cage. The old man pulled a flint starter from the pocket of his trousers while we all watched in silence. He opened Maher's pack and covered him with his tunics and wool blankets. Once he was shrouded, Tomas walked the banks of the river until he returned with five large driftwood logs. He arranged the pyre to his satisfaction, then lit the blankets. Tomas worked as if the rest of us didn't exist, and no one dared interrupt. The ceremony was so simple, just a fire in the night, unnoticed by the island of Casted hundreds of miles away. None of their funerals were public, if they held them at all. Dying was reserved for the poor. Tomas gave Maher a dignified sendoff only a working classman could do.

"Goodbye, Maher," I whispered. I'd barely known him, but I felt his loss somewhere adjacent to my mother. They weren't on the same scale necessarily, but those were the only two deaths that had touched my life. Never experiencing something like this was a distinct Casted privilege that I'd been too naive to see before.

"Let's get out of this place," Nix said, and I agreed.

I dozed in and out of awareness while Nix carted me like an infant over mountainous trails, until he finally laid me down at a location Nix deemed safe for our weary party to rest for the night. In the haze of comfort and safety brought by Nix's nearness, I'd neglected to consider where we were headed. I honestly didn't care, so long as Nix was carrying me there.

"He won't take this route," Nix said in a hushed voice as he prepped our tent. "The maps make it look impassable so he'll go around." My mind flashed to the tick marks on the map. We were going to traverse directly over the spine of the Andalls, the highest point in all the Dominion. Dejectedly, I scanned over my wrapped arm and tattered pant legs, knowing that was only the surface.

He intended for us to reach the final passage back to the training ground before any of the other teams. We'd lay in wait for them to make their descent with their objects, and then we'd act. I inched my way into the lean-to and hunkered down into my parka, considering the possibilities of what that could mean. Nix leaned back next to me, his shoulder grazing my uninjured arm.

"I know," I said. There were so many other words hanging between us, but I lacked the capacity to say them. It was probably for the best; nothing on the tip of my tongue would help this situation. Nix shifted. Maybe he sensed the weight of things unspoken, or maybe he was just trying to get comfortable in the tight confines of the tent.

Even in the restricted space, the cold seeped into my pores. My fingers trembled until untying my bootlaces became a chore. I gave up and yanked my feet free, and then chucked the shoes outside the tent. Nix arched his eyebrow at me with a shadow of a smirk. I'd deal with him, and whatever critters found my boots, tomorrow. I undid my hair and started to comb it with shaking hands, but the clawing ache in my bicep stole what little dexterity I had left. Instead of tying it back up like I should have, I hurtled the leather strap across the tent in frustration. My eyes welled from the mounting frustration, but I squeezed the dampness away.

Wide arms pulled me backward and wrapped around me. It was too much. His kindness and his comfort were more than I could bear, and I came undone. Hot, wet tears flowed into Nix's tunic, leaving it stamped with salt. He laced his fingers through my hair in gentle strokes, wiping the damp clumps of curls from my temple. I wept until I went still, nothing left in me to give. But Nix didn't release me from his arms. Instead, he lowered us into our parkas and tucked me against him, the same wall of security that carried me out of that ravine and all the way here. I clung to his arms like they were my lifeline in a churning sea.

We laid like that for the rest of the night, not quite sleeping but unmoving. I prayed to stave off daylight, to postpone stirring free from the safety net woven around me. But it came tumbling in anyway. When the light broke through, Nix rustled out of the tent. I sensed his hesitation in the entrance before he walked away to check on everyone else. Alone in the vacant tent, my skin prickled in the cold where Nix's arms had just been. I looked down at my rumpled tunic, pleated from his bodyweight, and refused to admit the remnants of his presence were affecting me in unspeakable ways.

To compound the growing list of things I didn't want to acknowledge, Andren had been dead silent. He had to have felt my turmoil no matter the state of our Sewing, but he'd kept his distance from me. I'd known it down in the ravine, but hadn't put my finger on it–a night of restlessness solved that, though. Tar stained my emotions as I put the series of events back together in my head. While I was being attacked, beaten half to death, fighting for my life, Andren hadn't been there. But Nix was. It was Nix who carried me back, who dressed my wounds, and who held me while I was most vulnerable.

But Nix was forbidden. I clamped my jaw. My heart tore under the strain of my treacherous sentiments. Andren was my fiancé, a powerful Governor who had gone to great lengths to bring us together. He had committed himself to me in a deeply sacred way, and I had given myself over to him. I loved him. I loved Andren so much I was traipsing through a literal hell to be with him. I lost my mother for him. My chest spasmed until I doubled over. I had to get out of this stupid tent.

I wet the sleeve of my tunic with my canteen and started dabbing the dried tears from my face. I knew I was falling victim to my own inexperience. Nix was Andren's confidante, his most trusted advisor, and he was doing nothing more than Andren had asked of him. I was the one fabricating ghosts of emotions because Nix had shown me kindness, my childish feelings misdirected.

And there it was. Right as I swallowed away my duplicity, dressing myself in a fresh tunic, welcoming the sting from my wounded arm, I felt it. *Andren.* Andren tapped against my navel, distant but steady. Maybe nearly dying had been enough penance for him—I'd shown enough remorse. He was here, just as he promised, and I needed to do everything in my power to get back to him. *No more distractions.* The stakes had been raised to a staggering height—people had died to complete the Trials—and I couldn't indulge my frivolous emotions. What other choice was there? Dressed and recentered, I emerged from the tent.

Finally out of biscuits, Abe had spent most of his watch scrounging the forest for food. He had a smorgasbord of berries, mushrooms, and even two rabbits he managed to trap. For the member of the team who'd been chosen last, he was certainly proving his worth.

"My father is a wild-game hunter," he said with a shrug. Tomas knelt with Cecil and Ophida, showing them how to ignite kindling with flint. Once he had a spark, he sent them to fetch firewood from the forest floor while Abe skinned the rabbits. The smell of meat roasting transported me back to Oberin with our elaborate dining room and golden serving platters. I envisioned our butler standing over me as I took my first bite.

If the message from Andren hadn't done the trick, the hearty meal did. My belly was full and my head clear, washing away any specks of doubt with a swig from my canteen. After our impromptu breakfast by the river, Nix and Tomas once again spread out the map on the ground with the rest of us looking over their shoulders.

Nix had removed one of his boot laces and was pinning it to the map as a makeshift protractor, marking different lengths and assessing various points in the mountains. I noticed he had scrolled several new markings on the map, adding in more land features and detail to the ground we had traversed. His talent as a cartographer was undeniable.

"We're cutting Rior off here." He pointed where the path in the mountains appeared to drop off several miles from the road back to Hanover Hall. "We will head off the other groups as they pass." Nix's outline sounded so simple, but the thought of being face-to-face with Rior made the rabbit roil in my stomach. The cloud of hesitation emanating from the group was palpable, but no one wanted to let Nix down. We cleaned up our camp and marched back into the snowy peaks like the dutiful soldiers we were.

The river began to narrow as the day faded away, growing rougher and more demanding as we pushed into the highest elevations. Dusk swept in a damp chill that quickly overtook the remaining glow of sun. Tomas and Nix hiked side-by-side, the gray-haired man taking two strides to every one of Nix's, but still keeping up. I fell towards the back of the line, letting the rest push ahead.

The line came to an abrupt halt, sending me tumbling into Della. I stood on my tip-toes to try to see around the row of bobbing heads, but it was too dark to make anything out. Exasperated, I side-stepped the gaggle and ran to the head of the line where Nix and Tomas had frozen. Immediately, I saw why.

Even in the dark, I could clearly discern all of the land unfurling in front of us was pitch-black, like a cancerous tar that had bubbled up from the earth. It reeked of abomination, setting every hair on my head on end. Everything in my line of sight was painted black. All of the foliage was dead and the trees jutted from the ground like unholy daggers. The whipping breeze evaporated, leaving the air stale and thick. Sulfur and decay permeated my nostrils. My muscles twitched with uneasiness, actively trying to restrain me from advancing any closer.

"Ain't right," Tomas said as he absorbed the desecrated landscape. Nix's entire body was petrified, suspended from any animation. His typical mahogany complexion had gone sickly gray and his jaw was slack. I tried to catch his attention, but his glazed eyes were transfixed on something unseen. Tomas didn't need to expand his statement; the mounting dread in my gut was proof enough. It wasn't right.

"Nix," I called, but he didn't respond. I reached out to grab his arm and realized he was shaking. I tasted bile and a sourness I'd come to dread. *He's scared.* The unyielding beast of a man was scared, and it staked me straight through my core.

Panicked, I extended my arms to Nix's face while Tomas and the others looked on in disbelief. I clamped his jaw in my hands and cranked his face toward mine. He made no attempt to resist, but he wasn't there to fight back. His pupils bled over into the brown of his eyes, making him look inhuman. The sight of him against the blackness of this place turned my blood to ice. Dread crushed me, and my brain spiraled trying to figure out why. Nix had no weaknesses, but something was horribly wrong with this place if it could reach him.

"Nix," I screamed at him. A beat later, his eyes focused on mine as horror materialized across his face. I released him.

"What's wrong?" Rashel cried as she pushed past me. "What's wrong with him?" She made a move to grab Nix's arm, but he jerked and angled it as if unhinged, forcing her to reconsider. She crossed her arms tightly over her chest.

"I-I don't know," I said. Helplessness tumbled from my words like fat drops of failure. Nix had saved me several times, and I could do nothing to pull him from this.

I pivoted around to try and see what had triggered Nix's reaction, what had set him off in such a way. The stagnant air rang with a blood-curdling shriek, snapping my attention into the landscape. Ophida had veered off the trail, standing erect in the gnarly black tree line. She screamed again, pointing to something in the forest. I glanced at Nix, who was still out of sorts. His condition didn't seem to be changing, so I rushed to Ophida. The others followed me, forming a circle around her and straining to see into the tarry woods.

"They're all dead," Rashel murmured.

Dead? Her words bit me like a rabid animal, and as I scanned the horizon closer, the disease threatened to seize hold of my own veins. There, intermixed with the abandoned stumps and decrepit trees, were the shapes of carcasses scattered across the ground. The arms and legs were distinctly human. *Dead. All dead.* A shiver rocked through my body.

Tomas took several steps forward but Cecil grabbed him by the tunic. The old man pushed him away and continued his pensive approach toward the remains. I'd seen enough carnage for the week; I wasn't about to get any closer. Anything that made Nix act like *that* was nothing I wanted to be involved with. Tomas walked side to side, inspecting the damage, before returning to us. His resilience would have been admirable if it wasn't teetering on insanity.

"It's one of the teams," he said.

"Deona?" My mouth betrayed me. Tomas stared blankly at me before shaking his head.

"Different team. Looks like wolves got them." That was all the information we needed to hear to send the others trampling back to Nix, who knelt in the spot where we left him. I inched my way back to the safety of the bank, wolves or otherwise. The whole place flipped my organs upside down, leaving me buzzing with frenetic energy. Pushing me to bolt. Pulling me at the navel to get the fuck out of there, where Andren should have been.

Nix had managed to emerge from his catatonic state, looking subdued but still very turbulent. I reached my hand out to touch his shoulder, but he flinched at the sudden motion, and I pulled back. He rubbed his eyes with flattened palms, as if he could erase everything he'd just seen. I looked from Rashel's pale face to Tomas's, all of us mirroring one another's expression.

"This place," Nix said, the air stuck in his throat. The rest of the team circled around him listlessly, shifting as he uncurled himself back to his full height. His complexion was sallow and his eyes were matte and dull, but he managed to focus on me. *What the hell just happened?*

"Let's go." His voice was hoarse and distant, sounding nothing like the man I'd come to know, but his eyes lingered on mine. They pleaded with me, saying all the things his mouth didn't. I grazed his cheek with the side of my hand, his eyes unblinking when I made contact. The best thing I could do for him was to get him far away from that horrid place. We all needed Nix back, and the longer we stayed, the more we lost him. I signaled for the team to press on, looping my arm through his to lead him somewhere safe. I owed it to him. Andren would want me to take care of him.

Chapter
Twenty-Five

I awoke with a start, my heart beat slamming in my ear drums. Too afraid to move, I kept my head against the ground and leaned over to listen closer. The pine needles rustled about, something heavy shifting in the layers of rock and dirt. Nix hadn't joined me in the makeshift tent tonight, leaving me to grapple with my thoughts alone, and fend off the shadows lurking out there. *Damnit.* The shuffling persisted, no more than a dozen feet away. Whatever was making the noise was close, and large.

I made the tiniest adjustments to lift my neck up and squint through the darkness without alarming the mystery creature. An enormous silhouette slunk around the trees, rasping hard in and out. *Please be a deer. Please be a deer.* But the black shape was far too large. It moved too liquidly to be a boar, and as it drew closer, I realized it stood apex. Not a deer, a *bear.*

My pulse thrummed into a single note as the creature padded closer. The air passing over me shifted the strands of my hair as it chuffed and wheezed. *Don't move.* My muscles fired against the abuse they'd already sustained earlier as I clenched everything as tight as possible. I had no hope of defending myself against a bear, and I was in no state to run. But when it bayed into the night, a surge of chills jerked me into animation. *Shit.* Where the hell was Nix when I needed him? Or had I grown so used to him saving me I just expected it? He had his own problems to contend with, but none of them were carnivorous predators. *Shit. Shit. Shit.* The thing sounded like it was being tortured, cawing and grunting pitifully. My ears pricked. It silenced for a brief second, then erupted in a bitter wail into the wooded canopy. I froze–the sound wasn't a bear at all. *It's human.*

I bolted upright, letting my eyes adjust to the night before I scrambled after the figure. My mind raced back to the ghostly bodies strewn on the forest floor, but the grisly shreds in my memory weren't enough to stop me. Someone was out there, and they were in distress. *Stop letting things happen. To me* and *to my team.* The figure was only a few feet away and I stalked toward it, running right up onto its heels with my heart pounding so loudly I was sure it could hear me. I shrieked a clipped, airy sound as it dropped to the ground in front of me.

Nix.

The familiar shape of his shoulders and shaggy hair illuminated in a beam of moonlight. Nix was now on his side, flailing and arching his back. He gurgled and strained as the oxygen squeezed out of his airway. *He's hurt.* I raced to his side and shook him, calling his name over and over. The flailing slowed, but he continued to mumble and pant. The disoriented movements weren't in pain, though his face suggested otherwise. They were from a dream. *Or a nightmare.* I stroked his sweaty, matted hair and shushed him into a lull. It was disconcerting to witness such a force drowning in vulnerability, compelling me to sprint back to my tent so he could suffer in privacy. But he was in such a defenseless state I couldn't bring myself to abandon him. I sat against his back, consoling him.

"Selah?" He turned toward me, his eyes so wide the whites glowed in the darkness. A sharp wave of embarrassment washed over me to see him like that–so childlike and vulnerable. I should have given him privacy, should have minded my own business and let him work through whatever was happening. His forehead creased as he screwed up his eyes, smashing his palm against his head to silence something deep within. Stabbing pain pinched inside my chest, and it pinned me to the spot. *I can't leave him like this.* I wrapped my fingers in my tunic to keep from running them along his skin, smoothing the lines, letting him know I was there with him. Nix made no noise, just sat in that position, shuddering. I had to do something. Hesitating, I rested my hand on his shoulder in a feeble attempt to steady him.

When he looked at me again, his eyes were sharp and stormy. My stomach squeezed into my esophagus. All of Nix was there and present, focused on me like a vulture to carrion, along with some part I didn't recognize. A new and terrifying part. My muscles pulled at me to run from it, but his stare held too much of a grip. The pin inside me pushed harder. I had to help him, but he was poised to attack at any sudden movement. Nix didn't speak; the only sign of consciousness was the flare of his nostrils. My own voice clogged my throat as I sat suspended, waiting.

Without warning, Nix grabbed me under the arms and lifted me on top of him roughly, just a wisp in his mighty hands. I yelped when he engulfed me with his torso. He was everywhere around me, invading all of my space, consuming me. His warmth, the foreign but familiar feel of his arms around me. It would've all felt *so damn good* if his mannerisms hadn't terrified the shit out of me.

Pushing against his forearms, I struggled to get free, but he only tightened his squeeze. I opened my mouth in protest, and he filled the void of my hesitation with his mouth. Instant shock paralyzed my brain. I could have convinced myself it was a dream if it wasn't for the stubble of his beard stinging my bruised lips. My vision sparked with bright white lights. *I can't do this. This is* Nix. *But damn.* He pushed harder, forcing his way through my resistance. It was pretty flimsy anyway, but the second I stopped lying to myself was the second I was damned. Nix pulled back and stared straight into me.

His lids were half-open but the squall was very much alive, emblazoned. He knew I was lying; I knew I was lying. I'd been so careless to dance around that fact for weeks, and now he was unraveling the facade, demanding me to look back at him. To actually see him for what he'd been this whole time. *I have to stop this. For Andren.* But I couldn't move, and my own voice was pathetically far away. A powerful undercurrent swept all around us, pulling me under, until I drowned in the despair, the trauma, and the raw, unbridled *need.* Without another thought, my restraint snapped and I brought his face to meet his, and I kissed him.

Fuck.

I had nothing between us any longer, no physical distance or invisible rules I was prepared to follow. Nix took my mouth without any hesitation, hungry and steaming in the cold air. My mind raced in a blur of colors and smells, the forest moving at lightning speed past me, and yet I couldn't form any coherent thought. He let his tongue close the distance between us and I tasted him. Salty, earthy, and more real than anything I'd ever experienced. *Stop this, Selah. This is too far.* But that voice wasn't mine, and I didn't have to listen to it.

I dragged my lips to the corner of his mouth, hanging on its fullness. Is this what I'd been missing, this *high*, from keeping everything locked down so tightly? Could people really exist so *unrestrained*? Those lips I'd watched from afar, never once letting myself wonder what they'd taste like. Anything I could have come up with would have paled in comparison. They were off limits, kept on the highest shelf out of my reach. But now that I had them on me, right in my grasp, *I needed more.*

I proceeded to work my mouth along his square jaw to his neck. His skin flamed under my touch, and I devoured it in the cold. When I circled back to his mouth, Nix inched away, keeping the prize just out of reach. I could've screamed in rage but I was panting too hard. This was so bad. No amount of training would give me the strength to stop though. Not after I finally got my fingers on what I'd been withholding. My whole mouth tingled for more and I ached for him in ways that should have scared me, but I didn't give a shit about consequences, so long as I got his mouth back.

A whimper escaped my lips, my desperation betraying me. Whatever control Nix had been yielding flitted away with the wintry breeze, the angles of his face morphing into a predatory sneer. My mouth ran dry. Kissing him had released the spools of tension between us, but this–this was dangerous. He growled low, a noise that undulated through me, touching parts I had to ignore. *I can't let this go on. Too far. This is too far.* His jaw clenched as he locked sights on his prey, and then he pounced.

The full force of Nix hit me like a rock. His body on mine, heavy and hardened. The weight of him smothering away all the emptiness that had grown and festered within me. The dam broke, and all the thoughts I'd buried came flooding out. He felt *so good*–the itch I hadn't been able to scratch for months. Everything I'd been missing. *Craving.* In spite of all my sensibilities, I wanted him even closer. I needed more of that delicious weight to drown out everything else.

As if he read my mind, Nix groped at my flimsy tunic and tore it away like shreds of parchment. A shock of cold bit my skin, but the heat from Nix burned so intensely I feared the flesh would melt off my bones. The contrast made my insides coil but I held steady, fully on display before him. I clenched my abdomen, bracing for the discomfort of my exposure, but it simply wasn't there. Being this close to Nix was more natural than each ragged breath I sucked in, which proved to be a challenge under the circumstances.

Nix worked his large palms around my back and pulled me in, gripping me possessively. I was his to do with as he pleased. *Why doesn't that scare me? What's so wrong with me that I want to be his, no matter what?* But in response, I snuck my own hands under his tunic, skimming the mound of each of his muscles as they reacted to my touch, tensing on my path upward to his chest. That single feeling, of my skin on his, was enough to convince me of anything. He could tell me I was a bird and somehow I'd figure out how to sprout wings and fly around. I'd stifled this for so long, maintaining the ridiculous farce that he was nothing but a companion. Just a servant. There was no way I could keep that up now, not anymore. And I didn't want to. Like a frenzied bird set free, I awkwardly flapped, testing the air, but I wasn't about to go back to the ground.

Nix tracked my movement when I tossed his tunic aside, his shaggy hair tousled on his forehead. I succumbed to the impulse and reached for it, tangling my fingers in the black strands. Damp with sweat, but unexpectedly soft. Just like the rest of him. Nix leaned into my touch, resting his cheek against my forearm. It was such an innate gesture it made my chest squeeze. Feeling me shudder on top of him, Nix sat up and pressed my bare breasts against his chest, cradling me in his lap. The direct contact smoldered endlessly after he pulled away.

"Selah," he whispered into my ear, his mouth leaving a damp trail down my lobe and into the crease of my neck. I angled my head to give way to his mouth. He nipped the tender skin, forcing my own animalistic needs into overdrive. That tiny voice warning me to pull back was drowned out by the sound of Nix's breath in my ear. Hell, if that was the last thing I heard, I'd die happy out here in the woods. I wrapped my legs around his waist, triggering him to lift his pelvis hard into me. The firmness pressing against my neediest places sent me squirming uncontrollably, grinding my hips downward. *Oh, fuck.*

"Fuck," Nix echoed, biting into me before sucking away the resulting pain. He was such a paradox in everything, even the way he kissed me. Nix was rugged, violent, hard, delicate, gentle, attentive. He was every emotion, every sensation spiraled into something far out of reach. But I had him meshed with my flesh, in between my legs, and in my mouth. I could touch him, hold all of him now.

I choked back a scream when Nix flipped me over, hooking his arm under my waist in one easy swoop. He forced me down on the ground, pressing into my back with all of his weight. He growled and pushed his erection right between my legs, daring the trousers between us to hold tight. The air ripped from my lungs and my head swam at the sensation of his rigid manhood against my opening, the friction moistening my undergarments. His mass was overwhelming, bombarding every inch of my space. I begged for him to press harder, to suffocate me.

Nix kept his arm laced under me, harnessing my body against his hips. He forced the loose trousers away, working them around my tangled legs. He wedged his hand deep between us and cupped my budding desire. I cried out when his calloused fingers made contact, hot white sparks of pleasure ringing in my head. Nix worked against my cleft, touching me with a roughness I didn't know I would like. But from Nix–I fucking loved it. My body anchored to the painful sensation, propelling me to a level of intensity threatening to tear me open. I felt myself dripping into his palm. Nix felt the wetness, too, and ferociously shoved my trousers the rest of the way down. I heard the fabric tear under the strain, but I would have ripped them to shreds if it meant I could get closer to Nix.

"Please." I groveled under the force of him, raising the bare curve of my backside. Suddenly Nix backed away. He planted his palms into the dirt and pushed off me, every millimeter of space between us progressively more excruciating. I heaved inwardly against the void, sucking sharp, cold air into my lungs.

"We can't do this." Nix's voice was a rough snarl. I convulsed under the pressure to hold back, and I cried out in actual pain from his absence. I could have hit him, demanded him to come back. Anything to stop this torture. To get him back on me, where he belonged. I'd never be able to convince my body otherwise after this.

"I will never be able to forgive myself if I let this happen," he whispered, his lips pressed into a firm line. My heart sank but I gritted my teeth to fight through the devastation. He was right. His jaw flexed maniacally. "But I might die if I don't." Nix leaned over me, skin so close I could feel it radiating into mine. He was waiting for my signal, hanging by the threads of an impossible decision. I whimpered in response.

"Nix," I started, turning my head to face him. The look in his eye was hazardous, pure recklessness. I watched him against the black night, his chest heaving in and out. His muscular physique was unlike anything on this earth and it was poised to take me if I said the word. Everything in my existence had been so fragile. My home, my life, the Caste, everything was scaled. I had stumbled my way through, looking for something sturdy, something that could support me, all of me. I didn't want to be handled delicately. I wanted to be *fucking shattered.*

He looked at me expectantly, his face softening when he saw my hesitation. I couldn't do this to Andren, and I couldn't let Nix do that either. A shiver rattled over me–a warning. I inhaled, pulling my mind back into my body, and I swallowed the ice away.

"I don't want to hold back anymore."

Nix's eyes clouded, his jaw once again granite as he slid his trousers away in single motion. I had ushered us to the point of no return.

Nix attacked me, forcing me to turn away from him, then ramming me against his body. I felt the satiating weight on top of me, felt his abs flex against my lower back while he lifted my hips to meet his. He singed my skin everywhere he made contact, his legs against my thighs and his fingers kneading at my hips, moving downward. The way he growled when he felt my eagerness for him echoed inside me, vibrating clear down between my legs where Nix stood in wait against my exposed skin.

He reached across my chest with his other arm, completely covering my breast, and pulled me back against him. He staged his knees between mine and shoved them open. My skin scraped against the ground as he spread me wider, throwing me off balance. The movement was rough and jarring, but it was the precise level of dominance I needed. I craved submission after everything today, and I was desperate to forfeit all thought and control to Nix.

He held me suspended into the forest floor, supporting me entirely, pressing his palm into my wetness. The force of his hand against my peak created shockwaves surging low in my gut. I pitched forward to open even more until I was splayed out to him in the night.

Over my shoulder, I heard Nix emit a ravaged snarl. Never letting go of his possessive grip, he jerked my hips backwards and entered me with full force. My cries cut through the trees as I leaned into his thickness. Seeing clusters of stars, I cried out as he pulled back, leaving me quivering with emptiness. Nix thrust again, hammering me with that exquisite, overwhelming pain.

The hollowness of my demolished Sewing was filled with Nix. I was starving for it, receiving it greedily over and over. Our bodies were clammy in the night air as he drove into me harder. But I still needed more. The soul-wrenching ache in my bones left no room for inhibition. I reached behind me and clawed at anything I could make contact with to pull him all the way in—to ravage me completely. He shuddered and choked out a muffled sound before he collapsed into my back. I was enlivened by the power I had over him, despite being very much in his trap. He'd awakened something feral within me.

Nix sank his teeth into my shoulder as the frenzy grew, anchoring himself to keep me from undoing him completely. I cried into the dark as his canines pierced my flesh. We were in a battle to overtake the other, consume them whole. Whatever there was to be lost was already gone and we both knew it. I bucked back and pulled Nix into me, the unbearable tension winding through every cell. He sensed the necessity in my movement and rose to meet it.

Over and over, Nix pushed into me with all of himself, building an explosive, primal energy. The thrust that finally destroyed me was violent, shattering a wall I didn't know I had. I screamed as I shook with an electrifying ecstasy. Nix roared one more time, pushing me over the limit. He pulled away, and the heat of his orgasm melded into my skin as Nix fell to the ground, bringing me with him. I was bruised and battered, barely human, and fully surrendered to him.

Chapter
Twenty-Six

Mounds of dried pine needles were matted in the dirt, the odd dunes amplifying the vacant spot on the ground under the harsh morning light. I swallowed away the grit of slumber and dread that was quickly filling the hollow space in my chest. Nix was gone, but the evidence of our actions still clung to me like my own skin. The stark, bitter sunrise didn't reveal some twisted dream; I had actually done that. I'd crossed the line I didn't consciously know existed until last night. And right then–rumpled and achy from the inside out–my only regret was being foolish enough to think he'd stay the night with me.

I fished in my bag to find fresh clothing. The campsite around me was abuzz with movement and I needed to catch up with the rest of the group. When I peeled one sleeve away from my arm to dress, I saw them–translucent blue and purple marks. I lifted the rest of my tunic away to find bruises forming underneath, and the fraying bandage around my bicep. Ratcheting my neck to survey the damage from Rior, I spied the teeth marks on my shoulder. The spot ignited under my touch. Nix had marked me, branded me as his to the point I worried the others would be able to see his signature straight through my clothing. *But where is he?* And what would he think when he faced all this in the light of day?

Reality sped into me, escorted by a queasy restlessness. My little game of pretend was over–Nix knew how I felt about him, and I couldn't lie to myself anymore, either. Somehow I'd have to drag myself up this damn mountain with Nix in my view and Andren in the folds of my brain the entire way. How had I let this get so fucked up? Wasn't the outlook bad enough without throwing in a one-night stand with my fiancé's most trusted advisor? I keeled over, overcome by the brewing turmoil that felt like soot in my belly. There was nothing but ash where Andren should have been, and it was my fault.

"Selah." A deep voice jerked me from my frenzy. I wiped my crusted eyes, not wanting to face him. If I ignored it a little longer, maybe it would all fade away.

"Selah," he said again, softer this time. "It's time to go." A heavy hand landed on my shoulder, covering the fresh bite wound. I flinched, but his hand didn't retreat. Instead, it moved down the side of my forearm, dodging my injury, while his other arm rose up to meet it. He held me in his grasp, ducking down in front of me. Then his hands were on my chin, tugging it gently, nudging me in his direction. *Resist him.* Like I should have last night. But his pull was too strong and I looked up at him.

"You okay?" he asked.

My stomach twisted in its turbulence. Of course I wasn't okay, but my neck creaked as I nodded anyway. I wasn't going to feel okay again, but saying otherwise wouldn't help anything right now. I just needed to get up, force my limbs to move, and to put as much distance between whatever *this* was. At least I could help my team, since it was too late for me.

Nix saw right through my feeble gesture, however. His eyes darted from my face to the trail of scattered clothing, quickly stacking everything up. The rush of his sigh sent a tendril of hair tumbling over my cheek. I swiped it away, hoping to preemptively wipe away the wetness forming in the corner of my eyes. *Don't fall apart. Not now.* But Nix bent over and gathered me like an infant. I couldn't be back here–back in his arms. This was the very spot that both comforted me and catapulted me into ruin. I pushed against his chest, but he squeezed tighter, until the screaming in my ears faded just enough.

"The others are about to push out, but we can wait here as long as you'd like," Nix said. *Forever*, I thought. "And I'm sorry I wasn't there when you woke up. I assumed you'd want to avoid the line of questions if someone found us...like that." I snorted in reply. I couldn't help it, as inappropriate and juxtaposed as it was to the gravity of *this*. Nix raised a black eyebrow at me.

"I'm sorry," he repeated, resting his hand on my knee. I stared at him, the sunlight drawing out the warm brown dimension in his dark eyes. Before I could mouth the words *for what?* Nix beat me to it. "For last night. For everything. I should have never put you in that position, and I-I should have never been so rough with you." The words peppered me, and I flushed in response as wisps of our rendezvous flashed in my mind. *Shit, am I supposed to feel guilty for that?* The weight of his stare on me told me yes, but I'd be lying to the universe if I said otherwise.

"Don't," I said. "I'm not sorry, and I'm not some breakable Lady."

"I know that," Nix replied. He squeezed his fingers on my bruised knee, summoning my pulse beneath his hand. I relished in the pain, knowing he'd branded me. As if my whole situation wasn't fucked enough, I relished the aftermath of Nix. He exhaled loudly in resignation, as if there was anything else we could say to one another.

I looked out at the crowd of team members lining up along the hill, blissfully lolling about as they waited for the signal. How nice that luxury must have been; they had a clear path out of the Trials, ready to follow a singular direction. There was nothing pulling them backward. Even if the Ancient Ones could split me in half and send one piece to complete the Trial with every ounce of it focused on the life I'd left behind, leaving half here with Nix would never be enough. This beast of a man had encroached on my entire existence. As if the trail of his marks wasn't evidence enough. I softened as Nix gazed at me. *Does he always have to be so supportive?* I deserved exile at best.

Nix allowed me to marinate in his presence for a few more minutes before I rose to my feet. Somehow I had to pretend I was still human, like my whole life hadn't shifted last night. *Better get this over with.* Sensing my unease, Nix marched ahead to rejoin the others, staying far ahead in the line as we marched into the morning. The separation was both tortuous and the exact relief I needed to think about anything but him, especially as the hike took a treacherous turn mid-day.

The rocks along the trail grew craggy and sharp, and the trees became fewer and fewer as the walkway dwindled. The wind cut at my face, tearing open my swollen lips. My heart strained beyond its normal capacities, for more reasons than I wanted to consider right at that moment, and forced droplets of sweat down my temples in spite of the temperature. At least the burn in my thighs and limited oxygen supply kept my head clear.

Eventually the line of competitors moved almost vertically, the incline much more severe than our original path down. Nix hadn't been kidding about going straight over the mountains. The air was paper thin and glacial, inflicting pain anywhere it clipped exposed skin. I shrugged the heavy parka higher on my shoulders and hastened my gait to catch up to Nix at the front of the line. We had paused our march. *Finally*. He and Tomas were huddled over a stack of timber against the granite, working a piece of flint in a tuft of kindling. We were well above the tree line, and I briefly wondered where they'd stashed the wood.

"We shouldn't risk a fire." Tomas spoke before I had a chance to come up with something to stay. I hung back awkwardly while the two deliberated.

"I know," Nix said. "But would you rather someone find us alive or frozen to death?" Tomas shrugged and continued to strike the flint rock. It seemed to groan against the frigid air, resisting every spark it released. I couldn't blame it. After a bit of effort on both the stone and Tomas's part, he finally produced a plume of fire that attracted the weary travelers like moths.

"My toes feel like icicles," Rashel said, untying her boots to hold up her stockinged feet. Even that small amount of work seemed too taxing, and I plopped down exactly where I stood.

"At least you can still feel." Ophida rolled her eyes before drawing herself into a tight ball at the base of the flames. Nix wrapped his arms around me and reeled me into his lap. *What the hell is he doing?* Everyone could see us. Panic warmed me faster than the open flames, and Nix's body on mine made me sweat. I bounced from face to rosy face around the campfire, each one distorted with long, orange shadows.

Nobody gawked at us. In fact, nobody even noticed us sitting together, as if nothing unusual was happening. But it was anything but usual. I had my complete betrayal and utter undoing on display, so why weren't they as appalled as I was?

Nix rubbed his gloved hands up and down my arms. I'd been burying my tension under layers of clothing all day, but it rapidly melted away with the snow near the fire. Even when he was the source of my problems, Nix managed to help ease them.

"Do you regret it?" he whispered into the back of my head. His warm, damp breath startled me, and I choked on my own saliva. He'd caught me somewhere I couldn't escape from his question, not without attracting a large audience. *Well done, Nix.* I swallowed hard, trying to remove the paste that had formed on the roof of my mouth.

"No." The answer was out of my lips before my brain considered otherwise. The atmosphere was too thin and raw–*I* was too raw–to lie.

I should have regretted it. I should have never given in to that unspeakable part of me, and my stupid weak emotions. I should have considered my fiancé. But I didn't, and my lack of regret was the source of all my guilt. Because that was the cold, ugly truth–I'd do it again if given the choice. Whatever depravity was within me, I didn't know. I didn't *want* to know. But my body had been polarized in its dark fixation. And if I was being completely candid, it was something much more than a fixation. No strength of will would have stopped me from accepting his invitation. Even stacked up against my worst moments, it never *felt* wrong.

Nix's chest heaved up and down against my back. "Do you?" I asked. He had almost as much to lose as I had.

"No," he whispered. "You're all I've wanted since I first saw you in the market, way too fucking beautiful and rare for the Caste, but way too far out of my reach." The gears in my head wound so tightly I thought it would explode. I guess on paper it would seem that way to him, but really, he'd been out of *my* reach.

"This whole time?" I hadn't been dreaming of the magnetism between us, because we'd both wanted this all along. When I thought I'd lost him in the cave and felt my soul crawling out of my body, it hadn't been over the Trials or Andren; it had been Nix. He'd known it as well as I had.

Nix shifted and held me tighter until I could smell the saltiness from his cheek against mine. "I thought it had been obvious." Apparently, I'd had one very large, Nix-sized blindspot.

"Do you think he knows?" *Why in the hell would you bring that up now?* I had to go and ruin the moment, and braced for the impact.

Nix sighed and pulled back slightly. "Many say Sewing is just old lore." I sucked in a large blast of frosty air. Could it really have been possible I'd imagined all those feelings of Andren? "But Noala is renowned for her work among Lower Oberin, and I don't think either of us are destined to get off that easily," Nix said.

I deflated all the way into him. Of course Andren knew. My judgment was obviously clouded in these mountains with all the lies it was trying to ingest. "What are we going to do?" My voice sounded as brittle as my nerves.

"He will still have you," Nix said. "If you want."

If I want? I pushed away from him, letting the cold snake between us. Turning to face him, I glowered at his stony face. His expression melded perfectly with the scenery.

"But I can't do that. Not to him, and not to you." My eyes darted back and forth between his. "Nix–I can't go back to the way things were. Not now."

His temple flexed in the orange glow of the fire. If the others were still seated around us, I was totally unaware. There was nothing else in the world but the two of us right then.

"You don't have to worry about me," Nix replied. "Though I'm not mad you do." He conjured an impish grin that made my palpitations worse. That mouth was so divinely formed, with lips fuller than any Casted man's, and teeth so strikingly white against his skin tone. It looked dangerous; it *felt* dangerous. And I had tasted it.

"H-how do you know he'll still have me?" I gulped, trying to pry my eyes away from his mouth. Even if there was some way my indiscretion had bypassed our Sewn connection, if it truly was a fable, there was no possibility I could live with a secret that huge. And it would be huge in the most literal sense, with this prodigious man looming over my life as a

Governess, constantly reminding me of the unrestrained passion we had shared. That couldn't possibly be what he had in mind for him—for us.

"It is exactly what I told you, Selah," Nix said. "Andren will not risk his pride. The sooner you realize and accept that dynamic in your engagement, the easier it will be for you as his Governess. He cares for you, but he cares for his pride even more." Nix could have slapped me in the face and I would have been less stunned.

"And before you say it, I realize I am not in the position to make a statement like that," Nix said, quieter this time. "I'm not naïve to my bias in the situation, so I don't want you to think I'm being unnecessarily critical of Andren. But I know him better than anyone." Nix watched intently for my reaction but I couldn't produce one. "I know I'm being unfair," he continued. "And you have to deal with repercussions you didn't ask for. But Selah." The way he said my name made my hair stand on end. "I could never regret one second with you. Not when it was the one time in my whole life I was truly free."

I gasped, too dazed to function. Nix's words weighed more than he did. What we did was a betrayal to Andren, but Nix's loyalty wasn't sourced from some exquisite bond—Andren *owned* him. Just as he found a way to own me by sending me here, when I had no other choice.

"And I'll do whatever it takes to stay near you, in whatever capacity that might be. I was never meant to have someone like you, so the fact I was able to have this much is nothing short of a miracle."

I had no response, nothing with enough substance, to form any coherent thought. The look in his eyes was undeniable, and the logical part of me knew it put him at risk just to say what he had out loud. I simply let his words replay over and over, storing them as the fuel I'd need to make it out of this frozen hellscape. Not that anything beyond this would be improved. At least I had Nix here; at least he and I were the same out here.

"Better put the fire out for the night." Tomas spared me from stringing together a response, not that I could. I whipped around to face the group, breaking the spell Nix had been holding over me. Ophida eyed me with mild interest, and Rashel and Della were already asleep. Tomas seemed to be the only member to acknowledge our exchange, but it wasn't disapproval on his face. It wouldn't be. Caution, maybe, but I'd heard his story. Of all people, Tomas knew what we had at stake.

Nix squelched the flames into smoke with his canteen, sending ash into the swirling mountain winds. I tracked the white flakes until they dissipated, jealous of the way they could move so freely in any direction they liked.

"I saved you a spot next to me," Nix called over my shoulder as he scaled the loose shale around us. "If you want it."

The question wasn't whether I wanted it–it was whether I *should* want it. We were well beyond respectable boundaries and there was no need to add hypothermia to the list of my mounting problems. I gathered my things and followed him. He didn't bother with the tent, layering the extra wool blanket over us for additional warmth instead.

I shimmied beneath the blankets, turning to face Nix. He draped his arms around me and pulled me into his chest possessively. His body encapsulated mine, forming a shield that felt too good, too secure, to let the guilt penetrate it. I laced my legs between his and let my body melt into him. Nix leaned in and planted the lightest kiss on my forehead. *At least we can be free for the moment.*

The next day and a half were slow-moving up the frozen face of the mountain. None of us were conditioned for the extreme demand and had to force our bodies to make each step toward the objective. Nix had calculated Rior's arrival to the passage based on the most likely route his team would go, and with the lead they'd had, there was no reason for them to risk traversing the spine. As far as Rior knew, we were no longer a threat to him.

Nix and Tomas pushed us until we had ascended the white crests of the Andalls. Despite the bleakness in our faces, particularly Ophida's matching snowy pallor, Hanover Hall was less than a day away and the passage was within our grasp. We decided to make our final camp just west of the point so we could be well-rested when we executed tomorrow's plan. If my run-in with Rior in the ravine had been any indication, we would need all our strength.

I sat by the dancing warmth of the fire long after the others had retired to their packs, thawing my toes inside my boots. The blissful flames kissed my hands and cheeks, reminding me of sultry lips against my bare skin.

"I'm going to rustle up a few more logs," Nix said as he squeezed my shoulders from behind. My insides went warm from the contact, and the refreshed memory.

"What are you doing?" A high-pitched voice cut into my dreamy state, instantly returning my body temperature to normal.

"Just getting warm," I said to Ophida. She plopped herself in the spot where Nix had been, invading the space I had reserved for him. So much for the intimate moment.

"I know I didn't have fancy tutors or grow up in a mansion, but I'm not stupid, Selah." Ophida curled her knees into her arms, but her stare didn't move off my face. My chest heated in annoyance.

"I know you're not stupid, Ophida," I replied.

"Then what are you doing—with Nix?" My tongue glued itself to the roof of my mouth, making it difficult to swallow my shame away. I looked down at my boots, deciding it was the perfect time to untie them before I retired for night. "Selah," she said again.

I turned to face her pale eyes, glowing red in the fire. "I don't know," I said with a rasp, my voice abandoning me. "But I'm the stupid one."

"Yes," she said. I looked up at her, swearing she hadn't blinked since she sat down. "You're betrothed to a Governor."

"I know." I shook my head. God, did I know.

"Nix is his Hand," she continued. I was used to her snark by this point, but she wasn't being argumentative. She was just speaking the truth.

"Ophida, I know. I don't have a plan here. I never expected Andren to propose to me, and the Ancient Ones all know I didn't deserve that. I didn't intend for any of this to happen." I rambled on and on, not sure if I was talking about Andren, the Trials, or Nix. That was open to her interpretation, I supposed.

She shook her head. After the last Trial, I thought we had make some progress in our...relationship. She'd kept her assaults to a minimum, and had actually been pleasant on occasion. A rare occasion, but it was still something. And it made her judgment sting twice as badly.

"I'm sorry," I whispered. "For letting you down." Ophida straightened her legs and propped herself upright.

"You've never let me down."

"I—what?" I turned to face her, mouth hanging open.

"And you do deserve to be a Governess." She angled her chin in the same familiar manner when she wanted to make herself look bigger—when she didn't want to be challenged. I couldn't think of a single coherent thing to say. "You're not like the other Casted Ladies. You were kind to me, even when you had no reason to be. Casted aren't kind. Which is why you need to be careful."

I still hadn't connected my lips together when Nix plowed up the hill in a rush. He didn't have any logs and his face was twisted into a serious expression.

"What's wrong?" I asked. He shushed me and focused his eyes somewhere in the distance.

"Something is off." He crouched down between Ophida and me, poised in a low squat like he was ready to pounce. I couldn't see or hear whatever he had detected, just quiet mountain air whistling between the rocks, but icy cold dread filled my gut.

"Go wake the others and take them that way." He pointed toward the southern passage in the mountains. "Something is coming."

The urgency in his voice racked my rib cage like a xylophone. Abandoning my gloves and hat, I sprang to my feet and sprinted to the first tent I could find in the dark. I had to get there. I had to tell them. *What*, I didn't know.

"Go get everyone up," I said to Ophida. Her eyes were as wide as dinner plates, but she stood on command and ran off toward the tents.

"Get Tomas," Nix said, then disappeared into the snow-covered crevices.

I found Tomas still upright in his tent, whittling a piece of wood with his knife.

"Nix needs you," I said breathlessly. "Come quick."

Tomas didn't need any other explanation before he, too, jumped to action. Ophida had managed to rouse the others, guiding them toward the cut in the hillside in a file. Their faces were all ghostly and solemn in the dark.

"Go with them, Selah," Tomas said. "I'll find Nix."

I hesitated, struggling to picture the old man fending off a pack of wolves, wielding a sword larger than he was. I should've been the one to stay with Nix, but the look on his face said he wasn't open to debate. Nix wanted me to take care of the others, and I couldn't let him down.

Not now. I nodded before heading toward the opening. As I stepped away, Tomas grabbed my arm hard. I yelped in surprise.

But when I turned around, Tomas wasn't there. I was eye-to-eye with Rior, his ruddy face lit bright red against the firelight. *No.* This wasn't supposed to happen. This couldn't happen. My stomach dropped to my knees when I spied Tomas on the ground, Bodney standing over him with a muddy boot lodged against the old man's back. *How? How did they beat us here?*

"Let him go," I yelled, adrenaline choking out the panic inching up and down my spine. I summoned every drop of bravado I could muster and squared my body to the two men, ready to leap between them and Tomas.

"I know better than to let this group go, now," Rior said, his greasy voice slithering over my ears. "Best to remove a few appendages to keep you all from getting away."

I had to do something. Tomas looked so small and frail on the ground. He needed help, but shadows of my last encounter with Rior pulsed over my flesh. *Where is Nix?*

"Don't touch him," I yelled at Rior, and then I turned and screamed for Nix. My voice fizzled in the cold mountain air. The men just laughed at me and ratcheted Tomas from the ground. This was bad. This was so fucking bad. And it was about to get worse if Nix didn't get here soon.

"Tell you what, *Madame*," Rior sang. "You take his place and I'll let him go. I could go for some *red meat* right about now." I shook with rage, and complete disgust. I needed to run. I needed to find Nix so he could get Tomas to safety. *But I can't leave Tomas with these monsters.*

"Fine." *What the fuck am I doing?* I took a tentative step closer.

Tomas eyed me wildly. "No!" he yelled. "Run, Selah!" But I planted my feet, ignoring the shrieks inside my own head. I didn't have control over my life, but I could at least choose not to tuck my tail and run. I could choose to stay and help Tomas.

"What do you mean?" Rior said to the old man. "This is a wonderful agreement."

I wanted to claw his smug face from his skull, but Bodney kicked Tomas so hard the man cried out. I shrieked and tried to reach for Tomas, but Rior dug his fingers into my arm, leaving his imprints over the yellowed bruises he'd given me before. Several other faces materialized behind Rior–the rest of his team coming to reinforce his threats.

"That's okay," Rior said over his shoulder to his teammates, staving off his dogs. "I can work for it. This is a Trial, after all." He nodded to Bodney, who proceeded to thrust his boot into Tomas's side again. Tomas wrenched into the fetal position and wheezed. *Do something, damnit,* I wailed to myself.

I drove my body downward, pulling it free from Rior's grasp with the swift, unexpected motion, then lunged into the stocky man and tackled him into the ground. As fast as I could, I clambered on top of Rior to gain control with whatever means possible. I straddled him like I had before, but I wasn't letting go of his arms this time. I rammed my elbow against the side of his head and pinned it against his neck. He cursed and thrashed belligerently underneath me.

I pressed my forearm across his neck with my entire weight, forcing the blood and air in his body to halt. I had no intention of stopping until the life drained from his ugly face. He turned a shade of red that shone iridescent against the moonlight, and it catapulted me into a frenzy to push harder. If I survived this, I'd have a dress made in that exact shade. I laid into him with everything I had, determined to silence him forever. A jolt of blinding pain slammed against my temple, swarming me with white hot sparks, and I slumped over.

"Little bitch," I heard somewhere far away, but I couldn't focus on anything around me. Then the second blow came, violent and gut-wrenching to my back, and I felt myself fall from my mount. Rior bucked away from me while I pawed at the earth to keep everything from spinning. He grabbed hold of my injured arm and buried his thumb into the split flesh. I screamed at an unrecognizable pitch, my every cell sizzling in pain.

"I'm done playing with you," he spat. "Where's the rest of your group? You're missing your servant again." *Fuck. Where is Nix?* I didn't dignify Rior with an answer and braced for another blow. Instead, Rior called out into the darkness.

"Go find the others!" He barked at the leering members of his team behind him, who obediently fled into the mountains.

Tomas erupted in an agonizing cry and I scrambled to reach him. I had to get those animals off of him. The dull thuds of bone and meat sickened me, but I teetered back onto my feet, my knees threatening mutiny. I prepared to launch myself back at Rior but this time Bodney intervened. He threw me to the ground, my skull cracking against the granite. The ringing in my ears stunned me, except for the single pervasive thought: *I have to get up.* Tomas was going to die. I was going to die. But I had to get up. I fought against gravity, against my own body, gritting my teeth until a sliver cracked away. But I couldn't do it. I couldn't move. Helplessly, I laid in the cold, listening to Rior and Bodney close in on me.

"What's this?" Bodney asked. The attack was imminent. This was it. But when nothing happened, I forced my eyes open. Rior was huddled over my backpack, now busted open against the rocks with its contents scattered. It was my chance to run, for me to try to get up again, but something in Rior's hand caught my eye. I squinted against the sand in my lids to make it out.

"*The Geomancer?*" He presented the cover to me. "The perfect little *Madame* has been hiding contraband?" The depraved look in his eyes shown brighter than ever.

"Guess she's not so perfect after all," Bodney said.

"I think you're right." Rior's voice dripped menacingly. "I think she *wants* to be bad." I tensed, working my good arm under me to sit up. The last thing I wanted was to face him laying down. Nix wasn't coming to save me, and there was nothing I could do to save myself. This was how it was always going to end. I realized that now. But I sure as fuck wasn't going to die on the ground. He'd have to kill me standing up, like the fucking Lady I was. *More than a Lady*, something whispered. Rior flashed the book over my face, then reached down to skim the edge of my tunic with his grubby fingers. I jerked back, flinging myself away from his grip, but he held onto my tunic and split it down the front.

"Don't fucking touch her." The sound echoed off the mountains, and Rior froze. Relief flooded over the pure rage festering in me, and the ground shook as Nix approached.

"You think I'm afraid of the Governor's overgrown pet?" Rior yelled.

"You should be," Nix replied. I braced myself as the ground lurched.

I must have hit my head harder than I realized. But Rior and Bodney turned to each other, as if they'd felt it, too. Before I could speculate any longer, the pair turned back to Nix. Rior tipped his head and Bodney dutifully forged ahead with his dagger brandished. I could only watch it all unfold in slow motion, my organs wrapping themselves around each other as I looked on.

Instead of lunging for Nix, Bodney swooped down and hoisted me to my feet. He cranked my back against him and held the blade to my throat. Bodney's scent assaulted my nostrils, thick and ripe. I felt the steel graze my esophagus as I swallowed hard. *God no, not like this.* Everything in me beat at a dangerous rate, trying to pound Bodney's hands off of me. Clawing to get to Nix.

"Let her go," Nix said coolly as thunder rumbled in the distance. My ears pricked, luring my consciousness away from the threat. *Stay sharp. Get away.* But then another cadence of thunder sounded, closer this time. I'd never heard thunder in the winter.

"Your girlfriend belongs to me now," Rior taunted from Nix's side. The muscle in his jaw flickered to life–Nix had a plan. He always had a plan.

"This is your last warning," Nix said with a lethal edge in his tone. Lower. Silkier. Deadlier. I shuddered when it rippled over me.

Bodney pressed the dagger against my skin and I let out a ragged cry, a warm trail of blood trickling its way down my neck. Nix closed his eyes and inhaled. *Hurry Nix!* This time I jumped when the thunder boomed all around us, followed by a deafening crack before everything gave way beneath me. Dust and debris pelted the air in a thick cloud. I pushed away from the knife but Bodney's grip tightened on me.

When the cloud of dirt settled, I gasped. The whole mountain face had split open in an angry fissure. *What the hell is happening?* My chest shook with the violent rattle of the earth churning underfoot, like the rock was boiling to life from the inside. It quaked again menacingly.

The whole mountain was liable to crumble around us at this rate, but Bodney held me tighter. Mercifully, the next jolt of the mountain sent me to my hands and knees, throwing Bodney somewhere behind me. I craned my neck to watch the fissure spread from the top of the peak, splintering rapidly toward us. Rocks tumbled and bounced, knocked loose from their resting place.

Rior and Nix had been tossed to the other side of the crack, but Nix was already on his feet, stalking toward Rior. I could practically taste his sickly sweet fear as Nix closed in. His eyes bulged from his head and his nostrils flared with each calculated step Nix took. God, it was so satisfying to see his ruddy face wiped clean of that stupid, smug look. I prayed for Nix to tear it clean off his face.

Debris flew past him, rocks clinking like little pellets, but Nix was unflinching as he swept Rior up by his collar. He lifted him from the ground, the stocky man's feet kicking as he dangled. Nix extended his arm, Rior no more than a wisp in his clutch, and held the swinging man over the chasm. My own stomach somersaulted from the bottomless opening pulling on Rior. Even I doubted what Nix prepared to do.

"N-n-no," Rior cried. Nothing but empty, stinking terror left. Nix had robbed him of what little power he'd had, just as he'd done to me. Bodney looked on, immobile on his hands and knees as the downpour of rubble plummeted around him. *Good, you vile bastard. You're next.* If Nix didn't take care of him, I would.

"You will *never* touch her again." Nix sliced each word into Rior's ear. He reined the flailing man in close before releasing him into the gaping void of the mountain. The stench of him overpowered my senses as Rior plummeted into the broken void. His screams echoed against the stones until they faded into the grumbling ground. I actually felt bad for the mountains that would contain him until he rotted away into the true decay that he was.

Nix bounded across the rift to the other side with an inhuman liquidity. He reached down and pulled me to my feet. I fell into him, letting go of all the strain and force I'd been harboring. He kissed me, hard and unbridled, until I tasted blood and my insides burned white hot. My mind went completely blank under the onslaught of relief.

When Nix released me, he was looking over my shoulder instead of down at my face. His jet black pupils narrowed, tracking movement somewhere behind me. I pivoted, spying Bodney slithering off into the mountains. Rage refilled the void in my brain. We couldn't let him get away. *Go Nix,* I urged. But he made no move in Bodney's direction. *Go!*

The tension in Nix's muscles melted away, as if he was relaxing after a long day's work, and he went perfectly still. *He's going to get away!* I practically jumped onto Nix's back to ride him like a steed after Bodney, but he closed his eyes instead. He held them closed as deafening cracks blasted over the mountain. My heart pounded while I searched for the source of the noise, which grew louder with each *thump*. An enormous boulder bounced from high up the summit, striking viciously as it tumbled down.

Bodney heard the commotion, too, and cut left to get out of its path. I stood frozen, watching the scene like I wasn't actually there. Bodney sprinted in the opposite direction, racing toward the cut in the side of the mountain, but the rock veered sharply and changed courses. I rubbed my eyes. *The whole fucking rock just shifted.* If I hadn't known better, I would have sworn it *purposely* turned toward Bodney. It bounded one more time before it careened into his body, slamming him down and sandwiching him into the stone before it rolled to a gentle stop. Bodney was left contorted at impossible angles, nothing moving but a tuft of his hair in the residual breeze.

Roused by the noise, the remaining members of Rior's team funneled into the clearing. Rior and Bodney may have been gone, but we still had to contend with the rest of their group. The men took in Bodney's lifeless body before turning back to us. I thought I heard one of them mutter Rior's name, but it could have been the quaking earth around us. The mountain trembled ruthlessly, and one of them dropped to his knees. The other charged toward us, carrying on the mission Bodney had started. We'd gotten lucky with the inexplicable, yet well-timed disaster. I didn't think we'd be so lucky if all of them charged at once, no matter how big Nix was.

The earth quaked and quarreled around us, heightening its demand and pulling a whimper from me. Nix squeezed my hand, but he remained statuesque. Why the hell wasn't he doing anything? We needed to run, before one of the boulders got a piece of us. Or one particularly savage-looking candidate, who was moving swiftly toward our location. Urgency bled into my chest, but Nix still didn't ruffle. He held us in place, hand-in-hand, as the mountain unleashed.

I gritted my teeth to brace for impact. Through the narrow slits of my eyelids, I watched a thunderstorm of rocks bounding downward, smashing and cracking as they rolled across the steep slopes. It was louder than anything imaginable, and my eardrums ached at the assault. Any trees or debris in their path snapped like twigs under the battery of destruction. I choked on the dust spilling through the air, but I primed my legs and tried to retreat. Nix didn't budge though.

"Nix!" I yelled but he either couldn't hear me over the barrage of rock, or he simply ignored me. Instead, he raised his free hand into the air, as if conducting a symphony of screaming stone, and closed his eyes. His flesh against my hand burned at an impossible temperature, but I held on for dear life–too petrified to release my lifeline.

The cascade grew even larger, now a full-blown landslide crashing and shaking the mountains like they were nothing more than eggshells. I flinched with each shrieking snap of rock breaking apart, swallowing us up in the flurry of shrapnel. We had to get out of here, but he wouldn't budge. Nix was going to kill us all, as if granting me my wish to stay in the mountains with him. The sickening thought doubled me over, but Nix wrapped his forearm around my torso and steadied me.

I screamed his name again as a massive boulder the size of a small house plummeted down the side of the mountain, heading directly at us. He straightened his back while I tugged frantically at his hand. Every hair follicle stood to try and run.

"Nix, let's go!" I begged, tears turning to clay on my cheeks from all the dust. "Please!" But it was too late. The bolder bounded at us, a beat away from where we stood. I squeezed my eyes shut and turned into his arm.

Nix threw his hand into the air, pulling my face with it, but I didn't understand anything that happened after that. My eyes detected the images in front of them but my brain failed to reconcile the events against any logic or reasoning. The boulder stopped in its tracks. Even more impossibly, Nix *moved* it. There was no way Nix could have actually shifted that boulder, but that was the lie my brain told me as I watched from my paralysis. There was nothing else to explain the way the rock followed the direction of his hand. *Except I've finally lost it.* I was honestly surprised it took that long to go crazy here. The boulder veered around us before swallowing the remainder of Rior's group in one gulp. I gagged on the dirt and carnage, falling to my knees at Nix's side.

Nix gestured again, seemingly lulling the maelstrom of gravel with a flick of his wrist. The cacophony of everything screeching to a stop in front of us jostled my head, blurring my vision in and out of focus. When I blinked it away, everything stilled. I opened my mouth to scream, or just to breathe, but my jaw hung in disbelief.

"Are you okay?" Nix asked.

No, I am not okay. I was either dead or hallucinating, but I sure as fuck wasn't okay.

My mouth opened and closed several times. *I'm not okay. Nothing is okay.* Nix cranked my eyes up toward his then wiped the sediment from my cheeks. He searched my face and I focused on the little creases spidering out from the corners of his lids. This whole fucking scene couldn't be real, yet here he was, in the flesh. Warm, breathing, sweating flesh.

I asked the only question I could think of. "What are you?"

"It's all true," Nix whispered to me, eyes glistening with each word. *What the hell is he talking about?* "The book." I sputtered and coughed on the thick air. Nix was shaken up, and he wasn't making sense. "I'm one of *them*, Selah."

One of what? I didn't know if I'd said the words in my head or out loud, but Nix squeezed my shoulders in response. The bruises activated another realization, a much more tangible one.

"Tomas!" I yelled. The old man had been left unconscious, right in the rockslide's path. Nix's chaos would have to wait. A fresh wave of nausea overtook me. We had to find him, if there was anything left to find.

"He's alive," Nix said, walking way too calmly toward the location we'd last seen him. I almost asked how he knew that, but nothing else would've struck me as unbelievable by that point. As long as we could find Tomas *alive*, I didn't care how he knew.

Nix paused near a pile of rubble and sifted through the debris. I went lightheaded and had to catch myself on a nearby chunk of stone when he retrieved a limp silhouette from somewhere underneath. Nix slung Tomas over his shoulder.

"He needs help," he said, as if I needed clarification. That was the one answer I had.

I looked around at the foggy scene—everything painted gray from the thick coating of dust. "Let's find the others and get the hell out of here." I eyed Nix warily, but he nodded and marched toward the pass where we'd told them to hide.

My spine tingled knowing that our teammates were somewhere out there. There was no time to consider what had just happened. And definitely not *how.* I pushed all my questions into a corner and forced my legs to run in spite of the nagging pain in my hips. A dozen feet away from the fold in the mountain, where the passage began, Nix paused to examine something in the rubble. I caught up with him as quickly as I could, fearing the worst. What if Rior had gotten to them first? What if they'd been out here when it all came down?

I followed his gaze to a patch of sandy hair and waxy fingertips poking through the rock pile. My gut twisted into a sharp knot, pushing bile into the back of my throat. I looked at Nix in horror as he kicked at the rocks. Ophida's hair flashed in my vision. *Please don't be them.*

"What are you doing?" I yelled, terror bleeding into my voice. Nix kept digging at the debris, ignoring my demand. But then I saw why and clamped my lips closed. He reached down and shook something free. The gold sheen poked through the thick layer of dust on the object.

"The shield!" I gasped. *He found their shield!* With the beginning of the Trial just a distant memory, I'd completely forgotten about our objective out here. After our run-in with Rior, it had shifted to *survive,* never mind anything beyond that. But if we wanted to advance to the final Trial, if I still held onto anything of my old life, we needed our shield back.

"Both of them." Nix beamed, flipping it around to reveal one more shield tethered to the back. I should have been overjoyed, but dread weighted my boots to the earth. The shields in his hand solidified it. We still had to live through another Trial, and the first two had nearly killed me. Worse than that, I had no idea what else they could possibly throw at us after all this. Clearly there were no limits to what they'd do to test us. And I had no assurance I'd have Nix at my side.

I only caught my first taste of relief when I spotted Cecil's vivid red hair against the monotone collage of mountain. A muffled squeal escaped my mouth. Standing at his shoulder was Abe, arms crossed as he spoke to Della. Rashel lingered behind them, and Ophida crouched on the ground, fixated on something far in the distance. Her eyes sharpened when we took another step forward.

"Look!" She alerted the others, triggering all their faces to turn to us in unison. I noticed *more* eyes off to the side. Another group jumbled together, too frightened to pose much of a threat. I quirked my eyebrow at the intruders, but clearly our team wasn't worried about sharing a hiding place with them.

"We found them on their way up the passage and warned them about Rior," Rashel explained. "They just want to get back safely." Nix looked down at me, chewing on something unspoken before walking up to the others. One of the men cowered as he approached, taking in the unconscious body over Nix's shoulder, but Nix didn't slow. He pulled the shields from the straps of his backpack and held them up. It took the man a second to process what he was looking at, but he snagged it from Nix's hand when he extended it forward.

"Thanks to Rior, we have an extra."

The boyish-looking man turned the metal object over in his hands, mouth slackened and eyes wide. "Thank you," he said to Nix, who tipped his head in acknowledgment.

My heart squeezed. Somehow I'd shuffled through every emotion in the spectrum in just a few short minutes. It was exhausting, and my legs shook beneath me as if the mountain was still quaking. I wiped a bead of sweat from my forehead, then reached for Nix's free arm.

"Let's get back."

Chapter Twenty-Eight

"Congratulations on the completion of your second Trial," the Commissioner announced across the dining hall. Even with only two teams inside the sprawling room, the domed ceiling pushed down on us, and the walls constricted my windpipe. Nothing about being inside felt natural, even with its radiating warmth and platters of food. I craved the freedom of the wilderness.

"We need a healer," I yelled. The Commissioner didn't react, but Officer Pickham stepped forward, peering at Tomas over his nose.

"In due time," Pickham said. We didn't have time.

"He needs help now!" My plea echoed against the stone walls. Pickham and the Commissioner whispered something too quiet to detect. If they wouldn't do something, I would. "We're taking him to Medical." I yanked at Nix's sleeve but the Commissioner held up his palm.

"Stay and eat," he said, too softly for the situation. "You must rest before your final Trial begins in the morning. We will get your *friend* to the healer." He folded two fingers, summoning a team of men in red cloaks. They glided at us, retrieving Tomas from Nix's arms, letting his head bob against their red sleeves. He didn't look good. Thankfully, they didn't waste any more time and carted him out of the hall.

I couldn't go through this again. A third Trial was unfathomable, and it only guaranteed more suffering. And no way to Nix. No matter the outcome, I had no way out of this twisted loop. I studied Nix's profile, taking in his angular jaw and straight nose. Even if I got out of here unscathed, I was still bound to lose him.

I didn't sit down. My legs gave way and I fell to the bench, the other six members of our team taking their seats around me. My fingers were still numb but I attempted to pick at the plate of meat and potatoes, sliding pieces around with my fork. It was all so dense and rich, the overpowering flavors turning my stomach sour. I wanted rest, but I wasn't ready to be alone with my thoughts.

My footsteps echoed against the floor of the dorm after the Commissioner released us, the bunks looking like strange monuments as I passed. Nothing had moved, yet everything had changed since we'd last been here. Our bunk loomed in the corner, the very last in the row, but I didn't want to sit down. Not yet.

I threw my pack up top, not making eye contact with Nix, and rushed to the bath house instead. Maybe the warm water would wash away whatever spell I'd fallen under out there. I found the bath house completely deserted, a victory better than the second Trial, and the water was boiling hot–the exact temperature my weary bones needed.

Once clean, I padded back to the dorm, but Nix wasn't in his bunk. Too tired to climb, I plopped on his mattress. He'd left his things on top of his covers, so I picked up his comb and aimlessly started brushing the knots and brambles from my hair. At first it felt like an invasion of his personal belongings, but then that seemed ridiculous after all that we'd exchanged the last few days. Sharing a comb should be nothing.

"They wouldn't let me see him." Nix startled me from my trance. He held onto the top bunk and leaned in, watching me maneuver through my long, wet strands. If he was upset about his comb, he didn't show it.

"What are we going to do?" If that wasn't the question of the century. The mattress dipped as he sat down next to me, tilting me toward him. My body pulled to his warmth on its own volition—practically reflexive. Despite the calm of his touch, I shuddered at the flash of rock and silt, and the ghosts of crashes and screams in my head.

"Right now? We're just going to do whatever we have to," Nix said, taking the comb from my hand and gathering my hair in his. He didn't say anything else. He just worked his fingers through sections of my hair, braiding it with a wrinkle of concentration painted across his forehead. I ran my hand along his work absentmindedly, wishing everything could be wound together just as easily. Every strand of my life was a tangled, frizzled mess.

"I don't have a good explanation for everything." Nix broke the silence, catching my wrist and pulling my hand in his lap. "But I know you're a part of it." I thought I'd be able to stave off this conversation until the morning, if not forever. Everything was still so disjointed in my mind, flashing at random intervals, slicing what was left of my nerves. *Boulder flying. Rior falling. Nix and me. Me and Nix. Nix and the boulder.* I doubted any explanation he could produce would help, especially when it was far easier to chalk it up to my head injury.

"Nix, I–" He nudged my chin with his fingers and eased my mouth closed.

"It's okay. I should have told you sooner, but I didn't know how. And then everything I did know changed when I met you." He released his hold, but my mouth flopped open. "I don't expect you to understand right now, because I don't understand it. But I think the book is true, Selah. I think I'm a Geomancer."

I clamped my mouth shut with a snap. "That book is fiction. And even if it wasn't, the Geomancers would have died hundreds of years ago." I shook my head so hard I lost sight of his dark eyes. Nix was always upbeat, playful even, but he wasn't one to tell tales. That startled me more than anything. "It's impossible."

He braced his massive palms around my cheeks, then brought his face directly in front of mine. His pupils had consumed every spec of his irises and his breathing quickened against my nose. *Heat, steam, cold. Heat, steam, cold.* "Selah," he whispered mere millimeters from my mouth. I wasn't in any danger, but my heart pounded furiously against my sternum. "I think I was there."

This time I laughed out loud. Nix's hands fell into his lap but he maintained the same intensity in his stare. As strong as he was, even he had to be rattled by the events of the Trial. Maybe this was his way of dealing with it, rationalizing the carnage away. He had to be in shock–what human wouldn't be?

"I'm serious." His voice had an edge he didn't normally use with me. "I wanted to tell you after the fire, but there was no way I could explain it without making you think I was crazy. And maybe I am. But Selah, I don't know how old I am. I don't know when I was born, or where I came from." Nix hunched his shoulders as the words poured out of him, leaving him deflated in front of me. I summoned the night he sat in this very bunk, telling me about his childhood and how his adopted father had found him wandering the mountains. He'd looked just as fragile then, like the truth had infiltrated his brains and bones.

"I know," I said. "But you can't be more than a quarter century old, not *hundreds* of centuries. Only the Casted live that long." I hated drawing attention to his lesser status, but we were well past niceties.

"That's the thing–I don't live that long. I haven't lived that long. But I do know I've lived multiple lives."

"You *what*?" I coughed, nearly throwing myself off the side of his bunk. When I regained my balance, I put my palm up to his forehead to see if he was feverish. Nix swatted it away, but gave my knee a gentle pat before he rested his hand.

"I don't know how or why, but I can't die," he said. I inched backward. This was going too far. He needed rest and so did I. We'd barely survived out there, and it was very clear that the effects weren't going to release their chokehold on Nix right away.

"You are the most amazing person I've ever met," I said, going breathless to let everything inside come out in the open. "But it's very dangerous to think like that here. You can't be reckless." Nix blinked at me, one eye at a time, then shook his head. He gathered up my hands again, cupping them between his, and drew me in conspiratorially.

"I mean, I can die," he whispered. "But somehow I *come back*. The details are fuzzy because most of my memories are wiped clean when it happens, but there are shreds of the old ones. Shadows of me before. When Ephraim found me on the mountain, it was after I'd died. I remember that part."

"You... come back." I repeated him, not in question–no explanation would fill in those gaps–but to ensure his words weren't getting lost in my bewildered state.

"As far as I know, I always come back as a child. I start over. And it's happened dozens of times, maybe even hundreds." He peered at me expectantly while I chewed on his last statement. My heart sunk and the room spiraled around us, leaving everything but his face a whirl. I knew far too well that some injuries weren't physical.

"I think we both need to get some sleep," I said. "We can talk about this tomorrow."

"You don't believe me." Nix yanked his hands from mine and folded his face into them. Dark curls tumbled over his fingers as he rubbed his forehead. When he emerged, he appeared every bit as old as he claimed to be.

"Nix, I–"

"I expected that. But I owe you the truth regardless," he said. I pressed my lips together to let him finish. Nothing I could say would help right now. Not in this state. "When we walked through that dead marsh, I had been there before. I can only remember tiny pieces of it, but I was there when the others died. When they killed us."

I narrowed my eyes. "When *who* killed you?" I couldn't believe I was indulging this fantasy, but he'd piqued my curiosity, and his insistence was way stronger than my will right now.

"The River Clan. The book is true. I know it is because I was there, because I am one of the Geomancers. I had forgotten it all until I saw that *place,* but I know I was there." His speech was even, articulate, unwavering. Whether it was true or not, he believed it. That, I didn't question.

"Their whole team was killed there. The wolves, remember? It's natural for your body to try and rationalize what you saw." I said. That eerie place had really affected him—it made perfect sense he'd imagine a way to come to terms with it.

Nix shook his head, hair falling around his eyes. "I can do what they do, too," he whispered. I stilled, letting my hand drop.

I paused. "You can do—"

"I've always been *connected* to the land, but since I found you, it feels like that connection evolved. And the closer I am to you, the stronger it is. When Rior trapped us in the cave and I didn't know where you were, I could *hear* you through the ground. Like the earth could talk to me–my own little spy. It told me you were hurt, and I–I tore the cave down to get to you."

The smoke, the flames, Maher's lifeless body on the ground. But the worst part was fearing I had lost Nix in that cave. I shook my head. It was just a coincidence. Admittedly, I didn't have an explanation for what I'd seen out there, but this... *this* was inconceivable. I ran the side of my hand down his face, over his proud cheek bone and into the scruff of his beard. Raw, organic, and powerful–but beautifully broken like me.

"And tonight. When he had you again, I couldn't bear it. I couldn't stand to see his hands on you, to see him hurt you again. I had to stop him." His voice cracked.

"You moved the boulder." I exhaled the words before the thought had fully formed. A chill slid over me despite the roaring fire behind us.

"I did," he said.

"And you stopped the other one before it hit me." My airway clamped shut, forcing me to work twice as hard to draw in a breath. *What am I saying?* I couldn't possibly buy into this, but voicing it out loud clicked something deep inside my mind. I felt the snap of the puzzle piece, finally finding its home.

"I had to. Selah, I couldn't make it through this life, or any others, if I let something happen to you. It sounds unbelievable, because it is. But I've lived countless lives, and I'm convinced each one was trying to find you." His eyebrows were nearly to his hairline and his temples flashed furiously as he spoke. Heavy waves sloshed around my skull and I had to look away from the blazing intensity of his stare. All my rational parts dangled over a cliff, hanging on by a thread. But my gut nagged at me, reminded me of all the impossible things I had witnessed with my own eyes. If Casted people could extend their lives for centuries through the magic of a few parchment rolls, why was this any less believable?

I wanted to believe him. He *compelled* me to believe him.

Something clinked inside my head, like a paper-thin shard of glass. Another puzzle piece falling into place. "The Scrolls," I said. "Nix–"

"I know," he replied, twisting his thumbs together in his lap. "If it's true, then that means the Scrolls were stolen. They never belonged to the Caste."

I caught the side of the bunk before I toppled forward. Lightheaded and filled with more questions than answers, I allowed Nix to lower us down into his bed and cover us with his quilt. I pressed my face against his chest, clinging to its solid comfort.

Morning was a thief that came too soon, eager to rob me of the only peace I'd found since coming to Hanover Hall. Nix was still fast asleep, his face at rest and lips slack. He was so fucking beautiful. If any being in this world could do the things he'd described last night, it was him. It felt sinful to wake him, but we were the last ones left in the dorm and my stomach growled angrily.

Nix and I slid into the empty dining hall, still entranced from everything we'd exchanged the night before. I dragged my feet to keep from clicking my heels, which echoed too loudly without the fullness of the crowd. Pickham perched himself like a vulture in the doorway, but we sidestepped him without regard. He sniffed as we passed, but I didn't look back to witness his irritation. The aroma of coffee and bacon called to me, and I was eager to temper my emotions with food.

"You have done well to make it this far, but there is still one Trial remaining, and it is the most important Trial of all," Pickham said as we chewed. "You must prove your devotion to the Caste through the Trial of Creed, and you must do it alone. We are stronger as a society, but only you can truly determine your commitment to it." I paused my jaw, moving a pasty glob of biscuit around with my tongue. I couldn't bring myself to swallow it.

"We have to do this *alone*?" Ophida cried, letting her mug clank against the wooden table.

"That's right," Pickham said, far too gleefully. "Over the next few days, I will come to retrieve each of you to carry out your final Trial. Those of you who complete all the requirements to become Casted will then be cleansed." He held onto his *S* as he spoke, making him sound like a serpent. Nix reached for my leg under the table, steadying my bouncing foot. *Alone.* We had to do the final Trial without each other. Even a Geomancer couldn't help me.

"And Candidate Brown," Pickham spoke to Ophida. She eyed him sharply over her plate. "Once you're finished with your meal, you can go first."

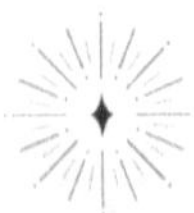

Chapter
Twenty-Nine

I gripped the edge of the heavy table, preparing for the tantrum that was sure to erupt at any second. But it was far worse; Ophida sat in silence, face turning redder and redder as she melted down from the inside out.

"Phi," I called, but she didn't respond. Officer Pickham materialized behind her, sending her face to an unearthly shade of purple. Her plate was untouched, the discarded food exactly where it had been dished.

"Candidate Brown, it's time for your final Trial," he said, looming over her head. Ophida didn't react.

"Phi, you have to go," I said.

Her lashes fluttered.

"Phi." I tried again.

She flashed her eyes to mine before blinking rapidly, shaking her head in tiny twitches.

"Come on, Candidate Brown. I'd hate to fail you before you even started."

Her features stilled briefly, emphasizing the bags under her eyes, and the new creases that had formed between her brows. She flared her nostrils and pursed her lips, making them go stark white against the purple hue of her skin. Without looking our way, Ophida followed Officer Pickham out of the double doors. Or at least the shell of

Ophida. I feared the Trials had finally broken her this time. I looked to Rashel, and then to Abe, before landing on Nix. Everyone was thinking the same thing but we couldn't do a damn thing about it.

Pickham had pushed the final Trial on us so quickly, I'd gotten whiplash from the ups and downs of the last several hours. Tomas was still in the medical ward, status unknown. Ophida, of all people, had no time to prepare. Not that there was any preparation to be done since no one knew what to expect. How did one test their *creed*? I tucked my trembling fingers under my legs to still them before someone noticed.

Nix followed behind me on the way back to the dormitory, so close he crowded my own shadow in the patchy light. When I planted my foot on the side of the bunk to hoist my weary body to my bed, Nix hooked me around my waist and lifted me back down to the ground. My insides clenched at his unexpected contact, but I welcomed the steadiness of his hands. Without a word, he guided me onto his bed, tucking me away into his nook. I would have forgone food and water, even oxygen, just to live there forever.

He was quiet, eyes fixed in front of him, letting me sync my breathing to his. I wanted to memorize the feel of him against me, the sound of his inhales and exhales, the way he smelled fresh out of the bath house. I had no idea how much longer I had with him, but it wouldn't be long enough. As real as he felt with his body curled around me, this was just a fantasy–a temporary delusion before everything would crumble away.

The wooden door of the dorm banged against the wall, reverberating in my sternum. Nix's weight disappeared, and he shot up from the bed before I could gather my bearings. He took giant strides across the room to face the intrusion head on. *Not yet. Please, not yet.* But it wasn't Officer Pickham in the doorway; it was Tomas. I sprinted at the old man, elbowing a candidate from the other group out of the way. Tomas had his arm in a sling and a bandage around his head, but I hugged him around the shoulders anyway. He winced, but I didn't let go.

"You're okay," I said, tasting the salt of my own tears. "You're okay." My relief leaked out of my eyeballs at an alarming pace but Tomas was alive, and he was up and walking, albeit painfully. I released him, wiping the moisture away. Tomas never smiled, but the corner of his mouth moved a fraction of an inch. That was more than enough.

The doors to the dormitory slammed open again, and this time Pickham barged in. I pivoted to face him, but quickly decided it would be better to avoid eye contact, and hurried to my bunk. He couldn't pick me if he forgot about me. Pickham held his chin at an angle, scanning the mostly-empty bunks overtop his nose as he marched. Della pressed her back against the wall, attempting to use my technique. It seemed to work, because Pickham walked past two more bunks before he stopped immediately in the center of the room.

"Candidate Offler," he said.

No. They can't do that. Tomas peered at him from under his bushy, gray brows, face steeled. He wasn't going to give Pickham the satisfaction, and I admired the fuck out of him for that.

"It is time for your final Trial."

"But he can't–" Rashel argued fruitlessly at Pickham's back while Tomas rearranged his weight, refusing to let any flicker of pain show when he marched solemnly from the room he'd just entered.

I pinched the bridge of my nose, trying to anchor myself back in the moment. When Nix's shoulder brushed against mine, I turned my head up to face him. The look that passed between carried everything unspoken. Pickham had illustrated so plainly what I'd watched my entire life; I'd just never had the context to see what was happening.

The Caste wasn't some elite society. Sure, they lived longer, never felt sickness, and all had the same, refined features, but there was nothing glamorous about being Casted. They'd been made to look like that so those unlike them would stand out. And the longer they lived, the longer they could stay in control. That's what it had always been about–control. Pickham didn't care about curating the perfect Casted inductees to carry on the bloodline; he wanted to remind Tomas he was in control. And even if Tomas passed his Trial and was made Casted, he still wouldn't have control. Of all people, I should have seen that long ago.

Nix kissed my forehead, then planted another on my cheek. Our lips connected, and everything about the Caste faded away. *This* was organic, unaltered, and undeniably real. I kissed him hard, tasting the hint of maple and coffee lingering on his tongue. The dorm was occupied, and daylight poured in through the dirty window, but I didn't care who saw us. What did it matter anyway?

At some point I dozed off, still tucked safely in Nix's arms. Funny how it was the only way I could get sleep these days. Nix flashed me a lazy smile that made my bones melt. Tracing my finger over the curve of his shoulder, I wondered how being cleansed would change him. His perfect, deep complexion, the rich texture of his midnight hair, and the warmth of his eyes were all liable to fade into yet another Casted Lord. It was a crime of the worst degree to alter that kind of artistry.

The doors clanked open, driving Nix's lids wide open. *Not again.* I huddled into his chest, clinging to him for dear life. This couldn't be the last time I got to hold him. But Nix sat up, pulling from my grip.

"Selah," he said. The tone of his voice pricked my ears, and I eased myself off the bed to face the door. My intestines flipped around and then back again, filling me with a furious blaze of relief. Even my cheeks and neck burned hot as I watched Tomas hobble down the dorm unassisted. Nix rushed to his side with me close on his heels. Abe also took off running, and we all intercepted the old man in a whirlwind.

"What happened?" Cecil called from behind Tomas.

"I passed," Tomas replied. He pushed past Della's face to clear a path to his own bunk, but the group followed like a swarm of gnats. Tomas proceeded to peel off his boots while the others bombarded him with questions.

"What was it like?" Abe asked.

"Awful," Tomas said.

"Awful?"

"Yes," Tomas replied without looking at him.

Rashel loomed at the foot of his bed. "But you passed..."

"Come on, you have to give us something," Della said. "Ophida is still gone, so how are you back already?"

Tomas sighed a breath that sounded like it had been clinging to his lungs for decades. He gazed at the semi-circle of eager candidates around him, an involuntary father figure to his children. What a fucked up family we'd all become.

"They design the final Trial just for each candidate, so mine was nothing like yours will be. But they're going to pick something that can hurt you." A bitter stone clawed its way up my throat.

"So how did you make it out so quickly?" Cecil asked, crossing his arms.

"They already took the only things that can hurt me," Tomas replied matter-of-factly. "There's nothing left they can do."

"Candidates Holliday, Armor, and Vero, come with me." I reeled around to find Pickham had appeared in the center of the dorm. *Sneaky bastard.* Della started to cry but Rashel draped her arm over Della's shoulder, then whispered into her ear. Whatever she said did the trick, and Della silenced. Cecil's face ignited into brilliant crimson as he drudged behind the women.

Pickham hadn't picked anyone from the other group yet, and there were only three of us left standing from ours. My name would be called, and they'd rip me away. I paced back and forth until I'd all but worn a trail in the stone floor. Nix planted his hands on my shoulder so I couldn't continue my pointless parade.

"Let's go to dinner. Get your mind off of this," he said, gesturing to the walls. Whatever they had seen over the years of candidates, they were just innocent bystanders in all this. Food was the last thing on my mind but I went with Nix just for something to do, and for something other than these walls to look at.

The only respite I got, however, was Nix telling me I needed to eat while I drew patterns in my potatoes with lumpy, cold gravy. When Nix finally gave in and ushered us back to the dormitory, the sun had already fallen behind the crests of the mountains. Even the sunlight didn't want to hang around for this.

I'd withdrawn so far into my little cocoon of misery, I didn't flinch the next time the doors opened. I traced the hem of my sleeve over and over with the pads of my fingers, counting the stitches to clear my mind before my name was called. The odds were stacked high against me now, and all this anticipation had pulled so tightly, I was about to crack. The button from my cuff pinged on the floor when I heard a woman's voice, not Pickham's. *Ophida is back!*

"Thank the Ancient Ones that's over," Rashel yelled into the silent dormitory. I should've been relieved to see her return, but I couldn't shake the look on Ophida's face when they'd dragged her away. She'd been so vulnerable, smaller than ever, and I hadn't been able to help her this time. *And they still have her.*

"Whatever you imagine, multiply that by ten," Rashel said. Apparently some of the math we'd learned had stuck. But what was wrong with her face? I pushed up on my elbows to get a better look. Mottled bruising peppered her, complete with matching raccoon eyes and patterned lacerations striping her cheeks. And her *hair.* Strands were everywhere, chopped at harsh angles and ripped down to her scalp in places. *What did they do to her?* If I hadn't caught the hallmark sass, I wouldn't have believed it was Rashel at all.

"What happened to you?" Tomas asked before I could. He had come back unfazed, at least on the surface. But Rashel's Trial looked personal. She sniffled into her palms, retracting her hands before they could graze the injuries on her face. *Torture.* They'd taken this Trial to the point of actual torture. My insides roiled and I clamped the sides of my bunk to keep the room from spinning.

"It was awful!" She wailed. "They wanted to make me ugly, told me I'd be made Casted just like *this.* They took *everything* and wouldn't stop. But I did it. I did it...." Her words came out in one long chant as she rocked back and forth. Abe reached to hug her, but pulled back in hesitation. Her injuries were gruesome, leaving no unharmed spot he could safely touch. Rashel flung her arms around his waist anyway, and he gingerly patted her back with his fingertips.

"Do you think they'll come for anyone else tonight?" Abe asked, overtop her head.

"I don't know," Tomas replied. "I don't know."

Chapter Thirty

This was mental warfare, and I had yet to make it to my Trial. Based on Tomas's account, and Rashel's face, the possibilities of what they could do were endless. And it was the scenarios I couldn't imagine that truly shook my core. I couldn't exist in this suspended hell much longer.

Time ticked by based on our trips to the dining hall. Nix rotated me between naps and meals, foregoing any further conversation after the night before. I'd lost track of where I was floating next but thought it was lunchtime, when the doors opened again. Still not Pickham. The waiting could have been a Trial all its own.

This time Della crept in, and she looked to be in much better condition than Rashel had. She drew closer, revealing her ghostly pallor and complete absence of pigment in her lips, as if they'd already tried to cleanse her. The haunted look in her eyes made my skin crawl more than the butchered meat of Rashel's face. Nobody spoke to her. Slinking away, the others cleared a path to her bunk, where Della laid down with all her clothes.

Maybe I could delay this thing forever. Ophida had been gone since the very beginning, no sign or indication on how she was doing. Whatever they were subjecting her to, it was dragging into days. Rashel had faced physical abuse, and Della's appearance rattled me far more.

Nothing was worth that amount of torture. Nothing but Nix, and the Trial only solidified a wedge between us if I passed. *Ultimate control.* They'd truly found the perfect leash to bring me to heel.

But his hands on my waist didn't have the chance to comfort me. The swing of the door and clank of Pickham's boots, the way Nix's fingers flexed into my sides, spliced away what little calm I had left. Pickham strolled in with his arms tucked behind his back, cloak fluttering in his wake. A peacock with no feathers. Each *thump* of his boot drove a nail into my heart, closing out any desire I had for this Trial. *Thump.* No half-life on Oberin was worth this torment. *Thump.* Andren would never see me in the same light. *Thump.* My mother had died in vain. *Thump.* My father would lose us both. *Thump.* I could never, ever have Nix. *Thump.*

The footsteps stopped.

"Candidate Sharpe," Pickham called. I gripped Nix's fingertips as hard as I could. *Not yet. I'm not ready. I'll never be ready.* "And Candidate Emrys." Dread rushed from head to toe, so unbearably cold it burned. He'd taken three candidates last time, but this was deliberate. It had to be. *Something that will hurt you.* "Time to go," Pickham said. He sneered at us then swung on his heels to exit. What choice did we have? The sooner I accepted I couldn't control any of this, let loose and accept my fate, the sooner it would be over.

"We have quite the special Trial for you two," he said as we walked. I scraped my feet along the polished stone. "It's not often we get our very own romance." I tripped over my laces, only staying upright because I had a death grip on Nix's arm. The words played back to me in my head. *They know. They know how to hurt me.* "So we're trying something unconventional in your honor," Pickham continued. I couldn't hear anything else Pickham said over the ringing in my ears. Nix touched the back of my elbow to prompt me to follow him through a large set of arched doors.

The arena, no, the *stadium* opened before me—so expansive I nearly lost my balance. I stepped onto the soft dirt floor to root myself to the ground, the staggering high walls trying their best to swallow me whole. There was another open archway across from me, and a rack of gleaming steel to the side. Pointed, jagged, steel.

I turned to Nix in a frenzy, then back to the rack of weapons, my eyes pleading with anything they made contact with. I'd never even seen half of their spiked, heavy forms before, but each one looked progressively more lethal. Oh god, there was no way those were for decoration. Not in this place. Not with *him*. Pickham leered with his arms crossed, a smug feline grin painted on his face.

"We haven't opened the fighting ring in nearly a century, but it is an honor to accommodate such a high-ranking official and our...special guests." In a second, my soul fled from my body and floated high above my head. The color scale of my vision ran from the entire rainbow down to a flat black and gray. I almost didn't notice him at first, until a flash of gold flickered in my awareness, flashed in my memory, and assaulted what was left of my sanity.

"Thank you, Officer Pickham," Andren said, strolling through the double doors. "And welcome Selah, Finix." He left a trail of tidy footprints in the dirt as he marched toward us. I brushed the side of Nix's hand with my pinky, transferring the clammy chill from his skin to mine. Andren's razor sharp eyes cut to the slight contact, then burned holes through the back of my skull with their raging blue. *Fuck.*

"Welcome to your third and final Trial, Candidate Sharpe and Candidate Emrys. We will make this quite simple for you, since this is a Trial of Creed after all," Pickham spoke with an extra thick layer of diction. "*You must choose.*"

The blood inside my vessels evaporated, until I felt like nothing more than a shriveled shell. *Oh, god.* I whipped my head from Pickham to Nix, and back to Andren. I couldn't be hearing correctly.

"Choose–"

"That's correct, Candidate Sharpe. You must choose between the Caste and a life of servitude. *Prove your allegiance.*" The words fell from Pickham's mouth like a curse. And that's exactly what he had done. He had cursed me.

"But I–"

"Selah," Andren said. "It's okay. We know everything." *How is that okay?* "I know I left you alone, and I understand why you were mad at me. I don't blame you." *He knows. He knows about Nix and me.* I'd suspected it all along, but to hear it out loud drove a nail into my heart. "All is forgiven, but you must choose me over him."

How could I ever choose anything over Nix? He'd been the one to put me back together when I was so irreparably broken, collecting all the missing pieces that had been scattered–by the Caste, by my mother, and by Andren. There was no way I could go back. Not without Nix.

"But what about Nix's Trial?" I asked. The old Selah would have known better than to ask foolish, hopeful questions. That Selah was used to being kicked after the first blow had come. "How does he pass?" I grabbed hold of his icy fingers, standing solidly as one unit in defiance. There was no point in pretending now. Andren's nostrils flared, just slightly, but it was enough to make me squeeze tighter to Nix.

"By your choice," Pickham replied. "The whole Trial boils down to your decision on who to kill."

Kill?

"No," I said. "You can fail me. I don't care." The Trials were brutal, and they were deadly, but there had been an answer in each one. But this wasn't a Trial at all; it was revenge. Andren had planned this just to punish me. Why else would he have traveled all this way, just to watch me squirm? I refused to give him that.

"Unfortunately not choosing will escalate the Trial, and your inaction will result in both their deaths." Pickham puffed his chest. He couldn't do that. He *wouldn't* do that. Andren was a goddamn Governor.

"Yes, Selah. They would do that," Andren said, pulling the thoughts straight from my head. I would scorch every day that had passed since that fucking Sewing if I could. "The Fifth Governor is expendable. I knew that when I accepted the job as head of the Barrier. Why else would they appoint a twenty-four year old?" The room began to spin, and I grew woozy, but he kept talking. "It would be quite senseless for both of us to perish when you could save two out of three."

If it had been my first day at Hanover, I would have laughed in his face at the ludicrous notion they'd actually go through with this. But it wasn't my first day here, and I had witnessed every grisly second that had transpired. Dozens of candidates had been slaughtered without a second thought. Rior had never been held accountable for murder, rather, rewarded for making it ahead in his Trial. There was no humanity here—only the demand for compliance. And now, for allegiance.

"I can't. I can't kill someone." I couldn't kill either man, even with the unfiltered loathing I had for Andren at that exact moment. My mind still held the warmth he had shown me, even still. *And Nix....*

"Oh, Selah," Andren said. "Don't start growing a conscience now." Never mind. I could kill him on the spot and not bat an eye. *Bastard.* I opened my mouth to tell Andren to go fuck himself, in fewer words, when Nix clamped his hand around mine so hard, I yelped.

Selah.

Electricity coursed from his hand to mine, tingling on its path through my shoulder and my neck.

Selah, listen to me.

The current spread, coming from the ground up my leg. My entire body thrummed with a charge. The voice was too deep to be Andren, too powerful. Even with him standing so close to whatever thread still remained intact between us, it wasn't Andren speaking to me. It was Nix.

You have to pick him, Selah. That's the only way.

I screamed back in my head, hoping he could hear me. *No! I can't!*

You have to. You have to trust me.

My mind raced to the threadbare quilt back in the dorm, where Nix had held me and told me his darkest secret. Truth or otherwise, he believed it. But could I take that kind of gamble? On speculation and an old, forgotten book? My heart raced as Andren and Pickham stared me down, waiting. Nix held his vise grip on my fingers, but I never wanted him to let go. I could never pick Andren; even if he would take me back, I *couldn't* go back to the way things were. And I didn't want to.

You have to. I was never meant to be Casted.

Every mechanical function in my body shut down, trying to clear space for my mind. Nix was right. He wasn't meant to be tainted by the Caste's blood magic. He wasn't meant to lose everything that made him who he was. *Everything I love.*

"Time to choose, Candidate Sharpe," Pickham said. Andren placed his hands on his hips leisurely, but his toe tapped over and over in the dirt. Nix had the ability to get us out of here, to collapse this whole damned place. But he wouldn't. *He can't.* He could never let them know that he housed something more powerful than the Caste, and I couldn't betray that to Andren–Sewing or otherwise.

"Fine," I said. The single word weighed more than all of Nix. "I choose Andren."

I couldn't look him in his eye, nor could I bring myself to let go of Nix's hand.

"Excellent choice," Pickham said. "Now follow through." He walked to the rack of weapons, which I'd done my best to block out. I couldn't ignore them any longer. God, they all looked dreadful.

The dagger. Pick the dagger.

I inched closer to the rack, where I found a row dedicated just to blades. Long, curved, barbed–all barbaric and impossible for me to wield. Seeing them up close ravaged me with violent nausea. I swallowed the gritty, sick feeling, but it wouldn't dissipate.

"I'm afraid you are almost out of time, Selah. The consequences remain the same, and your choice is not complete until you have eliminated the other." *Eliminated.* God.

Pick up the dagger, Selah. You can do this. You have to do this.

My fingers wrapped around a velvet hilt, burning on the scratchy fibers. It was lighter than the one Nix carried, but still impossibly heavy in my head. Nix turned to face me, still holding the tips of my fingers in his.

This is the only way.

I can't. I cried out, but my mouth wouldn't shape any coherent sounds. *God, I can't.*

You can and you will.

Nix let my hand dangle to my side, and I instantly yearned for his contact once again. The physical distance was excruciating; I'd never survive losing him forever.

You will survive because you will choose to. Because you have to. Trust me.

Trust him. Trust him.

"Time's ticking," Andren said, making me jump. I grabbed onto the dagger before it could hit the dirt. Every bone in my body had been conditioned to know what a dagger meant. Just like my Scrolling, Just like my mother. And now Nix.

Do it.

I lifted the dagger, holding it perpendicular to Nix's broad chest in the air, my joints completely immobilized. I could hear Andren breathing greedily but I focused on the sound of Nix.

"Selah," Nix said. "You have to let me go. You have to do this." I stared into his endless eyes, then peeked over at Andren. Black to blue. Back to the prison of my island. Back to the Caste. Andren nodded his head, urging me to raise the knife. Nix wrapped his hands around mine on the dagger, pulling me toward his chest.

I will find you.

The last sound of Nix.

Using the vaporized wisps of my strength to stay upright, I submitted into Nix's grip. He moved our hands and forced the dagger directly into his chest. Right where my heart lived within his. I knew it as soon as I struck it, because it carved the life right out of me.

What have I done?

His vibrance grew dim, subdued.

I love you, it whispered to me.

I grabbed for the shrapnel of it but everything left of Nix fell through my fingers like sand. The large, powerful man gave way, his knees buckling beneath him. And then I caved into my own personal hell, which I'd designed and executed. I had done this. All of my decisions had led me to this cursed, unthinkably fucked up point.

Stop letting things happen to you. The words echoed like thunder, louder but more distant than they ever had. I had chosen, but even as Andren cupped me under my arms and lifted me to my feet, I doubted that choice.

Chapter Thirty-One

Hanging high above everything, the sense of weightlessness and potential energy from being suspended persisted after the Proctors deposited me back in the dormitory. It had been so unceremonious, but I preferred it that way. The light, floating feeling kept me from touching the ground, because the second I did that, I'd have to return to reality.

I was vaguely aware of the dim lighting and stone walls of the dorm, of the glassy eyes swarming around me. The faces were things I recognized, but they didn't connect with any part of my brain. That piece of me had shut off for my protection, leaving my most primal instincts to steer the ship.

"Selah, what happened?"

"Where's Nix?"

"Selah?"

The sounds clawed at my ear drums when I needed silence. Why couldn't they see that? Why couldn't they see Nix was gone, and it was my fault? Why wouldn't they leave me the fuck alone? Eventually they gave up their line of questioning after I stared blankly at the wall, unwilling and unable to answer them. I thought I was finally by myself until one of them grabbed my arm, intruding on the fragile state I'd stitched together. The gray eyebrows and balding head passed in my vision, but I didn't care enough to focus on their face.

"Selah," the intruder whispered. "Selah snap out of it." A *crack* struck me in the cheek, instantly drawing my eyes to the man in front of me.

"What the fuck, Tomas?" I held my hand to the stinging patch where he had made contact with my face, but it was a feathery twinge compared to the force that plowed me over. It flipped me inside out, punching a Nix-sized hole right through my midsection.

"You can't give in to it."

I narrowed my eyes at him. How could I give in when it had beaten me long ago? I couldn't live in this unbearable torture, couldn't fight anymore. He needed to let me rest in acceptance.

"He's gone, isn't he?" Tomas asked. I gaped at his mouth, mostly hidden under his scraggly mustache. I didn't need to see it to loathe it, though.

"How dare you ask me that?" I hissed at him. He didn't back off and I balled a fist, ready to force him away if I had to.

"Because I know that look. And I know what it feels like," he replied.

I wanted to bite back, to cut him as much as he just did me, but his conversation leaked into my poisoned mind. I'd overheard him with Maher that evening in the mountains–knew everything that had brought Tomas here. He did know. Dropping my defenses, I quieted. Not in acceptance, but in resignation. There was nothing left of me with Nix gone.

"You have to pick up and go, no matter how bad you feel right now. Your life hasn't stopped, and he wouldn't want it to. If you give up now, they really have won." He patted my hand and walked away, leaving me in a ball on Nix's bed, marinating in the empty words. He meant well, but they would never bring Nix back. Nix didn't want this for me. He wanted us together, alive and breathing, no matter what it cost him.

I draped the pillow and blanket over me like a burial shroud, partly to block out other interruptions, but mainly because they smelled like Nix. His scent was very much alive even though the emptiness in my chest suggested otherwise. He'd sat here just days before and confessed his secret, that he could move literal mountains, and that he couldn't die. The longer I laid here without him walking through those doors, the more I knew that belief had been very misguided.

I admitted even I had believed it. The evidence on the mountain was so compelling, how couldn't I? With my very own eyes, I had watched the boulder shift its course on a hair, and come to a complete stop from a maddening speed that no natural force could have managed. *Something* had interfered; I was sure of it. But perhaps the book had given us both wild ideas, and we had filled in the blanks with outlandish assumptions. It made him reckless, and it made me stupid.

Somehow I'd have to make it through the Cleansing with the shreds of my Sewing monitoring everything, all while the rest of my insides had been obliterated by something much bigger. There was no doubt Andren knew my emotions, and I hoped he could feel exactly what I was sending him. Over and over, I cursed the day I met him. The day he brought Nix into my life, and the day he ripped him away. Even if Nix came back, even if I pretended like the past few months hadn't happened, it would never be the same.

I never saw Pickham again. The Commissioner was the one who stood in front of the gaggle of candidates in the excruciating cold, and Andren was nowhere in sight. Perhaps he had returned to Oberin, his work complete. Nix was gone and I'd been taught the one lesson I'd never forget—the Caste would win. Not me. Not the candidates. Just the Caste. Hanover Hall's lawn was covered in a blanket of snow and ice, muffling the sounds and numbing the excitement that should have been present, but I could barely conjure the energy to put one foot before the other.

"The time has come to advance our successful candidates to the final leg of their journey. To join the Caste, your blood must first be made pure as snow." He waved his hand around, the sky obliging him with a fresh swirl of fat snowflakes. Why was snow always used to display purity? My boots were soggy and my pants clung to my legs in icy, wet clumps. Purity sounded much better in theory than practice.

Just as quickly as the snowflakes came down, a whirl of motion broke out behind the Commissioner. Flashes of red hoods mingled with the precipitation until a large white curtain was drawn, revealing an oversized wooden structure. The Commissioner marched up a set of stairs off to the side, taking his place on the stage. It was higher than any stage I'd seen, putting him several lengths above the rest of us. Whether it was for function or for imagery, it fit.

Beneath the stage was a second platform, with something white stacked across it. The snow obscured the texture of the objects, but their curious shape drew my attention. They were long, with rounded edges, and draped in white muslin. Dozens of them, stacked like logs. One, in particular, was larger than the others. One had a familiar curve and taper. One threatened to upheave my breakfast and send me shuttling through the crowd like I'd been lit on fire.

Nix. If I needed any additional confirmation, two of the Proctors held torches to the base of the platform, spreading flames across the straw beneath it. They'd constructed a funeral pyre for all the dead candidates, sending them and their dead dreams up in smoke.

The way the Commissioner loomed over them sickened me at an elemental level. He really held that little regard for humanity, regardless of their societal status. They'd all lived lives, and in one case, *many* lives. Yet he'd wrapped them up and tossed them aside as if they never were. Only the smartest, the strongest, and the most loyal mattered. I had a hunch the latter was the sticking point.

"Tomas Offler, please come forward." I hadn't noticed Tomas at my shoulder until the empty space left me chilled to the marrow. The man blended into the gray and white scenery perfectly, but I tracked him like a hawk as he climbed the steps. The Proctor removed the robe Tomas wore, leaving the old man completely naked and exposed in the elements. Nothing could shock me by now, but the sight of his slender, curved body trembling up there was jarring. Just an animal–a shorn sheep trying to be a wolf.

The Proctor took Tomas's right arm in his hand, then revealed a shiny, hooked dagger in the other. Using the lethal point, he drew a thin line down Tomas's forearm. His blood pooled before spilling over onto the stage, but the Commissioner grabbed his hand and redirected him over the pyre. There, Tomas bled freely onto the burning bodies. Horror kicked me in the spine, nearly knocking me from my feet. Putting them on display was vile, but this–*this* was utterly inhuman. My own death would have been preferable–then Nix would still be here, and I wouldn't have to see his body desecrated. No ancient mountain reincarnation magic would wipe this from my core.

Tomas shook harder, and his knees rocked together; between the blood loss and the relentless cold, he was about to go down. The Commissioner released his hand and he tumbled into the Proctors, supported purely by their robed arms. The Commissioner reached for something behind him and returned with a small vial. When he held it over the white, snowy backdrop, I recognized it from the Sponsorship. We'd kept them this whole time, but in my stupor since Nix had gone, I didn't recall anyone asking me for mine.

"The blood of your Sponsor will renew what has been lost. You have stood over the others to prove you are worthy of Cleansing." *Worthy.* What kind of worthiness did this prove? But Tomas didn't bat an eye. He played the part perfectly, standing as still as possible as the Commissioner uncorked the vial and emptied its contents into Tomas's open wound. He never flinched when the Commissioner took an iron rod from another Proctor and forced the glowing end into his flesh. The sizzle was audible over the cracks and pops of the pyre, and I had to turn away to keep my consciousness intact.

When I swerved around once again, Tomas bore a fresh brand shaped like a circle with a single, straight line imposed. It was identical to the charm on the necklace Andren had given me before I left. Before I knew what it meant to be here, what it meant to wear that blasted necklace. Everything the Casted touched was tainted with veiled meaning; I'd just been too naive to know it was there.

Tomas returned to my side, his robe replaced and his arm cradled in the other. He didn't speak. There was nothing left to say. The Commissioner was already onto the next candidate, and Tomas was just another duty fulfilled. Make more Casted. Breed more Casted. Maintain the Original Bloodline. It had been so simple, hadn't it?

All of the bitterness I'd been housing for two decades floated away from the pyre in pieces of lonely ash. I'd been an outcast, even when I'd been one of them. And after I'd clawed my way to come back, the veil had been lifted and I'd seen the poison in the water. Why I had never fit in. And why I never would. How the hell was I going to carry on pretending like I didn't know this, and like I had never known Nix? How could I possibly return to Andren and play the part of a perfect Governor's wife, if he'd even take me back as Nix had suggested? But they had the control, and I would do it anyway, putting on the same charade Tomas just had. *Because I have no other choice.*

Plumes of black smoke rolled into the monotone sky. The fire had grown into a monster all its own, swallowing my last glimpse of Nix. Whatever remained of his body was carried away by the wind. Nothing but ash and snow. So insignificant, but something that would anchor me in this moment forever. I never heard the Commissioner wrap up the ceremony as I watched the fire burn. It wasn't until Tomas flung his arms around me in a tight hug, then kissed my cheek, that I realized anything was wrong.

The Proctor had me by my arm as awareness clicked into place. I was never called to the stage. *I wasn't cleansed.*

"This way, Miss Sharpe," he said.

"But wait," I called, digging my heels into the snow. "I wasn't cleansed." The Proctor didn't answer. He marched me through the trampled white ground where all the others had waited their turn.

"Gaine will see you the rest of the way," the Proctor said, then released me into a stable on the side of the fortress. *The rest of the way? But I wasn't finished here. I wasn't cleansed!*

"Why didn't they call me?" I yelled at the willowy man. I could break him with little more than my words.

"Ah, Selah. I didn't expect to see you here," the airy voice replied.

"What am I doing *here*?" Manure and wet hay struck my nose, my sense of smell delayed.

"I've drawn up a few mules, and we'll head out as soon as the others arrive," Gaine said, never answering me.

"Others?" I asked. The non-answers were a dangerous accelerant around my non-existent patience, but Gaine vanished from my awareness altogether. Andren pushed through the barn door, draped in riding pants and a heavy parka. He flashed me a half smile and a nod, then made his way to a steed in the corner stable.

"What's going on?" I demanded. Andren continued to tie up his pack and cinch down the saddle without looking at me. "Andren," I said, more forcefully. I had no capacity left for games. "What is going on?" Andren paused, giving the saddle one good jerk then letting the stirrups dangle at his horse's side. He kicked one foot in and threw himself onto the animal's back in a single, swift motion.

"You're leaving here with Gaine," he replied, looking down at me. "With all the other candidates who didn't pass."

"Didn't pass? What the hell are you trying to say?" The smell of livestock pitted my empty stomach in spasms. There had to be an error, some kind of mistake. "I passed all three Trials, so why didn't they call me to be cleansed? What exactly am I doing here?" I stepped toward Andren. The horse snuffed at my aggression, but I pushed closer anyway.

"I am sorry to be the one to tell you, Selah, but I assumed you knew. You did not, in fact, pass your final Trial. It's quite regrettable," he said. The entire barn fell out from underneath me, as if I was right back at the first Trial.

"What are you trying to pull, Andren? You made me choose, and I proved my allegiance by paying a very high price," I yelled. One of the mules thumped at its stall, as uneasy as I was in this place.

Andren gave a little cough before addressing me. "You did pay a price, but you can't possibly think I'd let you be rewarded after everything. That was a punishment."

I fell backward into the damp posts. Burning, stinking, sulfurous rage pounded at my temples, fire scratching at my throat. I should have killed him when I had the chance, and I still could have if Gaine hadn't grabbed my sleeve. I seethed at Andren's unbothered face, sitting on his haughty fucking horse. I should have known. I *did* know, but I was stupid enough to ignore all the signs.

Gaine smiled meekly at the war in my expression. "They are not always meant to be fair, Miss Sharpe. The Trials are meant to separate those who should and shouldn't be Casted, and you have a tendency to *default to inac-*

tion." There it was. At least he'd said something truthful. It was painfully obvious I wasn't meant to be Casted, but I already knew that. I had known from the moment of my wretched Scrolling that the Caste would end me, no matter what action I took. Andren eyed the man before kicking at his horse.

"Good day, Selah."

"What am I supposed to do now?" I asked flatly, my face numb. Andren bobbed down the hill, fading away into the snowy landscape. His travels would never take him far enough from me.

"Go home, if you'd like. You can return to Oberin and work for a nice Casted family, find respectable labor and live out your days." I looked away from Gaine. Going back wasn't an option. "Or you can go elsewhere, if you'd prefer," he added. "You have the entire journey down the mountain to consider your options."

His advice was far from comforting, and for the thousandth time, my world stood juxtapose to the one everybody else lived in. I had less than a day to decide where to take my life–as a servant. The best I could hope for was a nice family who didn't abuse me. Oberin was out of the question. Just the thought of running into Andren turned my face green. And my father didn't deserve to see that. He'd be better off thinking I'd died out here. Lilah would be there to comfort him–his legitimate daughter who wouldn't disappoint him like this.

My knees faltered when I pictured my beautiful sister—flawless in every way. The daughter my father deserved. *Not me.* I'd let everyone I had ever met down since I was born, marked with whatever curse my mother had gifted me from the beginning. The only people I could call friends were lost to me—Myran, Martock, and now Nix. I could never see them again.

"Ready?" Gaine asked with raised eyebrows. Two more males had joined us, one with colorless hair and gray eyes, and the other a man at least ten years older with sallow skin and haggard, peppery hair. The lines of his face revealed this wasn't his first hurdle in life. They looked to each other, then to me, as if one of us was going to say no. *As if we could say no.*

"Wait for me!" A shrill voice rang from behind. I snapped around to see Ophida struggling to run in her oversized parka. The rush of consolation hit me first, but quickly faded into sinking dread. Ophida was alive, but she hadn't passed either. As much as she annoyed me back in Oberin, she didn't deserve to lose her place. And I strongly doubted Lord Frier would find anyone else willing to wed him.

"What are you doing here?" I asked. She seemed uninjured and in good spirits at least.

"I'm coming with you," she replied with a shrug.

"Excuse me?" I didn't try to hide my incredulity.

"I'm not going back." She turned her nose up indignantly. "I backed out of my Trial. I wasn't cleansed."

"What–how? You didn't do your Trial? Was that even an option?" My patience and good nature died with Nix, and Ophida's evasive answers were as maddening as Gaine's. Did everybody here have to speak in riddles? Gaine and the others lurked in the background, either too afraid or too invested to interrupt our reunion.

"I didn't go through with the Trial. I don't want to be Casted."

I gawked at her. Nix had revealed his darkest secret, and I held onto that belief like a beacon of hope. But *this* was too far. Nothing Ophida could say would convince me she didn't actually want to be Casted. She'd practically stabbed me with a dinner fork at Debut.

"But what about Lord Frier?" I asked, putting my hands to my hips. She shrank, but only enough for me to notice. The others would have missed it if they weren't watching closely.

"I don't like him. I never did. I just wanted to be a Lady and he was the only way I could do that." She shrugged her shoulders. "But somewhere in that blasted mountain, I realized I'd rather wash clothes and darn socks until my fingers fall off before I spend the rest of my life tied to that miserable man. He wasn't worth all this." If I wasn't so numb, I would have appreciated Ophida's diatribe. Instead I continued to stare at her wordlessly.

"And I can't let you go alone," she said under her breath. Ophida looked at the ground and kicked at a piece of clumped dirt. I hoped it was dirt, at least. When she looked back up at me, she'd fortified her fair eyes, her jaw squared. This wasn't the petulant child I'd met at Debut after all. She was stronger than I'd been through all of this, and she'd made her choice definitively. And she was the last person in the world by my side.

"You're choosing me over being Casted?" It amazed me that anything could still manage to surprise me.

Ophida rolled her eyes. "Don't let it go to your head. I was just starting to like you." She stared at me after her deadpan delivery. I wasn't ready to smile. Not yet. But she had earned one from me sooner or later.

"I'm not going back to Oberin," I said. She nodded as we followed Gaine and a string of mules out of the courtyard. Thankfully, she didn't ask where I intended to go.

The ride down passed by much faster than it had on the way up. I had nothing waiting for me, no anticipation to build, nothing to look forward to. Ophida trotted next to me atop her mule, her knee occasionally grazing mine. The contact was both foreign and assaulting. Aside from Tomas, no one else had touched me since Nix, and I didn't want anyone rubbing away the feel of him. But I let her stay and tried to focus on the passing trees and rhythmic rumbling from the wooden wheels against the rocky dirt path.

By evening, we'd reached the humid, temperate weather of Esson. My bones no longer ached from the persistent cold, yet another wave of regret took its place. I longed for the mountains. Without their jagged fortitude surrounding me, I was exposed and vulnerable. The space was too expansive and Nix was too far away. I was desperate to recapture the smell of earth and pine, to keep him alive in my senses, to be encased by his unwavering strength like the stony summits.

"I want to go to Windton," I said.

Ophida stared at me blankly, giving away nothing. We'd ridden in silence for hours, and neither of us were very good at chit-chat. Windton was a village northeast of Esson, tucked in the folds of the Andalls and named for the mighty winds that blew off the coast. It was so far north the beaches stayed frozen, and the crags were capped with snow year round. Though I had never been, Father had traveled there for his trades and always described it as a hidden arctic gem.

"Okay," she replied. Whether she liked my choice or not–whether she even knew where it was–she agreed. I'd been defining *alone* as without Nix. How could I have guessed *this* is what it would look like, with Ophida of all people in tow, heading to a brand new place?

"How far is Windton?" she asked as we searched for our bags in the storage room where we first met the Navigator.

"I'm not sure." I only knew its general direction in relation to Esson, and I hadn't fully baked my plan. I just knew it wasn't near Oberin, and that's all that mattered.

"It's two days by horse, five by foot." The weathered man spoke up, his voice just as scratchy as his skin. "It's where I'm from." I eyed him with more regard now. He was short, not much taller than Ophida, with mousy brown hair falling into his eyes.

"I'm Eamon," he offered, noticing I was studying him.

Ophida spoke for me. "I'm Ophida and this is Selah."

"What do you want with Windton?" he asked, hoisting his bag onto his back.

"We're going to live there," Ophida said. For once I was glad she couldn't keep her mouth shut. It spared me from having to contribute.

"Why would you want to live there?" Eamon's face wrinkled further.

"To disappear," I replied. He shrugged but didn't ask anymore questions, quickly adding the pieces together.

"Well we can rest up for the night here and push out in the morning, if you'd like me to escort you." Despite the crackle in his voice, it was gentle as he extended his offer. "It's cold, but it's a nice place. Not many Casted there." *It's perfect.*

"We would be very grateful for that."

The next morning, Ophida and I rose early to pack the provisions Gaine laid out, still a Navigator despite our failed Trials. The irony of all his promise of help and guidance in the Trials wasn't lost on me, even in my current state. The withering man was as useless as I had been when it mattered most. His words bounced around in the silence as we packed up. *Default to inaction.* He'd certainly be able to recognize that attribute, wouldn't he?

While I funneled through my trunk, bitterly digging away at the remnants of my former life, I found Andren's locket buried in my stacks of clothing. It had only been a few weeks but that all felt so long ago. The expensive metal was alien in my hand, but I strapped it to my neck anyway. I hadn't been branded, but I wanted to brandish it as a reminder of everything I had lost. Or maybe it was everything I hadn't accepted. The outcome was the same regardless.

I shoved a few garments into my bag, then abandoned the trunk and the rest of my belongings. The portrait of my family was locked away so I didn't have to see their disappointment, even in oil paint. Eamon met us behind the house with three horses tethered to a pole. I didn't ask how he got them, observing their ragged coats and stringy musculature. They appeared to be very old mares, but they were better than nothing.

I mounted a sorrel horse with a swayback, feeling a little guilty as I bowed her more under the weight of my pack. She didn't protest, however, as I climbed up. Ophida opted for the smallest mare, a deep chestnut palfrey shifting her weight from side to side as Ophida perched in the saddle. Eamon took the third, loading his gear onto the dapple gray back.

"Ready?" Eamon asked. Of course, I wasn't ready, but I had no options left. The only thing I could do was trudge towards something reminiscent of acceptance. I'd never had control over my life, and this wasn't any different. Ophida's lips twitched with a small flash of excitement. Maybe this wasn't as hard for her because she hadn't had as much to lose. She'd never been Casted. But I had, and I had seen the grotesque inner workings of it all. But she had seen it, too. I would never be the Caste's only victim, and it would keep taking.

She made a choice. I defaulted to inaction. Was it society conspiring against me, or was all this self-inflicted? I couldn't deny that I'd been the common denominator in my self-destruction. *That's* what I needed to accept. And now I had Nix's death to contend with, and the constant battle with the hope that he'd come back. I hadn't displayed creed in my Trial, but I would now have to hold out faith in Nix. I'd lost him, but I could choose to believe the world hadn't.

"Yes," I said anyway. I swallowed the bitter taste in the back of my throat and kicked the sides of my horse. She trotted forward after Eamon, and Ophida trailed behind. We had a long journey ahead of us, and not just the travel to Windton. But I kept my eyes planted on the mountains in the horizon.

...I would say "the end," but it's only the beginning of Selah's journey. The story of the Caste continues with Alloyed: Book Two of the Stolen Scrolls series.

About the Author

Author by night, healthcare finance weirdo by day...in that order. As the former kid who always had a book or notepad in her hand (oftentimes both), Ashley started writing her first fantasy series to satisfy the itch other books weren't scratching. From that premise, she spawned the world of Casted.

She's a mom to four badass girls and frequently uses them as inspiration for her characters. Her biggest hope is that they chase their passions just as relentlessly, and that they don't read her books until they're at least twenty.

She also really loves dogs. Big dogs, little dogs, fluffy dogs. But especially her dogs, otherwise known as the barking assholes/her shadows/the Corgis. Her husband is pretty okay, too. He doesn't bark.